A MATTER

OF

INTOLERANCE

Bernadette Mackenna Cases
Book 5

D.R. BAILEY

Cover Design by Sarah Bailey
Photographer: LVAB
Cover Model: Lily V Brazier

Published by Twisted Tree Publications
www.twistedtreepublications.com
info@twistedtreepublications.com

Paperback ISBN: 978-1-913217-34-1

*I would like to dedicate this book to my niece Thomasina.
I've known her all her life, obviously, and can vouch for
the fact she's a lovely girl. In fact, she has just finished a
master's at the University of Exeter in Physics no less. She
has always loved playing sports, particularly hockey,
both at home and internationally, and apparently can
solve multiple forms of Rubik's cubes which is an art in
itself. Thomasina is a bright star, I say that unreservedly
and I wish I knew her better, but time and location often
mitigate against such things. Over time Thomasina found
her sexuality took her in the direction of girls rather than
boys in her teens. She had a tough entrance to love when
she fell for a girl who really struggled with her sexuality,
religion and her parents' expectations. It's quite apropos
as readers of this book will find. Young love hits hard,
that's for sure, I know that from my own youthful
experience. However, from heartbreak comes perhaps a
life lesson and Thomasina tells me she has learnt that it's
better to find someone who is proud of having you and
wants to share your love with those close to them. I am
glad to know, she has found this in her current
relationship. Thomasina says she was lucky enough to
feel she could explore her sexuality as a teenager and*

young adult without fear, and only wishes for the lives of the LGBT community to continue to be respected and accepted by all. Of course, we know that this isn't the case in many parts of the world, and it behoves all of us to continue to support the cause of tolerance for LGBT everywhere. Thomasina is a caring person, and I well know her love of chocolate as she always got the most eggs on the annual Easter egg hunt at her Grandmother's. Everyone has a story, and hopefully, Thomasina's will be a long and fruitful one.

CHAPTER ONE

"*D*arling, it's OK, honestly it's OK."

Bernadette sat in a meeting room at the Criminal Courts of Justice with her arms around Imogen who was bawling her eyes out, and comprehensively wetting the collar of Bernadette's jacket in the process. Bernadette smiled softly and sympathetically. She had black hair which was hanging loose, brown eyes and was held to be exceptionally beautiful, particularly by her wife, Eve, whom she had recently married.

"It's not, it's fucking not alright," Imogen sobbed, "I have fucked it all up, I'm crap, I'm useless."

"You're not darling, don't be silly," Bernadette chided her gently whilst stroking the silky red locks of Imogen, her pretty junior partner and junior barrister.

"Yes, I am, I'm a failure." Imogen sat up with red puffy green eyes. Her smooth translucent skin denoted her being in her late twenties, and the summery weather had brought out her freckles. Imogen's fiancée, D'Arcy Brown found her devastatingly attractive. The feeling was mutual, and Imogen was equally besotted. She regarded Bernadette, her friend and senior partner with a face of abject misery.

"You are not a failure!" Bernadette shot back firmly but implacably.

"I don't know why I even bothered to become a barrister when I can't even win the easiest case in the world!" Imogen was determined to castigate herself it seemed, no matter what Bernadette said.

"I wouldn't say it was the easiest case in the world, darling."

"It was, it was, you would have won it easily."

"That's actually not true, you weren't to know the witnesses would change their testimony on the stand."

"Well, no," Imogen conceded.

Bernadette was gradually getting Imogen to lead with some of the smaller cases under her supervision. She had taken on the defence of a man accused of a common assault causing harm, there had been a brawl and he had broken someone's nose. Prior to the trial, there were several witnesses who swore the accused was provoked, was hit first by the plaintiff and retaliated acting in self-defence. However, on the stand, they decided to say it was an unprovoked attack instead. When challenged, they simply said they had realised they had seen it all wrong before. It was ridiculous, Bernadette felt, but there was nothing to be done. The judge in a summary trial had found in the prosecution's favour based on the evidence heard in court. Although Imogen had argued valiantly, it was to no avail. She was devastated and had broken down as soon as they got out of the courtroom.

"Darling, even I couldn't successfully defend against overwhelming evidence against our client."

"I know but..."

"They'd obviously been got at or something, you can't do anything about it." Bernadette shrugged.

"I feel so terrible for the client, he nearly got a prison sentence and everything."

Bernadette gently took hold of her shoulders. "Darling, I love you to bits, you know that. This is how the cookie crumbles. You're going to take some losses. God knows I did. You just move on from it to the next one. I know it's easier said than done, of course. It seems the worst thing in the world, right now."

"If you say so." Imogen sniffed, wiping her eyes.

"I do say so."

"I bet you didn't cry your eyes out like a silly schoolgirl."

"I did cry actually, quite bitterly sometimes, usually in the toilet." Bernadette gave a low laugh.

"Really?" Imogen looked surprised.

"Yes, really, so stop beating yourself up about it."

"OK." Imogen cracked a weak smile.

"That's better, my darling, now let's freshen up and I'll take you to lunch, hey?"

"Yes." Imogen nodded, not particularly mollified it seemed but looking a little happier than she had been when a few minutes earlier.

✳ ✳ ✳

Mama Mia's was one of their favourite haunts. It was a cosy restaurant near their offices with red stripy tablecloths and a limited but excellent menu.

Imogen chose the *Pasta Boscaiola* which came with ham, mushrooms, green peas and fresh cream, while

3

Bernadette had selected *Gnocchi Sorrentina* which had tomatoes, and mozzarella. She felt they needed something a bit more substantial than a panini for a change and chose a mixed leaf salad to accompany the mains.

Bernadette sipped her Lemon Pellegrino with ice and said, "Feeling better?"

Imogen smiled taking a mouthful of her pasta before speaking. "Yes, I guess so, it was just so annoying."

The case had at least moved from being the worst thing in the world, to annoying. This was progress, Bernadette reflected in amusement.

"That's the life of a barrister, darling, you have to take the rough with the smooth."

"You seem to have more smooth than rough." Imogen gave a hollow laugh.

"I've been doing it longer than you, my sweet, and I've had more than my fair share of failures. Each of them has been hard to take in its own way."

"I just wish we'd known the witnesses were all going to change their minds beforehand."

"Look, it wasn't as if it was a serious case."

"It was for me." Imogen pouted.

"Sorry, I didn't mean it like *that*."

"I know you didn't. Anyway, are we going to appeal it?" Imogen looked only half hopeful.

"I don't see we have any grounds for it, unless we can prove the witnesses changed their minds or were tampered with. Also, the client has to have an appetite for it, and I suspect, since he got away with a fine and a community service order, he doesn't want to tempt fate. After all the appeal might impose a harsher sentence."

Imogen sighed. "Yes, I suppose you are right."

"Put it behind you, and let's move on. Close it off with the client. We got paid, we did our job."

"Yes, but not as well as I should."

"Stop!" Bernadette waved her fork in the air. "Darling, you have to stop. You did as well as you could. Now, that's enough."

Imogen shot her a sly look. "You know I love it when you get assertive."

"Oh you. You're incorrigible." Bernadette shook her head.

"And I love you." Imogen blew her a kiss.

"I love you too, but can we put this to bed now."

"Which part?"

"Oh!" Bernadette shot her a look of mock severity and returned her attention to her pasta.

Imogen giggled and resumed eating too. Neither of them said anything while they finished their food. Then she sat back with satisfaction.

"Delicious as usual," she pronounced.

"Now do you feel better?" Bernadette cocked an eyebrow.

"I do and you are right, I'm going to move on from this now."

"Thank goodness, I'll get us some coffee."

Bernadette signalled to the waiter who removed the plate and took the order for two lattes.

"Anyway, how are the plans for your wedding coming along?" she said changing the subject.

"OK." Imogen shrugged.

"So not OK, are they?" Bernadette read between the lines.

"We're at a little bit of an impasse, to be honest." Imogen gave a big sigh. "I don't really want a big wedding with all the pomp and circumstance attached."

"Like mine you mean?"

"Yours wasn't a big wedding."

"It seemed quite big to me."

"We have gone from a few guests to over two hundred, media and God knows what," said Imogen crossly.

"But why?" It seemed a little strange to Bernadette since previous discussions had centred around a modest style or so she thought.

"She got carried away I suppose. Yours was such a success she now thinks she's a wedding planner extraordinaire. Apart from anything else I think it's a mistake to have so many people around her house. I mean, you know what the press are like, nosy bastards prying into everything."

"Is there no middle ground?"

"Not at the moment, no."

"Would it help if I got Eve to talk to her?"

Eve had become firm friends with D'Arcy, and the two of them spent quite a lot of time together. D'Arcy was quite a demanding friend and insisted on taking her to lunch once a week. They often went on shopping sprees, which was more Eve persuading her friend not to buy things than actually making purchases. As a result, D'Arcy confided quite a bit in Eve and so this was possibly a way in.

"Maybe." Imogen didn't look particularly optimistic which led Bernadette to believe the rift over this issue was bigger than she was letting on.

"I thought you were the Domme in your relationship and she did what you told her." Bernadette was referring to the sexual proclivities of Imogen who had a marked predilection for spanking which found its way into her sex life with D'Arcy. D'Arcy had been rather submissive towards Imogen and although Bernadette was always a little dubious about the arrangement it seemed to work for them.

"As to that…" Imogen left the rest unsaid.

"Go on, what does *that* mean?"

"It means that I can't use my Domme powers for this. It's kind of off limits. She also hasn't wanted me to spank her for a while. I can't do it without her consent obviously, even when I want to. She can be such a little brat."

"Oh?"

Imogen gave another sigh, but it belied something deeper underneath which was troubling her.

"Yes, I don't really know what to do, I'm beginning to think she doesn't really love me anymore or she's getting tired of me."

Bernadette was suddenly quite alarmed to hear this, not least because D'Arcy and Imogen appeared to be besotted with each other. They seemed completely and irrevocably in love. To hear this might not be the case was concerning. She tried to probe it further in case Imogen was making more of it than it really was.

"I'm not sure how you can deduce that just because…"

"She's cold sometimes. She's less communicative and I don't know what's wrong. I know something is wrong though."

Tears sprung to Imogen's eyes.

"Oh fuck! How long has this been going on?" Bernadette wondered why Imogen had not told her sooner.

"A week or two, since we started discussing the wedding."

"Why didn't you say something before?"

Tears began to course once more down Imogen's cheeks. "I don't know, I was hoping it was just a phase or something, a bad day, but now it's turning into a bad two weeks..."

"Darling, don't cry, at least not here." Bernadette reached over and took her hand. "I'll talk to Eve. She'll know what to do I'm sure."

"I hope so," said Imogen miserably. She looked as if she was about to break down.

"Fucking hell!"

Bernadette called the waiter over to pay the bill anxious to get Imogen back to the office where she could vent her feelings properly.

✳ ✳ ✳

It was quite a while, sitting on Bernadette's sofa in the office before Imogen could be consoled. She had broken out into a hearty bout of weeping as soon as they got back. There had been nothing to do but hold her gently while the tears flowed freely. The way Imogen sobbed so quietly broke Bernadette's heart. She was determined to talk to Eve and see if they could solve it.

"Darling, can I ask you something?" Bernadette said when Imogen seemed to have recovered somewhat.

"Yes." Imogen retrieved a tissue and blew her nose.

"You're still having sex, right?"

Imogen nodded.

"And it's still... as good?"

Another nod and a slight smile.

"Then that's a good sign I would say."

"Yes... but..."

"No buts." Bernadette put her finger on Imogen's lips. "I'll talk to Eve, my darling, let's see what she has to say."

"OK."

There was a tap on the door and Alison's blonde head appeared around it.

"Sorry, Bernadette, sorry to intrude," she said tentatively.

"It's OK, darling, what's up?"

Alison slid into the office and closed the door behind her. She took in Imogen's tear-stained face in an instant. Alison was their PA, she was quite tall, slim, with a boyish figure and fair complexion also sporting a few freckles. Her blue eyes looked anxiously at Bernadette through her glasses with funky red frames, a new acquisition apparently.

"It's just there's a prospective client," said Alison quietly.

"Oh?"

"Yes, in the meeting room."

"How long has she been there?"

Alison bit her lip in a manner which Bernadette found incredibly endearing. She shook off the thought.

"Well, a few minutes or maybe ten, perhaps fifteen." Alison's expression was quite guilty.

"Why didn't you…"

"I was going to, but I didn't want to disturb you, as… well…" Alison jerked her eyes in Imogen's direction.

"Oh, yes, I see. Thank you for that." Bernadette smiled. "Anyway, I guess we had better go and see her, who is she?"

"I think she's a human rights lawyer or something."

"Great. Go and tell him we'll be there shortly, apologise for the delay. Say erm… there was something urgent to do with a case and get her some more refreshments."

"OK, sure. Is… everything alright?" Alison ventured.

"No, darling, it's not, but I'll tell you later," Imogen put in having recovered sufficiently to say something herself.

"Right, well, we're coming," said Bernadette.

"Sure." Alison regarded Imogen anxiously for a moment more and then disappeared again.

"Oh fuck!" Imogen said.

"Alison's fine, she won't tell anyone," Bernadette assured her.

"I know, but I feel like a right fucked up bitch."

"You are not and if you don't want me to slap that arse of yours, I suggest you stop putting yourself down," Bernadette said severely.

"You know that's workplace harassment, right?" Imogen said with a grin.

"Except you'd love it, wouldn't you?"

"God yes, I've fantasised about it endlessly." Imogen laughed and so did Bernadette.

"Great, well, I'm glad to see you a little more the thing. I'm not going to slap your backside now or at any other time. Made you smile though."

"More's the pity." Imogen gave an exaggerated sigh.

"Go on with you, freshen up and then let's go and meet this lawyer."

Bernadette watched her leave the room and smiled to herself. This was their standard banter. There was no denying something of a spark between them, but it was one of a deep and enduring friendship. Imogen liked to tease her, and Bernadette played along. In reality, there was nothing sexual about it. They were more like sisters, as was Eve and also D'Arcy. Bernadette was somewhat worried about D'Arcy's latest behaviour but hoped it was simply a passing thing. D'Arcy was incredibly volatile. This was often reflected in her relationship with Imogen. She pulled out a compact mirror and checked her makeup while she waited for Imogen to return.

Once Imogen was a little refreshed, she entered the meeting room with Bernadette. The meeting room was decorated with dark green walls like the rest of the office accommodation. It had a large meeting table and some sofas for more informal chats. The atmosphere was calming, which Bernadette liked.

A woman was sitting on the sofa with a cup of tea in her hands. She had long black hair and looked to be around thirty-five years old. Her eyes were brown, and she was certainly beautiful, with a long straight nose and full lips. She was wearing a casual outfit of jeans, a white blouse and jacket with strappy sandals. Bernadette noticed she had dark red nail polish on her toes which suited her complexion well, along with a matching dark red lipstick.

"Hello, I'm Bernadette Mackenna and this is Imogen Stewart, my partner, I'm sorry we kept you waiting."

"Oh, that's not a problem at all, I gather you had something urgent come up." The woman smiled and stood. She spoke with a slight accent overlaid with an Irish lilt. "I'm Maneet Johal-Lynch, I'm a human rights lawyer."

"Yes, nice to meet you," said Bernadette shaking her hand. Imogen did the same and Bernadette motioned for them all to sit. She took the opposite sofa with Imogen beside her. "How can we help?"

"I'm not sure if you can but I came to ask because you are known as the top defence lawyer in Dublin," said Maneet frankly.

"Thanks for the compliment, though there are many good barristers in this city," Bernadette demurred. She sometimes found it hard to take compliments.

"Not as good as you."

"You're right about *that*," Imogen put in. She would fiercely jump to the defence of Bernadette and was one of her biggest proponents.

"Right, well, anyway," Bernadette said moving things on. "What can I do for you? Is it a human rights matter?"

"Sort of." Maneet laughed. "It is about rights, my rights."

"Oh?"

Maneet sighed as if the disclosure of her problem might be painful.

"Yes, perhaps I should tell you the whole. You probably didn't hear the news about a recent rally we held in Phoenix Park."

"Who's we?"

"Oh sorry, IAD, Irish Against Discrimination."

"Which is?"

"It's an organisation fighting against racists, homophobes, people like that. White supremacists, you know."

Although Bernadette kept up with current affairs, she wasn't au fait with every kind of protest occurring in the city nor all of the causes being espoused.

"OK. I'm I sorry I wasn't aware of the rally."

Maneet shrugged and gave a slight smile, as if to say this wasn't unexpected.

"It's fine, I mean, it wasn't hugely high profile or anything. We're not very high profile ourselves usually. After all, this isn't a particularly racist country overall. However, we had noticed an uptick in incidents particularly in Dublin. I believe there has been some resurgence of racism. We monitor things like that, so we held a rally to speak out against it."

"I see." Bernadette didn't really see where this was leading but no doubt it would become clear. Beside her, Imogen sipped her coffee and kept silent. This was unusual but then Imogen was suffering a little and Bernadette was now well aware of it. Half her mind was still on that.

"Anyway, there was some trouble at the rally."

"What kind of trouble?"

"We were there minding our own business and the Garda turned up unannounced. To cut a long story short, I was involved in a scuffle and I was arrested for assaulting an officer of the Garda."

"What?" Bernadette looked a little incredulous at this statement.

"I know, it sounds bad, but I was provoked, and so I hit him, maybe a few times. Now I'm being charged with assault."

Bernadette found it was hard to keep a smile off her face at this almost disingenuous confession. Maneet picked it up in her expression.

"I know, you're looking at me and thinking what the hell?"

"Something like that, yes," Bernadette admitted.

"It sounds bad. A human rights lawyer accused of assaulting a Garda officer. Incredibly bad actually and it's very bad for our organisation if I get convicted."

Maneet looked down at her feet for a moment, as if she was quite ashamed.

"So, what was the provocation?"

"He... called me..." Maneet stopped because it seemed suddenly quite hard for her to confront the memory of it.

"He called you?" Bernadette said gently.

"A fucking Paki bitch, a stupid Indian whore, a fucking black slut who should fuck off to my own country... among other things. And I'm not even *from* Pakistan for fuck's sake!"

"What?" Bernadette was visibly shocked at this. It was unprecedented almost. She knew racism existed in Ireland but to hear it this graphically was rather different.

"Yes, I know, I'm kind of used to comments like that, though not usually as bad, nor as often. This just got to me. Things were heating up, confused, I got angry, and I lashed out."

"So, what did you do exactly?" Bernadette wanted to know the full extent of it.

"I full on punched him in the face, and then I slapped him a few times, and I kicked out at him. Then they grabbed me and arrested me."

"What happened after that?"

"I was taken to the nearby Garda station, charged and then released without bail."

"How were you treated during and after your arrest?"

Maneet shrugged. "That's the thing, I think they must have realised who I was because I was treated with great deference from then on. Nobody insulted me or called me names, or anything. It was as if it had never happened. I was formally charged, and the charges were read in a very formal way. Then I went home."

Bernadette paused for a moment, took a sip of coffee in order to think about it.

"What are you being charged with?"

"Assault causing harm. It carries a fine or up to five years in prison unless by a summary trial, which I don't want."

"Yes, I know. I mean, it's not a serious offence but it's serious enough now the Garda is involved."

"Exactly and... well, I'm ashamed, my family will be ashamed too if I go to prison." Maneet drew in a breath like a sob, as if she let her guard down.

"It need not come to that."

"I've fucked up everything I've worked for my whole career. Respect for me will be lost." Maneet seemed determined to indulge in self-castigation.

"But only if you lose." Bernadette felt it incumbent on her to point this out before Maneet began to pour too much scorn on herself.

"Yes, well, that's why I've come to you." Maneet looked up at Bernadette. Her eyes were soft, almost imploring.

"But you're a lawyer why can't you defend yourself?" It was a fair question and came from Imogen who had suddenly found her voice.

"I'm a human rights lawyer, yes, but I'm not a barrister and I've no experience of criminal law."

"OK, so you need someone else to defend you who can?"

"Yes, yes I do."

"Well, you've come to the right place." Imogen smiled.

"I hope so... I really do, because..." Maneet stopped as if there was something even worse, she had to tell them.

"Because?"

"Because my fiancé is angry with me. He's a big wheel in the finance world, you know, and he's worried about his reputation and we're supposed to marry, but now he's having second thoughts... and..."

"Is he..." said Bernadette pursing her lips with a martial light in her eye.

"You don't understand for my culture disgrace is everything, if I disgrace my family, I am nothing, I'm nothing..."

Suddenly and without warning Maneet began to cry, bitter tears. In flash and without hesitation Imogen was beside her and took her in her arms. Imogen was a natural comforter. Bernadette knew from the many times she had similarly cried in Imogen's embrace. She suspected also Maneet's distress was a deflection from Imogen's own. Bernadette watched the two of them and finished the rest of her coffee. It would not be the first time clients had cried in her meeting room. Many came distressed and upset, because innately criminal cases were exactly that to those who were accused or who were the victims of crime. She did not see victims so much since she was a defence lawyer, but she also never took on a case if she felt the person was guilty. It was not her job to defend the guilty, but it was her calling to get justice for the innocent. She had had her share of defending plainly guilty suspects until she started her own practice and could choose. Maneet did not seem guilty. She had evidently committed the assault but the racism which preceded it was a massive mitigating circumstance.

After a few moments longer, Maneet seemed to feel better and sat up looking gratefully at Imogen.

"Thank you," she said.

Imogen reached over and snagged a box of tissues which they kept on the table. She handed it to Maneet who took it wordlessly and blew her nose.

"Oh fuck," she said, "I've made a spectacle of myself already."

Bernadette laughed. "Don't worry about it, darling, both of us have cried more often than I can count."

"Really?" Maneet looked surprised.

"Yes."

"Oh!" Maneet said no more, as if she expected Bernadette to have been some kind of ice queen.

"Are you feeling up to a few more questions?"

"Sure."

"Do you have any witnesses to the racist taunts and insults?"

"No, it was very loud all of a sudden, chanting and stuff. The Garda was advancing on us and I went to speak to them... alone."

"Right." This wasn't good.

"I thought they would deal with a lone woman better, turns out I was wrong."

"And witnesses on their side?"

"The other Garda would have heard it but I expect they will close ranks and deny it. The officer who made the racist taunts will also deny it."

"OK." Bernadette wasn't surprised to hear this. "What about video footage?"

"There is some obviously but not close enough to hear what they were saying."

"We're going to need it regardless."

Maneet's head jerked up. "So you'll defend me?"

"Yes, I will, subject to the financial formalities which will need to be discussed with our finance manager."

"Consider yourself lucky, she doesn't take on cases just like *that*," Imogen told her.

"Really?"

"Yes, really." Imogen smiled reassuringly. "It means she believes in you and what you're fighting for, which is, of course, justice." She put out a hand and lightly touched Maneet's arm. Bernadette looked on approvingly when Imogen mentioned justice, her favourite word.

"Thank you, you are both so kind, I didn't expect..."

"Lawyers, to be kind?"

"No, oh I don't know. I'm just a bit emotional right now."

"We noticed." Imogen giggled and it was infectious. The three of them ended up laughing for a few minutes.

"OK," said Bernadette. "We are going to need all the paperwork you have, any video footage and anything else relevant."

"Yes. As to the financial elements, my fiancé will take care of it."

"He will?" Bernadette was surprised.

"Yes, he said if I get a lawyer who can get me off the charge, he'll pay for it."

"He will have to meet with us and our finance manager, Andrew Bond, then."

"Yes, I will arrange it."

"Great, then Imogen will sign you up as a client, we'll take some details. If you can get your fiancé to come in and see us, we can sort out the financial aspects. In the meantime, send us everything you can." Bernadette felt they had elicited all they could for the moment.

"Thank you." Maneet looked at them gratefully. "You don't know what this means to me."

"No, but I can certainly understand the stress you are under and that's very real to me."

Bernadette could not tell what it meant to her client. Each person was on their own journey. She could, however, see what her client was going through as this was obvious enough.

"It is?"

"Yes, of course, it's the same for any client facing the justice system."

"Yes, you're right I suppose." Maneet nodded.

"If there's anything else?"

"No, you've been too kind, more than I expected."

"Goodness, we must have a fearsome reputation then." Bernadette gave a light laugh.

"One or two people said..." Maneet trailed off and blushed a little.

"Said what? I doubt it's something I haven't heard."

"That you are a tough unfeeling bitch..." Maneet paused and then added, "From hell."

Bernadette looked at her for a moment and burst out laughing, as did Imogen. Maneet looked nonplussed.

"I must admit I hadn't heard that one," Bernadette told her once she had recovered.

"Oh?"

"Yes, we're known as those lesbian bitches usually."

"And are you?"

"Gay, yes of course, and Imogen is too. I don't think we're really bitches, except when we need to be. I hope you don't mind it?"

"I would hardly be living up to my reputation as a human rights lawyer if I minded it, would I?" It was Maneet's turn to laugh. She seemed to have become very much at ease in their company from when they had first met her.

"You know, it's just the profession. I'm successful, *we* are successful, and also women. These two things are difficult for many of the old school lawyers to reconcile." Bernadette laughed again.

"Well, you try being Indian and a woman," Maneet shot back. "Though of course, I'm not gay."

"Which would be three strikes I guess."

"Yes, for sure. Also, my parents are not so understanding about sexuality. I'm supposed to have a good profession, marry a man with a solid reputation and income. Settle down, have a family, all of that. I did pretty well on the profession and the man, even though I am a human rights lawyer."

"Oh?"

"My father doesn't think that's a proper lawyer, not like you."

"I see."

"You would be forgiven for being gay because you are very successful," Maneet said rather guilelessly.

"Thank God for *that*." Bernadette's tone was sardonic, but she was smiling.

"My parents must sound terribly shallow but it's how they were raised, and it goes from generation on to the next. Well... not this time." Maneet pursed her lips.

"I sort of understand, though I wasn't brought up that way."

"It's our culture." Maneet shrugged.

"Yes, for sure."

"Anyway, like I said I'm grateful."

"No need to be, it's our pleasure." Bernadette stood up.

"I'll take you to my office and we can sort out the formalities," said Imogen standing up too.

"Yes."

Maneet stood up too and she said goodbye to Bernadette before leaving the room with Imogen.

Bernadette watched them go, musing over what had just happened. The cultural differences added a different dimension to the case. She wondered at the idea that a family would be so concerned about their daughter bringing them into disrepute. Then she remembered how Eve's sister had been ashamed of Eve being gay and also what her sister had done. Her brow darkened a little at this. She still had not reconciled herself about it, somewhere in her mind the sister deserved some sort of payback.

✳ ✳ ✳

In a while, Imogen reappeared in Bernadette's office with two coffees.

"All done?" Bernadette asked her looking up from her computer. She stopped what she was doing and went to sit on the sofa.

Imogen joined her and handed her a mug of coffee.

"Mmm, thanks," said Bernadette sipping it gratefully.

"You're welcome, darling. And, yes, it's all sorted out for the moment. I've got her details and she will arrange for the fiancé to come in to see us. His name is Akshay Pandit, he's a banker or something, he works in one of the big firms in Dublin. Apparently, he's loaded."

"Also, a bit of a chauvinist it sounds like."

"Let's not judge him too harshly, yet."

"That's a change of tune, missy, usual you're the one doing all the judging." Bernadette's eyes twinkled.

"I know but maybe I'm trying to mellow."

"Or it's just your current mood." Bernadette sipped her coffee and regarded her friend perspicaciously.

"Don't remind me, at least this case will take my mind off things at home." Imogen sighed and sipped her coffee too.

"Don't do anything rash, darling, let me talk to Eve," Bernadette reminded her.

"You mean like giving D'Arcy the soundest spanking she's ever had?" Imogen opined bitterly.

"Perhaps *not* doing that?"

Imogen sighed. "I can't do anything unless she lets me, so not much chance of it."

"Is it maybe you that's backing off and not her?" Bernadette mused on this thought.

"I'm afraid to rock the boat."

Bernadette could understand this. It was true that once you became uncertain in your relationship the natural thing to do was to back away. The problem was it could then become a self-fulfilling prophecy from there on out. She didn't want this to happen to Imogen and was determined to help solve things for her.

"Let's see what Eve says, have some patience."

"OK."

Bernadette reached out and took Imogen's hand. Imogen accepted it gratefully.

"What do you think about this case?" Bernadette shifted the subject.

"I don't know. I mean, on the face of it, it's a straightforward case of assault. How are we going to get her off it?"

"Technically we can't, but if we can prove she was provoked then it may be possible to argue that it was a lawful excuse, or at the very least an excuse. We might be able to prove that she acted under duress whether by threats or circumstances."

"Can racial slurs and insults be seen as duress in the eyes of the law?" Imogen wondered.

"Are they not? We will certainly have to test it. I mean, if he had by any chance threatened her with violence it would help us tremendously, but we need as exact as possible wording of what he said according to Maneet."

"Which he denies."

"Naturally."

"And probably with witnesses."

Bernadette sighed. "I know and that will make it very difficult."

"But not impossible." Imogen smiled.

"Never say impossible, darling."

"I think we should also get Micky to try and get whatever footage he can dig up from the internet. People may have posted on social media, news agencies, stuff like that. Stuff which hasn't been published perhaps he could try some of the media outlets."

Bernadette was pleased to see Imogen taking the initiative, this is exactly what she wanted her to do.

"We'll get him in and talk to him about it."

"Yes, shall I?"

"Sit a moment, darling. Then by all means."

Imogen put her cup down, and Bernadette put an arm around her shoulders. Imogen sank gratefully into her.

"It will all come right, you'll see." Bernadette said it with more conviction than she currently felt and hoped Eve would be able to extract something out of D'Arcy.

* * *

Micky sat in Bernadette's office on one of the chairs facing Bernadette and Imogen who remained on the sofa. Micky was wearing a natty blue suit, collar and tie. There was no real set dress code as far as Bernadette was concerned, but most people looked smart or smart casual as would be befitting a lawyer's office. Micky liked to dress the part and usually wore suits. He was fresh faced and youthful in his early twenties, although now he had taken to a sporting moustache and a little bit of designer stubble, he looked older. This probably served him well as he would be taken more seriously by others. Bernadette also noticed he was filling out a little muscle wise and put this down to the gym and the karate training which the firm was paying for.

"How's things, Micky?" she said amiably.

"Oh, you know, same as when you saw me two days ago." He grinned at his own joke.

Bernadette was pleased to see he felt enough at ease to make a joke in her presence. It indicated perhaps he wasn't treating her quite like a goddess anymore and more like a colleague. This was good, since the last thing Bernadette felt was goddess-like. Only one person made her feel as if she was a goddess and that was Eve. Particularly during a Shibari session, something Eve had a prediction for, and was part of their sexual games. Bernadette recalled they were probably due for another very soon. Eve tended to get a little wayward and bratty when she was craving it. Bernadette knew perfectly well Eve did it on purpose to goad her.

"I'm glad to hear your life isn't *that* volatile then." Bernadette laughed.

"Me too."

She felt perhaps he wanted her to get to the point and so she began.

"Alright well, we've got a case, Micky. It's come in today. The client is Maneet Johal-Lynch, she is apparently a prominent human rights lawyer."

"Right." Micky extracted a small notebook from his pocket and began to write in it. It looked suspiciously like those carried by Garda detectives to Bernadette's amusement, but she refrained from commenting.

She wondered, before continuing, about Maneet's double-barrelled surname. One part was very obviously Indian but the other sounded Irish, and Maneet had said her parents were Indian. Bernadette wondered if perhaps one of her parents was really half European or something like that. She would ask Maneet if a suitable time arose, but it wasn't really important.

"She works with an organisation called IAD which stands for Irish Against Discrimination."

"Yes?"

"Recently there was a rally in Phoenix Park. She got into a scuffle with the Garda. She hit one of the officers apparently because he had called her some very nasty racist names."

"Oh?" Micky's face registered a slight surprise on hearing this, but he didn't comment further.

"So, she has been charged with assault, and it's our job to get her off and that's where you come in."

"What do I need to do?" Micky poised his pen for further action.

"Find out everything you can about her, past and present. Then find out about this IAD organisation, events, rallies, has there been violence before. Find out who the leaders are, we may want to interview them. Then search for rally footage and, in particular, anything at all you can get of the incident itself with Maneet. Search all of social media, YouTube, wherever. There may have been some people who recorded it on their phones and posted it. We need whatever you can find. Got all that?"

"Phew, yes, that's a tall order but, yes." Micky had been scribbling furiously in his pad and looked up at her anxiously.

"Should keep you out of trouble anyway, Micky, darling." Imogen furnished him with a radiant smile which made him blush.

"Yes, for sure I'll get onto this right away." He tried to ignore her remark. He was still prone to embarrassment when either of them played too much of their womanly wiles on him.

"Take your time, Micky," said Bernadette. "Do a thorough job, let us know when you've got something."

"I will."

Micky stood up to go.

"You're doing a fine job by the way. In case I haven't told you that in a while."

He blushed a deeper shade of red, mumbled something about getting on with it and disappeared with alacrity.

"You bitch, you know he doesn't take compliments well." Imogen laughed.

"What? I was trying to be nice and encouraging. I saw that flirtatious look *you* gave him."

"Poor Micky, we're probably the bane of his life."

"I think he just doesn't know how to handle us but then he's young."

"Yes, yes he is."

"So, darling, are we all sorted with a plan of action?"

"Yes, I think so. If the papers don't arrive from Maneet I'll chase them up, and I'll send you a copy once they do. I'll make an appointment with Akshay for tomorrow and make sure Andrew is aware."

"Thanks, darling." Bernadette squeezed her hand.

"Fine, I'll get on then."

Imogen sounded reluctant to go, as if the company was helping her to cope.

"If you need me, come back anytime," Bernadette said meaningfully.

Imogen nodded, leaned over and gave her a peck on the cheek.

"I love you, so much," she whispered.

"You too, my sweet."

She watched Imogen leave the room and then on a whim got up and locked the door. Eve had said to her not long ago she liked surprises, and so Bernadette decided to give her one.

* * *

Eve answered the phone almost right away, her dulcet tones gave a fillip to Bernadette's heart. "Darling, how nice to hear from you, aren't you coming home soon?"

Eve sounded hopeful. Bernadette knew Eve missed her when she was at work.

"Yes, I am but what are you doing at the moment?"

"I'm drawing, why?"

"And what are you wearing?" Bernadette dropped her voice a little lower.

"My robe, that's all, you know, I'm naked underneath it." Eve wasn't stupid, she picked up on things very quickly.

"Oh... good, well, go and sit on the sofa, darling."

"Why?" A mischievous note of anticipation crept into Eve's voice.

"Just do as you are told, missy." Bernadette injected an assertive tone into her voice, which she knew Eve liked.

"Oh... God..." Eve gave a little gasp, but the sound of her light footsteps indicated she was complying. "OK, and what now?"

"Are you sitting comfortably?"

"I'm lying down, but yes... why?"

"I'm going to fuck you when I get home that's why, and I wanted you to know that."

"Oh!... oh... oh God."

"Are you touching yourself?" Bernadette demanded.

"Yes..." Eve's voice was already ragged.

"Did I say you could do that?"

"No... oh... but can I please, Mrs Mackenna?"

Bernadette's voice became more sultry, sexy, the way she knew Eve liked it.

"Yes, I want you to touch yourself, I want you to imagine my fingers right there where you are touching, feeling, exactly what I'll be doing to you very soon..."

"Oh... oh... oh... yes... I want that... my God... honey... oh." Eve's breath became heavy, and she was moaning softly.

"Harder, do it harder, faster," Bernadette urged her. "After my fingers, I'll be using my tongue."

"Oh... fuck... you have no idea what that... oh... fuck... oh... my... ohh!" Eve screamed out as she climaxed very rapidly to Bernadette's satisfaction.

She listened as Eve's breathing steadied and she stopped gasping.

"What are you doing now?" Bernadette asked.

"Licking my fingers." Eve laughed.

"God, you're a horny little witch and so very, very bad."

"I'm not the one ringing up and starting phone sex." Eve giggled delightedly.

"Didn't you like it?"

"Of course, I liked it, couldn't you hear?"

"Yes."

"I loved it, and I love you."

"I love you too."

"I hope you're going to..."

"Keep my promise?"

"Yes."

"Of course."

Eve sighed a contented sigh. "OK. I'll get on with the dinner then, darling."

"Bye, darling."

"Love you."

"Love you too."

The phone disconnected and Bernadette looked at it indulgently. She was pleased with herself. Eve was usually the spontaneous one. Perhaps she should do it more often. To Bernadette's surprise they were still as horny as ever they were since they got together. She had a high sex drive and Eve's was more than a match for it. The two of them were quite explosive in that department. It was definitely a very important part of their makeup and their relationship. Bernadette decided she would check on Imogen one more time before leaving.

* * *

Bernadette drove her red Audi Quattro into the driveway. She watched the gate shut behind her as she got out of the car, pulling her bag after her. She punched the coded numbers for the door and went inside. As she put down her bag, Eve appeared in the hallway and sidled up to her. Eve was naked.

"Oh fuck!" said Bernadette at once her arousal levels shooting up at once.

"That's the idea," Eve replied snaking her arms around Bernadette's neck.

Their lips met and fireworks exploded in Bernadette's head. This was the usual effect of Eve's kiss and Bernadette's lips grew hot in response to her wife's soft pliant mouth. Eve began to divest Bernadette of her jacket, and Bernadette slipped out of her shoes still locked in the kiss. Eve's hands moved under her blouse and Bernadette felt her bra release with a snap. Her nipples grew hard immediately under the deft ministrations of Eve's fingers.

"Mmm..." Bernadette murmured softly allowing Eve to manoeuvre her until her back was to the wall. Then Eve was kissing her harder, more urgently and her hands pushed Bernadette's skirt to the floor, followed by her knickers.

"Oh... fuck..." Bernadette gasped as Eve's fingers found their way between her legs.

"Yes... fuck... I'm fucking you... that's exactly what I'm doing," Eve whispered.

"Oh my God... oh... oh fuck... oh... my darling... oh fuck... shit... shit... oh... fuck..." Bernadette cried out, arching her back pushing her crotch into Eve's hand.

"Do you like that... hmm... do you?" Eve murmured her fingers moving faster.

"Oh... yes... yes... oh... fuck... fuck... fuck..." the unstoppable wave was building inside Bernadette and then it crested, she cried out pushing harder against the relentless fingers. "Oh my God... fuck... fuck... oh... fuck... oh my God... fuck... Jesus Christ... oh... oh... ohh!"

Bernadette climaxed with her head laid back, shouting out at the top of her lungs. Eve smiled and held her gently in her arms. She laid her head on Bernadette's breast.

"I love you. I love you so much, honey," she said softly, quietly.

"I love you too."

After a few more moments, when Bernadette had come down from her high, Eve stood up straight letting Bernadette go. "Come on darling, let's eat now."

"But what about?" Bernadette always worried she had not reciprocated.

"Later, my sweetheart, I've made your favourite."

The familiar and delicious smell now assailed Bernadette's senses.

"Stroganoff?"

"Yes."

"I love you even more now," Bernadette said with feeling.

"Is it even possible?" Eve gave a low chuckle.

"Of course, it is." Bernadette let Eve lead her by the hand. "I love you more each day."

"Same."

Eve picked up a gold satin robe and put it on, then handed a similar red one to Bernadette. Bernadette slid it up her arms and tied it while following her wife into the dining room where the table was set as usual. Eve was their very capable housekeeper for the most part. It was a division of labour set by Eve herself. She was the homemaker, and she cooked, kept house. Bernadette liked to help at weekends, but Eve didn't insist and said it was her labour of love. She liked being at home, creating art, and she was now earning good money from it. Eve said she had everything she wanted, and everything she wanted was Bernadette. Bernadette was the main earner, and she loved her work. Eve's income might well eclipse Bernadette's one day but the firm and being a barrister was Bernadette's raison d'etre. Eve would never take it away from her. They lived a privileged life for the most part and they both knew it.

Bernadette sat at the table on the end, and Eve ladled a decent portion of beef stroganoff onto her plate, served with rice rather than the traditional pasta. This was supplemented by a fresh green salad on a separate plate with French dressing. Eve served herself and sat down on Bernadette's left. She poured a glass of sparkling water for both of them. Although Bernadette had been quite the wine buff when Eve first met her, they had both cut down on alcohol. Bernadette acknowledged she felt the better for it. They saved their wine for the weekends usually and then drank in moderation.

"This is delicious, darling," Bernadette said taking a mouthful of the stroganoff.

"As good as it always is?"

"Yes, of course."

"Must be the witchy potions I put in it." Eve giggled.

"Oh you, you and your witch behaviour." Bernadette waved her fork at her wife in admonishment.

"I've got to keep you under my spell somehow."

"No need for potions, *you* are the potion, my darling." Bernadette returned her attention to her food.

"I like it when you say those things." Eve's bare foot ran lightly down Bernadette's calf. She knew this turned Bernadette on, not least because Bernadette had a thing about women's feet. Something Eve played to her advantage whenever she wanted.

"Stop it, I can't concentrate on eating," Bernadette complained.

Eve gave a mock pout, moved her foot away and took a mouthful of her own food.

"Imogen is very unhappy," said Bernadette without preamble.

"What?" Eve looked concerned at once.

"She cried today twice. She said she's worried about D'Arcy. She said D'Arcy seems a bit cold towards her and well, they are having sex but no... you know what."

"D'Arcy's not letting Imogen spank her?" Eve didn't mince words over it.

"No, she isn't but it's not the point. Imogen is scared D'Arcy doesn't love her anymore."

"Oh!" Eve looked quite shocked to hear this.

"You haven't..." Bernadette began.

"No, D'Arcy has said nothing to me about it."

Bernadette knew Eve and D'Arcy were quite close as friends. This was a reassuring sign, since D'Arcy would no doubt have told Eve if there was something amiss.

"So, do you think, Imogen is worrying for nothing?"

Eve didn't answer right away but took a few mouthfuls of the stew and chewed them meditatively. Bernadette took the opportunity to finish her own plate. Eve laid down her cutlery at length and took a drink of water.

"I don't know."

"You don't know?" Bernadette was a little frustrated at this considered response.

"I don't know because even though she's said nothing, D'Arcy can be closed when she wants to be."

"Oh. Fuck it and I thought you would be able to be reassuring." Bernadette pushed her plate away and sipped her own fizzy water.

"Not completely but I'll have lunch with her this week, we are due to anyway, and I'll see if I can't get something out of her subtly, of course."

"Subtly." Bernadette chuckled. Nothing was ever really subtle with D'Arcy.

"I'll have to be circumspect because she'll want to know why I'm asking. I'll ring her in the morning and maybe even see her tomorrow."

"Good, that's good." Bernadette took another sip.

"Tell Imogen to try not to worry, at least let me see what I can find out first."

"Sure, that's good. Although I doubt, I can stop her worrying but I'll try."

"I made dessert." Eve smiled.

"Mmm."

Eve took the plates to the kitchen and returned with a plate of Tiramisu.

'Fuck, you really are spoiling me." Bernadette accepted her plate gratefully.

"Because I love you, baby, that's why."

"I love you too."

Bernadette made suitable noises of appreciation as she tucked into the dessert.

"I know and I've got some good news, the gym will be ready by the weekend."

"Really, how wonderful."

The gymnasium was being installed in the outbuilding at the end of the garden, which was being converted for the purpose. Although Bernadette had not been keen on the exercise at first, she had come to enjoy it, although Eve, who had been a personal trainer, was a real task master.

"So, we can christen it."

"OK. With a gym session?"

"Yes." Eve's eyes were twinkling.

"What are you thinking, missy? I know that look," Bernadette said suspiciously.

"Oh nothing, darling, you'll see."

Bernadette did not explore the subject further. She had no doubt Eve was planning something and she would find out soon enough.

"Once the gym is done, I'm getting the foundations laid for the conservatory," Eve continued.

"You have been a busy little bee."

"Oh, I have, you don't know the half of it." Eve smirked.

"I think I can guess. I suppose you used your vibrator when I got off the phone to you." Bernadette was certain she was right.

"Three times actually."

"Oh my God, you horny little witch." Bernadette let out a crack of laughter.

"Whose fault is that?"

"I wouldn't know."

"You do, yes you do." The insistent foot was back stroking Bernadette's calf.

"I give in, yes, I do. Anyway, I've got news, we've a new client." She wanted to tell Eve about her day before they moved things to the bedroom.

"Oh?"

Eve was attentive at once. She enjoyed hearing about Bernadette's cases and had attended several as she loved to watch Bernadette in court. She had been a party to D'Arcy's libel case, at D'Arcy's insistence. It was during these proceedings that Imogen and D'Arcy got together with explosive consequences. They had become engaged to each other just before Bernadette and Eve had been married. Bernadette told her about Maneet while Eve listened with rapt attention. She also explained how Imogen had been very upset about her own performance in court that day, and Eve was suitably sympathetic.

"Do you think you can get Maneet off?" Eve asked when Bernadette had finished.

"I'm going to try."

"I'm sure you'll do more than try."

"Yes, I will."

Eve knew Bernadette put her heart and soul into her cases. Her confidence in her wife was paramount and unstinting.

"Shall we go upstairs now?" Eve made bedroom eyes at her wife.

"What about the dishes?"

"Leave them until later, I want you... now!"

There was an urgency in her voice and Eve looked flushed and excited. Bernadette pulled her to her feet and led her to the stairway.

CHAPTER TWO

The sun stole around the edge of the blinds in the morning, waking up Bernadette. She was lying spooned against Eve who had her arms tightly wound around her body. The alarm was due to go off shortly and she eased her way out trying not to wake her wife. However, Eve's eyes opened as soon as she moved.

"Where are you going? Hmm?" Eve murmured. "Without kissing me good morning."

"I was trying not to wake you." Bernadette smiled and turned around to face her.

"Don't be silly. I need to wake up otherwise how do I look after you?"

"I love you. I adore you. I worship you." Bernadette kissed her softly, nibbling her lips.

"Worship? Does that mean I'm a goddess?"

"You are my goddess."

"And you're mine."

Eve pulled her closer kissing her more urgently. Bernadette surrendered to the moment as her wife's fingers stole between her legs.

The alarm had gone unheeded while Bernadette was in full flow. She lay back with spent passion.

"Come on then, lazy bones, up you get." Eve laughed.

"Oh you, you're the one keeping me in bed and making me late."

"Go and have your shower, honey."

"Honestly!" Bernadette made an exasperated noise, but she was smiling. She slid out from under the covers and padded off to the bathroom.

When she returned with her wet hair in a towel, Eve sat her down, as she did every day and arranged her hair. Eve decided to plait it after lightly drying it. She did Bernadette's makeup, and then left her to get dressed. The bed was made, and Eve had laid out Bernadette's clothes. Eve chose her clothes, as she delighted in dressing her wife. Bernadette enjoyed the pampering.

Today Eve had chosen a ruched above the knee turquoise skirt, cream blouse and turquoise high heeled mules with a twisted strap. She pulled on the black blazer jacket and checked herself in the mirror with approval. Eve always had the perfect choice. Bernadette liked not having to think about what clothes to wear. She made her way downstairs to the kitchen. Eve was just plating up creamy scrambled eggs on toast with bacon on the side. Bernadette took her place and accepted the plate, followed by a cup of coffee. Eve sat down beside her at the breakfast bar with her own food and began to cut into the toast.

"Delicious as always, darling," Bernadette said taking a mouthful of the soft fluffy eggs.

"You're not… tired of my breakfast?" Eve said suddenly concerned.

"Don't be silly, darling, I love them. I'm a creature of habit, don't you know by now?"

"So, I'm a habit?" Eve's eyes danced at her.

"No, you're an addiction." Bernadette lightly touched Eve's arm.

"I'm happy to hear the potions are working."

"Oh, you're incorrigible!"

"You say the nicest things, my darling."

Bernadette smiled and put her attention back on her eggs. Although she didn't have court, she tried not to be late. Even though she was the boss, she liked to set a good example. Eve's insistence this morning had already pushed her a little for time.

"You know I should really start compiling a list," Bernadette said giving her a sly look.

"Ooh, really?" Eve looked happy at once.

The list was the start of a game. A game of consequences which Eve had instituted when Eve wanted a Shibari session. Those were the consequences. Although a little shy about it at first, Bernadette entered very much into the spirit of it now. She always started with a list of Eve's misdemeanours which Eve naturally perpetrated deliberately.

"Yes, really and the fact that your horny behaviour made me late is going at the top."

"So, I have to watch my behaviour now?"

"Yes, yes you do my girl," Bernadette said sternly.

"I'll have to see how much I can misbehave then."

"Don't say I didn't warn you."

"Mmm." Eve looked like the cat who got the cream.

Bernadette drained her coffee and made set it down on the counter.

"I have to go, my darling."

"OK."

Eve followed her out for her goodbye kiss. Bernadette turned to her and melted into her kiss. The goodbye kiss was an immutable tradition. When their lips met, it was like fire and ice all at the same time. A firework display went off in Bernadette's head just as it always did from the very first day. Eve always told her it was a witchy spell to make sure Bernadette did not forget her. Eve always said she was a witch, and it was Bernadette's pet name for her. Bernadette half believed it was true.

Their lips parted and Bernadette picked up her bag. She got into her car and gunned it into life. As she turned to pull out of the drive, Eve was standing in the doorway with her arms folded, barefoot, waving, wearing only a robe pulled tight around her curves. She would probably stay that way all day unless she was going out. Bernadette knew full well Eve used the toys from the drawer upstairs and probably watched porn too, in between her art sessions. But she didn't mind. They had reached a point of true honesty between them, and as far as she was concerned wedded bliss. She knew Eve felt the same way. There had been some fairly big bumps along the way, but they were in a good place. She pulled out into the main road and thought about Imogen. It seemed she had hit a major hump in her relationship with D'Arcy. She hoped she and Eve would be able to help her fix it. As she began her short drive to the office, she turned up the radio and began to hum to the latest tunes.

* * *

Bernadette pulled up in the road outside her offices, happy to have found a rare parking space just outside. Parking time was limited, so she would drop the keys off with Juanita their receptionist and Andrew's PA. She walked up the steps to the black front door. There was a swipe card entry and CCTV all courtesy of D'Arcy who had insisted on paying for its installation during her court case, due to a very real threat from D'Arcy's psychopathic ex-boyfriend. Bernadette walked down the long narrow hallway which comprised the entrance with its green walls, and white ceiling.

Juanita, a Spanish beauty, was sitting at the L-shaped reception desk reading Hello magazine. It was common knowledge that Juanita didn't do much work, but Andrew would not hear of getting rid of her. He had a soft spot for Juanita who apparently had a sick mother in Spain.

"Move my car please, honey," said Bernadette dropping her keys on the counter just as she always did.

"Of course, I move, I move, I always move," said Juanita not looking up from her magazine.

Bernadette who was used to her ways, and had developed a fondness for the indolent Juanita, just smiled. "Thanks, darling, is Imogen here yet?"

"Yes, she is here, she came early."

"OK, thank you." Bernadette headed for the kitchen at the back to get a coffee for herself and for her junior partner. The kitchen was long and narrow with green lacquered scallop front cabinets, and windows on the other side and tables where people could sit if they wished. She obtained two coffees from the machine and went upstairs to Imogen's office.

Imogen looked up when she entered, she could tell at once that her junior was unhappy and assumed things were still not going well.

"Hi, darling," said Bernadette sitting down at Imogen's sofa.

Imogen moved across and took the mug of coffee from her, she looked at Bernadette expectantly.

"I talked to Eve." Bernadette knew this would be the first thing on her mind.

"And?" Imogen was eager for news.

"She doesn't know anything, darling, but she's going to have lunch with D'Arcy and see if she can find out what's going on."

"OK." Imogen's expression was crestfallen at once and she sipped her coffee to cover the evident distress.

"My sweetheart, don't fret. We are going to get to the bottom of these or my name's not Bernadette Mackenna." She said this with more confidence than she felt.

"OK." A solitary tear trickled down Imogen's cheek, wringing Bernadette's heartstrings.

"How were things last night?" she ventured.

"OK, I guess. We watched TV, made love. But D'Arcy was distant, non-communicative. It's so hard to take, because we always talk about everything usually and she's on fire for me when I get home."

"Oh. Did you try talking? Making conversation?"

"I tried, but how hard can you try? The conversation peters out very quickly and so you don't want to try anymore... oh... fuck... fuck... fuck."

Once more Imogen burst into tears, and once more she ended up in Bernadette's arms for comfort. While she stroked her friends flaming red hair, Bernadette hoped Eve might even see D'Arcy that day and gain some insight into what was going on. She certainly hoped so, because, at this rate, things were heading for a showdown and it wasn't going to be pretty at all.

"It's OK," she soothed, "It's going to be OK."

"I'm breaking, Bernadette, she's breaking my heart," came the muffled response.

"I promise you it will be OK."

"You can't do that, nobody can," Imogen sobbed.

Bernadette fell silent. Imogen was right, and there was no promise she could give her that D'Arcy wasn't going to break up with her. She just hoped it wasn't going to be the case. Imogen would be a mess and Bernadette was going to be very angry with D'Arcy indeed that was a given. As far as allegiances were concerned although she did love D'Arcy, Imogen was like family to her, a sister, and anybody hurt her at their peril. D'Arcy would be getting a piece of Bernadette's mind in the event she broke Imogen's heart, and she would not be holding back. Bernadette pursed her lips and hoped it wouldn't come to it, although the signs were definitely not good.

After several minutes, Imogen began to recover and sat up. She picked up her coffee, took a sip and grimaced in distaste as it was cold.

"I'll get you another," Bernadette said at once.

"No, it's fine. I need to pull myself together. We've got Akshay Pandit coming in about half an hour to discuss the finances. Andrew is aware."

"You don't have to sit in on the meeting if you don't feel up to it."

"No, I want to, I need to take my mind off this or I'm going to implode or something."

"OK, well, why don't you freshen up and we'll do the meeting, have lunch together? How's that?"

"Yes, that's grand." Imogen gave her a weak smile. Bernadette leaned across and kissed her lightly.

"You are going to get through this, one way or another."

"Thank you, and for being my friend."

"Always, darling, I'm always there for you."

"Don't I'll cry all over again." Imogen laughed.

"Don't do that, my jacket won't stand it."

They both laughed at this and it relieved the tension.

"I'll see you shortly then." Bernadette squeezed her hand and left the room. She was smiling but inside she was sorely troubled for her friend.

In a short while, Bernadette, Imogen, Andrew Bond and Akshay Pandit were sitting around the small meeting table in Andrew's office. His office had been tidied for the occasion Bernadette noticed. The filing cabinets and his desk were usually strewn with papers and files. These had all miraculously disappeared, and the office looked almost immaculate. It had the same dark green walls, and a white ceiling with mouldings matching the décor of the rest of the office. Andrew also had a window which looked out onto the street and gave him some natural daylight. However, for the most part, Andrew was usually found at his desk typing nineteen to the dozen. He was very hard working and kept the firm's finances ticking over, as well as bringing in revenue from the outside doing various accounting jobs for local businesses.

Andrew was in his fifties, with short cropped grey hair, and a kindly face. He was English and married to an Irish Titian haired beauty, who was also exceptionally volatile. Today he was wearing a black suit, white shirt and blue spotted tie and looking very dapper. He kept the suit at the office for important clients.

Akshay was every inch a banker. He had a very expensive blue suit with brown brogues, a pin striped shirt and red tie. He was around thirty-five with slightly greying ample locks. He was well turned out and sported a closely cropped beard. He had a Rolex gold watch and a heavy gold signet ring on his finger. It was evident he was a man of expensive tastes judging from the cut of his clothes.

"So, I understand you will be, ahem… footing the bill for Maneet, who is your fiancée," Andrew said opening the bidding. The formalities had been completed along with the small talk, and refreshments served.

"Yes, that's right but first I would like to ask a few questions about the case," said Akshay urbanely.

"Ask away," said Bernadette.

"You know this is a serious case for… for my family and myself," he began.

"It's a serious case for Maneet."

"Yes, of course, but you know, it has the potential of bringing some great disrepute onto her family and mine, as we are to be married."

Andrew noticed a martial light enter Bernadette's eye at this statement and decided to attempt to intervene.

"Yes, I'm sure it is of course very concerning for all parties connected with the case, but if we can discuss the proposed daily rates…"

"Yes, yes in good time," said Akshay waving a dismissive hand. "I am more than able to cover the expense of the court case but that is not my point."

"Oh? What is your point in that case?" Andrew looked nettled.

Bernadette and Imogen exchanged glances it took a fair bit to rattle Andrew's calm demeanour but Akshay seemed to be doing a good job.

"My point is, are you going to win?"

Andrew looked at Bernadette expecting her to take the lead on this.

"We are going to do our best to win of course…" she began mildly. It wasn't an unusual question but the way he phrased it was somewhat insulting.

"Doing your best is not good enough, in my business you win, or you get out and cut your losses."

"And what is your business?" Bernadette kept her composure although to Imogen there were tell-tale signs of annoyance.

"I deal in stocks, currency, that sort of thing," he said airily. "I take risks on positions every day, millions of Euros, hundreds of millions sometimes, but I don't bet on something I can't win."

The way he puffed himself up did not impress Bernadette.

"I see." She eyed him askance. She couldn't resist a dig. "So, it's a form of gambling in effect with other people's money."

She wasn't stupid. She was perfectly aware of how wholesale banking and trading worked. Her father had told her all about this and other businesses when she was younger. At university, she had fraternised with all kinds of people and learned a great deal about how these things worked.

"If you want to put it that way." He gave a short laugh. "I prefer to call it strategised investment. I'm known in the City of Dublin as a sure bet."

"Good for you."

"Can you say the same about yourself?" He put this out as a challenge and the arrogance of the question vexed Bernadette. Beside her, she could tell Imogen was riling up.

"You know, the legal profession isn't like your little financial games. We throw everything we have into every case, but these cases are decided by judges and juries of twelve honest men and women. We make the best case we can within the law, based on evidence but the final decisions are made by them regardless of what we would like the outcome to be. There are no sure bets in law, Mr Pandit." Her tone was even, and she tried to keep the anger she was starting to feel out of it.

"So, you can't *guarantee* a win?" he said with a slight tone of division.

"No, I can't but I can tell you I win more than I lose."

"Yes, she does," put in Imogen.

"I don't like those odds."

Her bile was beginning to rise. His whole attitude was insulting, chauvinistic and potentially misogynistic.

"They're the only ones I've got, I'm afraid. The law isn't the same as wholesale banking." She regarded him implacably.

"If you'd like to discuss our rates..." Andrew began again hopefully.

It seemed Akshay wanted to still make his point.

"What about no win no fee then? If you win, I'll pay you more than it would cost you, double even if it helps and if you lose, you get nothing."

Bernadette was close to the edge now. He had annoyed her almost past the point of no return. Under the table, she felt the light touch of Imogen's hand as if to try and stay her wrath.

"We don't do no win no fee," she said tightly.

"Oh?"

"No."

"And why's that?" he shot it back at as a challenge.

"Because the people who engage us to defend them have every confidence we'll do the best job we can, and we do, but I've got people in this firm who work for me, who rely on me and my colleagues for their living. So, I'm not jeopardising my firm or their livelihoods to satisfy yours or anyone else's predilection for gambling."

"I can take my business elsewhere," he said smoothly.

"You can." Bernadette shrugged and sat back with her arms folded.

"That's it?" He looked incredulous as if he didn't expect them to turn him down. It was almost as if he thought his business was something she should not be able to refuse.

He didn't realise she did refuse clients and some very wealthy ones. She wasn't going to be held to ransom by anyone, and particularly not someone so arrogant.

"Pretty much, we didn't go asking your fiancée to take the case, she came to us. If you don't like our terms and conditions, then there are plenty of other legal firms in Dublin. I suggest you try them."

Bernadette was calmer now, she didn't like to turn away business, but at the same time, she wasn't going to be dictated to in this fashion. Apart from anything she knew if she acceded to his terms then he'd always call the shots. Nobody called the shots on her, and certainly not a client.

He wasn't expecting this. He was, no doubt, used to being on the winning side of negotiations and having people do what he wanted. When someone wasn't going to play ball, he didn't know what to do. Bernadette said nothing more, leaving the ball firmly in his court if he wanted to play it would be on her terms and not his.

For once Andrew was also silent. Bernadette knew he wasn't going to agree to a no win no fee either, so she was sure of her ground.

After a few more moments, Akshay stood up as if to call her bluff.

"Right then, I'll find another lawyer."

"As you wish."

They all stood up to and he turned for the door. Something in Bernadette snapped, she wasn't going to let him walk out without furnishing him with her none too favourable opinion of him.

"You know, frankly you seem far more interested in the money than in any chance of getting your fiancée off the charges. Regardless of the cost, if you love her and if you had an ounce of backbone in you then you'd support her choices. I've met her once and she's a beautiful person inside and out. I don't know what you think you're playing at doubting her in this way, and in her time of need. Frankly, if I was her, I'd dump you, but she is obviously head over heels in love with you, God knows why. So, I suggest you live up to it. Find another lawyer by all means where you can act the big shot banker since your family reputation evidently means more to you than her love for you."

He looked at her, gobsmacked. It was unlikely anyone usually spoke to him in this way, let alone a woman.

"Yes, well," he said not sure of what to reply.

"I'll, erm, see you out," Andrew told him, and took him to the door before he could collect his wits.

"Good day to you," Bernadette called after him.

"Fucking good job!" said Imogen firing up. "What an absolute fucking tosser! What an arsehole. Fucking hell, I was ready to lay into him and no mistake, particularly the way I'm feeling."

"Just as well you didn't." Bernadette laughed. "We'd have had to pick him up off the floor."

Andrew returned, with a slight smile. "That went well," he quipped.

"Sorry, Andrew, but it had to be said, supercilious prick," Bernadette replied angrily.

"Oh, I'm in total agreement with you." Andrew held his hands up. "Can't stand people like that. Up themselves and swinging their big dicks around because they've got money."

Akshay had obviously struck a nerve with Andrew.

"Sorry, we lost the client."

"Oh, it can't be helped, and anyway, you know my aversion to anything like *that*," said Andrew airily. By which Bernadette knew he meant working for free. Whenever she took a *pro bono* case he certainly acted up.

"Well, I guess we can get back to work then."

"Yes, off you go. I've plenty of work to do now that idiot wasted all our time. It was something I could well have done without."

"All of us I'm afraid, ah well, you win some, you lose some. Come on, Imogen."

They left Andrew to it and returned upstairs.

* * *

They went to Mamma Mia's for lunch, Imogen having fired off an email to Maneet telling her, unfortunately, they couldn't represent her, as her fiancé wasn't disposed to pay their fees after all. Imogen wasn't in the best of moods and Bernadette tried to keep up the conversation talking about their new conservatory and gym. Imogen smiled and laughed but Bernadette knew her mind was elsewhere, she hoped Eve would bring some good news later on.

As they passed by Juanita's desk on their return to the office, she said, "Oh, Bernadette, that lawyer is here to see you."

"Which lawyer?" It was typical of Juanita to talk in riddles.

"The one who got into the fight."

"You know about that?" Bernadette looked surprised.

"Oh yes, it was on the news. She hit the Garda man many times."

"You saw it?" Imogen was incredulous.

"Oh yes, on the television, on the news." Juanita looked at them both as if they were complete idiots.

"You watch the news?"

"Of course, what do you think?" said Juanita dismissively.

Bernadette and Imogen exchanged glances. The last thing they expected would be Juanita being up with current affairs.

"Right, we will want to talk to you later then, about what you saw," said Bernadette.

"OK, sure." Juanita waved her hand returning to her magazine.

"Where is Maneet?"

"In the meeting room, I give her a drink, don't you worry, I do everything."

This seemed to be the limit of the effort Juanita could expend on the whole subject. With a big sigh, she resumed reading.

"Come," said Bernadette to Imogen, "Let's get up there and see her."

They walked into the meeting room with a cup of coffee each to find Maneet pacing up and down the room in an agitated manner. As soon as she saw them, she rushed over to Bernadette.

"I am so sorry," she began.

"I'm sorry too," said Bernadette.

"No! You don't have anything to be sorry about but as for Akshay, I am furious with him, I can't tell you."

"Do tell us, though." Bernadette guided her to the sofa. She and Imogen took seats opposite.

"I didn't expect this to happen." Maneet was still annoyed. "When I asked Akshay to come and discuss the financial aspects I did not think he'd start trying to haggle with you."

"He didn't exactly haggle, rather he tried to force our hand into a no win no fee arrangement, and we just don't do that... ever."

"He's the limit! I am absolutely not speaking to him at the moment, he has made me so angry. I slammed the phone down on him."

"Right." Bernadette wasn't sure where this was leading.

"I wanted to come and apologise to you. Akshay said he was getting me another lawyer and I told him I didn't want anyone else. I want you!"

"That's nice but..."

"If it's the money you're worried about, my father will foot the bill. At least for the moment. My organisation may pay for it, raise the funds but he will cover it."

"I'm happy to hear it but I don't want your father to..."

"He's got plenty of money, don't you worry. He has properties all over it's not an issue." Maneet cut her off for the second time.

"OK, so do we need to get him in to sign something?" Bernadette said with a sigh.

"I'll do it, take me to see your finance manager and I'll sign whatever papers need signing."

"OK."

"Look, please. I know I'm a pain and this hasn't been a good start, but I really, really want you to represent me, please." Maneet was almost pleading with Bernadette, as Bernadette was being somewhat non-committal.

She said nothing more for a moment and as Maneet really did look like she might burst into tears again, she spoke, "Of course I'll represent you."

"You should have heard what she said to your fiancé," Imogen added mendaciously.

"Oh, thank you!" Maneet was wreathed in smiles. "He told me. I said bloody good job, Akshay, you stupid crass idiot making me look like a bloody fool. How dare you. I'm glad she said that to you and if I'd been there, I'd have said a whole lot more. Which I did anyway." She laughed.

"I think I'm really starting to like you," said Bernadette smiling too.

"I love you already," said Imogen.

"You two are so lovely, really. I can't imagine anyone else taking my case to court than you."

"It's good to hear. So, Imogen will take you down to see Andrew Bond and you can sign all the papers. We've already started anyway. I was quite disappointed when I spoke to your fiancé and thought we might have to pull out."

"It's nothing to how I felt I can assure you. I was fuming, absolutely fuming. Akshay is going to have to do some grovelling before I speak to him again, I can tell you." Maneet sounded so assertive that Bernadette almost felt sorry for Akshay after all, she was going to lead him a merry dance if they did manage to tie the knot.

"We have had a little bit of a volatile relationship," Maneet continued. "It's been on and off for some while. I'm afraid Akshay is a little, how shall I put it politely, like a pompous arsehole who is completely up himself and I can't stand that about him. I'm trying to change him but it's hard work."

"You must really love him," said Imogen.

"I do." They noticed how Maneet's whole expression softened. "There's another side to him which is so adorable, and he's so handsome, dashing. On his own, he's very funny, and charming, a romantic. All this other stuff he's picked up the city, the big I am, that's not him at all. I'll just have to knock these rough edges off him is all. Then I'm sure he'll be fine."

"Yes, for sure," said Bernadette with more conviction than she felt. Her experience of trying to change people was not an unqualified success. Rather, she had found that people were inclined to never change some parts of themselves and you had to love them and live with it or not. Only in Eve had she found there was nothing she couldn't love. This was rare she felt. She secretly wished Maneet well since her impression of Akshay wasn't that favourable at all.

"Anyway, I'm sure you must be busy, take me to your finance man and let's do the deed."

"Of course, but we will want to interview you more in depth shortly about exactly what happened. It would help if you can try to jot down the events of the incident, what exactly was said when. Try to get your thoughts in order if you can."

"I'll try, of course. It's all a jumble, a blur but I know you need something more precise so I will do my best."

Maneet was a lawyer herself. This was handy since it made it easier for her to understand what was needed and why they needed it.

"Great, then we'll speak soon."

Bernadette stood up and Imogen moved across to take Maneet to see Andrew.

"I'm really sorry again about Akshay," Maneet said.

"It's OK, it can't be helped and I'm sure we can move on from that. We've got a case to win."

"Yes, yes we do."

"Shall we?" Imogen asked her.

Bernadette bade Maneet a cordial goodbye and watched them leave. She sat down for a few moments to gather her thoughts. She was flattered Maneet wanted her to continue with the representation and had found a way to pay for it. There wasn't any way Bernadette could offer to *pro bono* it although the thought had crossed her mind. Andrew would have a fit, and since she'd turned down a no win no fee, which she would never do, she could hardly then do it for free.

In the back of her consciousness, a small but insistent voice was telling her this case could spell trouble. This was a little concerning. It hadn't got off to an auspicious start, and also when it came to issues like discrimination these topics could become very inflammatory. Not that Bernadette shied away from such things, but she didn't want to expose people in her firm to potential harm. She felt wholly responsible for their well-being at work. They had already had the security issues with the D'Arcy case to contend with and she did not want this to become one of those. However, on the other hand, was her overriding sense of justice, and this seemed to her to be a case which deserved justice to be done. Bernadette was a champion of justice and she wouldn't rest once she'd taken up the sword in defence of it.

As it was the rest of the day passed off without further incident. Papers were signed, Andrew was happy with the result and Imogen seemed in better spirits. Bernadette was looking forward to hopefully getting some news from Eve, assuming she'd managed to go out with D'Arcy.

Bernadette smiled all the way home, as she always did because she knew Eve would be waiting for her. Also, she never knew what might be for dinner and also what surprise Eve might spring on her. Eve was playfully by nature and also exceptionally horny much of the time. This suited Bernadette who matched her wife's high sex drive, and it made for some interesting times. They texted during the day and even called but it was mainly endearments or naughty suggestions for later. When she got home, they would talk about their day.

She pulled her Audi into the drive and went into the house while the gate closed behind her. She shut the door and put down her bag. There were no smells of culinary delights which was a little disappointing as Eve usually had a meal prepared. Just as she was wondering as to the whereabouts of her wife, Eve sauntered into the hallway. She was wearing an exceptionally short black ruched mini dress, with shoestring straps and an open V back. She had strappy heeled mules on and her hair was hanging enticingly loose.

"Fuck!" Bernadette exclaimed.

"You like?" Eve smiled.

"Yes, I very much like."

"Good, because we're going out to dinner."

"We are?"

"Yes, I want to and I'm taking you. Now go upstairs and get changed, your clothes are laid out on the bed."

"Ooh, but my hair, and makeup..."

"Is fine as it is, and I'll touch up your lipstick, now go on."

"So assertive."

"I can be."

Bernadette giggled like a delighted schoolgirl and went upstairs to see what her wife had picked out for her. It turned out to be a royal blue ruched midi length dress which she had not seen before, and silver strappy mules. It had shoestring straps also but wasn't backless like Eve's. There was also a silver sparkly jacket and silver clutch bag. Bernadette got dressed and admired the outfit in the mirror checking her makeup and hair before returning downstairs.

"Someone's been shopping," she said as she sashayed towards Eve.

"But you look drop dead gorgeous and I love you in that outfit."

"Thank you. You look sexy as fuck."

"Thank you, and you can kiss me now."

Bernadette kissed her almost hungrily and adoringly. She let the fireworks pop in her head savouring Eve's sweet soft lips and nuzzling against them gently.

"I quite like it when you take charge," she murmured.

"I like it too, sometimes." Eve nuzzled her back. "But you're still the boss."

"Am I?"

"Of course, and that's the way I want it," Eve said firmly.

"Shall we go then?"

"Yes, the taxi should be here any moment."

"Where are we going?"

"You'll see."

✳ ✳ ✳

The taxi arrived outside Marco Pierre White's Courtyard Bar and Grill a short drive from their house. The unassuming entrance led through to a pleasant, paved courtyard with tables outside and also indoors. The entranceway was lit by fairy lights, and there were shrubs and trees around the courtyard. The evening was on the cool side, Bernadette was glad Eve had booked a table inside the restaurant. The interior was lined with patio doors and had a pleasant atmosphere with subdued lighting. It consisted of a classic country house style look with pictures on the walls, a wooden floor and round tables each with a small lamp in the centre. The waiter ushered them to a table at the side and, since it wasn't too busy, it felt quite cosy.

Bernadette felt Eve's foot slide up her calf suggestively and Eve gave her a sultry smile.

"This is very lovely, what brought it on?" Bernadette asked her.

"I didn't feel like cooking today, and I wanted to give you a treat. I read about this place and wanted to give it a try, with you." Eve shrugged.

"It's a very nice treat, thank you."

"Also..."

"Also?"

"Extravagance is very naughty, and you should know that."

"Is it?"

"Yes," Eve said firmly.

"I'll remember to include it on my list then, although I feel it's churlish to punish someone for such a lovely treat." Bernadette gave a wry smile. She guessed there was more than one motive for this outing. Shibari was evidently very much at the forefront of Eve's mind.

"But firmness is important." Eve's eyes danced.

"Is it?"

"Yes."

"You're very bad, my darling." Bernadette slipped her hand into Eve's under the table.

"That's what I need to hear."

The waiter brought the menus, and it was simple slightly eclectic fare. Bernadette opted for *fresh scallops with Gubbeen smokehouse chorizo and celeriac puree*, followed by *belly of pork with Bramley apple and bubble and squeak*. Eve chose *Castletownbere crab, fresh herbs and mayonnaise*, and then *boned half roast chicken, grilled tomato, sauce Bearnaise and frites.* They ordered a glass of house rosé each and sparkling water. Bernadette did not want to consume an entire bottle between them since her capacity for alcohol was much diminished thanks to being more abstemious, a state which she infinitely preferred. They chose the wine as a compromise between red or white, though Bernadette usually preferred Pinot or Merlot.

"Now," said Bernadette quietly when the waiter had gone, "just so *you* know, I have decided you will be getting a Shibari session this weekend, because your misbehaviour has begun to escalate quite outrageously, and you need to be taken in hand."

She was well aware this was what Eve wanted and she decided to pitch it early rather than keeping Eve in suspense all week. They could move on to other topics with Eve well satisfied in anticipation of fulfilling her craving.

"Oh," was all Eve said but a tell-tale flush on her cheeks showed she was aroused, as did the insistent stroking of Bernadette's calf with her bare foot. This was making concentration difficult for Bernadette since she found it particularly stimulating, something Eve knew only too well.

"Darling, stop it for a moment, please. I promise I'll fuck you when we get home," she whispered.

"But I want you so badly," Eve whispered back.

"Well, you'll have to wait."

Eve turned a little mulish around the mouth at this.

"Will I?"

"What?"

"Come on, to the ladies, now!"

"Eve!"

Powerless to resist, she left the table with Eve in search of the toilet. This was a potluck undertaking since there was no telling what kind of loo the establishment would have neither of them having been there before. However, it turned out to be a suitable sized cubicle and Eve pulled her inside frantically locking the door.

"Oh, you are so..." Bernadette whispered but was silenced by Eve's insistent and urgent kiss which blew away any reservations she may have had. In a trice Eve's hand was pushing up Bernadette's skirt and making its way into her knickers.

"Oh fuck..." Bernadette gasped as the fingers found their target, "Fuck... oh... Eve..."

"Hush," Eve whispered continuing to make Bernadette want to scream her head off.

The situation was so horny, and the need to stop herself from speaking or moaning was so great that Bernadette climaxed in short order tensing hard around Eve's hand and suppressing the urge to cry out.

"Oh... oh... oh... fuck... oh... oh... oh... fuck... ohh," she breathed as the orgasm took her.

Almost immediately and urgently, Eve took Bernadette's hand and pushed it between her own legs having hitched up her skirt to her waist. Bernadette could feel her wife was dripping wet and no sooner had she touched her than Eve was shuddering deliciously with her head laid back.

"Oh... fuck... yes... fuck... oh my God... fuck... mmm... oh God... that was quick... oh my God... ohh," Eve whispered quietly as her whole body tensed and untensed in response to her climax.

After a little while as Bernadette held her gently, Eve relaxed, Bernadette let her go and kissed her softly. It was deliciously naughty, and Bernadette had enjoyed the clandestine nature as Eve knew she would. Eve had certainly led her to places she had not previously explored as regards sex.

"You are very bad, very, very bad, my girl, and you are going to pay for this little escapade as I'm sure you are aware."

Bernadette rearranged her dress, and washed her hands, as did Eve.

"Oh yes, I am, I certainly am, and I'm so looking forward to it." Eve smiled and kissed her back.

They sauntered back to their table, and no sooner had they sat down then the waiter brought the first course.

"Mmm, delicious and still OK," said Bernadette as she took a mouthful of scallops' conscious of the fact they may have had to keep it warm while she and Eve were otherwise engaged in the toilet.

"Lovely." Eve sampled her crab.

"You seem to have a predilection for toilet sex," Bernadette murmured recalling several other occasions in restaurants where Eve had pulled a similar stunt.

"I just like sex." Eve grinned cheekily.

"That too."

They finished the first course. Bernadette pushed her plate aside and took a sip of her wine.

"So, did you see D'Arcy today?" she said at length. Now Eve's libido had been temporarily assuaged she mused that perhaps they could have a normal conversation.

"Yes, I did." Eve sipped her wine too.

"And?"

"I didn't learn a lot, to be honest."

"Oh fuck!" This was disappointing.

"Sorry. I tried. I asked her in as roundabout a way as possible how things were going, and stuff like that. I tried to probe but it didn't really get anywhere."

"What *did* she say?" The news was very frustrating to Bernadette, as she had hoped for something a little more concrete, particularly since Eve and D'Arcy were quite close as friends.

"She said things are fine. Imogen is fine. Sex is fantastic as always. She likes being at home and with Imogen. They can't agree on the wedding plans and she spent quite a lot of time talking about that."

"Is *that* the problem, do you think?" Bernadette ventured after hearing all of this.

"No, I don't think it is." Eve's tone was frank.

"But you think there *is* a problem?" Bernadette could pick it up from Eve's voice.

"There is something wrong, but I don't know what it is. She's not her usual self and something is bothering her, even I can tell." Eve shrugged almost as nonplussed as Bernadette.

"Fuck!" Bernadette said in frustration. "Poor Imogen cried again today, and I can see she is almost at the end of her tether. I can foresee an explosion soon if we can't get to the bottom of it."

Eve thought for a bit and drank some more wine.

"Maybe that's part of the problem."

"What do you mean?"

"From what I can gather from D'Arcy, Imogen hasn't been getting to the bottom of things for a while. D'Arcy's bottom to be precise." She laughed at her own pun.

"Imogen did mention she'd not spanked D'Arcy in a while, yes."

"Perhaps she should."

Bernadette frowned. "Really? Imogen said D'Arcy didn't want her to and that's why she stopped."

"What D'Arcy wants and what she needs might be two different things."

"She can't force her. It has to be consensual."

Eve shook her head and smiled knowingly. "Yes, of course, it does. But when one partner stops doing something, particularly sexual, you know that in itself can cause doubt and problems in the other partner. Then it becomes a self-fulfilling prophecy."

"You really think it's so simple?" Bernadette was surprised at this little nugget of wisdom, and it seemed to her unlikely to be the entirety of the issue.

"No, darling, I don't but I do think Imogen needs to be herself and not pussyfoot around with D'Arcy. Maybe the truth will come out eventually, but Imogen isn't helping herself at all the way she's acting around her. She needs to stop walking on eggshells and just be herself, as if everything is normal even if it's not."

"Oh!" Bernadette was much struck by this viewpoint which had never occurred to her before. She mused on it for a few moments and then said, "So it's like if I stopped doing Shibari on you for no reason."

"Yes." Eve smiled. "But you wouldn't." She looked very firmly into Bernadette's eyes.

"Oh?"

"Because I wouldn't let you and because you love me too much. But yes, it would be like that, to answer your question."

There was a message in that statement, and Bernadette knew it. However, much Eve said Bernadette was the boss, Eve was very much also in control of things in their relationship. Instead of bothering her, Bernadette found this comforting, in that both of them were making the running and this was as it should be.

"Also," Eve added, "I love you too much too. Anyway, about Imogen and D'Arcy, that's what I think."

"How did you become so wise?" Bernadette had always been full of admiration for Eve's seemingly old head on such young shoulders. She put Bernadette to shame sometimes with her insight into relationships and other things. By the same token, Bernadette had learned a lot from her and from being with her, and she was still learning every day.

"I don't know and I'm not really, not all the time."

"You are to me."

Eve blew her a kiss, and the waiter brought the main course.

"Ooh this looks lovely," said Bernadette, cutting into the pork and taking a mouthful, "And it is, meltingly so in fact."

"Beautiful," Eve agreed, trying her chicken.

They ate together for a few minutes, feeding each other little bits from their own dish, just like young lovers in their first flush. There were a few surreptitious glances from other diners, almost envious at two people so harmoniously and obviously in love.

"You make me so ecstatically happy," said Bernadette as she laid down her cutlery for a moment.

"If I do then it's mission accomplished." Eve smiled.

"Do I make you happy?"

"I knew you would ask that. Darling, you should never have to ask. I'm so happy some days I could cry with it."

"Oh!" Bernadette flushed a little at this declaration.

"Finish your food and tell me about your day."

"OK, well, we lost our new client and got her back again..." Bernadette laughed.

"Do tell."

Bernadette spent the rest of the main course relating the events of the day, and all about Akshay's dreadful behaviour. Eve giggled about what she had said to him and endorsed the view that he sounded like a "right prick". She explained how Maneet had been very angry but was evidently besotted with him. However, they could at least proceed with their investigations and putting together their defence.

"Do you think you can get her off the charges?" Eve asked her at length finishing off the remains of her chicken.

"I don't know but we're going to give it a shot. It all depends on what evidence we can dig up, to be honest."

Bernadette put the last piece of the pork belly into her mouth and ate it with evident satisfaction. She had saved it until the end so it would be the last flavour she tasted.

"You've got Micky on the case?"

"Yes, I have, and I found out today Juanita saw the incident on the telly apparently and, surprise, surprise, she watches the news."

"Now that is a surprise." Eve had no great opinion of Juanita's intellect, in the sense she had, up to then showed no interest in anything apart from fashion and gossip magazines, and very little motivation to do any work.

"It just goes to show you can't judge a book by its cover, darling."

"You're right." Eve sighed. "I've been a bit harsh thinking of her as just a bimbo."

Bernadette couldn't help chuckling at this. "People are full of surprises, you told me yourself."

"I know, I've been very judgemental and..."

"Your list is going to be a long one this week."

"Yes." Eve sighed again happily at the thought.

They were both full, and so declined the dessert menu, but elected for a coffee instead. Eve talked about her plans for a new series of drawings and paintings focusing on self-love. This was news to Bernadette, and she asked Eve what she meant by that. Bernadette coloured up a little on discovering it was primarily focused on women pleasuring themselves. She was no prude but sometimes Eve's art exploits shocked her a little. It was one thing to talk about it, another to see it graphically depicted. However, Eve's art was fetching very good prices, so she did not demur.

"I'm going to have these amazing backgrounds, like fireworks and bright flowering explosions of colour, as if you can see what their climax looks like," Eve told her enthusiastically.

"And Valentino is up for this, is he?"

Valentino owned the gallery that syndicated out Eve's work. It sold very well and her last series of BDSM style pieces had done exceptionally well.

"Oh yes, he thinks it's marvellous, he has clients who will pay big money for them. I'm going to do some big canvases too and perhaps oils or acrylics."

"Really? When you say big money?" Bernadette knew the art was fetching a few thousand Euro apiece so far, and she had seen the receipts coming into their bank. Besides she acted as Eve's manager, although now Eve was up and running, Eve pretty much managed herself. Bernadette just made sure the contracts were all tight, and the books and tax was done properly. Andrew was handling the tax and accounting side of things which kept it in the family so to speak.

"Oh, anything from twenty thousand to fifty thousand," Eve said airily.

"What?" Bernadette almost spat out her coffee. "Did you say fifty grand?"

"Yes."

"Euros?"

"Yes, darling." Eve smiled mischievously.

"Jesus H Christ."

"I'm sure he wouldn't approve," Eve giggled.

"Wow, well…"

"Do you approve now you've heard how much it will earn us?" Eve regarded her teasing.

"I do but don't be like that, I didn't, not really."

"You were a little shocked though," Eve said candidly.

"I was taken aback by the idea, initially."

"Now who's the bad girl?" Eve pursued her theme with relish.

"Darling I…"

"You doubted me, didn't you?"

"Well, I not exactly but I was just." Bernadette bit her lip, when Eve became assertive, she went weak at the knees, and this was definitely one of those moments.

"I think it deserves a little punishment, don't you? Doubting the love of your life. So, it's going to be, hands on the wall upstairs when we get home, naked in stilettoes," said Eve firmly getting to the point.

"Oh, shit, fuck."

"I definitely *will* fuck you after a suitable penance."

"Oh God, oh fuck, Eve."

"I'm going to pay the bill," Eve said implacably.

Bernadette was in a state of sheer arousal at the thought of what Eve had said. Eve had turned a punishment she used to get from her parents into a sex game. She liked to spring it on Bernadette and had done so a couple of times in the past. They both found it so incredibly horny and now Eve had once more brought it up out of the blue, Bernadette was bereft of thought. It was amazing how Eve could turn the tables on her if she wanted to and added credence that she really had married a witch.

Eve settled the bill, asked them to call a taxi and gently led her wife into the cab with the smile of the cat who knew they were going to get the cream.

* * *

As soon as they returned home, the door had hardly closed when Eve said peremptorily, "Go upstairs, take off your clothes, choose some heels and stand with your hands on the wall, until I say you can stop. You can think about what you did and how I'm going to fuck you."

"Fuck," said Bernadette turning to go.

"Go on, darling."

Bernadette stood naked in a pair of her favourite mules, for what seemed to be an age with her hands on the bedroom wall. In reality, it was only fifteen minutes before Eve appeared, wordlessly stripped off herself and snaked her hands around Bernadette's body from behind.

"Have you learned your lesson?" she purred as her nails raked down Bernadette's naked skin making her hiss in her breath. She felt her nipples start to stand out as Eve's fingers teased her gently, and then harder.

"Yes, yes, please. I'm sorry I doubted you but fuck me, please, fuck me," Bernadette pleaded unable to stand it any longer.

"Lie on the bed then, my sweet."

Bernadette laid down on her back, and Eve began to work her over with her tongue.

"Oh fuck... fuck... fuck... oh... shit... fuck... I love that... oh... God... what you do to me... oh... Eve... Eve."

She arched her back and pushed herself harder into Eve's mouth.

"Oh... fuck... oh... oh... ah... fuck... oh my God... fuck... oh... don't... stop... oh." As the wave began to crest, she could hold it no longer, she began she move her pelvis in rhythm to Eve's tongue and finally she cut loose, "Oh fuck... oh my God... fuck... fuck, fuck... oh... oh... oh... ohh!" She screamed out loud. The scream she had wanted to make at the restaurant at the end of Eve's fingers.

As her body began to relax Eve was beside her smiling, holding her and kissing her softly.

"I love you," Bernadette whispered, "I love you so fucking much."

"I love you too, and I hope you enjoyed it?"

"Yes, yes I did, it was fucking well horny as hell."

"I know, I was turned on as fuck," Eve admitted.

"Mmm, I know. You certainly turned me on," Bernadette whispered.

"And did you learn your lesson?" Eve kissed her again.

"I'm not sure, maybe."

"How are we going to be sure?"

"Oh, I can think of one or two ways."

Bernadette's hand began to stray downwards. Eve lay back and let her wife make sweet love to her.

CHAPTER THREE

Bernadette leant over and silenced the alarm easing out of Eve's embrace. They had made passionate love into the small hours, as Eve had been exceptionally voracious and insistent.

"Where are you going?" Eve murmured as she stirred.

"To get ready for work."

"That time already?"

"Yes, darling." Bernadette kissed her gently and then slid out of the bed before Eve could do anything further and make her late.

She returned from her shower, to find Eve in her robe waiting to do her hair.

"I'll put your hair in a ponytail today, darling, if that's OK."

"Sure, whatever you want." Bernadette smiled. "I had a lovely night, darling."

"I did too." Eve deftly brushed Bernadette's long luscious locks and then bunched them tightly so she could put a hairband on them. She did so, changed her mind and started a French plait instead.

"Was it a full moon or something, last night?" Bernadette wondered while Eve completed her ministrations.

"Maybe."

"It's just that I read witches are more active during a full moon."

Eve giggled, and having finished Bernadette's hair, she started on her makeup.

"And you were certainly active, insatiable even."

"Perhaps it was."

Eve finished Bernadette's makeup and left her to get dressed. She had laid out a green midi wrap dress with puff sleeves. Black strappy sandals and black blazer style jacket for Bernadette. After a brief check in the mirror at Eve's good taste, she went down for breakfast.

As she entered the kitchen Eve placed two poached eggs on toast with bacon on the side on the counter along with a cup of coffee. Then Eve took her own seat.

"Poached eggs today, for a change," Eve said. "So, you don't get bored."

"You never bore me, and your cooking certainly doesn't."

Eve smiled at her and cut into her eggs. Bernadette took a mouthful of her own breakfast which was perfectly cooked as always. Eve was a perfectionist in the kitchen, even though Bernadette would not have minded if the food was less than perfect. Bernadette felt thoroughly spoiled.

"So, when are you starting on your masturbation series?" Bernadette asked her with a sly grin.

"I've made some preliminary sketches," Eve replied. "Of course, I've had plenty of time to research it."

"No doubt, first-hand."

"Naturally." Eve giggled and ran her foot up the side of Bernadette's leg.

"No," said Bernadette firmly. "I'm not being late today!"

"OK." Eve did a mock pout and returned her attention to her food. After a moment she said, "You're not supposed to say no to your wife, you know."

"I never say no to you." Bernadette shot her a look.

"But you just did." There was another pout.

"Oh God, but you are being a brat. I know you weren't really being serious just then."

Bernadette saw the little smirk which appeared on Eve's face after she said this and shook her head. She sighed.

"I know, I'm easy to tease, you little minx, and you just want more things for the list."

"Exactly!" Eve looked triumphant. "I have to make it worthwhile."

"But why?" Bernadette wondered since it really was just a game.

"Because then I can pretend I deserve it and it makes me very horny."

"I wonder if I'll ever really understand you." Bernadette finished her food and pushed her plate aside.

"But you can spend our whole life trying." Eve laughed and pulled Bernadette around to kiss her full on the lips.

"I'm helpless, helpless in your hands," Bernadette whispered.

"Do you not think you do the same to me?"

"You've wrapped me around your little finger, you witch."

"I know." Eve kissed her again lightly.

Bernadette leaned across and picked up her coffee cup. She drained it and put it down.

"I have to go."

"Kiss me goodbye?"

"Always, you know I will."

"You know I won't let you go without doing it."

"Yes, and that's another reason I love you."

* * *

Bernadette dropped the keys with Juanita and said, "I want to see you later, darling, to pick your brains about that rally."

"Sure of course, sure, when you want," Juanita replied dismissively. She was reading Hello magazine and did not look up.

"My car."

"I know!"

Bernadette chuckled and went to get herself and Imogen a coffee before going up to Imogen's office. Imogen was waiting eagerly when she arrived and sat down on the sofa at once. Bernadette knew she was anxious for enlightenment and disappointed she would not be able to give her too much comfort.

"Well?" Imogen said expectantly, taking the cup of coffee from Bernadette.

"Eve had lunch with D'Arcy yesterday." Bernadette took a sip from her cup.

"I know D'Arcy told me."

"I don't have anything really concrete to tell you though. Eve said D'Arcy wasn't forthcoming when she tried to probe to see if anything was wrong."

"Oh!" Imogen's face fell ludicrously as if the sun had suddenly gone in and gloom descended once more.

"She's really sorry, she did try."

"But what did she say? How did she find D'Arcy, what's Eve's take on it all?"

"The truth?"

"Of course."

"She thinks there is something D'Arcy isn't saying but she won't even say it to her."

"I knew it! I fucking well knew it, that fucking little bitch. I'm so cross with her right now." Imogen slammed her cup down on the coffee table, got up and started pacing the room. "I've given everything to her, my heart, everything. I'm hers, body and soul, and that little fucking tart is hiding something from me. We are supposed to tell each other everything, everything!"

Bernadette was a little taken aback, not having ever heard Imogen address her thoughts about D'Arcy in those terms.

"She doesn't think she's cheating on you or anything like that," Bernadette hastened to add this rider since Imogen appeared to become agitated.

"I didn't think that either, but it's something. By God, I'm angry, I'm so angry."

"Sit down for goodness' sake," said Bernadette trying to soothe her ire. "It's no good getting worked up about it."

"I can't help it. I've been worried sick and now Eve's confirmed it. There *is* something and that's what I'm annoyed about."

"I get that, and we must get to the nub of it somehow."

"Yes, perhaps I should ask her outright!" Imogen exclaimed. "Insist she tells me."

"I'm not sure that's wise." Bernadette thought a full frontal assault was probably not the best course of action particularly if Imogen was in full flow.

"Oh? Then what *do* you suggest?"

"There is one thing, Eve mentioned it actually."

"What? What? Tell me at once."

"Well, you should normalise your relationship again."

"What do you mean?" Imogen regarded her nonplussed.

Bernadette sighed. "There are things you said, you weren't doing at the moment, in the bedroom, and Eve said that's a bad idea. You should continue to act as if there is nothing wrong, and not withhold yourself the way you've been doing. I mean far be it from me to say it but..."

"You're telling me I should give her a damn good spanking, is that it?"

Bernadette rolled her eyes and shrugged. "In a nutshell yes, because that's what the two of you are used to."

"Oh my God. Why didn't I think of that before? Eve is right!"

"Eve said it would become a self-fulfilling prophecy if you stopped doing the things you normally do." Bernadette warmed to her theme.

"Yes, absolutely and I'm going to rectify that right now."

Bernadette sipped her coffee somewhat bemused as Imogen got up and marched over to her phone. She picked it up and texted something furiously. There was an almost immediate response, and she texted again followed by another response.

"There," said Imogen triumphantly showing Bernadette the screen.

The first text from Imogen said, "You best leave the paddle out tonight, darling, because you are going to be getting the spanking of your life!" This was followed by "Why?" from D'Arcy. "Because I said so!" Imogen had replied. D'Arcy had simply replied "OK xxx."

"Is this a sample of your normal texts to each other?" Bernadette asked when she had read them.

"Yes, absolutely. I'm the Domme remember, and I've stopped being the Domme. So, I have to be the Domme again."

"I guess, well if it works."

Bernadette shrugged. If she felt Imogen had gone a little over the top, she didn't articulate it. It was perhaps a relief to Imogen after all her worry. She wasn't sure how D'Arcy would appreciate it though when Imogen cut loose with her paddle, particularly after the mood she had been in for a few days. She put it out of her mind. Eve was far more interested in Imogen's antics than she was and would no doubt require a made-up rendition of it later.

"It will!"

"The kisses seemed like a good sign."

"Yes. They were, that's how she normally is. Things will be fine, you'll see, after tonight."

"OK, that's good."

"Tell Eve, thank you."

"I will."

Imogen picked up her coffee and began to drink it with relish.

"What's next on the agenda?"

Bernadette was happy Imogen seemed to feel she could solve her relationship issues with a paddle, but she wasn't quite convinced. Eve had said there was something else and even though what Imogen was planning might normalise things if there really was another reason it wouldn't quite go away just like that. However, as Imogen seemed so much happier, she didn't want to rain on her parade.

"You know tonight, if you are getting things back to normal, as it were, I wouldn't try to quiz her too much on anything," Bernadette said lightly.

"Oh, don't worry about that, I'll just tell her she hasn't been attentive enough or something, and I'll find some things she's done to misbehave recently. I won't try to rock the boat." Imogen waved a hand airily.

"Good, very good, so I think we need to talk to Juanita this morning and also to Micky to see what he's found out, he must have discovered something by now."

"Yes, good plan. Let's tackle Juanita first." Imogen's mind seemed more able to focus on work now she felt she had a solution to her troubles.

"No time like the present, let's get her up to the meeting room."

"Sure, I'll ask Alison to man the reception while she's with us."

"OK."

✳ ✳ ✳

Imogen and Bernadette sat opposite Juanita on the sofas in the meeting room. They had a cup of coffee each and Imogen had thoughtfully provided some chocolate finger biscuits from the kitchen supplies. Juanita leaned forward showing more cleavage than seemed quite decent to Bernadette and picked up a chocolate finger with her beautifully manicured fingers, and long nails. Today they had azure blue polish on them. Juanita seemed to change her nail colour with the same frequency as her underwear.

"Juanita," Bernadette said. "You watched the rally on the news, that's what you said. The one with the lawyer Maneet."

"Yes, yes I watch."

"Right, and can you describe what you saw?"

Bernadette took a sip of her coffee and waited while Juanita thought about this for a moment.

"It was in that big park you know, the Phoenix Park. By that big stone, you know, the big stone penis."

Imogen snorted at this unable to help herself.

"You mean the Wellington monument, the obelisk?"

"Yes, yes that one, like a big penis into the sky, yes."

"OK."

Bernadette shot a sideways glance at Imogen who was struggling to contain herself.

"What?" said Juanita somewhat aggrieved noticing this. "Is like a penis, no?"

"Yes, it is, very much like one in certain ways, yes." Bernadette didn't want to upset her as she might just clam up and refuse to say anything further. Apart from the fact, the monument was in fact square going up to a point with

83

sharply defined edges, she felt it possibly could be likened to a phallus, if you were Picasso.

"Yes, well, all of these people were there, speaking and there was a big crowd. Then next to that... thing... you know... the lawyer was there and all of some other people. Talking about racism and stuff like this in Ireland. Yes."

"So, the speakers were at the base of the monument and they were making speeches and there was a crowd?"

"Yes, that's right."

"What were they saying?"

"Ah just about how racism is wrong, and we don't want this in our country. Things like this and they are right. They are right. We don't want these, we don't need such bastards saying this kind of racist stuff."

Juanita flashed her eyes furiously at the thought of racists in Ireland. It seemed to be something she could at least be passionate about. Her long eyelash extensions emphasised her angry expression.

"Absolutely, no, you're right about that, and then what happened?" It seemed a good course of action to agree with Juanita and encourage her to divulge more, although naturally, Bernadette was no fan of racism either.

"Ah well. Then came some Garda you know, in the yellow jackets and so, with the big sticks and the plastic shields for the riots. But this was nothing, no riot. They were coming, coming closer." Juanita's voice took on a more dramatic tone in the retelling.

"And then?"

"So, the lawyer, she was speaking, and she stopped. She walked towards them and then the Garda they also stopped.

Then some came forward, to talk to her. Maybe three or four, five, more, I don't know?"

"Were they carrying shields?"

"No, nothing, they just came out from behind to talk."

"Did you see them up close?"

"Oh yes, I saw. They zoom in I think from a drone or something from the TV. The Garda he looked at her, but I didn't see if he had spoken to her, I don't know, but then this lady she just went crazy. She went crazy, she hit him in the face, and then another time, and kick him, slap him. They grabbed her the others and handcuff her, then they took her away."

Juanita shook her head at this inexplicable behaviour.

"Wow, right. Could you tell at all why she got so angry?"

"Ah no, I can't tell nothing. But she looked angry just angry. She was very angry."

"Did she start out angry?"

"No, not angry at first, but afterwards then she was mad, very mad. Such women can become very angry you know, very, very angry."

Bernadette forbore to enquire what sort of women 'such women' were and how Juanita had determined Maneet was one of these. To Bernadette's mind, Maneet would have been the least likely person she knew to react like that.

"So, they arrested her?"

"Yes, they took her away, I didn't see her after that. This is the fate of such women." Juanita pronounced this in ominous tones.

"What happened then?"

"The others, the people, they just started to walk away, they all left. It was the end."

"Was there any more trouble that you could see?"

"No, no trouble I didn't see no trouble."

That seemed to be all, so Bernadette decided to reiterate it to make sure.

"In summary then. The Garda came, and they arrested Maneet after she went to talk to them, and then the rally broke up."

"Yes, yes that's right, it's what happened."

"That's great, Juanita, really, really helpful, thank you so much."

"It's OK." Juanita waved her hand dismissively as if she discussed topics like this with them every day.

Imogen, who had recovered her composure somewhat, decided to pick up on something Juanita had said.

"What kind of woman is Maneet, would you say? Because you said, 'such women.' What kind of woman is that?"

Juanita regarded her for a moment as if Imogen was truly stupid, rolled her eyes, and said, "Ah you know, she is a strong woman, tough. Yes, she knows what she wants. Like me."

"Oh."

Bernadette could tell Imogen's idea of Juanita was very far removed from the picture she had just painted.

"Yes. You can push such a woman too far and then boom."

"Boom?" Imogen repeated.

"Yes, boom. Just like this what happened."

"So, she's volatile?"

"Yes, yes, of course, you should know this, Imogen. You know with this colour hair. Boom. That's you. It's you." Juanita furnished Imogen with a knowing smile.

"Right." Imogen blushed.

Juanita laughed lightly at her own joke.

"Can you think of anything else?" Bernadette decided to intervene.

"No, nothing else." Juanita shook her head.

"Well, thank you for your help, it was very useful."

"You are welcome. I go now?"

"Sure, thanks again."

Juanita leant forward and took another couple of biscuits. She popped one in her mouth, got up and sauntered out on her very high platform shoes.

"Oh my God, I can never look at the monument again without thinking of it as a penis." Imogen broke off into peals of laughter after Juanita had gone.

Bernadette joined in the merriment. She had found it very funny too.

"Was that much use though, what she told us?" Imogen wondered after their mirth had subsided.

"Not as much as I'd hoped but it gave us a general idea and it supports what Maneet said about it."

"I'll get Micky, shall I? We can ask him where he's got to."

"Why not."

* * *

Micky sat in the meeting room, a few minutes later. He seemed much more relaxed in their presence these days. He had done a fair few assignments for Bernadette now and she always made sure she praised him highly for his work. He was getting used to their banter around him too and it didn't faze him nearly as much as it used to.

"Micky, have you found anything out so far?" Bernadette asked him.

"I've found that Maneet is a pretty highly respected lawyer," he said nodding, "She's spoken at the UN, she writes articles on the rights of immigrants stuff like that, she's had some interviews."

"So, she's well known?"

"Yes, I'd say so. If you google her quite a lot of stuff comes up."

"Anything negative?" Imogen wanted to know.

"Only the rally thing. The media have got hold of the story she's been charged with an offence. I think the Garda must have released it to the press."

"So, it really could be a blot in her copybook, like she said." Bernadette exchanged glances with Imogen.

"You could put it that way, I suppose. I mean, so far, the press reporting wasn't too negative, to be honest. There was some speculation she must have been provoked because it's out of character." Micky shrugged.

"Have you managed to get footage of the incident?"

"Yes, I've got some mainly from the press stories. I'm still looking."

"What can you tell from it?"

"Not much. She was speaking at the rally and she went to speak to the Garda who were approaching in force. Then some officers came to speak to her, she lashed out and she was arrested. The rally broke up."

This endorsed what they already had heard from Maneet and also Juanita.

"Could you tell if they said anything to her or what they were saying?"

"No, not really. It's not clear enough or a good enough view of their faces. I mean, we couldn't get a lip reader to decipher it from the angle, I would say that's impossible."

"We need different footage then?

"Yes, we would I would say. I'm trying to find it like you said, in case someone posted something from their phone but it's not so easy. For a start, it would have to be posted publicly."

"Yes, yes of course."

Bernadette paused for a moment.

"Could you show us what you do have, or at least the best one?"

"Sure, I'll just get my laptop."

Micky disappeared for a few moments and returned with his laptop. It was a fairly heavy duty one and with a high spec. This was much against Andrew's wishes but Bernadette, as usual, had overridden them. Micky needed whatever he needed to do his research in her view.

Micky put the laptop on the table and played a video. They watched it through, and it was almost exactly as Juanita had described. There was no scope to see if the Garda had said anything at all to Maneet, which made it more difficult.

"I wonder if any of them had bodycams?" Bernadette said when the video had finished.

"I can ask, and in fact, I will ask the prosecution for it," Imogen replied. "I'm expecting the answer 'no' but it's worth a shot. If they had bodycams which I doubt, then they would be obliged to release the footage."

"Sure, we might as well try."

Bernadette turned her attention back to Micky.

"What's your assessment of the incident?"

"OK, well..." he began flushing slightly with pleasure to have his opinion canvassed. "I would say she must have been provoked. Looking at the various videos I've watched she didn't approach the Garda in an aggressive manner, and she didn't seem aggressive beforehand. So, I would say something happened during the exchange with the Garda which made her lash out. You know, people don't lash out for no reason unless they are on drugs or have been drinking and then you can tell beforehand."

"You seem quite knowledgeable about this," Imogen observed.

"Ach, you know I've had my nights at the pub and clubs, you can tell when someone is looking for a fight. Also, now I've been doing martial arts, you know we talk about stuff like this."

"Very good, Micky," said Bernadette. "This brings one or two things to mind. Maybe we can find an expert witness, a behavioural specialist who could say what you said about the footage. I mean, it's just they would have the qualifications otherwise we could put you on the stand."

"Sure, I know." He nodded. "The qualifications count in court."

"Alas, you're right. I think we also need a character witness. Someone who can vouch for her being calm under pressure that sort of thing. We should ask to talk to some of her colleagues at the organisation she works for, pick someone suitable."

"I'll get onto it and set something up," said Imogen.

"Excellent, this has been very productive." Bernadette smiled.

"Is there anything else you need right now?" Micky enquired.

"Not immediately but please keep trying to find that footage, it's vital evidence if we can get it."

"I've another idea," he said after thinking for a moment. "I could go onto Facebook groups which are allied with the IAD and ask if anyone has any footage."

"Sure but try to keep a low profile if you do."

"You can count on me. I've got several, erm, alternative profiles for stuff like this." Micky grinned.

"Oh-ho! Looks like we've got a double oh seven in our firm," Imogen quipped. "I'm Doyle, Micky Doyle. I like my women stirred, not shaken."

Micky laughed and blushed slightly.

"Very good, Micky, as long as you're not planning on leaving us for the secret service," said Bernadette laughing.

"Ach, not me. No way. I'll be here as long you want me." He sounded so sincere all of a sudden that it touched Bernadette's heart.

"Oh, Micky, darling, you're so sweet."

Before he could do anything, she moved over and gave me a big hug. He blushed furiously at this.

"Sorry," she said a little contrite. "It was just such a lovely thing to say."

"Ach, Bernadette..."

"So, Micky, is there a lucky woman in your life?" Imogen came to the rescue.

"Ach well, you know..." Micky looked as if he definitely didn't want to talk about *that*.

"Oh, there is I can see... I can see." Imogen pursued her theme.

"Leave the poor boy alone." Bernadette intervened.

"Oh no, I want to know who it is."

"Well, I..."

"You don't have to tell us if you don't want to, Micky." It was Bernadette's turn to rescue him.

"Um, well, I'd better get on you know." He said hastily shutting his laptop and getting up.

"I'm going to ask Alison!" Imogen shot after him as he beat a hasty retreat. This only served to make him blush scarlet.

"Imogen, honestly!" Bernadette chided.

"So... spank me."

"I know perfectly well that's your biggest fantasy and it's not happening!" Bernadette told her in admonishing tones. This was a standing joke between them, although Bernadette suspected there was a little bit of truth to it on Imogen's part.

"You really are no fun!"

Bernadette shook her head, but she was secretly pleased to see the banter return.

"I'm glad to see you are back on form."

"Oh, yes I certainly am, as D'Arcy is going to find out later."

"Poor D'Arcy."

"I'll be able to get rid of all my frustrations," said Imogen with relish.

"Doubly poor D'Arcy."

"Shall we get lunch?"

"Mamma Mia's?"

"Why not. You can tell me all about what happened last night."

They left the meeting room and went via each other's offices to pick up their respective purses.

"How do you know something happened?"

"It's bound to have where you and Eve are concerned."

"You must think Eve and I have sex all the time."

"Is the Pope Catholic?"

"Oh you!"

✳ ✳ ✳

After an amicable lunch, Bernadette returned to her office to catch up on some other casework, and Imogen went to hers in order to arrange various things they had discussed on Maneet's case. Bernadette shut her door and went to sit down, as she was reading the first email her mobile rang. It was Eve.

"Hi, darling," she trilled.

"Are you alone?" Eve asked her at once.

"Yes, why?" Bernadette was instantly suspicious of Eve's intentions and she was not disappointed in her assumption.

"Lock the door."

"What? Why?" Bernadette asked whilst doing it, all the same, suspecting Eve was going to be quite naughty. It sent a bit of a thrill up her spine at the thought. She returned to her chair and sat down. "OK, now what?"

"I didn't want you to be disturbed." Eve giggled.

"Because?" Bernadette thought she knew the answer and it was not long in coming.

"This..." A familiar buzzing noise sounded followed by a gasp from Eve.

"Is that what I think it is?"

"Oh yes... oh yes indeed... oh... fuck... Jesus... oh... Fuck!"

Bernadette bit her lip hearing her wife using what she assumed was their rabbit and was immediately aroused herself.

"Where are you?" she asked Eve.

"Oh... in... the bedroom... oh fuck... I'm naked... can you imagine it?... oh my God! Oh... oh... fuck... fuck... ow... yes... oh my God."

"You are so naughty," said Bernadette spellbound listening to this performance.

"I know... I can't help it... I'm thinking of you... yes... oh... yes... yes... oh... oh... oh... oh... oh... ohh!" The rabbit seemed to work exceptionally fast, and Eve climaxed on a scream.

"You are so bad," Bernadette whispered after a few moments, "teasing me like that."

"Did I make you horny?" Eve sounded hopeful.

"Yes, God yes."

"Good!"

"Oh... oh... you're so... bad... so very bad!"

"Aren't you going to?" Eve wondered.

"I want to, but no, I've got work to do. You'll have to do it for me, later."

"I will. Oh God, but I want to do it *now*." Eve's voice was pitched low and lustful, it was all Bernadette could do to resist it, but resist it she did.

"You will have to wait. You horny little witch," Bernadette said firmly. "If you're finished, I'll see you later."

"Is it going on the list?"

"Yes, in fact, I'm going to write one right now, as soon as I put the phone down, while I remember."

Eve gave a little sigh of satisfaction.

"Bye then, darling. I love you."

"I love you too, you misbehaving little brat."

"You say the nicest things."

Eve clicked off the phone and with a mental effort, Bernadette tore her mind away from what she really wanted to do. Besides it would be very difficult in the dress she was wearing.

Instead, she unlocked the door and sat down to write the list of Eve's misdemeanours. She had just completed this task when Imogen came into her room. Imogen was very much used to coming in unannounced and Bernadette was happy she hadn't arrived a few minutes earlier. She had no doubt Imogen would have wanted to listen and that would have been a little awkward perhaps. Imogen and Eve were two of a kind very sexual and extremely naughty with it. Bernadette was a little more restrained.

"What's that you are doing? And what have you been doing?" Imogen said at once missing nothing and setting down a coffee for Bernadette at the coffee table.

"Why?" Bernadette said attempting to look innocent.

"You look a little flushed, and I'm very familiar with *that* look!"

"Oh! Well, I'm writing a list for Eve, if you must know." Bernadette came and sat down on the sofa.

"Let me see it." Imogen held out her hand.

"My God, you are like a schoolmistress." Bernadette handed the list over.

"I'm practising for tonight." Imogen looked it over. "There's a few things on here. Making me late for work several times. Being extravagant. Being judgemental. Eve's quite the minx, isn't she?"

"She's a brat when she wants to be," said Bernadette laughing.

"For sure, and what's this at the bottom? Using her rabbit while on the phone to you in the office?" Imogen's eyes grew wider.

"Um..."

"*That's* what you've been doing, I see."

"I wasn't doing anything. I was listening," Bernadette protested.

"Sorry I missed it."

"I'm not."

"You really are no fun."

Bernadette laughed. "You are incorrigible."

"It's my job."

"Talking about jobs, did you make some arrangements?" Bernadette tried to steer the subject back to the case.

"Yes, I've set up meetings with Maneet and a couple of her colleagues for tomorrow at their offices."

"Excellent."

"I was also wondering if that psychologist Patrick might be good for the expert witness thing?"

"The one you fancied?"

Patrick Kelly was a psychologist and a good friend of Bernadette's. They had got to know each other at university and become best mates. Patrick was an out and out ladies' man who left a string of broken hearts behind him. Imogen had set her cap at him, but he had declined to play ball, much to her annoyance. However, that was before she found out she was actually gay.

"Yes, well, I don't fancy him anymore. But what do you think?"

"He might feel qualified to do it, why don't you ring and ask?"

"I will and if so, we'll get him in here to look at the footage."

"Great."

Alison popped her head around the door at that moment.

"Oh, hi," she said spying them both.

"Alison, what can I do for you?" Bernadette asked her.

"I wanted to go over the shortlist for the PA position."

"You can do it with both of us then."

Alison came into the office and sat down in one of the chairs. She handed a list of names to Bernadette and Imogen craned over to see. There were six people on it. The PA issue had been ongoing for some time. Andrew had taken a little persuading to allow them to get another PA in the first place, and then when they had obtained the agreement, there were the usual adverts and so forth to be placed. She had let Alison run with it since the new PA would primarily be working with her. Bernadette looked the list over, but the names didn't mean a lot.

"Which of these is your favourite?" she asked after a moment.

"I suppose it would be Lucy Ferguson," Alison replied at once.

"Why?"

"I don't know. I like the look of her CV. She's worked in legal before and she sounded like fun, I guess. I think she's Scottish."

"Scottish, hmm? OK, well if you can, Imogen, maybe you can sit in on the interviews?"

"Sure, why not. It would be interesting," Imogen agreed.

"After all the new PA will probably end up doing a lot of your work."

"Yes, I'll soon whip her into shape."

Bernadette looked at her sharply and Imogen gave a smirk.

"Not literally of course."

"No, of course." Bernadette said this for Alison's benefit as she was looking from one to the other of them. Imogen's proclivities were not common knowledge and Bernadette certainly didn't want them to be.

"That's settled then," said Imogen. "Just work around my diary."

"Will do."

"Is everything OK otherwise?" Bernadette wanted to know.

"Yes, shouldn't it be?" Alison looked puzzled.

"It should be, but I like to make sure."

Alison smiled.

"Oh, yes, it's all fine. The new PA can have Micky's old cubbyhole for now. I don't think three of us can fit in our office."

"Sure, I mean unless Micky wants to..."

"No, he doesn't and... I don't want him to," said Alison a little too quickly.

"Oh, sure, OK, well whatever suits you, both of you." Bernadette shrugged.

"Anyway, I better get on because I want to finish on time today. Micky and I are going bowling." Alison flushed perhaps having said more than she wanted to.

"Oh? Bowling? Well, have fun." Bernadette said no more but she and Imogen looked at each other as Alison left.

"Bowling my arse." Imogen burst out laughing.

"They might very well be going bowling," Bernadette chided her.

"And after bowling, no doubt Micky will score a strike or two."

"You are..."

"Incorrigible, I know."

"I never would have thought those two."

"An unlikely pair but then you never can tell, after all, D'Arcy and I were an unlikely pair to start with." Imogen shrugged.

"I'm not so sure about *that*. I thought you fancied her when you started dressing up before we went over there to interview her," Bernadette said wryly.

"Was it so obvious?" Imogen blushed.

"Pretty much, yes. I just didn't know you were gay at that point, but I began to suspect from the way you were acting."

"And then you knew for sure when you saw us together at the swimming pool."

"Oh, don't remind me." Bernadette coloured up herself. "It was quite improper of me in hindsight."

"Oh, don't sweat it. I know I tease you about it but if someone was going to watch me having sex, I'd rather it was you."

"Really?"

"Yes, silly because I know you wouldn't make a big deal about it, darling. And anyway, we're practically family now. Don't you go all prim and proper on me missy."

Bernadette chuckled. "Perish the thought. There's no chance of it, not with the little witch of a wife I married. I just sometimes feel I shouldn't have crossed so many lines and I always seem to do so around D'Arcy."

Imogen patted her arm. "You think too much, and you worry too much. Stop it. If I don't care, then you shouldn't either."

"You're right, I'm a worry guts."

"Yes, you are, now stop or I'll tell Eve."

"Oh don't, I don't want another wall session quite yet."

Imogen went off into a peal of laughter. "What would I without all this, the way we are together?"

"It is not normal in business though. You do know that." Bernadette smiled.

"Oh I do, and that's why I love you. You make life fun and exciting. I just love it."

"You do?"

"Yes, and I'm going back to my office now, so I can go home on time. D'Arcy's arse isn't going to spank itself."

"Good luck with it." Bernadette smiled feeling a little sorry for D'Arcy's impending fate.

"She's the one who needs it not me."

"Oh you." Bernadette shook her head and accepted a light kiss from Imogen, before she watched her flame haired friend leave the office.

She mused on their conversation. It was true, she did worry too much and perhaps refined far too much upon the past sometimes. Imogen was a devil may care, and she evidently didn't care that Bernadette had seen her and D'Arcy together, in fact, she got the distinct impression Imogen quite liked it. She had no idea how they had evolved into the relationship they now had, but she quite liked it too. It wasn't conventional, but then Bernadette never set out to be conventional. She looked forward to coming to work because of Imogen. They certainly had an inseparable bond. She glanced at her watch and decided she had better get some work done before heading home. God knows what Eve had in store for her.

* * *

Bernadette pulled her car into her driveway and the gate closed behind her. Eve might be lying in wait in the hallway for all she knew. She opened the front door with a little trepidation and slipped inside. She hung up her jacket and kicked off her shoes. There was a delicious smell emanating from the kitchen indicating dinner was underway and probably in the oven or slow cooker. Bernadette peeked into the lounge, but Eve was not there drawing like she often was. She wasn't downstairs and so Bernadette went upstairs. As she walked quietly into the bedroom, she found Eve asleep in the bed, her blonde hair suitably tousled on the pillow. On the floor beside the bed were a couple of vibrators, and Bernadette could only assume Eve had worn herself out.

She disrobed and slid under the covers, to snuggle up against her sleeping wife who was deliciously warm. Eve stirred slightly as Bernadette put her arms around her and pulled in close. Eve sighed softly but did not wake. Bernadette closed her eyes, and within a few moments, she was also asleep.

When she opened them again, full of sleep, Eve had turned to face her and was looking at her smiling.

"You're awake," said Bernadette unnecessarily.

"Yes."

"Were you tired, darling?"

"I was. I just lay down for a nap and then I found you holding me tight."

"Are you feeling OK?"

"Yes, of course." Eve chuckled. "I'm not sick if that's what you are worried about."

"I'll try not to."

"No, don't do *that*, my darling. I'm perfectly fine."

Eve kissed her then, igniting the flames of desire very quickly. Bernadette's ardour of the afternoon had been unrequited and now she wanted Eve more than ever. Her wife obliged her by tracing her hands lightly down Bernadette's naked skin, caressing and causing ripples and tingles in her nerve endings.

"Oh... oh... my," Bernadette sighed.

"I think I owe you something, don't I, darling?" Eve whispered and her head disappeared from view.

Bernadette found herself turned onto her back, and then she felt the thrill and the wetness of Eve's tongue.

"Oh fuck... oh... fuck... oh... Eve..." Her hands clutched at the duvet clenching the fabric as the insistent flicking of Eve's tongue made her dizzy and she could feel the wave building inside her.

"Oh... fuck... Eve... oh my God... I love... that... Eve... fuck... fuck..." Her hands went down to push Eve's head harder into her groin as she tilted up her pelvis, pushing into Eve's mouth.

"Oh... ah... oh... oh... oh... oh... oh... oh... oh... ohh!" The wave broke, and her climax rushed through her making her tense and then untense, curling her toes as she shouted out loud. "Oh... fuck... ohh... yes!" She bucked and writhed though Eve held her fast, pushing her to greater heights until she could stand it no longer and let out a long low moan before relaxing. Eve let her go and came up again to lie beside her.

"Is that better?" Eve said in a soft loving way.

"Yes, it was mind blowing if you want to know."

"Good, that's good because I wouldn't like you to feel deprived." Eve giggled.

"Highly unlikely, you minx."

"You know I just love you so much." Eve kissed her gently nibbling her lips.

"I love you too and I should..."

"Let's have dinner first, hmm, tell me about your day."

"Well you know some of it." Bernadette's eyes twinkled in the half light.

"Oh?"

"Yes, a naughty little brat rang me up and got herself off with my rabbit on the phone."

"Oh, goodness, well she deserves to be thoroughly punished for such outrageous behaviour."

"She will be."

"She knows it."

Bernadette chuckled at the way Eve manipulated her into doing exactly what she wanted.

"Then let's eat, my darling, I'm a little hungry I must confess."

"I've made a very chicken casserole."

"Sounds lovely."

Eve got out of bed, and put on a robe, tossing one to Bernadette.

"Come on then," she cooed, waiting for Bernadette to put it on before taking her hand and leading her downstairs.

CHAPTER FOUR

he morning came around all too soon. They had not repaired to bed immediately after dinner as Eve declared she was not tired. So instead, she contented herself with sketching idly while they watched a movie together on the sofa. As a result, they had gone to bed a little late and Bernadette still felt sleepy when the alarm woke her.

Eve didn't wake, so she got out of bed and went to have her shower. She expected Eve to be up when she got back, but Eve was still fast asleep. Bernadette did begin to be worried at this because it was very unlike her to sleep in. However, she didn't want to wake up Eve and so she sat down at the dressing table. Bernadette was unused to doing her own hair, since Eve had now styled it for her every day for so long.

She began to brush it and stared helplessly at it, as if she never fixed her hair before in her life. With Eve she never had to think and now as she did start to think, the thought of Eve not being there crossed her mind. Eve was never ill, what if this was something serious? A tear squeezed out of the corner of her eye and it ran down her cheek. She closed her eyes and began to silently sob at the thought.

Two strong arms encircled her, and Eve was nuzzling her back.

"What's wrong, darling," Eve asked full of concern as she felt Bernadette's sobbing frame.

"I... I..."

"Good God, what is it?"

Eve came and knelt down in front of her looking at her tears in alarm.

"Baby, what's wrong, why are you crying?"

"It's because... because I don't want to lose you... I can't lose you," Bernadette blurted out.

Eve looked at her in shock. "Lose me? Why on earth should you lose me? I thought we had put all that to bed now we are married."

"Because, because you were tired and I'm afraid maybe it's something bad and then I just got to thinking and..."

"Oh you are silly, silly girl." Eve pulled her close kissing away Bernadette's tears, murmuring softly and stroking her hair. "Why would you even think such a thing?"

"I don't know," Bernadette whispered, choking back a sob. "It's just you are always so full of beans and then I came home and find you sleeping like that and this morning again... and I had to do my own hair... and..."

"Come here, come on here for a moment."

Eve pulled her up and sat beside her on the bed.

"What do you think? I've got some dreadful disease or something? Is that it?" she enquired softly.

"Well..."

"It's a long stretch from me being tired to having a life-threatening illness, even for you, you silly goose."

"I'm sorry, I'm just afraid, I can't lose you. I'm not a goose!" Bernadette pouted.

"More like a duck when you pout like that. You are silly though. Look, yesterday I didn't eat enough for a start, so my protein levels were down. I was busy drawing. I also haven't been exercising as much. I probably did overdo the vibrator just a bit, I used it more than ten times. But to be honest I have been feeling a bit tired lately. It could just be a deficiency of some kind. I'll go and see the doctor today if it will make you happy. OK?"

"Yes, OK." Bernadette smiled a looked a little more cheerful.

"Good, so let me do your hair and makeup, you'll need to wash your face. No more talk of losing me. You cry-baby."

"I know, I'm sorry."

"Don't be. You are *my* cry-baby and I love you for it." Eve kissed her.

Finally, when Bernadette was dressed, made up and with her hair straightened and hanging loose, she went downstairs to eat. She was wearing a black skirt suit, and a light pink blouse, with block heeled mules. As she was seeing clients, she needed to look a little more formal than usual.

Eve put a plate of scrambled eggs and bacon in front of her, and a cup of coffee. She sat down herself and tucked into what appeared to be a double portion.

"Making up for yesterday?" Bernadette said amused.

"Yes, and I'm going to be doing exercise every day too."

"I thought you were." Bernadette raised an eyebrow.

"Not *that* kind of exercise."

"Did you say ten times?" Bernadette put a mouthful of egg and toast into her mouth.

"Yes, I got carried away I guess."

"I'll say."

"Was I very bad?"

"Yes." Bernadette said this in matter of fact tones, suppressing a laugh, and continued tucking into her breakfast.

"It was a bit much even for me. I was just ultra horny."

"Why, how many times is it normally?"

"Three or four I suppose." Eve laughed self-consciously.

"God, you are horny as fuck, you little witch."

"This is what you married." Eve shrugged.

"I know and I'm not complaining."

Eve smiled and they finished their breakfast. Bernadette drank her coffee while holding Eve's hand.

"But you will still go to the doctor?"

"Yes, I will, OK? I promise."

"Thank you."

"I know, you want the peace of mind, and so I do I. It's only sensible. Although I don't think it's anything, and certainly *not* what you were thinking."

"I wonder how Imogen got on last night," Bernadette mused, changing the subject and drinking the last of her coffee.

"Or how D'Arcy did." Eve smirked.

Bernadette knew full well Eve would want a report from her, and a made-up story that evening.

"I'm going to be at a client's today, so no surprise phone calls." Bernadette looked at her with mock severity.

"OK, I suppose I'll be good." Eve pouted.

"You better had," Bernadette said with mock severity.

"Yes, Mrs Mackenna."

"Come on, kiss me goodbye, I've got to go. But do ring me or text me and tell me about the doctor, ok? To save me worrying."

"Yes, sure. I know how much you worry. Silly billy."

"I'm not silly... well, maybe just a bit..."

✶ ✶ ✶

Bernadette was sitting in her office and was just logging in when right on cue Imogen breezed in with two mugs of hot coffee.

"You are looking happy," Bernadette said accepting a cup and taking a seat on the sofa.

"Oh yes, very happy."

"I take it last night went well then?" Bernadette sipped her coffee.

"Very well, I unleashed my inner bitch on D'Arcy, and it did wonders for my self-esteem. I felt so much more in control of the situation, Eve was perfectly right."

"I'm glad to hear it and how did D'Arcy take it?"

Bernadette wondered exactly how much unleashing Imogen had indulged in but didn't want to enquire too closely.

"Let's just say she got the spanking she deserved and then some."

"Right."

"And afterwards she was perfectly loving towards me and so gentle, and lovely, just like normal." Imogen smiled happily looking very self-satisfied.

Bernadette forbore to ask for any further details, although she knew Eve would want them. However, Bernadette had, perforce, become very adept at filling in the gaps and making up naughty stories.

"So, do you think that's all it was?"

"Who knows, but if it did the trick then I'm happy."

"Great."

Bernadette did not feel quite so optimistic. From what Eve had said there was something deeper troubling D'Arcy but perhaps the return to normality had helped things along. As Imogen seemed in better spirits it was all to the good. Hopefully, things would improve from here for both of them.

"How was your evening?"

"Oh, well..." Bernadette told her about her concern for Eve's health and how she was apparently suddenly tired. She did not omit to tell Imogen about Eve's highly sexed escapades.

"Ten times! I should think it would make anyone tired."

"I just worry it's a bit more than that. It's not like her." Bernadette allowed a little of her concern to show in her face.

"I'm sure Eve is right, don't fret so much, darling. She's seeing the doctor anyway."

"I know."

"Then stop it."

"OK, I'll try." Bernadette's lip trembled and she controlled herself with an effort.

It seemed so silly to her, to worry the way she did about what was probably nothing. It underlined the deep insecurity she had over losing Eve. After they were married, she stopped worrying Eve would leave her, but this was a different kind of leaving.

"We're going over to Maneet's workplace shortly. So, will you be OK?"

"I'll try."

Imogen shook her head and leaned over to give her a kiss.

"Do more than try, come on. This isn't anything until it is. You are magnifying this in your mind."

"I know, I can't help it. I just love her so much. She is my whole life to me."

"Don't think I don't understand how you feel. Look at me these last couple of weeks."

Bernadette nodded, and impulsively put out a hand to take Imogen's for reassurance.

"What do I have if I don't have Eve?" she whispered.

"You have me," Imogen said looking her right in the eyes. "You will always have me."

* * *

On the way to the offices of Irish Against Discrimination, Bernadette reflected on the exchange which had taken place earlier between her and Imogen. Imogen was a fierce friend, incredibly loyal and kind. She had as much told Bernadette she would always be there for her. It was incredibly comforting somehow, to know someone always had your back. There are many different kinds of love. She and

Imogen had something enduring, not a sexual love but far beyond it.

The offices turned out to be a short distance from their own office and on their side of the river, in a large building called Marine House. On the exterior, it appeared to be built in the seventies style with red brick and white windows. The lobby was very plain with a wood faced curving reception, lemon coloured walls, and grey tiles on the floor. However, once they arrived at IAD's offices on another floor it turned out to have been furnished in quite a modern style. It was large, with an open plan industrial theme. The ceilings had chipboard blocks suspended on metal stalks. A large mauve carpet ran through in a big swathe interspersing with grey stripes. There were desk clusters, and on one side a kitchen area, plus chill out sofas. In one corner was a meeting room with glass walls and fancy designs etched into it.

Maneet met them at the reception desk with a smile.

"Hi, great to see you again, I'll take you to our meeting room and you can conduct your interviews in there. Can I get you something to drink?"

"Sure, coffee for both of us," Bernadette replied and allowed her to escort them to a glass panelled room.

There were a few curious glances as they walked across the room, but generally, it seemed like a busy space and a hive of activity. Quite a few phone conversations were in progress, and most probably some of this, by the sound of it, was fundraising. They entered the room with a purple carpet and white furniture and sat down at the main meeting table.

"Would you like to talk to me first or..." Maneet enquired.

"We'll talk to you last, if that's OK," Bernadette told her.

"Sure, whatever way you want to play it, I'll get some coffee and your first victim." Maneet laughed at her own joke and disappeared from the room.

Imogen laid out their notebooks and also a recorder, as it was preferable for them to record the conversations if they could.

After a few moments, Maneet reappeared with two cups of coffee, some biscuits. She put these down on the table and left them. Shortly there was a light knock on the door, and a tall thin man with thick glasses and a bushy beard entered. He had a lumberjack style red shirt, green cords and desert boots.

"Hi," he said in a thick American accent which Bernadette thought was probably from the West Coast, "I'm Judd Garford, I'm the campaign coordinator here."

He advanced on the table and held out his hand. Bernadette shook it and introduced him to Imogen. They sat down, and he placed a mug of black tea on the table.

"I'm sure you are aware why we are here," Bernadette said taking a sip of her coffee.

"Sure, you are representing Maneet in the assault case, yes?"

"That's right, and if you wouldn't mind us recording the conversation?"

"Sure, I don't mind, I'm not one of these conspiracy theorists," he laughed.

Imogen turned on the recorder and picked up her pen to make notes.

"Great, so could you perhaps give us a bit of background. How you come to be working here, what you do here?"

"Sure. For my sins, I'm the campaign coordinator as I said, which in a nutshell means I am in charge of all of the campaigns we do. The buck stops with me, so to speak, as far as that is concerned."

"So, you are pretty high up in this organisation?"

"Yes, well, Maneet is, of course, our figurehead and you could say our CEO in effect although we don't subscribe to such corporate labels here."

Bernadette could tell from this where he was likely to lean on the political spectrum, though it wasn't particularly material to the case. She was very liberal in her views, herself, but as always justice was her primary concern.

"How did you come to be working here?" She smiled.

"Oh, in a roundabout way. I've been involved in all kinds of protests in the US for years. You know I was one of those hippy types, spent my youth in a VW Combi van, smoked weed, protested against everything whilst happily milking the system at university paid for by my rich parents."

The speech was self-deprecating, as if he despised his upbringing and his well-off roots.

"So anyway, I came over for a visit to Dublin some years ago, there happened to be a rally by the IAD. I happened to attend it and then I happened to bump into Maneet. Shall we say we became a little more than just friends for a while, we dated and stuff..." he trailed off wistfully.

"You two were an item?" said Imogen pouncing on this at once.

"Yes, we were perhaps for a year until the idea of marriage hit her. Then I'm afraid, tradition rules over love or perhaps it was never really love in the first place."

Bernadette glanced at Imogen. The casual way in which he disclosed this was a little disconcerting and perhaps it was because he hailed from across the pond.

"And yet you are still here."

"Yes, I stayed on because I like Ireland, it suits me. There are causes to be had here and I'm tired of America and its eccentricities. I far prefer the eccentric nature of the Irish, and then of course there are still many Irish women to get to know." He smiled, and it was a little lascivious. Bernadette could tell perhaps his attachment to Maneet hadn't been all that deep.

"So, if you don't me asking, how do you and Maneet get on as colleagues?"

"Fine, fine. The past is the past. We moved on, both of us. Although I'm not sure her choice of moving on is the best one, but you can't pick who you really fall in love with can you?"

"No, that's very true." Bernadette and Imogen smiled at this.

"You've worked here for some time, I take it you know Maneet quite well," Imogen added.

"Yes, I do, very well. She's a very special lady."

"I gather she is well respected?"

"Oh, for sure, she's moved in some exalted circles, far higher than I could ever aspire to. She's been to the UN, spoken in front of world leaders."

"Does she have any enemies?" Bernadette said suddenly. It occurred to her this was a good time to ask it.

He paused for a moment and seemingly thought this over.

"I'm sure she does, though I can't think of anyone specifically. White racists are not big fans of hers I should imagine." He chuckled.

"You can't think of anyone by name, or a group?"

"No, I can't. Organisations like ours make enemies because of what we stand for. In this country they aren't quite as exposed as in the US, I'll say that. Over there it's much more blatant. Here it's undercover and so we don't see them put their heads up over the parapet."

"Right. Then, if we can turn to the rally, can you tell me what you remember of it, specifically the incident of assault and what you saw or heard?"

This was the nub of the issue. His answers had really not told them much although they still needed to ask him about her character, in case he would make a character witness. Bernadette was dubious as he was an ex-lover and if the prosecution got wind of that then they would use it against the defence.

"Yes. The rally. It was all well organised. We had decided to hold it at the memorial in Phoenix Park."

"Had you informed the Garda of your intentions?" Imogen asked him.

"Under the constitution, we don't have to. We have the right to protest, assuming we're not promoting hate or violence which we weren't. We can choose to tell the Garda and they will usually help with the arrangement. In this case, we chose not to."

This was something which needed to be explored further.

"Why?"

"We suspect, and bear in mind I said I'm not a conspiracy theorist, that there are some sympathies in the Garda with white supremacy, racism. We didn't want them to give the racists a heads up. So, we decided to keep it low key by word of mouth without too much exposure on Facebook until the very last moment."

"I see and did it work?"

"Well, as you can see it did not. The Garda turned up anyway just when we hitting our stride. We just simply wanted to go and make some speeches, and then go home. The Garda arrived with a show of force, done up for a riot when there was no riot. This isn't how they usually play things in this country. It took us by surprise."

He sounded very genuine in his explanation. Bernadette saw no need to doubt the veracity of what he said so far. It seemed odd to her, almost premeditated from somewhere in the Garda. She pursued it further.

"What happened when they arrived?"

"Maneet said she would talk to them. Ever the diplomat I suppose she thought that as a woman she would be able to defuse any potential trouble and they would listen to her."

His expression told them he wasn't of the same opinion but didn't like to voice it outright.

"And what actually transpired?"

"I was a distance away, as were we all. She told us to stay back and approached them on her own. We saw a group of uniformed officers come out from behind the line of riot shields, and they stopped when they got close to her. Almost as if they were there by design."

117

He paused gave her a significant look. It did seem strange. Would they have anticipated her actions? That seemed farfetched Bernadette mused.

"How many?"

"I think it was six officers."

"Really? Six? To talk to one female?"

To come mob handed to talk to a female lawyer seemed in itself like provocation.

"Yes, it seemed a little odd."

"Then what?"

"I don't know. Suddenly and without warning she lashed out at the lead guy, punched him in the face, and then she was slapping him, hitting him. They subdued her and arrested her."

He held out his hands as if to say he had no idea.

"Subdued her how?"

"The grabbed her arms and pinned them to her side, two officers, I think. They handcuffed her hands behind her back and took her into custody."

Bernadette grimaced although it could have been much worse. They could have tackled her to the ground. Their restraint was interesting, almost as if they wanted to be the innocent party in an unprovoked attack.

"Was there any retaliation from them? Did you see them mistreat her in any way?"

"No, not at all, once she was handcuffed, they just guided her away. One person had their hand on her arm but that was all."

"What happened afterwards?"

"You know what they say about the serpent, if you want to disable it cut off its head. It should not be in this case, but after what happened, we broke up and dispersed. Besides I wanted to see what they were doing with Maneet."

If the intention had been to break up the rally, Bernadette reflected, then they had succeeded.

"What *were* they doing?"

"They charged her and released her without bail. By the time we arrived at the station she was ready to leave."

"Strange, surely. No bail or anything?"

"I thought it was odd myself, but we were grateful for her release."

Bernadette and Imogen knew, of course, there was no bail. Bernadette assumed because the charge was none too serious, in reality, to justify it.

"However, here we are with the head of your organisation charged with assault. How do you think it will affect your cause if she is convicted?"

"I'm not sure. It will have a big impact for certain, but the show goes on regardless. She may have to step back and losing her would be a bitter blow for us. She is a person who can make things happen. She is the lynchpin. Without the lynchpin, the wheels start to fall off. It would be up to us to ensure it doesn't happen."

He was already thinking of damage control, this much was clear. However, Bernadette did not blame him for it. Any organisation would have to do the same. However, her interest wasn't in IAD's future but in Maneet's.

"I see, and what will happen to her?"

"Her reputation will be damaged for sure. I doubt forever but for some time to come. She will probably find invitations to the UN will be in short supply."

Imogen who had been writing notes, stopped for a moment. "You told us she hadn't any enemies, but doesn't it strike you as odd that the Garda turned up in riot gear, and she ended up getting arrested?"

"Of course, I've thought about it a lot but I've no explanation. We don't have intelligence on the other side, as it were. We're not the CIA nor do we want to be."

"Right." Imogen gave him a searching look as if she felt this wasn't a good move on their part.

"Can you tell us about Maneet's character and if this behaviour towards the Garda is out of character?" asked Bernadette.

"For sure. She is trustworthy, she is truthful, honest, fully committed to the causes she supports. She's a lawyer and of course level-headed. I've not ever noticed her do anything impulsive or out of control. Certainly not before. I've really not seen her lose her temper certainly not to that extent. She gets tetchy of course but not much more than that."

Bernadette was satisfied with this explanation. "You could vouch for her character if needed? What she did was out of character?"

"Absolutely one hundred percent. She's a person of goodwill. I wouldn't say she respected authority, but she does respect the rule of law, well, most of the time." He laughed. "I'm not doing a good job of this am I?"

"Not really no," Bernadette agreed. An ambivalent witness was no use to them. The prosecution would have a field day with it.

"I'm probably not your best character witness."

"We'll think about it, after we've spoken to the others."

"You might be better off with one of them."

"We'll see." She was non-committal. Such decisions couldn't be lightly made. They required a proper amount of thought.

"Is there anything else I can help you with?"

"That's pretty much all for now, thanks, you've been most helpful."

"You are welcome, if you need anything else, you can contact me here."

He pulled out a business card and slid it across to them.

"Likewise, if anything occurs to you."

Bernadette passed him her own card in exchange.

"I'll get the next person for you."

"Yes, sure, if you can give us about ten minutes before you do so?"

"Sure, nice to meet you, sorry I wasn't more helpful."

He obviously felt he hadn't really assisted them particularly.

"You have been."

Bernadette stood up. He nodded and left the room. She turned to Imogen.

"What do you think?"

Imogen turned off the recorder.

"We can't use him as a witness," she said emphatically.

"No, I don't think we can."

"He will get shredded and so will our case!"

"You're right, but there were some interesting points which have come out of what he said." Bernadette sighed.

"Do you think someone in the Garda is complicit?" Bernadette picked up the thought.

"It seems a bit too much of a coincidence. We should pick someone's brains on it."

"Like?"

"Olivia to start with."

Olivia Thompson was a Garda detective who had helped and even worked with them on previous cases. She had a soft spot for Imogen which had come in handy even though Imogen had not been happy about it at first. However, Olivia had accepted Imogen wasn't a prospect once she became engaged to D'Arcy. Now they had become friends. If anyone could assist them, Olivia could.

"Olivia, yes, good idea, she might be able to help."

Olivia wasn't one to necessarily close ranks with her colleagues if her colleagues were doing something they should not. She would certainly not hold with white supremacists in the ranks.

"If Olivia doesn't work then we should try Brogan next."

"Yes, but let's keep him in reserve for now."

DCS Brogan had turned into an ally of Bernadette's. He had been helpful on two cases so far, and particularly in their recent extradition case. If needed, Bernadette was sure he could help again. He was the big gun.

"So, let's see the next person."

* * *

Rachel Clayton sat opposite them at the table. She was a dark haired woman of around thirty years of age with curly hair and green eyes. She was wearing a summery dress, and pink crocs. It was an incongruous combination but somehow it worked. The formalities having been covered. They began the interview.

"Rachel, what is it you do here?" Imogen took the lead this time.

"I'm Maneet's PA I suppose. I help her with her cases, diary, well everything really." She spoke quite quickly, and her green eyes never seemed still.

"You know her quite well then?"

"Yes, I've known her for several years. We're quite close I guess."

"What is she like?" It seemed like a good place to start.

"She's kind, considerate, caring about others, especially everyone here. She was very good to me when I got into some issues with debt collectors." Rachel blushed, realising what she had said. "Oh, I shouldn't be telling you all that about me."

"This is confidential, and we certainly are not judging you," Imogen assured her with a smile.

"Oh. Oh yes, of course, good. Well, she helped me, got them off my back. She's good like that. She's an excellent lawyer. Of course, I'm sure you know she's been to the UN. I went with her actually. She's very well received, highly regarded in those circles. Honestly, you couldn't work for... well, I couldn't work for a nicer person."

"She's getting married soon, am I right?"

"Yes, she is but I don't know, recently she wasn't happy with him, not at all. Apparently, he's quite demanding and she doesn't like it. She's her own woman, so to speak. I mean, she's very independent and he's perhaps not used to a woman being like that, you know, in his culture. I'll be honest I'm not his biggest fan, he's very chauvinistic if you ask me, not at all suitable for her but she's madly in love with him, what can you do?"

Both Imogen and Bernadette had already formed exactly this impression of him. Imogen moved things on.

"Indeed, and are you aware of her having any enemies?"

The question had to be asked, Rachel seemed most likely to know if anyone did.

"Enemies?" Rachel looked shocked.

"Yes, I would be surprised if she didn't have enemies," said Imogen frankly.

"Erm... I'm certainly not aware of any, not overtly."

"So, she has never received any threats from anyone. Like white supremacists, anything like that?"

Rachel thought for a long moment before speaking again.

"We do get emails, stuff like that. We get phone messages threatening us. You know. We just ignore them. Delete them. An organisation like us is bound to get these things. They aren't particularly targeted at Maneet."

"Do have any of them, any emails, anything?" Bernadette asked her.

"Yes, we have some, we get them every week, though a lot more lately."

"Can we have copies of whatever you have? We would like to investigate them further and they may well be evidence we can use."

"Sure, I'll put some of it together for you and send it over to you."

"Great, thanks." Bernadette furnished her with a smile.

"Were you at the rally?" Imogen said.

"Yes, of course, I was right there."

"Can you tell us what happened?"

Rachel collected her thoughts.

"Sure, we were there, with all our supporters. Maneet was giving a speech and then the Garda turned up out of the blue."

"You hadn't informed them?"

They wanted to corroborate witness stories, so Imogen didn't mention what Judd had told them.

"No, we didn't not this time. Judd and Maneet said we shouldn't alert anyone to it. So, we kept it low key. Someone must have called them in though."

This scanned with what Judd had said which made Bernadette happy. It was best when everyone's account matched at least in the main details. Finer details might differ due to individual perspectives.

"From your point of view have you any idea who it might have been?"

"Someone in our ranks, is it what you are asking?" Rachel's eyes widened a little.

"Could it have been?" Imogen cocked an eyebrow, much in the manner that Bernadette was fond of doing. The mannerisms of her senior were rubbing off on her.

"I don't think anyone who works here, no. We are all very loyal and a close knit team. But that doesn't mean someone else, you know, wouldn't have alerted them. After all, we don't know who monitors our Facebook and other network communications like WhatsApp. We put the call out very late for that reason."

"OK, anyway for argument's sake somebody let the Garda know and they arrived, what happened afterwards?"

"Oh, they turned up in riot gear. It was ridiculous really. There was no riot and no trouble at all. Very peaceful. Maneet said to me, 'for God's sake now look. I'll go and talk to them.'"

"She said it like that?"

"Yes, yes she did, and then she walked over there. She said, 'you stay here, I will handle it, it's better if I handle it.'"

"What happened then?"

"As she walked over about six officers came from behind their ranks. It was weird. I mean they had no riot gear on, and it was almost as if they were expecting her to do that."

"Really? Why would it be?"

"Well, to be honest, and this is going to sound bad. At first, I wondered if she hadn't staged it herself. As a stunt, I mean it would be good publicity for us, if she got arrested."

Bernadette and Imogen looked at each other. This was a new idea they hadn't thought of and a rather disconcerting one.

"Are you saying it was staged?"

Rachel looked rather scared, almost as if she'd said too much. "Oh no, no, no. I said it's what I thought at first, but then when she started hitting one of the Garda, I thought it couldn't be."

Both Bernadette and Imogen were suddenly looking sceptical.

"It's true," Rachel insisted. "I didn't hear what the officer said, or anything, they were too far away. She suddenly lashed out at him though."

"How exactly?" Imogen wanted to know.

"She punched him in the face, full on. Then followed by quite a few slaps, and then kicked out, I think. Two of the others came and grabbed her arms, she struggled a bit, and then they handcuffed her hands behind her back. She stopped then and went away quietly with them."

"So, did you, or do you still think it might be staged?"

"No, I don't." Rachel saw their expressions, and said again, "No! I swear I don't think it was."

"But you've no idea at all what was said to make her hit out like that?"

"None, I'm sorry none of us was close enough to hear it or even see it. He may have said something, but I just don't know."

This seemed to be as much as they might get from her. Although, they could always talk to her again if needed. Imogen decided to wrap it up.

"Right. Well, thank you for your time."

"If there is anything else, we'll let you know," said Bernadette.

"My card, send me all the emails you can and anything else you have, notes, whatever it is, please." Imogen slid her business card over to Rachel.

"Thanks, I'll send it as soon as I can."

After Rachel had gone, Bernadette sighed.

"*Do* you think Maneet has made all this up and staged the whole thing?"

"I hadn't thought it up to now, but we should ask her directly."

"I will be very angry if she has," Bernadette said in dire tones.

"I'm sure it's not like that. Why would she go to all the trouble of a court case?"

"No, you're probably right. After all, why would she hit out at the Garda if so?"

"When you get those letters and stuff, pass them onto Micky to copy onto the server and see if he can use them to track anything down."

"Sure, I will. Any news from Eve?" Imogen changed the subject.

"No, I'm not sure when she's seeing the doctor though." Bernadette checked her phone.

"Maybe you should ring her after the next interview."

"Yes, perhaps I ought to."

✳ ✳ ✳

Lunara Younan was around twenty-five with long black hair, dark eyes, and an attractive face with nicely shaped lips. She was wearing a t-shirt with a slogan on it, jeans and sandals. She sat down and agreed to be recorded then waited patiently for them to start.

"Lunara," said Bernadette, "thanks for talking to us."

"It's OK."

The woman seemed a little nervous and had a pronounced accent. Perhaps she had not been a very long time in Ireland, Bernadette mused.

"We're just asking you some questions about the rally, you were there, am I right?"

"Yes, yes I was."

"What is your role here?"

"I'm an interpreter, I speak several languages. I talk to people who come with issues about racism, or other things." Lunara gave a tight smile.

"An important job by the sound of it." Bernadette wanted to put her more at ease. It often helped to say things of this nature, although she genuinely meant it.

"Yes, of course, this is why I came, to help people. We have many problems in my country, there is much discrimination, no freedom of speech. Here it is different but still, there are problems."

"I'm sure."

Lunara seemed to relax a little.

"Do you work closely with Maneet at all?"

"I do quite a bit of interpreting for her so, yes. When she is interviewing people to see if we can take their case."

"What's she like?"

Lunara suddenly looked a little guarded, as if this might be a touchy subject.

"We need you to be honest with us, we're here to help Maneet, but if you don't tell us what you know then it makes it harder for us." Imogen smiled at her and had chimed in. She was nearer Lunara's age and perhaps that might be reassuring for her.

Lunara considered her for a moment before answering.

"Usually she is very calm, caring. She listens very carefully to what people say and speaks kindly to them. She can also be quite tough. You know, if it's needed."

Bernadette felt this wasn't the entire truth and so she pursued it further.

"You said usually, what about the not so usual part?" It was quite direct, and she could tell Lunara didn't want to answer it. "Look, you might feel you are being disloyal but if we don't know everything then we can't defend her properly. We have to understand her weaknesses if she has them."

Lunara was silent again, for a while.

"She has a temper," she said at length. "I have seen it but not many have."

"Explain."

Lunara sighed. "When things don't always go her way, she can become very angry. I have seen her shout at staff in a restaurant because the dish was cold or not cooked well. I have shared hotel rooms with her when she travels, and I've seen her lose her temper over something on a case for example. She smashed some things, like a vase, once or twice in a hotel room. We had to pay for it, of course."

Imogen flicked a quick glance at Bernadette. A different picture was shaping up, of their client. Bernadette wasn't prepared to quite let this go and wanted to know more.

"How often does she lose her temper?"

"Not often and mostly in private or when she is with me, like in the restaurant."

There was still something not quite right about this, and Bernadette continued.

"You say you have seen it and yet you are not her PA. Her PA did not mention it, but I would have expected her to be closer to Maneet than yourself."

There were wheels within wheels here, and from Imogen's expression, it was dawning on her too. Imogen looked as if she meant to speak but Bernadette's hand on her arm stopped her. This had to be handled very delicately.

"Well... I don't know... why she wouldn't see her do so... I mean, of course, Rachel is close to Maneet but..." Lunara flushed slightly.

"But?"

Lunara looked away.

"The whole truth, Lunara, I need to know the whole truth. You said you shared a hotel room with Maneet, and it sounds a little unusual, wouldn't you say? Was it separate rooms or..."

Bernadette left the rest of the sentence unsaid, but it was perfectly clear what she was hinting at.

Lunara didn't say anything for a full minute before evidently deciding to stop prevaricating. She looked Bernadette full in the face.

"No, it was not separate rooms."

"So?"

"We shared a bed because... we were lovers... are... lovers."

There was a palpable sense of relief on her face when she disclosed this. Bernadette felt Imogen touch her hand under the table, a gesture to indicate things were starting to become a little clearer to her too.

"Right," said Bernadette. "And how long have you been lovers?"

"Perhaps two years or more, on and off, since I came here. Maneet has a preference for eastern looks I suppose you could say. Another reason I left Turkey is because..."

"Of your sexuality." Bernadette finished it for her.

"Yes. I am a lesbian and it's not favoured in my country. Many have suffered who show their true feelings."

"I'm sorry," said Bernadette. "So you came here to..."

"Fight for the rights which we can't get in my homeland."

"And you met Maneet."

"Yes, and then I had feelings for her, attraction, very strong attraction and it was mutual, and so."

"So, you got to see a part of her which is very private, I understand."

"Yes, nobody knows her like I do." Lunara seemed suddenly fiercely possessive.

Bernadette knew she had to ask the next few questions now the truth had been told.

"You know she's engaged to be married, right?"

"Yes, of course, I do."

"Is she bisexual then?"

"Perhaps?" Lunara shrugged. "She has to please her family and I know that. They want her to marry and have children."

"And she?"

"She is a product of her culture still. I am too but I can break free. Maneet cannot. It seems that way."

Bernadette was surprised to see much less emotion than one would expect from a person thus treated so she carried on, intrigued to know more.

"Where does this leave you?"

"Marriage is no barrier to love. I will still be the one who travels with her so..."

The implication was plain enough they would still share a bed after Maneet was married.

"Do you love her?"

"Yes." Lunara said it without hesitation. "And when one loves, then one must also be prepared to make a sacrifice if needed."

"And does she love you?"

"Yes."

Bernadette felt Imogen squeeze her hand this time, as if she really felt for Lunara.

"You're very noble, I don't think I could do what you are doing."

"I am practical. When you come from my background you learn to adapt and to change. You learn to survive and in order for love to survive then sometimes you find another way, a different way."

"Wow." Bernadette looked at her in awe.

"It's life." Lunara smiled.

"Have you met her fiancé?"

"Of course. I will meet her children too and they will never know, any of them, about us."

Imogen looked at Bernadette who nodded, feeling it was OK for her to speak.

"If her PA doesn't know about you two, then how did it work if you travelled together, since Rebecca also travelled with her?" Imogen said.

"In this case, we stayed in separate rooms, with an adjoining door. It's simple to do these things. Rebecca would book the rooms, and then I would ring up and change them." Lunara laughed.

"My God."

"God helps those who also help themselves," Lunara quipped, seemingly having overcome the difficulty of speaking, she was now prepared to be completely open.

"So, it seems."

"Rebecca thinks Maneet is very much in love with her fiancé Akshay," said Bernadette.

"She thinks. Appearances can be deceptive." Lunara smiled. "Perhaps she does love him, but she loves me more,

I know. I am the one who feels her lips and the passion in her kiss. I am the one who knows when she makes love to me how much it really means. I know because I have lived it." Her voice vibrated suddenly filled with intensity. A snapshot of her feelings and then it was gone.

Bernadette regarded her for a moment. She was definitely an enigma in many ways. She obviously ran very deep and so did her feelings which she concealed from view. When she walked into the room, they would never have guessed any of this from her demeanour. Perhaps Maneet did love her fiancé or perhaps she did not, but it wasn't important in the grand scheme of things. They needed to get to the heart of the incident as much as anything else.

"Returning to Maneet. She has a bad temper, as you said, but others rarely see it. You have seen it, has she ever lost her temper with you? Lashed out?" Bernadette asked.

"She lost her temper, yes, of course, this is the way of lovers. Also, we eastern women are a little volatile perhaps. But she would never hit me, no. She breaks things instead to take out her anger. I have never seen her hit anyone until that Garda."

"She didn't hit you, in a playful way, or you her?" Imogen posed the question, straying into sexual kinks.

"No, not like *that*. We don't do those kinds of things in bed."

"OK."

"Tell us about the rally," Bernadette said feeling they had everything they needed for the moment regarding Maneet's temperament and her involvement with Lunara.

"I was nearby with the speakers. She was speaking. The Garda came in force. This is nothing to me. We have seen this in Turkey many times. I was not afraid because this is Ireland. She went to speak to them, but I didn't think it was wise. Then she lost her temper. I've not seen her do so before in front of everybody. He must have said something very bad to her. Well, he did, she told me about the racism."

"But you don't know what he said, not first-hand?"

"No, none of us were close enough. If she had taken one of us with her then that would be different. Perhaps it would have had a different outcome."

"How so?"

"I would have hit him instead." Lunara laughed.

Bernadette and Imogen joined in the mirth. Bernadette wasn't sure. However, it was really a joke.

"Are you going to tell Maneet about this?" Lunara wanted to know.

"I haven't decided." It was best, to be honest. "It depends on what she says when we talk to her properly. In the end, we have to know the whole truth, or we cannot defend her. We're not here to judge her morals, or sexual behaviour, we are here to try and get her acquitted. If there are traps, then we need to know what they are."

"OK." Lunara seemed quite accepting.

"Do you think in any way the incident with the Garda was a setup?" Imogen put in suddenly.

"A setup?" Lunara knitted her brow at this question.

"Do you think it was staged?"

Her brow cleared and Lunara said, "Oh no, I don't think so. If it was, she would tell me, she tells me everything."

"OK, if you're sure."

"I am sure. The way she lost her temper wasn't an act. It was genuine. I've seen it before as I said."

"Right, fair enough." Imogen dropped the subject.

"Is this going to come out in court?" was Lunara's next question.

"Again, I don't know. I'm not going to put you on the stand if I don't want it to, as we don't want the prosecution exposing something we don't want exposed. You are a good witness in one way, but in another, your testimony could be damaging. If she is prone to temper tantrums, then we can't claim it's out of character."

"I see. I mean, I don't mind, but Maneet would probably not like it. It would not matter to me if our love was exposed to the world." Lunara sighed wistfully.

Bernadette felt sorry for her. She was hamstrung pretty much by Maneet into silence and destined to live in her shadow. If it came out Maneet was bisexual or a lesbian her marriage would not take place, and it might affect her reputation also. She would no longer be able to travel to certain countries either.

"We understand," she said. "Both of us do."

"You do?"

"I'm gay and so is Imogen. I'm happily married to a beautiful woman. Imogen is openly engaged to someone too. I can't imagine how hard it is for you."

This was the first time Lunara showed her feelings as a tear started in the corner of one eye and rolled down her cheek. "Thank you, it means a lot."

This was all she said but there was genuine heartfelt emotion in the statement. She was suppressing her grief, for certain. The grief of being forced to accept love on the terms of another with no way out of it.

"You are welcome. Thank you so much for your honesty, it has helped us a great deal."

"*You* are welcome."

"We'll let you go now, but if we need more we will be in touch."

"Yes, of course, you can call me at any time." Lunara was smiling once more. The grief had disappeared as swiftly as it had come.

"Thanks again."

Lunara left the room and Imogen turned to Bernadette.

"Well fuck, I did not see that coming, did you?"

"Not at all."

"Puts a different complexion on things doesn't it?"

"Yes, yes it does."

"What are we going to say to Maneet?"

Bernadette thought for a moment. "I think we shall have to play it by ear and then we'll bring it up if it seems right. What do you think?"

"Good plan," Imogen agreed. "Now what about Eve?"

Bernadette had not managed to get hold of Eve before the last interview and assumed Eve was at the doctor. She picked up her phone and saw a text, it said, "Everything is OK. Just having some tests to make sure."

Seeing those words had the opposite effect to what was intended, and Bernadette rang Eve at once.

"Hi, darling," Eve trilled picking up the call.

"What tests?" Bernadette demanded without preamble.

"I knew you'd do that." Eve chuckled. "Just a blood test silly, routine. Urine test too."

"What did the doctor actually say?"

"He said it sounded like fatigue. He's checking me for anaemia and things like vitamin D levels, but in any case, he's prescribed some for me in the meantime. He doesn't think there's anything to worry about."

"Thank God!" Bernadette let out a sigh.

"See, do you feel better now?"

"Yes, I do. But behave yourself, can you? Don't wear yourself out!"

"I won't, I promise." Eve laughed.

"And don't tease me either, I've been worried sick!"

"I know, I'm sorry. We'll have a nice dinner tonight to celebrate."

"OK."

"I love you."

Bernadette spied Maneet approaching the meeting room.

"I love you too, I've got to go."

"Bye, darling."

* * *

Maneet came in and sat down.

"How did it go? Have you seen enough people? I can get you more, if you want."

"I think we have enough for now, and we need to talk to you," Bernadette said.

"Sure, if you want, I'm at your disposal."

Bernadette glanced at her watch. "It's past lunchtime so perhaps we can take you out to lunch, and we can talk?"

"Oh, really? I was going to invite you to have lunch here, we have a group lunch usually. But, if you want to go out, let me take you!"

"If you insist, but out would be better. We need somewhere quiet though, and private, where we can talk undisturbed."

"I do insist and I'm paying, well, Akshay is going to pay with the credit card he gave me to use." Maneet giggled.

Bernadette reflected any rift with Akshay must have been short lived. Maneet picked up her look.

"Oh, I might not be speaking to him, but it doesn't stop me spending his money."

Bernadette gave a short laugh. "Thanks to your fiancé then, but if you'll allow us to pick the restaurant, we know somewhere secluded."

Maneet laughed too. "OK."

Bernadette drove them the Chapter One, a favourite haunt of D'Arcy's while Imogen phoned ahead to reserved their favourite cubby hole. They knew Imogen at the restaurant very well because she was D'Arcy's fiancée, and D'Arcy took Imogen there quite often. Maneet was full of admiration for Bernadette's car and enthused about it all the way there. She was evidently considering the idea of getting one like it herself. Bernadette reflected that for all the causes Maneet was dedicated to, she wasn't above an interest in the trappings of wealth. Maneet was obviously a woman of dichotomies.

Bernadette parked the car, and they went down the stairs from the road to the basement where Chapter One was located in Parnell Square. The entrance led them through the stone arched foyer, and they were immediately whisked to the Demi Salle, which was their usual private dining space. This was part of the cellar complex which made up the restaurant. The small room was secluded with an Elmwood table and plush leather upholstered benches. The walls were dark green with dark floor tiles, it was well lit however with subdued lighting.

"Oh, this is nice," Maneet pronounced as they took their seats.

"Yes, and it's very good food, D'Arcy comes here all the time," said Imogen.

"D'Arcy?"

"D'Arcy Brown, she's my fiancée," said Imogen smiling.

"Oh my God, *that* D'Arcy Brown, I hadn't figured it out. I should have known. I'm usually smarter than this, and more on the ball."

"It's OK, you've other things on your mind."

"Well, but even so. D'Arcy Brown, goodness me."

Further discussion was curtailed while the waiter brought the menus and they opted for the set lunch. Bernadette wondered if Maneet might be vegetarian, but it turned out not to be the case. Bernadette chose *Lamb Kromseki with pickle crown prince pumpkin, caper sprout cream, rosemary and Madeira jus* followed by *Braised Short Rib of Beef with cauliflower and pickled garlic, grilled king oyster mushrooms and colcannon.* Imogen opted for the *Game Terrine with Muscat grapes and foie gras parfait, rye bread crouton* and then the short rib of beef. Maneet who spent a while examining the selection eventually decided upon *Red Cow Parmesan with artichokes en barigoule, charred lettuce and mushroom duxelles* and then *Guinea Hen with David Byrne's sweetcorn, pressed leg with Lyonnaise onion and sage* to follow. The order was taken, and it was to be accompanied by sparkling water. In the meantime, a waiter brought a breadbasket of small rolls with butter.

"Now," said Maneet once the excitement of choosing food was completed, "what would you like to ask me?"

"May we record it?" Imogen enquired.

"Sure, of course."

Imogen placed the recorder which she had brought in her bag, on the table, and started it.

"We've had some very interesting conversations with your colleagues," Bernadette began diplomatically.

"Oh yes?"

"One thing they concur on is none of them could tell what the Garda officer said to you before you assaulted him because you were too far away."

"Sure, that's right, I asked them myself obviously." Maneet shrugged.

"Why did you decide to approach the Garda on your own?" It was a mild enough question although Maneet looked at her a little askance.

Perhaps she wasn't expecting some incisive or probing questions, but Bernadette was fully aware there were many of these which needed to be asked.

"I didn't want to involve any of my staff in any unpleasantness and I thought I could handle it on my own. Foolishly as it turned out."

"Were you expecting unpleasantness?"

"No, not as such but you never can tell in these situations. I also just felt a lone woman approaching them might appear less of a threat."

"Right." Bernadette nodded and glanced at Imogen who was watching Maneet rather intently. A person's body language could tell you a lot but Maneet did not seem particularly tense or defensive.

The waiter brought the sparkling water and poured this out, allowing for a pause during which Maneet buttered a roll and started to eat it. The waiter informed them the first course would not be long.

"I'm hungry so I'm glad to hear it," Maneet pronounced once he had left.

"One thing which I find curious, and I wonder if you did also," Bernadette continued, "the Garda turned up in full riot gear and then when you went to parlay six uniformed officers appeared from behind the line. Didn't that seem strange to you?"

Maneet sipped her water and considered this. "I don't know. I mean in the heat of the moment you're not really analysing things too much. You just react and try to act calmly. I saw them approaching and I hoped I could talk things down, as it were."

"So, you weren't expecting the Garda at all?" Bernadette floated this question very lightly to see what reaction it would get.

"Expecting them? No, why would we be..." Maneet trailed off and then said sharply. "I didn't set this up if that's what you're thinking."

"I didn't say you did."

"Not in so many words. But you might have been implying it."

"Why would you think that?" Bernadette regarded her implacably. She was testing Maneet for sure.

"Oh." Maneet sighed. "OK, well, I know Rachel thinks I did. She probably told you. She thinks I don't know but I heard her talking the other day, to some others when she thought I wasn't there. You know, I've done a lot of things in my time but I'm not going to get myself arrested for anyone's cause."

"Actually, she said she thought so at first but not now," Imogen told her.

"Ah Rachel, she's a gem, but perhaps I trained her too well, now she suspects everything, even me." Maneet laughed.

"Do you suspect everything?" Bernadette wondered.

"It's part of my job, as I'm sure it's yours. Things are not always what they seem, so I keep an open mind."

"Alright. I believe you didn't set it up, but I don't understand why the Garda came to your rally in riot gear and also why six officers came out to speak to you."

Maneet shook her head. "I don't know either."

"Do you perhaps have a plant or a mole in your organisation?" It was a reasonable question given what had occurred.

"I don't think so, no. We vet our people very carefully, all those who work directly for us. We check their social media, references, all sorts. We can't afford to have anyone who is not kosher or who might let our organisation down. We might seem to be quite informal, but we've got very high standards. Well, I do at least. It takes dedication to do what we do, and we need people who are dedicated, passionate and honest."

"Fair enough, then we have to assume someone on the outside tipped off the Garda, or your organisation is being monitored in some way?"

Bernadette wanted to try and get some perspective on the incident because some things about it did not gel. If it wasn't from Maneet's side, then there must be other forces in play.

"We probably are being monitored." Maneet grimaced. "There are far right groups in this country, and I doubt they like us. This kind of disruption is part and parcel of what they do to try and stop our rallies from being successful."

"So rather than direct confrontation?"

"We rarely get a counter rally. It would very likely rebound on them, so they go for more covert methods I suspect."

"We gather you get hate mail every week."

"Yes. Sadly, this is where we are. We choose to stick our heads up above the parapet and so we're going to get shot at."

"I certainly hope not literally!" Bernadette exclaimed.

"No, no, of course not." Maneet laughed.

The first course arrived and for a few moments, the conversation ceased while they addressed themselves to the food. Maneet said the subtle flavours were amazing and wondered why she had not been to the restaurant before. She then opined about bringing Akshay there and Bernadette caught a look from Imogen at this statement. She was beginning to come to the conclusion she would need to tackle Maneet about her sexuality, and about Lunara.

As they finished the remnants, Bernadette turned on the recorder to continue her questions.

"Rachel is going to get us copies of the abusive mail, we'll get our investigator to research it and perhaps run down where it's coming from," she said.

"Do you need to? I mean, is it relevant to the case?" Maneet looked surprised.

"I do, because frankly, this whole thing doesn't smell right at all. Something is off. The Garda arriving in riot gear, and then six officers coming out like that. It doesn't seem right."

"OK." Maneet smiled and it seemed she was happy with this explanation and to leave it to Bernadette and her team.

"What we do need to know, is what the officer said to you as exactly as you can remember it."

Maneet made a face, and then screwed up her eyes evidently trying to think back. This moment was prolonged a little more while the waiter came and removed the dishes.

"OK, well, I'll try."

"This is crucial, as you will have to repeat it on the stand and put it in an affidavit, and the versions can't be different under cross examination," Bernadette told her.

"I get you, yes of course. I mean, I am a lawyer. I do know that." Maneet was a little testy.

"Sure." Bernadette smiled.

"Sorry. I'll try to remember." Maneet closed her eyes again. "So, I was standing making my speech, and in the middle of the speech the Garda vans pulled up on Chesterfield Avenue. They poured out of them, must have been maybe fifty of them at least. If you've seen the video it was a lot. They were in full riot gear and they started advancing on us in a line."

She opened her eyes. "Am I doing OK so far?"

"Yes, go on..."

Maneet closed her eyes again. "I said to the others, I'm going to talk to them they will listen to me. Famous last words eh. Me the big I am, big shot lawyer, going to broker peace. What a joke that was."

Maneet let out a sardonic laugh and her mouth twisted into a wry smile. "Anyway. As I started walking towards them, these others came from behind and then walked up to me, just in normal uniforms. The riot police stopped behind them, and we ended up maybe three feet apart, me and those six. I mean, it was close, close enough to hear. They were sort of in a semi-circle and I was in the middle. It was quite intimidating actually."

"I can imagine."

"So, this officer. Sergeant Franklin Maguire, the one named in the pleadings. He was staring at me, like with real antagonism. I said to him, this is a peaceful rally, you don't need to be here, we aren't causing any trouble, just let us finish our speeches and we'll be gone."

"And what did he say?" It sounded like a reasonable request from Maneet, Bernadette reflected.

"He said, fuck your fucking rally, you Indian bitch. Why are you in this fucking country anyway? You fucking Paki whore. Go back to Paki land where you belong, you fucking little black slut, back to the gutter where your kind belong. We don't need people like you in this country. Fuck off you cocksucking black piece of shit Indian dog..."

"Fuck!" said Imogen, when she heard this. It was quite shocking. "I would have smacked him into the middle of next week."

"Well, that's exactly what I did." Maneet laughed.

"What did you do, as precisely as you can recall it?" Bernadette shooting a quelling glance at Imogen who poked her tongue out. Maneet still had her eyes closed so didn't see this exchange.

"I lost my temper, I saw red, whatever you want to call it and I landed a punch right in his face. With my right fist. I do, or did, kickboxing so I can punch for sure. He looked startled and was slightly reeling back. I slapped him hard, a few times, and I think I kicked him the leg. He retreated and the others, a couple of them grabbed me and pinned my arms. I started to come to, I relaxed, and they handcuffed me, led me away."

"Did he retaliate at all say anything when you were hitting him?"

"No, that's the surprising thing, he just took it almost as if he wanted me to..." Maneet stopped as if it was just dawning on her. "Oh fuck! Fuck! I've been fucking set up, haven't I?"

She looked at Bernadette and Imogen with her eyes wide in shock.

"We don't know for sure..." Bernadette began.

"No, I know for sure because the fucking arsehole was smiling at me, smiling while I smashed his fucking face!"

"OK." This again was an unexpected turn of events. Something, Bernadette mused, which seemed to keep happening on this case. Nothing was turning out to be what it appeared to be.

"Shit!"

"Did you say anything to him? While you were punching him?" Imogen wondered.

"I might have called him a bastard, arsehole, fucking arsehole perhaps. A few choice words like this but I can't remember, honestly, I really can't." Maneet gave a hollow laugh.

The waiter appeared with the main courses, and Bernadette turned off the recorder so they could eat. This gave her some time to reflect on things. She still felt they would need to bring up the issue of Lunara, perhaps even more now than before. Pushing these thoughts aside, she cut into her beef and ate a mouthful with satisfaction.

"My God, this is to die for. I mean, I usually go to Indian restaurants, but this is going on my favourite list for sure," exclaimed Maneet having tried her Guinea hen.

"Glad you like it, D'Arcy loves it and I'm getting to love it too," said Imogen.

"So, tell me about D'Arcy, what's it like being engaged to a celebrity?" Maneet shot her a sly look.

Imogen was more than happy to oblige, and so a pleasant half an hour passed while she rattled on about D'Arcy in the most besotted way imaginable. Bernadette looked on indulgently and with great affection. It was in these times it showed just how far Imogen had fallen. All the more reason to make sure she and D'Arcy made it to the altar and beyond.

With the mains being consumed, and when Imogen had finished waxing lyrical about her beloved, Bernadette decided it was time to return to the matter at hand.

She turned on the recorder once more and decided to take up the most controversial topic of all.

"You've got a bit of temper on you, am I right?" she said taking Maneet off guard.

"Who told you that?" Maneet shot her a look of defiance.

"Have you?" Bernadette ignored the question.

"Oh my God, you sound like a trial lawyer!"

"I am a trial lawyer, that's what I do." Bernadette was implacable.

"But I'm..."

"Not the one on trial? You are though, Maneet, you are the one on trial in court, and the prosecution will try to shred you piece by piece if I put you on the stand. So, it's my job to test you before they do."

"I can see why they say you're good," Maneet observed wryly.

"So, the question, Maneet, do you have a bit of a temper on you?" Bernadette was undeterred.

"Shit, you are fucking good, you're like a laser guided missile."

"It has been said about me, so..."

Maneet rolled her eyes and sighed. "Yes I do have a temper but hardly anyone ever sees it because I can usually control myself. So now who told you?"

"I am pretty sure you can guess, can't you? It was Lunara, and she told us other things too." There it was. The little bombshell Bernadette had been waiting to drop.

"Oh, shit." Maneet dropped her eyes.

"She's your lover, isn't she? You've been carrying out an elaborate charade while in actual fact you are in a relationship with your interpreter and have been for two years, is it? Yes?" Bernadette cocked an eyebrow.

Imogen smiled to herself, this was Bernadette at her most tenacious. She was like a viper, unrelenting and when she struck, she struck hard.

"Yes," said Maneet in a small voice. Her bottom lip pulled out in a pout.

"Who else knows about it, Maneet?" Bernadette ignored the impulse to tell her to put her lip away. She was on a roll and she wanted the whole truth.

"Nobody."

"Nobody?" Bernadette couldn't keep the note of scepticism out of her voice.

"Nobody I swear. Well, nobody important. I mean, obviously staff in hotels and stuff. They know we slept together but it's not as if they are going to say anything or care about it."

"They might if you become big news, which you will with this trial," Bernadette pointed out.

"We haven't been together in any hotels in Ireland. I mean, we rented a cottage way down south a few times but that's all."

"OK." Bernadette shrugged. "So Akshay doesn't know?"

"No, no he doesn't, good God."

"Right."

"Don't judge me. I have to do what I have to do. My parents, they expect it. I have to..." Maneet started to appear a little upset by this interrogation, but Bernadette needed to get everything out in the open.

"Do you... love... Akshay?"

"What's this…" Maneet started to say but seeing Bernadette's expression she stopped. "Yes, fine, yes I do love him, in my way."

"Your way?"

"He's very loveable, charming, funny. Lots of good things."

"But he's not Lunara, is he." It was a statement.

Maneet looked down at the table. "No, he's not and believe it or not I'm bloody good at putting on an act."

"You've got Rachel convinced. She thinks you are head over heels for him."

"Rachel thinks she knows me better than she does."

"And Lunara?"

"She knows everything. Everything about me, I'm an open book to her because I love her so dearly. It breaks my heart that I have to marry someone else." Maneet let out a sob for a moment, and then shed a few tears briefly before looking up.

"Why do you, though?"

"It's complicated, my culture. My heritage, the future, of my family."

"I see." Although really, Bernadette did not. She couldn't understand how a culture and tradition could subsume a person so completely.

"You don't," said Maneet candidly. "You weren't brought up like I was. You couldn't possibly understand the pressure of family."

"True. Touché. Can I ask you something else?"

"Why not? You've penetrated my most intimate secrets, which I never thought was going to happen. That's what I get for hiring a shit hot lawyer." Maneet laughed.

"Are you bisexual?"

"Oh, definitely not. You think because I sleep with Akshay that makes me bisexual? No, it doesn't. I can still sleep with him and enjoy it. Don't ask me but I can. My natural attraction has always been to women. Don't you know that's why I picked you, partly, because you're gay, and you're utterly beautiful, as well as being one of the best lawyers in Dublin? I would fuck you in a moment if you'd let me, but of course, I know you're taken."

Both Bernadette and Imogen regarded her in surprise, at this candid statement but they supposed things had moved beyond the boundaries of normal client and barrister conversation.

"I scored the treble then." Bernadette chuckled, unfazed by this statement. She filed it away later to tell Eve.

"Your wife is a lucky woman."

"Yes, well, it's me who is lucky." Bernadette smiled to herself thinking of Eve.

"Anyway. Now you've brought all this up, are you going to use it in court?"

"I don't want to and that's why I need to know if there is any way of the prosecution finding out. Apart from anything else, Lunara is the only one who really knows you have a temper and if the prosecution could bring that out in evidence it will hugely assist their case."

"Fuck!" said Maneet. "Are you using Lunara as a witness?"

"No, for the same reason. Not if we can help it."

"Phew, well, you've exposed the underbelly of my life now, I assume the recording is confidential."

"Your secrets are safe with us."

The waiter arrived and removed the dishes. He brought the menus in case they wanted dessert. Bernadette asked him to bring a selection of cheese as none of them wanted anything substantial, in spite of the tempting nature of items like *hot chocolate mousse*. The cheeseboard duly arrived with coffee, some fruit, and crackers.

Bernadette cut a slice of brie and took a few grapes. She ate it with relish. It was one of her favourites.

"Do you have any enemies? I don't mean the ones who send you hate mail but real enemies who hold a grudge against you."

Maneet ate some cheddar on a cracker with dried fig with evident enjoyment.

"I don't really know anyone who hates me to that extent, no. I haven't really done anything to anyone, not in a personal way."

"OK, I thought it might be worth asking. Just in case."

"I really can't think of anyone I've upset so much they'd have some kind of vendetta against me."

"Well, if you do then let us know, OK?"

"Sure." Maneet helped herself to some more cheese while Bernadette and Imogen sipped their coffees.

"Is there something else?" Maneet wondered, when neither of them said anything further.

"I think we've got everything for now," Bernadette told her.

"Phew, thank God that's over." Maneet ran the back of her hand dramatically over her brow.

"It's over for now, but you've still got court to endure."

"I know, but you've already pretty much just put me through the wringer."

"The prosecution will be worse, I assure you," Imogen said.

"God, really?"

"Yes, really, we've seen them in action plenty of times."

"Fuck."

"Criminal law is a very different kettle of fish to what you do," Bernadette said frankly. "Once you are on the stand it's no holds barred. Of course, it's the same for us with their witnesses."

"Heaven help them then!"

Bernadette laughed.

"You are a pair of bitches, that's what I've employed, bitches," Maneet complained with mock severity.

This only served to make Bernadette and Imogen laugh even harder. "That's what we call ourselves the Lesbian Bitch Lawyers."

"With good fucking reason."

"You've been a good sport." Bernadette became serious. "I'm impressed."

"I did something right then." Maneet laughed too.

"If we are all done, we should get back."

"I'm paying, well, Akshay is paying." Maneet brandished his credit card.

"There's no stopping her, darling." Imogen giggled.

"None whatsoever."

"Oh, you two, what did I deserve to get two lawyers like you!"

"You hired us."

"Well fuck, that was a mistake."

They all collapsed with mirth, having become firm friends in the space of a lunch hour now that the truth was out.

* * *

Bernadette drove back to Maneet's offices and dropped her outside. She felt they had obtained everything useful they could from the meeting so far, there was no need to go back in. No doubt Maneet would tell Lunara about their conversation, that was to be expected. The atmosphere on the return trip was quite convivial. Both Bernadette and Imogen now conceived a liking for Maneet which certainly helped. She had started to treat them as if they were old friends. Bernadette wasn't quite so far advanced in her feelings about it, Maneet was still their client after all. She tended to become friendly or friends with some clients, but one also had to respect professional boundaries. The only time this had gone completely out of the window was with D'Arcy, so many lines were crossed and that seemed to be D'Arcy all over, once in her orbit normal behaviour went out of the window. However, now D'Arcy was like family to them, and the past was the past as far as Bernadette was concerned.

After she parked, they repaired to Bernadette's office with coffee for a debrief.

"That was interesting," said Imogen as they sat together on the sofa.

"Very." Bernadette sipped her coffee.

"What are your thoughts?"

"What are yours?" Bernadette shot back, always liking to test her junior.

"OK." Imogen took a few sips of her own drink and thought about it. "I'm with you in that something doesn't gel about the way the Garda handled this, and I don't understand it at all. The guy who provoked her does sound as if he did it on purpose and I wonder if he's got far right connections or something. Somewhere in the Garda, something smells rotten about this, that's for sure. As for the rest, I never did guess Maneet was gay."

"Me neither, my gaydar must be off or she hides it exceptionally well."

"I cannot imagine doing what she's planning to do, marrying a guy, have children and still continue to be with her lover. It seems shockingly crazy to me. Although I suppose she has plenty of opportunity going away on business and so forth, to be with Lunara. Poor Lunara though, forever in the shadows." Imogen shook her head slightly in disapproval.

Bernadette nodded in agreement. "It seems insane and fraught with complications. I suppose when you've been lying to people your whole life then it becomes easier to continue lying."

"Yes, so where do we go from here?"

"For obvious reasons, we want to avoid using Lunara on the stand. She can't lie under oath. If the truth comes out about them both it will be damaging for Maneet professionally and personally. This isn't a case to bring out these kinds of truths I feel. Perhaps our best bet is one of the other two as a character witness and possibly Rachel who seems to carry a torch for her."

Something else occurred to Imogen. "That's another thing. She slept with Judd and had a relationship with him. We didn't ask her about it, maybe we should have."

"No, I don't think we needed to. It must have been before Lunara came on the scene. He said she broke up with him over marriage but maybe it was because he was a man, and she was really a lesbian."

Imogen pondered this for a minute and finished off her coffee. "She might not have realised it at first, just like I didn't, or perhaps she was genuinely attracted to him even though she says she's not bisexual."

"Exactly." Bernadette reached out and impulsively squeezed her hand. Imogen smiled at her. "I think we need to talk to Olivia, and also get Micky to investigate this Franklin Maguire."

"I can see if she's free."

"Sure, why not. You seem a lot happier by the way." Bernadette observed.

"Yes, I am. I might have to give D'Arcy a repeat performance tonight, for good measure."

"Poor D'Arcy."

"She's not poor D'Arcy, and she has deserved every one of the spankings I gave her. Well, maybe most of them..." Imogen trailed off seeing Bernadette's sceptical expression.

"I'm sure you're right."

"Don't humour me, you bitch." Imogen laughed.

"Such bad behaviour, darling."

"Well, you know what to do, if you want to correct it."

"Go, you incorrigible minx. And see if you can get Olivia in here." Bernadette's eyes were twinkling.

* * *

Olivia Thompson sat and stirred her tea in the maddeningly methodical manner she always did. She had brown hair, tied back in a ponytail although Bernadette had a suspicion it was longer than it used to be. She was looking exceptionally attractive that day, Bernadette mused. Olivia had brown eyes, full lips, which on reflection were entirely kissable. These thoughts were quite dispassionate, as Bernadette had no desire for anyone other than Eve, but it was her habit to size up other females. She did have a particular passion for women's feet, it was one of her predilections. Olivia was wearing court shoes and her feet were not on display. The shoes were coupled with a black skirt suit with a pretty pink blouse.

Olivia's passion lay with tea. Apparently, the tea they served in the office was incomparable to any other, for some reason. She became almost ceremonial when partaking of it and they just had to wait until she'd satisfied herself and taken the first sip. Bernadette and Imogen sat patiently sipping their own coffees. The two of them were very used to Olivia's ways by now.

"I know you're going to start with some social talk about Carole and me, so I'll tell you we are still together, remarkably. I think she might even be falling for me, although she hasn't said so," Olivia told them having sampled her tea with evident relish.

She leaned forward and took a Bourbon Cream from a plate of biscuits on the coffee table.

"I'm glad to hear it," Bernadette said. "And are you falling for her?"

"That ship has already sailed." Olivia gave a short laugh. "She's got me hook line and sinker."

"Have you told her?" Imogen wanted to know.

"Not in so many words, I mean, which one of us is going to be the first to speak, and all that?"

"Maybe she's waiting for you?"

"But I'm a coward, I don't want to get hurt."

Olivia took a sip of her tea.

"Sometimes you have to take the plunge, do what's right. I did with Eve. I was the first one to say I loved her, and it turned out she had fallen in love with me that first morning together."

"Really?" Olivia looked much struck but this.

"It's a risk, but you have to decide if love is worth the risk or not."

"She's right," Imogen added. "After all it was me who told D'Arcy first, and me who proposed."

"See!" Bernadette looked at her triumphantly.

"Alright, alright. Thanks for the relationship advice, and now what did you two reprobates actually get me over here for?" Olivia was smiling. They were on mutually friendly terms. Olivia and her girlfriend Carole had been invited to Bernadette's wedding. Bernadette had been instrumental in getting the two of them together, and she was happy it appeared to be working out.

"We need to pick your brains," said Imogen.

"Well, you're out there, I have none to pick." Olivia possessed a keen sense of humour.

"What do you know about racial prejudice in the Garda?" Bernadette asked her, smiling slightly at the self-deprecating quip but focused on their quest.

"Hmm, now there's a loaded question. What kind of race? Prejudice against whom?" Olivia regarded her keenly.

"White supremacists."

Olivia smiled a knowing smile. Picked up her cup of tea and sipped it before answering.

"You're asking if we have white racists in the Garda?"

"To put it bluntly, yes."

"Because?"

Olivia always gave them what they wanted, but never without asking why. She waited for a response.

"Because of the case we are working on."

"Which is?"

Bernadette sighed. She might as well tell Olivia the whole.

"We are representing Maneet Johal-Lynch, the lawyer who..."

"It's fine, you can spare me the details, I know all about it, it's all over the force." Olivia stopped her.

"OK, so that's why we want to know."

"Let me guess, you think she was provoked, or at least that's her defence. She's alleging the officer race baited her, and she reacted, am I right?"

"You seem to know more than just a little about it," Imogen said sounding slightly suspicious.

"Easy tiger." Oliva laughed. "I'm not involved in it, nor a racist but I make it my business to know stuff. Besides this is kind of high profile. The brass wants it put to bed without any fuss. Or so I've heard."

"Is that a fact!" Bernadette pursed her lips.

"Don't get all antsy with me, I'm just the messenger." Olivia held up her hands in mock surrender.

"Sorry."

"Don't be. Anyway, now we've established that, what exactly are you asking me?"

"I'm asking if you've come across or know of white supremacists among your colleagues."

"I see, and you realise you're asking me to betray fellow officers by telling you things like this. We're supposed to have each other's backs you know, close ranks, and all that jazz." Olivia smiled sardonically.

"If you'd rather not." Bernadette shrugged. You never could tell with Olivia whether she was being serious or sarcastic sometimes. Also, she didn't easily give up information without first having made you work for it.

Imogen scowled slightly. Though used to Olivia's ways, she found them irritating at times.

"It's OK, the pair of you don't need to look at me like *that*." Olivia laughed. "I'm not a fan of racists and particularly not in our force. Same goes for homophobes, and any other 'phobes. But to answer your question, yes there are. No, I don't know who they are, but I know there are definitely some white Garda who don't like people of another colour."

"Right," said Bernadette.

"What exactly do you need to know? Maybe I can be of more help if I actually understand what you are asking. Also, is there any more tea?" Olivia looked hopeful.

"I'll get it," said Imogen taking her cup and disappearing, to leave Bernadette to explain.

"OK. I'll be plain but it doesn't go past you," Bernadette told Olivia.

"Like everything you've told me, of course."

"Right. So, there are some odd things about what went down. Firstly, why did fifty or more Garda officers appear at the rally in riot gear? Then when Maneet went to talk to them why did six officers peel off and come to parlay, and they were not in riot gear? Finally, why did Sergeant Franklin Maguire tell my client to go back to Paki land, call her a fucking little black slut and a cocksucking black piece of shit Indian dog, among other things?"

"Well, fuck!" Olivia looked rather shocked. "I didn't know those were the allegations."

"They are."

"You believe her? You believe he said them?"

"Yes, yes I do. A person doesn't lash out for no reason, unless they are drunk or on drugs, mentally unstable. She was none of those. I've spoken to her more than once now and I think she's telling the truth."

Imogen reappeared with more tea for Olivia and more coffee for her and Bernadette. The tea ritual was repeated with the fresh cup while they waited once more until Olivia was ready to talk.

"Taking your questions in turn. The Garda in riot gear and in force. This might simply be because they were going to an unknown situation and wanted to be prepared. I take it they were not informed of the rally beforehand?"

"No, I think they felt it wasn't so high profile, and of course they aren't obliged to inform the Garda," said Bernadette.

"Somebody did though, obviously."

"Yes."

"So, they may have come out and moved forward in readiness for anything happening, which to be fair it did not. Some of this is standard training."

"OK."

Olivia drank some of her tea and thought for a few moments.

"The six Garda, I can't explain. Why six to meet one woman? It could be that if there was trouble, they had backup, though I can't say they should have expected it from one person alone. Admittedly she had the protesters behind her, but they were at some distance. So, it seems a little odd."

"Good." Bernadette was happy with this response. "That's how we feel about it."

"Now did he or didn't he say those words? Was he deliberately trying to provoke her? I don't know. If he said them, it's bang out of order. If I get the gist of what you're implying, he was trying to incite her to get herself arrested. Perhaps because, you suspect, there are greater forces in play here. Am I right so far?"

"You've got it."

"I don't have any other answers, off the top of my head, I'm afraid. Though that's not to say I can't get them. I just have to ask some very circumspect questions from people I can trust. In the Garda, like any organisation, there are little cliques. White supremacists will have theirs. I might be able to dig something up on the quiet."

"We'd be very grateful if you can."

"You are welcome. I'm not sure why I'm doing all this for you two, but it's probably because I like you." Olivia smiled.

It was true. She had no real reason to assist them in any way at all, and the fact she was, was very unusual and probably out of order in its own way. Per the terms and conditions of her job, she should not be discussing Garda business outside of the Garda. However, due to Bernadette and Imogen's efforts, she had made two important arrests and gained considerable kudos with her boss. Bernadette was fully aware much of her business hinged around contacts. Olivia was one of the best contacts they had. She and Imogen both regarded her as a friend rather than just a contact.

"We appreciate you."

"I appreciate you too, both of you." Olivia selected another biscuit. "My super still thinks the sun shines out of my arse thanks to the arrests I've made, and I aim to keep it that way. Also, if we have these kinds of people in the Garda then they don't belong. We should weed them out."

"You can't do it on your own surely?" Imogen protested, with a look of concern on her face.

"Of course not, but I can put information where it's needed to be found, if I know what the information is."

This was entirely cryptic, but Bernadette took it to mean Olivia would not endanger her own existence or job in the Garda. This was a good thing. She didn't want Olivia to cross any lines which jeopardised her own safety.

"Should we be concerned about these people?" The question had to be asked.

"I don't think you necessarily should, but it doesn't hurt to take a bit of extra care."

"Comforting," Bernadette said feeling precisely the opposite.

"You did ask, in any case, if you feel threatened in any way or for your personal safety just to get in touch."

"OK, well hopefully it won't come to that. After all, this is just a case of assault."

"Exactly." Olivia laughed lightly. She finished up her tea and stood up. "Now, I can't stay here drinking tea all afternoon. Duty calls and all."

"Thanks for coming."

"You're welcome. If I discover anything, I'll keep you posted."

They let Olivia see herself out. She was a familiar figure in their offices, and Bernadette had a high level of trust in her. They watched her go and then Bernadette turned back to Imogen.

"We didn't learn a whole lot then." Imogen made a face.

"No but it's at least got her thinking, and digging, she might dig up something."

"Or not."

"Don't be such a pessimist. You never know. Olivia has unearthed some very useful things for us in the past."

"Yes, you're right." Imogen sighed. "She just winds me up sometimes."

"Why?" Bernadette raised an eyebrow.

"Oh, because she's always so super self-confident, it becomes annoying."

"You know she isn't though, underneath. Think about it, she's a woman and a lesbian trying to make her way in a difficult profession. She needs to keep up a front. Acting confident is part of it. Just like we keep up the façade of being bitches, when we have to..."

"We *are* bitches though," Imogen protested.

"When we want to be, yes."

"Ask D'Arcy, she'll tell you."

"No doubt but I'm not talking about kinky sex."

Both of them laughed. Bernadette knew Imogen was sometimes ambivalent towards Olivia. Overall, Imogen and Olivia had reached a state of mutual understanding with each other which was all to the good.

"Shall I get Micky?" Imogen wondered, changing the subject.

Glancing at her watch, Bernadette could see it was getting late in the afternoon, and she'd had more than enough to take in for one day. She liked to let things gel and mull them over for a while.

"Let's talk to him tomorrow. In the meantime, let's see if there's a pre-trial date yet."

"Are we going to ask for a jury trial?"

"Yes, absolutely. We're not leaving it up to a judge. We've a better chance with a jury I think."

They could opt for a summary trial with a judge, but Bernadette knew this was a risk. She could appeal to a jury better and since the outcome was important, a jury was the best choice.

"Yes, for sure. I thought you would say so."

"We will cover it off at the prehearing."

"The prosecution won't want a jury."

"No, but it's not up to the judge."

"I wonder who we'll get up against us."

They wouldn't necessarily know who the prosecution was sending to represent them until the pre-trial hearing. They had gone up against most of the prosecution's lawyers by now and were old adversaries.

"I hope to God it's not Shane." Imogen grimaced.

"I doubt it very much, and in any case, there is a rumour he's heading back to the UK, joining a chambers there with his friend Mason."

"Good riddance!"

Shane Wilson was an English barrister who had come to Ireland to work for the prosecution. He and Bernadette had faced off more than once, but worse he and Imogen had had a fling prior to D'Arcy. It turned out Shane was a bit of a Christian Grey and had started Imogen off on her kinky bedroom antics. He had unleashed her wild side. However, following their last courtroom encounter he had got close to sexually harassing her were it not for D'Arcy's quick actions putting him on the ground with a martial arts move Eve had taught them. Although they did not pursue it further, all of them viewed him with distaste. It seemed his friend was trying to entice him back to the UK, in any case.

"I really don't think they'll put him on this," Bernadette said frankly. "I'm sure words would have been said, off the record."

"Thank God! I don't think I can really face him again after last time."

"I'm sure you won't have to. He won't be wanting to see you either I'm sure."

"No, well, anyway, I'll get hold of the court, check the lay of the land."

"Sure."

They cleared the cups and took them back to the kitchen. They went to their respective offices to wrap up some things before heading home.

* * *

Bernadette parked her car in the drive, entered the house which seemed rather quiet, dropped her bag and kicked off her shoes. Standing barefoot with some relief to be home, she could smell what she assumed was dinner cooking but there was no sign of Eve. After looking all around the house, Eve was nowhere to be seen, and then she remembered the gym. Eve had intimated it would be ready by the weekend, so perhaps she was out there. Bernadette slipped through the back door and walked over to their outbuilding. She noticed there was string marking out where the conservatory was going to go, and also there appeared to be quite a lot of new things in the garden, planters and the like. The outbuilding door was ajar, and she pulled it open. Inside, the floor was fitted out with soft landing tiles, and the walls were painted white. There was a large skylight in the roof which let light in, plus subdued spotlighting. There were a variety of weights and some exercise machines. Lying on her back, Eve was pushing up some weights. She was focused and exhaling on each lift with beads of sweat all over her skin. She was wearing close fitting Lycra which was hugging her curves, and training shoes. Bernadette could not help feeling aroused by the sight of her wife in this attire. Eve saw her after finishing a set, parked the weights and sat up. She bounced to her feet at once and came over to kiss Bernadette.

"Hi, darling, sorry, I was just trying out the new gym. It got finished early, as you can see," she said when their lips had parted.

"Mmm, and you look hot as fuck," said Bernadette unable to take her eyes off Eve.

"Do I?"

"And sweaty."

"Oh, sorry." Eve pulled away and grabbed herself a towel. She dried herself off. "Shall I show you around?"

"Sure, it looks lovely. Sorry that I haven't been paying attention as much as I should to everything at home." Bernadette felt contrite, there had obviously been a lot of work happening which she hadn't really registered. She chided herself and resolved to be more observant. Eve brushed this off.

"Yes, you have. You've been paying me attention and that's what matters."

She grabbed Bernadette's hand and led her around the room excitedly showing her the equipment and explaining its use.

"Wow," Bernadette said surprised. "And how much was all of this?"

She couldn't help wondering, although she knew Eve was excellent with their money and would not have overspent what they could afford.

"Oh! I knew you would ask that! I've got it all covered with my earnings don't you worry."

"I'm not, my sweetheart. It just looks expensive. I was curious is all." Bernadette didn't want to upset Eve, besides she didn't want to turn into Andrew.

"Oh you! It's an investment in our health, yours and mine."

"You're right, I'm sorry, I'll shut up about money. And what's this?" Bernadette wondered looking at a hanging punch bag.

"Oh, it's for kickboxing, I'm going to teach you to punch with the best of them."

"Sounds very energetic." Bernadette gave her a wry smile.

"Don't be like *that*, baby, I've done all this for us!" Eve pouted at Bernadette's seeming lack of enthusiasm.

"I know, I love it. I really do. I love everything you've done, my darling. I hope I can live up to it."

"Oh, you will! I'll make sure of it."

Bernadette giggled and kissed Eve soundly. She was lost in the kiss when her eyes alighted on the wall. She had not noticed a set of wooden bars going up it until just then.

"What are those?" she asked.

"Oh, now those, are for very special exercises."

"What kind of exercises? I only ever saw these at school, for climbing on, surely we're not going to do *that*?"

"I'll show you," Eve said mischievously. "Come over here and stand with your back to the bars."

Bernadette complied but looked at her wife suspiciously.

"What are you up to?"

"Nothing, just close your eyes and put your arms up above your head, bend your knees, keep your back straight and then grasp the bar with your hands. Yes, yes like that."

"What now?" Bernadette complied, wondering what Eve was doing, she could tell by Eve's voice she moved had away but then Eve's voice came right in her ear.

"This," Eve whispered, and simultaneously she snapped a pair of handcuffs onto Bernadette's wrists securing her to the bar.

"What? Why you fucking little witch!" Bernadette's eyes flew open, and she found herself unable to move.

"Oh, yes, but I would be careful how you talk to your witch now you are in her power." Eve's lips were now very close to Bernadette's.

"And what is my witch going to do now?" Bernadette whispered, completely aroused by the feeling of helplessness, and the awkward position Eve had placed her in.

"This!" Eve unbuttoned Bernadette's blouse undid her bra and released her ample breasts. Her hands began to run over Bernadette's naked skin and circling her nipples with her thumbs and then her tongue.

"Oh, Jesus... you... witch... oh... fuck... oh shit..." Bernadette breathed, gasping at the intensity of the touch.

Eve's hands strayed lower, and she deftly removed Bernadette's skirt and her knickers, her nails raking across Bernadette's tummy and then lower still.

"Oh... shit... Eve... oh... fuck... fuck... fuck..."

Eve's fingers lingered lightly teasing before she knelt down and put Bernadette's legs over her shoulders. Her tongue slid lightly and began to flick at Bernadette's sweet spot.

"Oh, fucking hell!" Bernadette screamed. "Oh... shit... oh my God... oh Eve... fuck... fuck... fuck... fuck... fuck... Jesus Christ... I... I... I... I'm going to... oh... oh... oh... ahh!"

The wave had been building inside her, welling up with each flick of Eve's insistent tongue. Coupled with the tension of the position, with her arms secured above and her legs wrapped tightly around Eve's neck. It broke hard and fast, and she climaxed her shouts echoing around the gym. She tensed and her toes curled, as wave after wave washed through her until she finally relaxed. Eve lifted her up and removed the cuffs. She kissed Bernadette fiercely.

"I love you, so much."

"I love you too, but you took advantage of me, tricked me." Bernadette smiled, though with the satisfaction of someone having received a beautiful treat.

"I know, I've been planning it all day."

"You are a bad witch, a very bad witch." Bernadette put her arms around Eve's neck pulling her close.

"I know." Eve's eyes twinkled.

"You know this is going to the top of the list don't you," Bernadette murmured.

"I was counting on it, my darling."

Bernadette regarded the wooden bars with renewed interest. "I think we can have a good Shibari session right here."

"Oh God, I was hoping you'd say so." The room tinkled with Eve's laughter.

"You had them put up just for *that*, didn't you!" Bernadette said with mock severity. "They are not for exercising at all."

"They could be used for exercise, I guess." Eve was still laughing.

"Just you wait until I get you tied to those bars, my girl."

"Some rope and toys are in the cupboard," Eve said pointing at another thing Bernadette had not noticed. She retrieved a robe for Bernadette from the wardrobe and handed it to her to put on.

There was a large wardrobe and chest of drawers in one corner, and also a cubicle which she found contained a shower and toilet. Eve said it would be useful for the gym and the hot tub outside in the garden.

"And that?" Bernadette pointing to stainless steel pole running from floor to ceiling.

"I'm going to learn pole dancing and then I'm going to give you a show," Eve informed her.

Bernadette sighed with pleasure. Eve really had thought of everything.

"You are truly amazing. I'll look forward to it."

"Are you really happy about this, all this?" Eve regarded her anxiously.

"Yes, of course, I am it's lovely, beautiful. You've done a fantastic job, really, my darling. I'm so impressed."

"I'm glad, so glad." Eve was beaming with the praise.

"I really do love it, darling. You're such a little minx though." Bernadette pulled her close again and kissed her softly, savouring the feel of her lips.

"Let's eat," Eve said after a few moments.

Eve had made Salmon en croute, with mashed potatoes and salad, accompanied by a white sauce.

"Oh God," said Bernadette tasting a mouthful of the flaky pastry. "This is to die for, you made this pastry?"

"All by my lonesome." Eve smiled.

"It's lovely."

"What happened today then?" Eve took a mouthful of mash and salad.

"We did some interviews at Maneet's office and then we went with Maneet to Chapter One to interview her a little more privately."

"Living it up I see." Eve smirked.

"You would be surprised by what we've found out..." Bernadette proceeded to relate the results of the interviews, and the discoveries they had made about Maneet.

"Oh my God, so she's gay, and she's hiding it and she's going to get married?" Eve's eyes widened as everything was revealed.

"Yes, I know we were as surprised as you. Also, get this... Maneet said she'd fuck me in a minute if I'd let her." Bernadette looked at her very slyly.

"Did she? Well, she's not having you."

"Of course not. I mean, she's very beautiful, of course."

"Oh, don't tease me!" Eve pouted.

"Darling, you know I only have eyes for you."

"I'm not jealous," Eve said haughtily. "Well maybe a bit, a teensy bit." She giggled. "Anyway, what's next on the agenda?"

"You mean for us or the case?"

"Both."

"We've got to figure out who tipped off the Garda. We have to find out who is behind this whole thing. It seems like a setup, and I don't know why someone would want to set Maneet up. There's something very odd about the whole thing."

"It's quite a conundrum then?"

"It certainly is."

"How about some dessert?"

"I won't say no."

"I've made tiramisu and then..."

"Sounds delicious. Also, I notice some new planters in the garden..."

"I'm going to grow some vegetables." Eve blushed a little.

"Of course, you are. You're full of surprises and I'm just a dull old stupid lawyer."

"Never say that, don't you dare say that. You're mine, and you're my beautiful wife, and you are perfect in every way."

"Thank you my darling," said Bernadette.

CHAPTER FIVE

They spent more time that evening talking about Eve's plans for the garden and the conservatory. Bernadette realised she had been neglectful, and she felt it too. Eve wouldn't hear of an apology, but she could tell Eve was pleased Bernadette took the time to listen to her. Bernadette reflected upon how things had changed. When Eve had first come into her life, she had seemed determined but shy, even reticent. She was reluctant to step up and make decisions other than around keeping house. Eve becoming a working artist had unleashed something in her, a newfound confidence. She became her own woman and started to take charge of things more particularly now they were married.

It turned out to Eve had been doing quite a lot in the garden albeit it was already well into spring, and the conservatory was being marked out soon to be built. It would revolutionise their living and give Eve a proper studio space. The conservatory room would run the full length of the side of the house, be fully double glazed and have heating. Eve had chosen a more traditional Victorian style which was a mite more expensive but was going to look amazing. It was funny to Bernadette to think about Eve choosing it, and that she'd had very little say in it herself other than to approve the design Eve had shown her. Bernadette had always been the independent one. Now she was relinquishing her independence for good and loving it to boot.

Bernadette lay awake pondering all of this in the early hours.

"What's wrong, darling?" Eve's voice came out of the darkness, as always, she sensed Bernadette's anxiety.

"Oh..." Bernadette turned to face her.

"Tell me." Eve kissed her softly.

"It's just... are you sure you don't feel I've been neglectful? I haven't paid attention to all the things you've been doing for us."

"No, stop it, darling. You've got your work and it's absorbing. I understand." Eve smiled in the half light.

"OK. I just feel such a heel." Bernadette pouted.

"You can make it up to me, if you want to. If you feel you must."

"How?"

"Take me out, wine and dine me. Something like that maybe. Couples stuff. We could go to the theatre, movies..."

"OK, OK, I will." Bernadette kissed her.

"And in the meantime..."

"In the meantime?"

"We can start in the bedroom..."

Eve moved Bernadette's hand to exactly the place she wanted it.

"Oh, yes... I see... you mean like this?"

"Oh... yes... fuck... yes... oh..."

✱ ✱ ✱

Morning arrived all too quickly. They had made love almost frantically and it had sent them both to sleep. Eve stirred with her arms around Bernadette, who reached out to silence the alarm.

Bernadette was feeling much happier. She would take Eve out more, just like she'd asked. She would pay more attention to Eve and the things she did at home. She resolved to do so, as she began to ease out of bed. Eve's arms tightened around her.

"Kiss me first," Eve whispered.

Bernadette turned around and did so. "OK, but no funny business." She giggled.

Eve kissed her and let her go to get her shower. When she returned, Eve was waiting to do her hair and makeup. She put Bernadette's hair into a ponytail and when her makeup was done, Bernadette stood up and kissed her.

"Thank you, darling."

"It's the same thing I do every day," Eve said surprised.

"Well, I should appreciate you for it every day."

Eve laughed and skipped off downstairs.

Bernadette followed once she had dressed, in a grey suit skirt, with a pale lilac blouse, and strappy black heels. She checked in the mirror and felt good. Her feet looked nice in the sandals too.

She joined Eve in the kitchen, where her wife placed the usual plate of scrambled eggs, toast and bacon in front of her, with a cup of coffee. Bernadette thanked her and cut into her eggs. Eve sat down beside her with her own plate.

"Delicious, as usual, darling," Bernadette said.

"Thank you." Eve put down her fork and squeezed Bernadette's hand before returning her attention to her food. When Bernadette had finished, she drank her coffee, and then remembered something important.

"Stay here," she said to Eve, who shot her a look of expectation. Bernadette went to retrieve something from her bag. It was a list of misdemeanours Eve had committed and she quickly added the episode in the gym to it. She put the list on the fridge and stood back. Eve had been watching her with interest.

"Now, you know what to expect when I get home," Bernadette told her with a little severity.

"Mmmhmm." Eve wrapped her arms around Bernadette's neck.

"And don't you dare use that vibrator more than twice today."

"Yes, Mrs Mackenna."

"Make sure my red stiletto mules and my corset are put in the cupboard in the gym."

"Yes, Mrs Mackenna, anything else."

"Try to behave." Bernadette sighed theatrically.

"I won't."

"Then it will be the worse for you."

"Oh good!"

"The wooden bars open up all sorts of possibilities," Bernadette whispered her lips close to Eve's.

"I know," Eve whispered back.

"I've got to go."

"I know."

"When I get home, you know what's going to happen, don't you?"

"God, yes..."

* * *

On the way to work, Bernadette reflected upon her plans for the evening. She had to make it a good session for Eve, and part of that was the strictness of her manner. She hadn't quite decided how to tie Eve up to the bars but had several ideas she was mulling over. One thing she did wonder, was what would happen if she was to pass out or something, and Eve was tied up. What would Eve do then? It had not occurred to her before, but they had recently watched a movie about a man who had had a heart attack while his lover was handcuffed to a bed in a remote cottage. It had rather dire consequences for the woman. Bernadette didn't want the same thing to happen. Not that she felt it would, but she was going to talk to Eve about it. Perhaps there could be an alarm button or something. In any case, the alarm would need to be extended to the gym, if Eve had not already thought of it.

Putting these fears from her mind until later, Bernadette parked outside the office, and dropped the keys off with Juanita. Shortly afterwards Imogen came into Bernadette's office with coffee for them both.

"How was your evening?" Imogen asked passing the cup across to Bernadette who had been sitting on the sofa in anticipation of her arrival.

"It was unexpected." Bernadette sipped her coffee.

"Oh?"

"Well, the new gym is done and..." Bernadette furnished Imogen with an account of the events in the gym which she knew Imogen would be eager to hear.

"Fuck *that* is horny!" Imogen pronounced at the end of it.

"It was, and the bars are going to be used again tonight for Shibari."

"Oh, has Eve been a naughty girl?"

"Very and last night's escapade is heading the list."

"It's a shame we don't have any bars like that," Imogen said sadly.

"I'm sure D'Arcy will get them installed if you want them." Bernadette chuckled.

"It sounds fun, and also I could tie her to them, in readiness for chastisement."

"How did I guess?"

"You know me."

"And last night?" Bernadette asked knowing Imogen would want to tell her.

"Oh well, D'Arcy won't be sitting comfortably today, not after the riding crop."

"Oh God!"

"I didn't break the skin, don't worry. I'm getting very good at it you know. With all the practice I've had." Imogen laughed.

"I should hope not!" Bernadette looked shocked. She felt sometimes Imogen was a little too blasé about her behaviour in the bedroom.

"Yes, I gave it to her after breakfast, before I came to work," Imogen said in a matter of fact way, ignoring the pointed tone of her friend.

"Because?"

"Oh, I just felt like it and she was snappy with me this morning, so I put her back in her place, little brat."

Bernadette decided not to enquire further to avoid being treated to too many details. Although she knew Eve would want to hear them if she were there. She changed her focus to Imogen and D'Arcy's relationship.

"Are things...?"

"OK? Yes, for the most part."

"For the most part?" Bernadette didn't like the sound of that.

"She was being a bit distant again, even after all the attention I've paid her. But I'm ignoring it for now and just carrying on as normal, like Eve suggested." Imogen imparted this information without seeming to be fazed by it.

Bernadette looked at her keenly, but Imogen returned a bland expression.

"OK."

Bernadette wondered for a moment if perhaps the kind of attention Imogen was giving her was what she really wanted, or perhaps not all the time. She shelved the thought. It wouldn't do to worry Imogen just on a hunch.

"You'll be the first to hear if it's not going well, I can assure you," Imogen said firmly.

"I'm sure."

"Anyway, I'm going to ring her later, and tell her how much I love her, and I'm sending her some flowers today. I'm trying to be more loving to her. Perhaps that is the part I've not been doing, I don't know."

This struck a chord with Bernadette. Firstly because of what she had just been musing about. Secondly, it made her think of her wife.

"Oh! Shit! I need to send Eve some flowers."

"You do?" Imogen looked at her strangely.

"Yes, I feel I've been neglectful." Bernadette explained how she was feeling and why.

"OK."

"Eve was fine about it, but she'd like me to take her out more, and I will. Flowers are a good idea, you just made me think of it that's all." Bernadette shrugged.

"Well, if it was me, you'd be straight over my knee and no mistake." Imogen giggled playfully.

"No doubt," Bernadette said wryly. "Thankfully Eve isn't you."

Imogen gave her a sly look. "I doubt you could handle me anyway, darling, I'm very high maintenance these days. Plus, I think I'm quite compulsively dominant. You'd have to become very submissive, and I don't really think that's you. Mind you, your assertive side is pretty horny as I've told you, perhaps I could get used to being the submissive one..."

"Oh, Imogen, now really!" Bernadette rolled her eyes.

They both laughed. It was a standing joke between them. Imogen reached across and took Bernadette's hand affectionately.

"You know I'm only teasing 'cos I love you to bits."

"I know, darling." Bernadette returned the squeeze and picked up her coffee cup.

"Anyway, enough of all that, what's on the agenda today?" Imogen changed the subject.

"We need to speak to Micky about investigating Franklin Maguire, and we need to find out when our pretrial hearing is going to be."

"OK, I'll get Micky then, and some fresh coffee."

"Yes, please."

Bernadette watched her leave the room, smiling to herself. Imogen was so much part of her life now, just as much as Eve.

✳ ✳ ✳

Micky sat in Bernadette's office once more, in a visitor's chair, whilst Bernadette and Imogen sat on the sofa.

"Micky," Bernadette began.

"Yes, Bernadette?" He was attired in a black suit which showed off his spare frame and a crisp white shirt with a yellow spotted tie. His shoes were black and shiny.

"You look very smart today." She smiled at him distracted by this.

"Oh, that..." He shrugged. "I'm going out later."

"With whom?" Imogen demanded at once fixing him with a beady eye.

"Imogen, don't tease him, poor lad." Bernadette shot her a quelling look.

Micky was blushing furiously.

"Come on spit it out to Aunty Imogen, Micky, is it Alison again?" Imogen was unperturbed.

"Well," said Micky, "yes, it is Alison, we're going to the movies."

"I knew it!" said Imogen triumphantly.

"We've gone out a few times, as it happens," he said shyly.

"I know, like bowling the other night."

"How did you?"

"I have my sources, Micky."

"Right now, we've got that out of the way, Micky, have you got anything more for us on the Maneet case?" Bernadette said shaking her head at Imogen, but she was smiling at the same time.

Micky looked contrite. "Sorry, Bernadette, I've not managed to get any footage like you wanted. At least, not yet. I'm still trying."

"Thanks, Micky."

"It seems very odd nobody has any footage of it." Imogen was looking puzzled. "Usually at these events, there are loads of recordings and Facebook lives."

"Everyone was too far away, for a start, to take a video with their phones, so it would have to be someone with a decent camera. Nobody has come forward from any forums I've been on asking about it."

"I can't believe there's no footage, someone must have taken it. Perhaps they won't come forward for a reason," Bernadette mused.

"What possible reason could they have?" Imogen wanted to know.

"Fear? Perhaps. This thing is going deeper than we realised."

"Maybe, maybe you're right."

"Micky," said Bernadette turning her attention to him, "we want you to widen your investigation. Look into Sergeant Franklin Maguire, find out everything you can about him. We are wondering if there is a connection to white supremacists here. You might need to go undercover online to do it."

"I already do, Bernadette, as I told you. I can fake up a profile which will work for that." He smiled.

"But what about the thingy, you know tracing you back to here?" Imogen asked him.

"Oh, it's easy. I've got software which spoofs the IP address, they'll never track it back to me or this firm. Don't worry. I'm up on all this stuff. I run it all out through a VPN for a start."

"If you're sure, not that I understood a word of what you said."

Bernadette laughed at Imogen's face.

"What! I'm a lawyer, not an IT expert!" Imogen poked her tongue out.

Micky sniggered.

"See, see how disrespectful she is to me, Micky. Me, the boss of the company!" Bernadette said in mock indignation.

"Oh, don't worry, Micky, she's going to chastise me soundly for it when you're gone." Imogen smirked.

"Oh honestly!" Bernadette rolled her eyes, and the two of them laughed. Micky joined in. "Whatever you can find out about this Maguire will be helpful. He's the key to this case I'm sure of it."

"Sure, I will, I'll do my best."

"You always do, Micky." Bernadette furnished him with a beatific smile.

"We are pretty sure he said the things he said to Maneet," Imogen added.

"What did he actually say?" Micky wondered.

"If I remember correctly it was 'fuck your fucking rally, you Indian bitch. Why are you in this fucking country anyway? You fucking Paki whore. Go back to Paki land where you belong, you fucking little black slut, back to the gutter where your kind belong. We don't need people like you in this country. Fuck off you cocksucking black piece of shit Indian dog.'"

"Shit!" Micky's face registered shock at this language.

"You see, this guy isn't a nice piece of work."

"A nasty piece more like." Micky looked grim.

"That's why we need you to find something on him. If there is anything linking him to white supremacy, then it's going to strengthen our case."

"Sure, I will, I'll get to it." Micky stood up to go.

"Have fun with Alison, later." Imogen smirked at him.

"Yes, well... thanks." He beat a hasty retreat.

"You really shouldn't tease him so much," said Bernadette.

"But he's such an easy target."

"You are a very bad girl!" Bernadette told her severely.

"Ooh, that's more like it. I love the assertive Bernadette."

"Have you found out anything from the court?" Bernadette ignored this banter.

"It looks like we might get a prehearing date in under two weeks. Might even be the end of next week."

"Really? So soon?"

"Maybe it's because it's the Garda, I don't know." Imogen shrugged.

The workings of the courts were a mystery to them in that respect. Normally the court system was slow but then sometimes, and more often lately, a window had opened up quite quickly. The last time it was because of meddling by a member of parliament.

"Regardless of that, we need to be ready. Push the prosecution for whatever witness statements they are putting in, and any other evidence they are intending to use."

"Yes, Mrs Mackenna."

"Don't you start, Ms Stewart!" Bernadette shot back with a giggle.

"I absolutely adore you, darling. I'll get on with this."

Imogen leaned over and gave Bernadette an affectionate peck before gathering up the cups and returning to her own office.

* * *

The rest of the day brought nothing fresh on the case. It appeared the pre-hearing would happen very shortly. A date would be given on Monday, but it seemed as if it could happen as early as that Friday or the Monday after. There were too many unanswered questions for the moment, as far as Bernadette was concerned. This was a difficult case and one they might face going into with very little evidence in their favour, which was not a position she wanted to be in.

With a sigh, she closed down her computer for the weekend, shut her office door and wandered downstairs. She picked up her keys from Juanita's desk, there was a note as usual as to where the car was parked. It was impossible to park it in the road outside all day due to restrictions, so it was customary for Juanita to move it for her. The parking was charged using a token which Bernadette kept on a keychain and she topped up monthly.

As it happened her car was conveniently parked not far up the road after all. As she approached it, she noticed one of the tyres was down at the front. When she finally got there, it was dead flat.

"Fuck!" said Bernadette crossly, wondering how on earth it could have happened. She took a photo of the tyre and texted it to Eve, letting her know she'd be late. Then she dialled the AA and after giving the details went back inside the office to wait.

Although she was very capable and could probably change the tyre, she didn't have breakdown insurance for nothing. Also, she did not want to get her clothes dirty.

Eve amused her for a while, sending naughty texts back and forth in anticipation of later. Finally, the AA man arrived, and she went outside. He was a friendly looking young guy with a beard. He glanced over at her car after scrutinising her membership card.

"Got a flat tyre, have you?" he added unnecessarily.

"Yes, I can't understand it." She forbore to be sarcastic even though he had stated the obvious, she was just pleased to see him.

He examined the tyre carefully and said he couldn't see anything wrong with it.

"Tell you what, I'll pump it up and let's see if it goes down. It could be a leaky valve or a slow puncture. We'll wait a wee while and see what it does."

"OK, whatever you think best. I just want to get home."

"Ach, you'll get home alright. If it seems dodgy, I'll put on the spare." He smiled reassuringly.

The AA man pumped up the tyre then stood back to wait. They chatted amiably and he asked her what she did for a living. Then she asked him, politely about his job, and he was more than happy to regale her with terrible tales of breakdowns he'd attended. He tutted at how owners did not look after their cars but said hers seemed to be in excellent condition. As the car was her pride and joy, she explained it was kept well, valeted regularly and serviced on time. She received his commendations on this information with a smile. After twenty minutes had passed in this fashion, he examined the tyre again.

"It seems right and tight," he pronounced, "but I'd get it checked at a tyre place in case there is a slow puncture. If it goes down overnight, call us out, we'll put the spare on, and you can get a new tyre fitted."

"Thanks, I appreciate your help."

"You're welcome."

Bernadette signed the appropriate paperwork and walked to her car while the man returned to his van. As she reached for the door handle the hairs on the back of her neck started to prickle. It was uncanny but now she thought of it, it was almost as if someone had been watching her this whole while. She panicked slightly looking up and down the road. She could see nobody but the AA man in the van talking on his radio, no doubt picking up his next job. Still, with the strange feeling, Bernadette got into the car and pulled away heading for home. She glanced in the mirror frequently. She had been followed in the past and knew what to look for. It didn't seem as if anyone was doing so. Gradually the apprehension left her, and she relaxed thinking about the Shibari session to come.

* * *

She parked the car in the driveway and locked it. She made sure the gate was shut before going inside. Somehow the incident had rattled her a little and she tried to dismiss it from her mind. Once inside, she kicked off her shoes, made sure the front door was deadbolted. The back garden wasn't very accessible, and the garden gate was locked and bolted. They locked the patio doors too in any case. Bringing her attention to the hallway she saw at once a big pile of dirty washing in the middle of the floor. This was obviously part of the game, and Eve would be waiting somewhere close by for it to start.

Summoning up her resources she said loudly and assertively, "Eve Mackenna, get in here at once!"

In a moment Eve appeared wearing her maid's outfit with black stiletto mules. Bernadotte looked at this revealing attire approvingly. It was definitely arousing.

"Yes, Mrs Mackenna?" said Eve looking a little flushed.

"What is the meaning of this?" Bernadette demanded pointing at the washing.

"Oh, that, well, it's dirty washing."

"How dare you be so insolent," Bernadette shot back at once, striding over to her. It immediately became hard for her to keep her hands off Eve, but she succeeded. "I'm tired of your slovenly behaviour. You are going to be punished. Go to the gymnasium now!"

Eve didn't move, goading her, she ran her tongue lasciviously around her lips. So tempting for Bernadette but she resisted valiantly.

"I said now! You dreadful little witch!"

Bodily turning Eve around she gave her a smart slap on her posterior. Eve squeaked and hurried off into the living room. Bernadette heard the patio door open and close before following her at a more leisurely pace. She left her jacket on the sofa and went outside to the gym locking the door behind her.

When she entered the gym, Eve was standing in the centre, her eyes shining with anticipation. Trying not to smile, Bernadette assumed a more severe demeanour while bolting the door from the inside.

"Now then, Mrs Mackenna, your behaviour recently has been appalling, hasn't it?"

She moved closer to stand in front of her wife.

"Yes." Eve nodded.

"Yes, what?"

"Yes, Mrs Mackenna."

"Better. You've misbehaved at every opportunity. Making me late for work several times. Being extravagant. Being judgemental. Ringing me up for phone sex in the office. Tying me up to the gym bars and having sex with me. Leaving washing in the hallway and God knows what else."

"Yes, Mrs Mackenna." Eve dropped her eyes demurely although Bernadette could tell from the timbre of her voice and the flush on her face, she was very aroused.

"Did you use your vibrator today?"

"Yes, Mrs Mackenna."

"How many times?"

Eve stayed silent. This was Bernadette's cue. She went up to Eve and tilted up Eve's face with one finger under Eve's chin. Eve looked at her in mock defiance, her blue eyes flaming with desire.

"I said how many, and don't lie to me, missy," Bernadette said softly.

"I... well... it was five..."

"Five?"

"Yes."

"And how many did I say you could do?"

"Two, Mrs Mackenna."

"So, you even disobeyed me in that!" Bernadette's eyes bored into Eve's. She was trying to be strict and holding onto the game only just because the proximity of Eve dressed like that was almost too much.

Eve was silent.

"You are nothing but a disobedient little brat. What happens to disobedient little brats?" Bernadette whispered.

"They get punished, Mrs Mackenna."

"Yes, they do, very severely." Bernadette raised her voice once more. "Get over there and stand facing the bars, put your arms out to the sides."

Eve didn't move, wanting to be coerced.

"I said now!" Bernadette said sharply.

Eve's eye's widened as if the tone was a surprise even for her, and then she hurried to do as she was bid. Once Eve was in position. Bernadette went to the cupboard and extracted her favourite corset and mules. She stripped, put them on and feeling even more mistress like, she picked up the ropes and strode over to where Eve was waiting. Bernadette deftly removed Eve's clothing, so that she was naked, but left her mules on. It pleased her to have Eve in heels, which arched Eve's feet so prettily and it turned her on too.

"Now you're going to find out what happens to naughty girls who misbehave..."

Bernadette began starting to tie Eve to the bars. She worked methodically whilst scolding Eve gently and chiding her for her behaviour, she knew Eve liked that, wanted it. After a while Eve ended up securely trussed to the bars, with her arms out sideways and her legs spread. The frame had given Bernadette far more scope for tying Eve up compared to the bed and she had made full use of it. She stood back and examined her artistry with satisfaction. She had become very good at Shibari with all the practice on Eve. Although it didn't really appeal to Bernadette to be tied up, Eve evidently derived immense pleasure from it, and it satisfied whatever kink lay deep in Eve's psyche. Bernadette had noticed Eve's camera in the cupboard and took some photographs because she knew Eve would want them. She expected them to appear in Eve's drawings at some point in the future. Smiling to herself she approached Eve from behind, as Eve was tied up facing the bars with her head turned sideways.

Bernadette began to nuzzle Eve's neck, kissing and lightly running her tongue up the nape.

"Oh... fuck... oh... God..." Eve breathed with the touch. "Oh...fuck! Fuck!"

Bernadette raked her nails across the exposed flesh and teased her whilst planting kisses on her skin. Eve moaned with every tantalising move which went lower and closer.

"Oh... oh... ah... fuck... oh... God... oh... ohh!" Eve squealed as Bernadette's fingers found her sweet spot and began to work.

"Oh you are so wet, Mrs Mackenna, aren't you... so very, very wet indeed. Because you like to be punished, don't you, Mrs Mackenna," Bernadette murmured in her ear.

"I want you. I want you so badly," Eve half cried out.

"At my pace, Mrs Mackenna, at my pace."

"Oh... you bitch... oh fuck... oh..."

"You are so very bad, aren't you, what should I really do with you, hmm?" Bernadette's fingers began to move a little faster building up the rhythm.

"Oh... oh... I don't know... oh... fuck... oh," Eve gasped.

Bernadette knew how to bring her to the edge and toyed with the idea of doing it a few times before allowing her to climax, but it felt cruel, and Eve was so ready. Bernadette knew the words which would bring it to a close. With her other hand, she dug her nails into Eve's buttocks.

"Oh fuck... you bitch!" Eve cried out but Bernadette could tell she was loving every moment.

"Your arse is such a great target, isn't it, Mrs Mackenna? Especially in that position." Bernadette whispered softly her fingers working all the while. "If only I had one of those floggers, hmmm, then you'd find out what naughty girls really deserve, hmmm... imagine one stroke, and then another with a swish... and... a nice thwack across that naked backside of yours... it would sting wouldn't it... oh so nicely..."

"Oh... fuck... fuck... fuck... God... yes... oh... fuck... don't... oh... oh my God... ohh... ahh!" Eve let out a big sigh and shuddered as her climax hit her. Bernadette felt Eve's body tense against the bonds and then relax, before tensing again a few more times. Eve had told her this was one of the best parts feeling the ropes cutting into her during her orgasm as her muscles strained against them. Bernadette stopped gently when she could tell Eve had had enough. She stood there holding Eve tightly.

"I love you," she whispered, "I love you so much it hurts."

"I love you too, so much, my darling. Thank you."

"For what?"

"For this, for indulging me."

"Oh *that*, well you deserved it." Bernadette giggled.

"Bitch." Eve was giggling too.

They stayed that way for many minutes while Bernadette savoured the closeness these sessions somehow brought to them. Eventually, when she felt ready, she released her wife from the bonds before they began to chafe too much.

Before Bernadette could do anything sensible, Eve had gently persuaded her to lie on the floor. Without further ado Eve's head was between her legs and Eve's tongue was causing all kinds of sensations Bernadette was unable to resist.

"Oh, shit. Fuck, fuck, oh my God. Fuck... shit... oh... Eve... Eve... Eve... oh God... my God." It didn't take much for the wave to build inside her, she had been close to the edge herself whilst ministering to Eve and so it broke without further ado to Bernadette's loud cries echoing around the room. "Oh... fucking hell... fuck... fuck... fuck... ahh!"

She bucked hard pushing into Eve's mouth, wrapping legs around her wife's body, tensing hard as she climaxed. She started to relax, and her head began to clear from the pleasant fog which had pervaded it. Eve was lying beside her on the spongy surface of the gym floor. Eve kissed her softly, and then more urgently. The passions rose again, and they made love a second time before lying once more breathless side by side.

"Are you insatiable or what?" Bernadette laughed.

"I think those vitamin D pills are doing the trick." Eve's eyes twinkled.

"Something is."

"How about dinner?" Eve asked her.

"Sure, what is it?"

"Oh, it's takeout, I've been a lazy slut today. I'll order it from our favourite Indian."

"Oh, you are a lazy little so and so." Bernadette giggled. "Should I start another list?"

"No, I've had enough, please, Mrs Mackenna." Eve's eyes were dancing.

"I wouldn't anyway, you do so much around here."

"Come on."

Eve stood up and pulled Bernadette to her feet. Then she got a robe for each of them, put away the ropes and gathered up the discarded clothes. She led Bernadette back to the house.

* * *

Eve ordered from Spice Guru which was a restaurant nearby and paid for delivery. They sometimes ate from there and it was one of their favourites. She chose *Bhaji* and *Pakoras* to start, *Chicken Dhansak*, *Rice*, *Aloo Gobi* and *Nan*. They sat together with the spread and a glass of Merlot each.

"This is a lot," said Bernadette ladling a portion of each main onto her plate with rice.

"We can have some for lunch then, darling, it's always nicer the next day."

"For sure."

They ate in silence enjoying each other's company, and the delicious food. Both of them made suitable 'mmm' noises of appreciation.

"Was that to your liking?" Bernadette asked her at length.

"The food?"

"You know what I'm talking about."

Eve giggled like a schoolgirl and blew Bernadette a kiss. "I loved it, of course, I did."

"Oh good. I worry I'm being too strict or not enough or..."

"You do it perfectly and it's because it's you, my darling, that's the difference."

"There is one thing," Bernadette said, satisfied with this answer.

"What?"

"Well, what if I collapsed or something and you're all tied up like that, how would you get free?"

"You're thinking of that movie we saw." Eve laughed.

"It's no laughing matter, what if it did?" Bernadette made her tone severe, but her unserious expression did not match it.

"I don't know, honey, you've got a good point. I mean, we could ask Imogen or D'Arcy to check on us if we didn't contact them the morning after."

"I was thinking more of a panic button or something."

"Maybe." Eve screwed up her nose. "I'll look into it."

"The gym needs to be connected to our alarm system and it does need a panic button in there at least anyway," Bernadette persisted.

"It's already in hand."

"I might have guessed, you're so efficient."

"So maybe I didn't need punishing after all."

"What?"

"I'm teasing."

"Oh you!" Bernadette caught her expression and shook her head.

Eve became pensive then. "Maybe I should get one of those floggers you mentioned..."

"Stop it."

"Well, you might find one in the cupboard next time and then you'll have to use it." Eve stuck her chin out defiantly.

"I thought we weren't going down *that* road." Bernadette raised an eyebrow.

"It might be fun." Eve shrugged.

"I can't keep up with you, honestly!"

"That's what you get for marrying a younger woman."

"I seriously am thinking of putting you over my knee if you carry on!" Bernadette smiled.

"Now you're making me horny."

"Really, darling. Stop it!"

"Oh fine. Tell me about your day then." Eve pouted.

"We're no further forward really on anything and I think we've got a pre-trial hearing at the end of next week or the beginning of the following one." Bernadette sighed.

"What will you do?"

"I don't know. We may have to fight this on what we have and that's something I don't like to do."

"It will be OK, you'll see." Eve took her hand reassuringly.

"I wish I could share your optimism."

"It will, trust me."

"More of your witchery?"

Eve chuckled. "No, I just have faith in it coming right, it usually does. Anyway, how was the tyre?"

"Oh, I'll look at it in the morning in case it's a slow puncture or take it to a tyre place to get checked out."

"OK."

"Seems strange," Bernadette mused, "just going flat like it. Never happened before."

"What are you worried about?" Eve picked up her tone at once.

"I don't know. Just when I was out there with the AA man, I felt like I was being watched. I couldn't see anybody. But you know how you get the feeling."

"Yes, for sure." Eve nodded. "I'll go and lock the gym."

"Didn't you lock it?"

"No, sorry I was distracted."

"Naughty girl, I'll come with you."

They walked out of the gym and secured it. Then returned indoors. They already had security lights outside courtesy of D'Arcy who had paid for their new alarm and security system. Bernadette watched Eve lock the door with some relief. Talking about the flat tyre had brought back that uncomfortable feeling.

She turned to Eve and wrapped her arms around Eve's neck pulling her in for a kiss.

"Shall I wine and dine you this weekend?" She smiled, remembering her promise to Eve and also contritely that she had forgotten to buy the flowers. She would remedy this the next day.

"Just take me for a ride, out to the sea, we'll have lunch somewhere maybe a little pub, explore the beach."

"Done."

"Now let's put away the dishes and I'll show you my latest drawings."

"Oh, you've actually been drawing have you, in between the porn sessions?" Bernadette said wryly.

"I'm not that bad!"

Bernadette just laughed.

CHAPTER SIX

ernadette devoted the weekend to pleasing her wife. She ordered flowers online which were delivered that afternoon. Eve was more than just delighted. She was touchingly grateful. They went out to a different beach each day and ate in a pub at lunchtime just as Eve had wanted. They walked barefoot hand in hand on the sand in summer dresses. They worked out in the new gym, watched movies together and made love. It was a wonderful weekend.

The car tyre had not deflated overnight, and on the way to the beach Bernadette had dropped in at a tyre place, and they had said they could find nothing wrong with the tyre. Bernadette was a little puzzled by this, but she let it go. There was time to ponder this during the week.

"Thank you, for such a beautiful time, this weekend," Eve told her over a dinner of steak, chips and salad, with a pepper sauce.

"It's my pleasure."

"It was special, and also for my beautiful flowers and for taking care of me."

"It's you who takes care of me."

"We take care of each other." Eve smiled, unwilling to consent to taking all the honours in the relationship. "If you didn't work and have such a great legal firm, we wouldn't have this, all this. A good life."

"We do have a good life, don't we?" Bernadette looked worried.

"Stop it, darling, of course, we do, we're lucky, very lucky to have each other too."

"Yes, yes we are."

* * *

Monday morning came around all too quickly. For once Bernadette had not allowed work to cross her mind all weekend. She hadn't thought about the case or pondered it at all. The alarm went and she slid out from under the bedclothes, after stealing a kiss from Eve.

Eve plaited Bernadette's hair, then did her makeup before skipping off downstairs. Bernadette followed after putting on a tan jacket over a cream blouse with wide plaid turnup trousers. She slipped on the black low mules and followed after her wife to the kitchen.

"Hey, beautiful, that suits you." Eve examined her admiringly as Bernadette did a twirl. The jacket and trousers were a recent acquisition Eve had made for her.

"Thank you." Bernadette kissed her and sat down. She gratefully accepted the poached eggs on toast with a side of bacon. "Delicious."

"I hope so."

"Very." Bernadette cut into her eggs and tasted a forkful.

"Good." Eve addressed herself to her own eggs.

They ate while idly chatting about Eve's plans for the day which included the start of the conservatory. There would be workmen and materials in the driveway for a while, during its construction. Eve told Bernadette there would be room for Bernadette's car.

At length, Bernadette drained her coffee while Eve accompanied her to the door. Eve kissed her goodbye and made Bernadette feel giddy as always. She admonished her wife to keep the doors locked and drove away watching Eve standing barefoot in her robe waving goodbye. She turned into the main road and headed for the office turning up the radio as she went.

✳ ✳ ✳

Bernadette logged into her computer once at work and waited for Imogen. Her junior partner arrived shortly with coffee and they sat in customary fashion on the sofa.

"How was your weekend?" Imogen said at once, no doubt wanting details of the Shibari session.

Bernadette obliged her while Imogen smirked as she heard about Eve's idea of getting a flogger.

"I knew you'd like that part," said Bernadette once she'd finished the story.

"Don't knock it until you've tried it." Imogen laughed.

"And what about you, no doubt flogging your fiancé?"

"I didn't actually, not once. We went out like you for a couple of meals and stuff. D'Arcy has been distant again. I'm fed up with it." Imogen made a face.

Bernadette thought for a moment and then made a suggestion. She wasn't sure how it could help but it might.

"How about we come for the weekend? It might cheer you both up."

Imogen latched onto this at once and brightened up a smidgeon.

"Yes, and then you can force her to tell you what's wrong!" she said vehemently.

"It wasn't quite what I had in mind." Bernadette adopted a soothing tone.

"It's what *I* have in mind if she won't stop this."

"It's OK, it'll be OK." Bernadette put her hand out to take Imogen's knowing the signs of her friend's imminent distress.

"I hope so."

"I'll talk to Eve, we'll come, maybe it will do you both some good to have company."

"OK," said Imogen suddenly in a small voice.

Bernadette did not want her to break down again, so she changed the subject.

"I had a flat tyre on Friday."

"Oh?"

Bernadette told her about the incident and how there seemed to be nothing wrong with the tyre. Also, the feeling of being watched.

"Hmm, that is odd." Imogen was diverted. "I wonder what it means."

"What do you mean, what it means?" Bernadette cocked an eyebrow.

"Was it deliberate, do you think?"

"Thanks. I hadn't thought it until now, and now you are freaking me out."

"Sorry. Look it could just be kids playing pranks. They do stuff like that." Imogen squeezed her hand.

"I hope so."

"Don't worry about it. I'm sure it's nothing."

They finished their coffee and Imogen returned to her own office to check on the court date. Bernadette went back to her desk. There was some disquiet in her mind, however, because of what Imogen had said.

Later on, Imogen returned to announce that she'd spoken to the court.

"It's Tuesday week, the pre-hearing with a date not long after that, probably within four to eight weeks."

"OK, it gives us time to prepare what we can in the meantime. Have you chased the prosecution for their evidence?"

"Done and I've asked to see what they have as soon as possible."

"Good, good. What else can we do?"

"Not much, Micky is doing his bit. We have to decide who if any of the staff we interviewed are going to be a witness."

"Sure, we'll make the decisions by Friday."

"Great. Well if anything occurs to you in the meantime. We can talk to Micky again midweek."

"Got it. I'll get on."

Imogen left the office and Bernadette turned to other cases which were underway and needed her attention.

✳ ✳ ✳

At the end of the day, Bernadette went down to her car which was again luckily in the road outside the office. About to open the driver's door, she noticed another flat tyre.

"Fuck! Is this a fucking joke?" she said out loud. She looked up and down the street suddenly angry. "It's not funny, if anyone is doing this. I'm not amused." She spoke loudly and to nobody in particular.

The same AA man turned up after a suitable wait. She would have told Imogen about the tyre, but her junior had already gone home. She didn't want to worry Imogen so didn't phone her.

"Making a habit of this are we?" he said in wry amusement at her latest predicament.

"No, I'm definitely not but whoever is doing it is making me quite annoyed."

"It's a different tyre I see," he mused fetching his portable electric pump.

"Yes, it is. I had the other one checked, there was nothing wrong with it. So, I was starting to think it was deliberate, and now this."

"It's probably kids," the AA man told her kindly, pumping up the tyre.

"But why me, why my car?" she demanded looking upset.

"It's red, it's a bit flash, the sort of thing kids target I'm sorry to say."

"Well if it is, they are little bastards!" she said loudly looking up and down the street.

"Oh, they'll be long gone, don't you worry. There was a spate of this on an estate once. They had to put up CCTV cameras. They caught them. The Garda put the fear of God into them. Stopped after that."

"I won't be answerable for my actions if I catch them, I can tell you." Bernadette's eyes flashed.

"No, I reckon they'll get the sharp end from you." He chuckled. "All done."

"Should I get it checked again?"

"No, I don't think you need to. The chances of two flats like that on different tyres is very unlikely. Plus, those are very new tyres."

With visions of flat tyres every day, she felt compelled to ask him. "What if it keeps happening?"

He smiled and shrugged. Fortunately, the solution was simple.

"Get yourself some locking tyre caps, I would. You can get them at Halfords, places like that."

"Thanks, I will. I'll go there now and get them fitted today."

"Good plan. Will you be OK now?" He regarded her with slight concern. She appreciated that he seemed to care at least.

"Yes, thanks, you've been so helpful."

"It's my job." He smiled and got the paperwork to sign.

She watched him get into his van and went to get into her car. The same feeling assailed her, the prickling feeling in her neck. It was starting to concern her. She called Eve, picked her up and went with her to Halfords to get the locking tyre caps.

* * *

Sweat dripping off her, Bernadette landed another punch on the boxing bag in their gym at Eve's urging.

"Come on, again, hit it again, one two and then kick."

"Jesus fucking Christ, how... many... more times..." Bernadette panted doing as she was bid.

"Until I say you can stop!"

"Fuck... I thought... I was the assertive one..." Bernadette hit the bag once more with a punch combination.

"And again!" Eve ordered ignoring this.

"Please, I can't do it... please..." Bernadette was reaching the end of her resources.

"OK, that's enough for today then." Eve's tone was reluctant.

They had been at it since getting home. Eve had insisted Bernadette was to start kickboxing lessons under her tutelage. Bernadette had acquiesced.

"I'm not having you out there not being able to defend yourself," Eve had told her. "We're starting your training today."

"Holy shit." Bernadette sat down on the bench while Eve handed her a bottle of water. "You're a slave driver and no mistake."

"It's for your own good. Tomorrow we're doing throws and self-defence moves, and then more kickboxing all week."

"Are you trying to kill me?" Bernadette smiled weakly at her own joke.

"No. I'm trying to protect you. Whoever is letting down your tyres might do something more and I don't want you not to be ready for it."

"OK, OK, you're the boss." Bernadette shook her head which was starting to clear after the exertions. The idea of being ready for something which required physical intervention on her part was not particularly appealing though it was comforting to know she could punch like that.

"In here and only for your training."

"And what about *your* training?" Bernadette shot Eve a sly look.

"That's an entirely different matter."

They both laughed.

"Come on, let's go and shower and eat." Eve pulled her up to her feet.

"I'm aching all over, what have you done to me?"

"Don't worry, I've already got that covered. I'll give you a nice massage later." Eve patted Bernadette's behind affectionately.

"You will?" Bernadette turned and wrapped her arms around Eve's waist, dropping a kiss on her lips.

"Yes, I'm starting an online course, so I need a willing subject."

"I'm definitely up for that."

"You'll have to be naked."

"I'm definitely up for that!"

＊ ＊ ＊

Over a dinner of spaghetti Bolognese with salad, they discussed the tyre issue.

"Do you think it really was deliberate?" Eve said coiling her spaghetti with a fork and spoon.

"Yes, yes I do. What else could it be? Two different tyres, nothing wrong with them. I can't imagine it was accidental."

Bernadette ate a mouthful of Bolognese with evident satisfaction.

"But who would do something like that?"

"I don't know but I can't help wondering if it's something to do with this case." Bernadette sprinkled some more parmesan on her plate.

"What?" Eve looked a little alarmed.

"Well, I don't know maybe it's a warning... I don't know!" Bernadette felt nonplussed, angry and confused by what had happened. It was a small thing but also potentially a big thing.

"A warning? What the fuck have you got yourself into? You're worrying me now. Shouldn't you talk to the Garda?"

"It's the Garda who are involved!" Bernadette laid down her fork a moment and thought. "OK, yeah, I will talk to Olivia about it, although, I think she'll tell me it was kids."

"I'll feel better if you do."

"OK, I will. Now what about the conservatory, I don't see any sign of workmen." Bernadette changed the subject. There was no point labouring it and now she had a plan of action. Also, Eve was becoming worried, and she did not want that either.

"They had to postpone."

"Postpone, why?" Bernadette was surprised, not that it really mattered to her if it was delayed but she knew it was important to Eve, as it was to partly become her studio.

"Oh well, because I ordered the Victorian style one, there were delays in the manufacture. Shouldn't be long though until they can start."

"As long as you're OK about it."

Eve shrugged and took a forkful of salad.

"It can't be helped. Anyway, darling, eat your dinner so I can do your massage."

"And what brought this on?" Bernadette's interest was piqued.

"Oh, I've always wanted to learn it."

"Well, you can practice on two other people this weekend if you like."

"Oh?"

"Yes, I suggested we go to D'Arcy's." Bernadette went on to explain the latest predicament Imogen felt herself to be in.

"Honestly, D'Arcy she needs a good..."

"Spanking? She's already getting those and it's not helping their relationship," Bernadette said firmly.

"Oh dear."

"So, you're alright for us to go?"

"Of course, why shouldn't I be, my sweetheart?"

"Great. Maybe we can talk some sense into them."

Bernadette reached across and took Eve's hand.

"Finish your dinner," Eve told her after giving her hand an affectionate squeeze.

"Yes, Mrs Mackenna." Bernadette returned her attention to her plate.

✳ ✳ ✳

The following day Bernadette waited, as usual in her office, for Imogen to arrive, a little impatiently. She felt relaxed from the sensual massage Eve had given her which was inevitably followed by sex. The sex had been relaxing too, easing the tensions of the day. She was feeling the kickboxing session in her aching muscles, however, and winced at the thought of more training to come.

On cue, Imogen arrived with coffee.

"Hey, darling," she said settling herself on the sofa and handing one cup to Bernadette.

"Thanks, sweetness." Bernadette accepted it and took a sip of coffee savouring the bittersweet liquid.

"How was your evening?"

"Well, not an auspicious start, I had another flat tyre."

"What?"

Bernadette related the events of the previous night and how she had to get special anti-theft valve caps.

"Fuck! You should have called me," said Imogen looking very concerned. "Maybe I should get some too?"

"Perhaps though I seem to be the target of whoever or whatever. I didn't call you because you had gone home and what was the point? The nice AA man sorted it for me. Anyway, you don't need them, darling, Carragh brings you to work and drives you home again."

"Yes, true, I didn't think of that. However, but you should have called me afterwards. I worry about you, you know. Anyway, what should we do?"

"I'm sorry for not calling you, darling. I didn't want to worry you, I will if it happens again. We'll speak to Olivia today, rather than officially report it..."

"Because the Garda might be involved... or someone in it..." Imogen had cottoned on at once.

"Yes."

"Fuck! You weren't wrong about the rabbit hole."

"No."

"I'm a little worried, to be honest."

"Don't be, anyway Eve has been training me half the bloody evening and making me do kickboxing." Bernadette rolled her eyes. "I'm aching all over today and there's more this evening from my sergeant major wife."

"Oh, my darling, you are funny." Imogen's laughter tinkled around the room.

"She also gave me a massage, to be fair."

"Ooh! Was it nice?"

"Orgasmic." Bernadette smiled like the cat who had got the cream.

"Oh you horny bitch!"

"Eve's doing a course on it."

"God, I envy you. Your own personal masseuse. You've got a perfect relationship, and all of it. Everything, and what have I got?" Imogen's voice cracked.

"You've got a beautiful woman who loves you."

"Does she? Does she fucking well really?" The pain showed in Imogen's face.

"She does, I'm sure she does." Bernadette's voice became gentler and more soothing. She reached out to Imogen who set down her cup and practically launched herself into Bernadette's arms. Imogen began to sob.

"Oh dear, oh dear, oh dear. That's right let it out, darling, let it out." Bernadette stroked her hair.

"Fuck, fuck, fuck," Imogen cried. "I don't know what to do, tell me what to do."

"You'll be fine, everything will be fine, my darling. I promise you."

"I wish I could believe you."

"Let's see at the weekend, my heart."

Imogen let out a big sigh, and after a while, she stopped crying. She sat up.

"Listen to me," said Bernadette. "No matter what you think, I believe she loves you. We are going to sort this out my honey, we really are."

"I hope so." Imogen sat up and dried her eyes.

"Try to be calm this week, sweetie pie, OK."

"Yes." Imogen nodded miserably.

"Help is at hand."

"What are *you* going to do?"

"I don't know, but Eve and I will figure something out, I promise. I'm great at off the cuff solutions."

"OK." Imogen laughed at this.

"Now, let's get Olivia in here. Tell her about the tyre."

✳ ✳ ✳

Olivia sat in the meeting room once more, methodically rotating her spoon in her teacup. Bernadette had thoughtfully provided a teapot, milk and sugar for her to replenish the cup when she wanted, as Olivia invariably drank at least two cups of tea when she visited.

"So where did this teapot come from?" Olivia asked. She was wearing a black suit, with a pale blue blouse, and low-heeled pumps. She seemed to wear quite formal attire most of the time in her role as a detective. Her hair was pulled into a ponytail as it quite often was.

"I had it bought especially for you," Bernadette replied.

"No, you didn't. Did you?" Olivia blushed a little on hearing this.

"Yes, I did actually. Nobody else is to use it."

"I'm flattered."

"You should be," Imogen put in wryly.

"I am." Olivia picked up her cup delicately and sipped the tea with satisfaction. After a few sips, she set the cup down. "What can I do for you anyway?"

"Strange occurrences of late, in the last two days which we need to speak to you about in confidence," said Bernadette.

"Go on."

Olivia sipped her tea and listened carefully to the story of the tyres. Then she poured herself a fresh cup and stirred it saying nothing. Imogen watched this curbing her impatience.

"It could be just kids, you know, fooling around," she said at length.

"But then wouldn't they do it to the other cars?" Imogen said reasonably.

"A fair point." Olivia inclined her head.

"You know why I'm worried," Bernadette cut in. "This white supremacy thing has got me rattled and concerned. The whole case does stink a little of some deeper goings on. I find it hard to believe it's a coincidence. Two flat tyres like that."

"Anyway, you put those valve caps which lock, so it shouldn't happen again."

"No, but..."

Olivia held up her hand. "I'll look into it, discreetly. If it's coming from one of us, then I'm not going to log this formally. If there's CCTV in the road, I can check that. I'll let you know."

"Thank you."

Olivia smiled and sipped her tea. "You two do get some cases, I'll say that for you. I thought legal stuff was terribly boring until I met you."

"Oh, we try to get only the exciting cases." Bernadette let out a hollow laugh.

"It's upset you, I can see," said Olivia gently. "Just take care and keep me posted OK. I promise I'll check it out for you. We'll see if it's kids or not."

"Wouldn't the person doing it think of CCTV?" Imogen asked her.

"Yes, ordinarily but they also would think you perhaps wouldn't go to the Garda, and also they could probably tamper with the CCTV if they were concerned."

"Oh my God!" Bernadette exclaimed.

"Easy tiger, it's not so simple to do. I'm just saying they could. I doubt they thought about it too much, to be honest. Also, there may not be CCTV in the road, so."

Olivia shrugged and picked up her teacup again.

"Any luck with…" Imogen began.

"Asking circumspect questions?" Olivia cocked an eyebrow. "Not as yet. There are rumours, of course, about Garda who aren't all they should be. I have to tread very carefully though, with this. These white supremacists are not nice people generally."

"You're telling us that now?" Imogen looked shocked.

"I mean, if you start nosing around in their business." Olivia sipped her tea.

"But that kind of is what we're doing, isn't it?" Bernadette said also sounding worried.

"Yes and no."

"You've done a lot to put our minds at rest, thanks!" said Imogen with some acidity.

"Ouch, sister. Ease up. I didn't mean to rattle either of you. You are right to be concerned, of course, but if this really was them doing your tyres, I'd expect them to be more overt."

"Like what?" Bernadette demanded.

"Well, make threats or something. They haven't, have they?"

"No, but..."

"Look, be on the alert, of course. So far though it doesn't sound too serious, that's all I am trying to say. I'm not playing it down. I'm trying to give you a more balanced view of it at this point. If something else happens let me know at once, OK."

"Happens like what?"

"Well..." Olivia hesitated, reluctant to say more.

"Just tell us the worst." Bernadette sighed. "I'm a big girl and so is Imogen."

"OK. So, such cases where people who are extremists get involved, usually result in verbal threats of violence or worse. They would leave voicemails, send anonymous letters, that sort of thing."

"Death threats, that is what you're saying isn't it!" Imogen glared at her.

"It could be, I guess." Olivia was reluctant to say more this much was clear.

"Fuck!" Bernadette said with feeling.

"But it's nothing like it yet, and maybe it won't be, and perhaps this was just kids."

"I felt I was being watched."

"Which still could be kids."

"OK." Bernadette was unconvinced. There was a gut feeling one had and once it took hold, it was hard to shake off, and her gut feelings were not often wrong.

"If anything, anything at all happens, phone me, day or night. OK? If your safety is under threat, I will pull whatever strings I have to don't you worry."

This was more reassuring, Bernadette relaxed slightly on hearing it.

"OK, yes, thank you."

"You're welcome." Olivia drained her cup. She regarded them both expectantly. "OK? Will you be alright if I go now?"

"Yes, of course, sorry for keeping you."

"I'm sorry not to be more helpful but I'm at the end of a phone day or night."

"Thanks."

Olivia stood up "Thanks for the tea and the teapot. I'll be in touch soon."

She sauntered out of the room with a nod.

"Well!" said Imogen crossly.

"She was just being honest."

Having recovered from the initial shock of what could be something more serious than just tyre pranks, Bernadette didn't want to direct their anxiety at Olivia. After all, she was just doing her job.

"Putting the fear of God into us more like."

"It was certainly alarming to think..."

"Are you worried about threats?"

"Until we have them no."

"What if we do?"

"Then I'll go to the top, I'll speak to Brogan directly," said Bernadette with resolution.

"Good plan, then we'll see some sparks fly."

"Indeed."

With that Imogen went to find Micky, perhaps he would have better news.

✳ ✳ ✳

Micky sat in the meeting room opposite Bernadette and Imogen. He waited expectantly for Bernadette to speak.

"Micky, I see a sheaf of papers in your hand, does it mean you've got something for us?"

"Yes, and no," Micky replied looking a little downcast.

"What does *that* mean?" Imogen asked him at once.

"I've found out Maguire has been involved in white supremacist groups but it's more than ten years ago."

"I see. Let's have a look then." Bernadette smiled at him and took the papers. She gave half to Imogen and leafed through them. Then they exchanged them to examine the other half. "OK, so from what I can see, he was a member of this group the *White Knights of Ireland*."

"Yes, that's right," Micky said. "It was disbanded when the leaders were arrested. Up until then they held some rallies and stuff, printed a racist type of newspaper. That sort of thing."

Bernadette spread the papers on the table. They were screenshots of news cuttings and some of what apparently a defunct website which had somehow never been deleted. Another website called *Irish Racewatch* put the identities of known supremacists on their pages. There were some incidents of racial harassment and so forth. However, the leaders had been arrested for those particular crimes. An ugly incident involved a conspiracy to attack a Sikh temple with a homemade bomb. The perpetrators were put away for a long spell. Bernadette shuddered at the thought. These were, after all, the types of people they might be dealing with.

"When did he join the Garda?" she asked Micky.

"After this. After the group was disbanded."

"Right. Well, it's quite good evidence overall."

"We've nailed him surely," said Imogen enthusiastically.

"Not quite, he will be forced to acknowledge he was a member but I'm pretty sure he'll claim it's all in the past. After all, had he been a current member he would have had some trouble joining the Garda." Bernadette didn't want to dampen her friend's enthusiasm."

"Yeah, that's what I thought," Micky added.

"Oh... well, fuck!" Imogen sounded disappointed. "But maybe the Garda didn't know about his past."

"I imagine they did not know about this when he joined. He probably did not have a record, a criminal one anyway, or even an incriminating one," Micky said.

"It's not all bad, we'll put this evidence in but unless we can find something more recent it's not quite enough to pile on the pressure the way I'd want to when he's on the stand," said Bernadette.

"I'm afraid it's all I can find. As far as I can tell there is nothing else controversial about him. He seems to not have done anything out of the ordinary since." Micky shrugged.

"I bet there's more recent stuff," said Imogen darkly.

"I do too," he replied. "But it's not on the internet or at least not the parts I can access."

"The Dark Web?" Bernadette said.

"Yeah probably, if that's even a thing. Well, it is a thing but it's on some kind of hidden servers, they are private. You probably have to be one of them to access it. I can look into it further. I think it needs a special browser and stuff."

Bernadotte shook her head.

"OK, we're not going down that road, you're just going to have to keep trying the normal way. I'm not putting you or this firm in jeopardy by pursuing those types of investigations. We don't know the sort of people on there. I mean, we can guess, and they're not good people."

"I will keep trying, of course. I just don't think I'll get much more." Micky nodded.

"I mean, of course the Garda could access it, they probably have a unit monitoring the Dark Web," said Bernadette. "But that doesn't help us either."

"They wouldn't do it for us anyway, unless it was an official investigation, even then..." Imogen pointed out.

"Yes, so we're a little at *Point Non Plus* right now, I suppose."

"Seems like it," Imogen agreed.

"Micky, just keep looking and also for anything else on Maneet."

"Sure, I will, Bernadette. I'll do my best."

"I know you will, Micky, and get us electronic copies of everything you can, screenshots, whatever, of all of the information you have found on Maguire. Also, with website addresses, dates, you know."

"Sure, I will get it all."

"Great, we need it for our submission of evidence. Though I think we'll delay it for as long as we can, so they don't have too much time to react to it."

This was common practice from both sides. Usually Bernadette tried to play fair, but this case was different, she felt the odds were being stacked against her by people she didn't even know. She knew how to play the system when she needed to.

"Is there anything else?" Micky asked her.

"Not just now but thank you for what you've done so far."

"Sure, I'll get back to it."

"Thanks, Micky... and how was the movie the other night?" Imogen asked him with an innocent expression.

"Oh, it was very nice. We enjoyed it. It was fun."

"Glad you had *fun*." Imogen smirked at him.

"Imogen, stop teasing the poor boy," Bernadette said intervening.

"It's alright, Bernadette, honestly." Micky smiled at her.

"Yes, Micky's a big boy now. Playing in the big leagues too."

"Oh, stop it! Now, Micky, I can only apologise for Imogen's bad behaviour."

Imogen was having a fit of the giggles and didn't reply.

"It's OK." Micky laughed too and got up to go.

"Sorry, Micky, I'm just teasing," Imogen said between giggles.

"I know."

He beat a hasty retreat.

"Honestly, darling, you are so very bad," Bernadette chided her, but she was laughing too.

"I'm sorry, it's just his face, I can't help it, I can't."

"I'll get us another coffee," said Bernadette getting up.

"I'm sorry, I really am." Imogen caught her hand.

"No you're not, you are just completely incorrigible and you know it."

"I am, I am." Imogen went into peals of fresh laughter. Bernadette pursed her lips in mock severity and disappeared to make two fresh cups of coffee.

When she returned Imogen was a little more composed. Bernadette handed her a cup.

"Sorry, darling."

"Oh, it's alright, I just worry about you teasing him, you know. Poor Micky." Bernadette had a soft spot for Micky and treated him a little like a favourite in the firm.

"He's a bit like a younger brother I suppose, that's why I do it."

"He doesn't seem fazed by it, I suppose," Bernadette mused.

"He's getting used to my ways, and yours."

"My ways are nothing like *that*."

"But he's in awe of you. Me being sisterly helps to balance it, it grounds him. See how much easier he feels in our company."

"Oh you!" Bernadette threw up her hands in mock exasperation.

"It's true!"

"Fine, anyway, that's enough about Micky. Let's get back to the case."

"OK. Who are we going to put down as witnesses?" Imogen turned her attention to the matter in hand.

"A good point. Maneet obviously, we need her testimony and an affidavit."

"Yes, obviously."

"I don't think we can put Lunara on."

"No, too dangerous." Imogen nodded in agreement.

"So Judd, or Rachel or both?"

"Do we need both of them? I think perhaps Rachel is the better bet since firstly she doesn't suspect anything about Lunara and secondly, she's not had a sexual relationship with Maneet."

"Good point, and on balance I think you are right. She's probably the better character reference."

"OK, I'll prep her up and get an affidavit from her too."

"It's a shame this is all we've got," said Bernadette a little despondently. "Don't put the affidavits in too soon, certainly not before they are required, we need to keep whatever slim advantages we can muster from this case."

"Are you regretting taking it on?"

"No, I'm not but it's turned out to be a lot tougher than I expected."

"We're up against an institution and institutions close ranks," Imogen said with some sagacity.

"You are right, but it's up to us to crack that unity."

"How?"

"We just have to find the right lever."

"I hope we can find it in time then."

"Me too."

* * *

Nothing further arose during the week to assist their case. Although Micky tried, he couldn't come up with anything else on Maguire. After an uneventful couple of days, where no further flat tyres had been discovered, Bernadette and Imogen were sitting in Bernadette's office fairly late on Friday afternoon discussing the weekend.

"I'm looking forward to you both coming, and D'Arcy is too," said Imogen.

"That's good. Let's hope it will be a good weekend."

"If you can fathom out what's wrong with D'Arcy, it will be."

"We will do our best darling, that's a promise."

With that, Imogen had to be satisfied, and she was just about to talk about wrapping up for the day when Alison popped her head around the doorway.

"Alison?" Bernadette smiled.

"Hi, Bernadette, erm..." Alison hesitated, and hovered looking as if she wanted to say something but wasn't sure how.

"What's up? Is it about the interviews for the new PA?"

"No, that's all in hand with Imogen next week." Alison shook her head.

"OK, so what's up?"

Alison took a breath. "I err... you've got a visitor?"

"Oh?" Bernadette regarded her with interest.

"Yes, she doesn't have an appointment, but she was most insistent. I couldn't stop her really."

Bernadette regarded her curiously. "Who is it?"

"Maneet." Alison shrugged apologetically.

"Maneet?"

"Yes."

"Where is she?"

"The meeting room, sorry." Alison pursed her lips contritely.

"Oh, right." Bernadette stood up. "Why are you looking so worried?"

Alison took a deep breath. "Well, it's just she's quite pushy and she practically barged in like she owned the place, and I tried to tell her she probably should have an appointment, but she wouldn't listen."

Bernadette and Imogen exchanged glances. "That sounds like her."

"Oh?"

"We've got to know her quite well." Bernadette laughed. "Don't worry, Alison, it's not a problem."

"Thank God for that!" Alison let out a sigh of relief. She was naturally protective of her boss and tended, like most PA's, to be the gatekeeper if she could.

"Yes, we'll go and see to her."

"I'll get some refreshments," said Alison heading off towards the stairs. Her job of preventing Bernadette from being disturbed having now been dispensed with she became the host instead who needed to ensure her boss' comfort.

"Thanks, darling," Bernadette called after her as she and Imogen made their way to the meeting room.

They entered the room, and Maneet who had apparently been pacing up and down feverishly launched herself at Bernadette.

"Oh, thank God, thank God, you're here, thank God," she said wrapping Bernadette in a crushing embrace. Bernadette slightly taken aback gently disentangled herself and led Maneet to the sofa.

"Whatever is wrong?"

"Fuck, oh fuck, I was so scared, so fucking scared." Maneet's eyes opened wildly, and she stared around the room as if her nemesis had arrived.

"Why, what's happened?" Bernadette wondered what could have ruffled Maneet so badly, she seemed, up to now, quite unflappable.

"I was followed. I'm sure of it. Followed by a car."

"What?" Imogen exclaimed looking at her in concern.

"Yes, I was just driving from the home of one of our clients, and I noticed this car behind me. OK, it was more of a big four by four monstrosity, hate those things. It was right on my tail. I tried to slow and let it pass but it just sat there. So, I tried going faster and it just continued to tail me. I was getting really worried."

"What did you do?"

"I rang ahead and got some of the guys to come down from the office and wait on the pavement outside. I drove and pulled in. I guess the people in the car saw them all and thought better of it. They pulled out and drove away at speed. Then I came here."

"OK."

This not being the reaction Maneet had hoped for, she continued, "Well, I didn't know what to do darling, I was just scared shitless. I got Judd to drop me off here."

"I see."

Alison entered the room with some coffee and biscuits for them, set it down on the table and after a curious glance at Maneet, she went out again. The intermission had given Bernadette time to think. She picked up a cup of coffee and indicated to Maneet to do the same. Maneet smiled and took a cup, sipping it delicately. Bernadette noticed Maneet was wearing a navy jacket and three-quarter length trousers with black stiletto mules. She had a pink blouse and had pink nails to match. There was no doubt she was incredibly attractive. A glance at Maneet's feet also showed she had nicely shaped long toes, and beautiful arches, something Bernadette always found very sexy. She pushed these thoughts out of her head. She wasn't above admiring other women but that was where it stopped.

"What do you think I should do?" Maneet ventured after a few moments of silence.

Bernadette turned to Imogen. "We need to get Olivia over here."

"Olivia?" Maneet looked from one to the other.

"She's our friendly Garda detective. She's helped us before."

"Oh!"

"Don't worry, she's not going to betray you to the white supremacists or anything. She's in our corner."

"Thank God for that!"

"I'll finish my coffee and call her up," said Imogen.

* * *

Olivia sat in her usual seat, next to Maneet and stirred her tea. Maneet stared at her somewhat puzzled while Olivia went through a ritual of pouring the tea, and then adding milk, sugar. The stirring followed. Bernadette and Imogen knew not to interrupt this process as it was also the time when Olivia thought things through. They were used to this behaviour by now. Maneet, not being familiar with Olivia's habits was becoming increasingly impatient. Fortunately, Olivia sipped her tea and spoke.

"So, tell me again exactly what happened?" she said to Maneet calmly.

Maneet did not look happy at this but complied with only a small sigh.

"I was driving back to the office, when I saw this big black four-wheel drive in my rear-view mirror up close."

"Did you happen to see what make it was?"

"No, not really it was just a car, a big black one!" There was a little hint of exasperation in Maneet's voice, but Olivia ignored it.

"OK, so then?"

"As I told you. I slowed down to let it pass, as I thought they were just being impatient. Then they slowed down too. I sped up and they did the same. Then I tried going up and down different roads, around roundabouts but they stayed right on my backside like a limpet."

Olivia nodded with interest and sipped her tea once more.

"You said they, could you see who was in the vehicle?"

"No, I just assumed, it was likely to be more than one person. I got scared OK, I started to think all kinds of things."

"I know, I know, I understand," said Olivia soothingly. "So, then you?"

"Then I called up our campaign director Judd and told him what was happening. He said to come to the office, and he'd come down mob handed. So, I did. Anyway, as I approached and indicated to pull over, the four-wheel-drive overtook and drove off at high speed."

"Did you get the number?"

"The number?"

"Did you get the number of the four-wheel drive?" Olivia asked patiently.

"Oh shit!" Maneet's face fell.

"I'm guessing no." Olivia sipped her tea again unperturbed.

"I'm sorry I didn't think, I was panicking."

"It's OK. It would have helped but if you haven't, you haven't." Olivia shrugged.

"Sorry."

"It does rather sound as if you were being followed."

"I was!"

"I know, I know." Olivia was evidently used to dealing with agitated people and Bernadette was impressed at the calm way she handled Maneet.

"Is there anything you can do?" Bernadette asked.

"Let me think on it a moment." Olivia poured herself another cup from the new teapot and went through the same ritual. Maneet flicked a glance at Bernadette in frustration but Bernadette's look in return indicated she needed to be patient. Maneet subsided albeit a little reluctantly.

"If you can write down the times and your route, I can try to get a look at the CCTV," said Olivia.

"I can do that."

"The number would help me get a lead on whoever it was, and some clue who it might be. I could get that from the CCTV."

"Are you going to make this an investigation?" Imogen wondered.

"No, based on everything that's happened I won't risk this going on the crimes database."

"Seems wise," Bernadette put in.

"I'd recommend you laying low for the weekend perhaps. Is there somewhere you can go?" Olivia said to Maneet.

"I don't know. I suppose my fiancé but I'm not really talking to him."

"Right. It's just that if these people are following you then it's best to go to ground for a couple of days. I'll try to look into a few things in the meantime, if I can. I'll need your address and so on, keys to your house, so I can give it the once over."

"Lunara!" Maneet looked in panic at Bernadette.

"Who's Lunara?" Olivia asked.

"There's a few things you should know, if I may?" Bernadette looked enquiringly at Maneet who nodded her assent. "OK, so Maneet..." she went on to explain about Lunara and Maneet's big secret.

"Wow, I didn't expect that!" Olivia picked up her cup. "Lunara should keep away from your house for now."

"She doesn't go there," Maneet said. "We meet at other places, her place. Our private place. I've got an apartment. Nobody knows about it."

"Great, maybe she can stay there for the moment, but what about you?"

Bernadette directed a searching look at Imogen who it seemed had the same idea.

"Look," said Imogen, "Bernadette and Eve are coming to our place this weekend. You are welcome to come, Maneet."

"What to D'Arcy Brown's?"

"Yes."

"I'd love to, but I've got nothing to wear, except these clothes."

"You look a similar build to me and Eve," said Bernadette, "we can lend you something."

"Great, that sorts that then." Olivia smiled.

"But what if someone follows us there?"

"Don't worry. I've thought this through. I'll borrow a squad car, and I'll escort you home, and then to D'Arcy's. Nobody will try to follow you with a Garda escort."

"Good thinking," said Bernadette.

"It's all very well, for the weekend," said Imogen, "but what happens after that? We have to go to work and so does she. We've got court on Tuesday."

"Worry not!" Olivia replied. "I'll have a think over the weekend, and we'll regroup on Monday. I'll see what I can discover."

"Is this an escalation, from the flat tyres?" Bernadette wondered.

"What flat tyres?" Maneet said at once.

An explanation had to be given to her, and Olivia, in the meantime, had a third cup of tea.

"Who the fuck let down your tyres?" Maneet demanded.

"I can probably help you there," said Olivia setting down her cup.

"You've found something on the CCTV?" Bernadette asked her at once.

"Yes, it's not very clear and the person was wearing a hoodie and also a scarf so they would be impossible to identify but it was definitely not kids."

"I knew it!" said Imogen triumphantly.

"I'm not so happy about it, to be honest." Bernadette frowned.

"It tells us you were targeted and that's concerning," Olivia continued.

"What exactly did they look like?" Maneet interjected.

"Fairly tall, I'd say, slim, wearing all black, and a scarf over the face so only the eyes were visible. Plus, a hoodie. The same person on both days, and yes, they did let the tyres down. I also saw they had walked a distance away from your car afterwards until they were out of shot, but it's very possible they were watching you."

Bernadette shuddered.

"Fuck!" said Imogen, "This is getting serious."

"Sure, but there's no actual death threats or anything," Bernadette pointed out.

"Death threats?" Maneet looked alarmed.

"OK, let's all calm down her, stick to the plan and then we'll meet on Monday, OK? By then I'll have a better handle on things my end," Olivia said trying to inject some perspective into the proceedings.

"Sure, OK, you're right," Bernadette agreed.

"Good, so why don't you all get yourselves sorted and give me a call when you need my escort?" Olivia got up to go.

"Thank you."

"You are welcome."

"Aren't you working on other cases and stuff, though?" Imogen wondered.

"Oh, I'm quite autonomous at the moment, free agent. The super is super happy with me so I'm a roving investigator for now. There's no major crime to pull me into so I can do what I want. Don't worry about me, I can manage things without being noticed."

"Great, that's good."

"I'll be off then, and I'll see you back here later on." Olivia left the meeting room.

"Is she always like that?" Maneet demanded once she had gone.

"Like what?" Bernadette asked her.

"Well, so weird, and doing tea stirring rituals and stuff, I mean..."

"She's a good friend. She's done us some favours in the past, we have, let's say a mutually beneficial alliance." Bernadette smiled.

"Sounds intriguing."

"I'll tell you later, but I've got to call Eve, tell her about the change of plans."

"Shall I get picked up as usual?" Imogen wondered. "Or come with all of you?"

"Come with us, it's probably safer," Bernadette replied after giving it some thought.

"OK, well, I'll call D'Arcy and tell her to expect Maneet."

"I'll call Lunara, and the office, and stuff," Maneet added.

"Sure, make yourself at home, we'll meet back in here when we're ready to go," said Bernadette.

She left the room with Imogen.

"Jesus fucking Christ," said Imogen as they paused outside Bernadette's office door.

"I know it's turning into some kind of lurid crime novel, but let's try to keep our heads."

Imogen put a hand on her arm. "You will still talk to D'Arcy even with..." She jerked her head back towards the meeting room.

"Of course, it goes without saying, don't you worry at all."

∗ ∗ ∗

Within a couple of hours, Bernadette was driving them all to D'Arcy's. She had spoken to Eve who met the new plans with her usual equanimity. They had driven under escort to Bernadette and Eve's house and having picked out some things for Maneet to wear, they had locked the house very carefully before heading off to D'Arcy's. The conservatory was still not started, something which Bernadette was thankful for.

They were all travelling in Bernadette's car and Olivia was following closely behind. It had been decided nobody should go with Olivia in case she was seen by other Garda officers. It wouldn't do to make out she was in cahoots, under the circumstances. As it was nobody would perhaps twig she was escorting Bernadette, but by the same token, the black four wheel drive was unlikely to show up, if they did they would beat a hasty retreat.

The drive was uneventful, and Eve chatted amiably to Maneet along the way. Maneet was perfectly happy to talk, and they were getting on very well.

"So, I gather you'd like to fuck my wife, am I right?" Eve said suddenly out of the blue.

"Darling!" Bernadette said sounding quite shocked.

"Your wife is very beautiful and if she was free, I wouldn't say no," Maneet said candidly blushing slightly.

"And I apologise for my wife's manners," Bernadette said severely.

"Oh, darling, we should just know where we stand, get it all out in the open," Eve shot back.

"Honestly it was just a passing remark, it didn't mean anything." Maneet began to backpedal sensing perhaps this was a contentious topic.

"Eve is just teasing you," Imogen said smoothly. "Though she's not usually quite *this* blunt."

"I'm just protective, marking out my territory." Eve laughed.

"She's a witch," Bernadette put in. "You need to know that, so I wouldn't upset her."

"God, what have I got into?"

"Nothing much." Imogen's eyes were dancing. "We've got a private coven at D'Arcy's of course, so we'll be having naked dancing and incantations around the bonfire later, that's before the orgy where we invoke the devil."

Maneet looked at her wide eyed before realising she was joking. They all laughed.

"Listen," said Eve, "don't take me seriously, I was teasing you, just a little. Anyway, I'm flattered. Bernadette is hot as fuck, so I'm hardly surprised you fancy her."

"Can we stop now?" Bernadette said interjecting and also blushing scarlet.

"Sorry." Eve blew her a kiss and slid her hand into Bernadette's affectionately.

"You're forgiven." Bernadette smiled at her but shot her a private look which told Eve it would be noted for another time. Eve smirked with satisfaction and lay back into the leather seat.

"I'm looking forward to seeing D'Arcy's place," said Maneet changing the subject.

"It's lovely, well amazing really, I'm lucky to live there," Imogen replied.

"You're lucky to be getting married to her I suppose."

"Yes, yes I am." However, Imogen's tone wasn't entirely convincing, and Bernadette did not miss the inflexion.

"What an amazing life you two must live."

"Yes," said Imogen with a hollow expression on her face. Maneet did not notice, she was too busy being starstruck.

Soon enough the mansion rolled into view, and Maneet made appreciative noises when she saw it. They stopped at the gate and waited for it to open. Olivia didn't follow them but peeled off and drove away as she had things to do. In any case, she had seen D'Arcy's mansion during Bernadette and Eve's wedding. She had told Bernadette to stay in touch over the weekend and let her know if anything eventful occurred.

* * *

Bernadette pulled up the car on the driveway in front of the wing shaped two story building which comprised the main house. Maneet gasped slightly at the size of it and then their attention was taken by D'Arcy skipping lightly down the path wearing a yellow sundress and flip flops.

"Darlings," she squealed making a beeline for Bernadette and hugging and kissing her soundly.

"Hello, D'Arcy," said Bernadette.

D'Arcy turned her attention to Eve in a similar fashion while Imogen watched her with affectionate indulgence.

"You must be Maneet," said D'Arcy raking her in a glance.

"Yes, that's me."

"Welcome to my house." D'Arcy held out her hand and shook Maneet's demurely. "Come in, come in, darlings I've got some dinner on the go, well, Cheffie has anyway," she sang out merrily and made her way back down the path with the others in tow.

Bernadette looked at Eve. They both had noticed how she had not greeted Imogen. This was very remiss of her and although Imogen had betrayed nothing it must have stung her. This wasn't good at all. It was almost as if her fiancé was an adjunct, and there wasn't even a kiss hello. Bernadette felt this was a terribly bad start to the weekend but hoped perhaps things could be turned around.

Once indoors D'Arcy commanded them to leave the cases, saying Constantina, her housekeeper, would see to it and ushered them upstairs.

"I have to say this is an amazing place," Maneet said somewhat in awe of her surroundings.

"Oh, do you like it, I should give you a tour, we've got time before dinner." D'Arcy sound pleased at this praise. She loved to show her place off, as Bernadette knew only too well.

"If you don't mind," came the eager response.

"Oh, not at all."

They had by this time reached one of the living rooms, which was the one she and Imogen used the most and had an outlook towards the substantial back gardens.

"I'll come, shall I?" Imogen said tentatively.

"Oh no, darling, stay with your friends. Maneet and I will be quite comfortable, won't we? Come along, Maneet."

So, saying D'Arcy tucked her arm under Maneet's and whisked her away, that latter being blissfully unaware of the thunderous look Imogen gave to their retreating backs.

"Do you see? Do you see?" Imogen turned to them with glistening eyes. "I swear to God I can't take much more of it. I'm going to blow, and it won't be pretty."

"Imogen, darling. I can see, we both can. Just please try. We'll do our best to intervene. Eve will talk to D'Arcy, won't you, darling?" Bernadette said touching her arm lightly in reassurance.

"I will try, I promise," Eve vowed with great sincerity.

"Just hold it in if you can, and no... *spanking*... ok?" Bernadette whispered the last part.

"Chance would be a fine thing." Imogen's eyes flashed. "You've no idea how much I want to put her across my knee and give her the finest paddling she's ever had in her life... but I won't."

"Good and we do understand, really we do. I mean, but especially, you know, with guests." Bernadette continued in soothing tones.

"We're going to sort this, Imogen, never fear," said Eve seeing how distressed their friend was.

"I hope so, I really do." Tears began to well up in Imogen's eyes and then she burst into tears.

Bernadette and Eve took her to the sofa to console her, which they managed to before D'Arcy breezed back in with Maneet in tow.

"Oh? What's happened?" she said at once noticing Imogen's puffy eyes, and hastily wiped cheeks.

"Oh, Imogen's just a little stressed about things at work, you know with the flat tyres and now these people following Maneet," Bernadette lied.

"Oh, yes, Maneet was just telling me, goodness what a to do." D'Arcy said this in an offhand tone.

This reaction was unusual. Normally she'd be much more concerned for Imogen, as she had been when they were pursuing D'Arcy's court case. Then nothing was too much trouble to keep Imogen and Bernadette safe. Now it seemed almost as if D'Arcy didn't care and this rather upset Bernadette on behalf of her friend.

"It is rather."

"I'm sorry it's so upsetting for Imogen," said Maneet contritely, thinking this was all her fault.

"It's OK." Imogen smiled weakly.

"She'll be OK, in a few minutes," said D'Arcy dismissively. "Come on let's go and eat."

She turned and went out of the room taking Maneet with her.

"I'm just going to freshen up," said Imogen sadly disappointed that D'Arcy had not even come to her side in her distressed state. She would usually be unable to bear the sight of Imogen in tears and would be the first to console her.

"Sure, we'll see you in the dining room."

"Yes," Imogen gasped and hurried away.

"Oh dear," said Bernadette.

"I'm going to end up chastising D'Arcy myself if this carries on," said Eve crossly. She had not missed the way D'Arcy was behaving towards her fiancé and she pursed her lips in annoyance.

"I know, God, I had no idea, we've got to sort this, darling. It can't go on whether Maneet is here or not."

"Yes," said Eve grimly. "Let's leave it for tonight and tackle it in the morning when we're fresh. I'll take D'Arcy aside and get to the bottom of this nonsense."

"Shall we get some dinner?"

"Yes, let's."

Dinners at D'Arcy's were usually delicious, and this was no exception. Her chef had laid on two main curries, *Beef Rendang* and a *Massaman* curry with lamb. There was rice, and some vegetable curry dishes, salad and naan.

"When I heard you were coming, I decided we'd go for Indian and Malaysian, the chef, my Cheffie, is very good at most cuisines, but this is one of his favourites," said D'Arcy as they began to help themselves.

Bernadette assumed D'Arcy had recently changed her chef, since she'd not heard her talk about Cheffie before.

"Wasn't your chef called Fernando?" she asked innocently.

"Oh, yes, well he went off to work at some restaurant with two Michelin Stars and I hired Cheffie. He's half Malaysian, cooks the most delicious food of all cuisines. He's been spoiling us royally. He's not called Cheffie of course, that's just my pet name for him."

This ingenuous and artless speech was typical D'Arcy. Bernadette did not enquire further suspecting D'Arcy could not pronounce her chef's name properly or some such thing. D'Arcy seemed blissfully unaware at times of the privilege her wealth and fame had brought her. She was, however, quite innocent of any malice, of that much Bernadette was certain.

"It all looks so delicious," said Maneet. "And I'm flattered you thought of me, thank you so much. You shouldn't have."

"Oh, it's my pleasure, really," said D'Arcy with an unmistakable flirtatious eye flutter.

From the corner of her eye, Bernadette saw Imogen reach for the Merlot of which two open bottles stood on the table and pour herself a sizeable glassful. She drank half of it in one go and filled up the glass again to repeat the performance.

"Eat something, darling," Bernadette told her.

"Sure, I will, it looks lovely."

Imogen helped herself to some generous portions of each and began to dig in, as did the rest of them. Unusually she did not join in the conversation confining herself to her food and the wine while listening to the others.

"Your chef has outdone himself," Bernadette remarked, trying to keep up the flow of innocuous topics.

"Oh yes, he trained with the best. I'm so lucky to have him," D'Arcy trilled.

"Wow, you are lucky to have a chef and all of this. A superstar lifestyle," Maneet said evidently a little envious.

Some people were more impressed than others with the trappings of wealth, Bernadette mused. She was not wrong in her assessment of Maneet, and it scanned with the fact she was determined to marry her rich fiancé.

"Oh, you know, it's good of course but it's not everything. There are other more important things to life." D'Arcy smiled. She did not elaborate further, but she did flick a shy glance in Imogen's direction, and Bernadette noted the veiled look of longing in her expression which was soon masked. Bernadette also realised that the wine bottle nearest to Imogen was going down fast. There wasn't much she could do about it but she very much hoped Imogen would not allow the alcohol to override her common sense.

"You must have an interesting time with refugees," D'Arcy said to Maneet, perhaps in an effort to shift the focus from herself for once.

"Oh yes, it's interesting for sure and enlightening. But it's a bit shit with these latest developments, I hate being so out of control of things," Maneet opined between mouthfuls of curry. "You know this really is delicious, D'Arcy, amazing."

"Oh, it's nothing but it's a great compliment coming from you."

Bernadette glanced at Maneet. This was a bit gauche, as D'Arcy was implying Maneet being Indian should appreciate it. However, she said nothing and Maneet did not look to be offended in fact quite the opposite.

"Oh, I know my Indian food, believe me," Maneet told her frankly. "And this is some of the best I've had."

"Well, I think it's brilliant," said Imogen her eyes a little bright from the wine.

"Thank you, darling." D'Arcy smiled at her for what seemed to be the first time that evening. "Anyway," she turned back to Maneet, "I understand what you mean about feeling out of control, in the movie business it feels that way all the time."

She proceeded to regale Maneet with tales of her past career some of which Bernadette had heard before, and doubtless, Imogen certainly had. This was more the D'Arcy she knew, being the centre of attention, something she simply could not help.

The others held their peace and addressed themselves to the delicious meal. Finally, Bernadette pushed her plate away feeling very full. She looked at the wine bottles which were now empty. Imogen was smiling a little inanely and she was evidently somewhat drunk. Bernadette was hardly surprised and readied herself to try to restrain her friend should she get out of order.

They all finally stopped eating and Constantina came in as if by magic and cleared it all away.

"I've got Kulfi if anyone cares for it, or coffee," D'Arcy asked them tentatively, having run out of stories for the present. Maneet had appeared to be quite enthralled listening to a real live celebrity.

All of them except Maneet refused the dessert on the grounds of not being able to eat anything else, but Maneet ate the Kulfi with evident relish. Bernadette wondered where she put it all and assumed, she must have a very fast metabolism, in which she was very lucky.

"Shall we go to the living room?" D'Arcy asked when Maneet had finished, again pronouncing it delicious.

"I'm a little tired," Imogen announced suddenly, "I'm going to bed, sorry." She got up and left the room abruptly.

"Well!" said D'Arcy looking slightly miffed at this.

"She's had a trying week," Bernadette told her in an attempt to mollify her.

"I suppose." There was a little pout, and then it was gone.

Bernadette and Eve exchanged glances but said nothing further. They all went to the living room and talked convivially until Bernadette also feeling tired, took Eve to bed too. They left D'Arcy talking to Maneet who seemed completely fascinated by D'Arcy's stories of her film star life.

"Do you think they'll be OK like *that*?" Eve asked her snuggling close in the usual bed and room they stayed in at D'Arcy's.

"Yes, she won't do anything, well, she'd better not," said Bernadette darkly.

"I don't think so, anyway Maneet loves Lunara, you said so."

"Yes, but she still sleeps with her fiancé."

"True, but let's hope it will all be OK. I don't think D'Arcy would."

"I hope to God not," Bernadette said with feeling.

"Did you notice how D'Arcy is saying *my* instead of *our*, all the time?" Eve changed the subject slightly.

"Yes, yes I did."

"It's not a good sign." Eve sighed. "They are supposed to be together, partners. She's talking as if Imogen isn't part of her life."

"What if she's not? What if this all turns to shit?" Bernadette wondered.

"I hope not, it would be such a shame."

"It will break Imogen for sure."

"We can't let it happen."

In the dark Bernadette saw Eve purse her lips in a determined fashion.

"Can't you work some of your magic, my witchy witch?"

"I can try," Eve whispered. "Shall I work some other magic, for now?"

"What kind?"

"This kind..."

"Oh fuck... yes... oh God... yes please..."

Eve's fingers began their magic dance between Bernadette's legs, and she gasped in response to the all too familiar touch.

Later that night they both awoke. Through the stillness of the night were the unmistakable sounds of Imogen's voice.

"Oh, D'Arcy, oh fuck... fuck... fuck... oh... fuck... I love you... I love you... ohh!" Then there was silence.

"That sounded good, auspicious, hopefully," Bernadette whispered.

"Let's hope so," Eve whispered back, kissing her softly before going back to sleep.

* * *

In the morning they were unceremoniously roused from slumber with a start, and to quite a different sound.

"How dare you! How dare you question me! How fucking *dare* you!"

It was D'Arcy shouting at the top of her lungs. Bernadette and Eve sat up in bed, in alarm.

"I just asked you a fucking question, and I deserve an answer!" Imogen shouted back.

"You fucking bitch. You asked me if I was fucking someone else! How dare you!"

"Well, are you? Just tell me because it fucking well feels like it the way you are treating me!"

"Jesus, we need to stop this," said Bernadette getting out of bed, and fumbling for their robes in their suitcase. Eve stood up too alarmed at the sudden escalation.

"I don't care, you've no right, you've no fucking right!"

"I do have a right, you're my fiancée remember, not that you seem to fucking care, do you? It's all *my* this, *my* that, *your* house, *your* everything else, what happened to OUR? What the fuck happened to US?" Imogen was shouting but they could hear the despair in her voice which was starting to crack through the pain she was feeling.

Bernadette threw on a robe, as did Eve, and hurried to the door opening it just in time to hear the denouement of the row.

"Get out! Get the fuck out of my fucking house, you fucking little bitch. I fucking hate you. I hate you! Get out!" screamed D'Arcy.

"Nooo! Don't say *that*! No... D'Arcy, no! Please, no, you don't mean it... tell me you don't mean it, darling... I love you... I love..." The cry from Imogen was heart-breaking as it floated down the corridor.

"GET OUT!" D'Arcy screamed at the top of her lungs. "GET OUT! I don't want you here anymore. Get out of MY HOUSE!"

"No, D'Arcy, no... you can't, can't, please... no... please..."

The sound of running feet assailed them and Imogen flew down the corridor unseeing her face streaming with tears.

"Shit," said Bernadette.

"You see to Imogen, I will deal with D'Arcy," said Eve.

Bernadette hurried after Imogen and found her in the living room, in a heap on the floor choking and sobbing as if her heart would break. She ran to her and put her arms around her protectively, holding her tightly while Imogen sobbed harder and harder unable to stop or say anything coherent.

Down the corridor Eve could be heard faintly trying to reason with D'Arcy who was still shouting hysterically.

"D'Arcy, come on now, you need to stop this, please, D'Arcy," Eve was saying.

"I want her out! Get her out! I hate the fucking sight of her!" D'Arcy shouted.

"You don't mean it, D'Arcy, now stop it, stop it at once!" Eve said severely.

"No! This is my house and I..."

She got no further.

"I said stop it!" said Eve sharply. There was the sound of a resounding slap and D'Arcy burst into tears.

Bernadette smiled to herself at this. She didn't know Eve had it in her. In her arms, Imogen was starting to subside a little and Bernadette coaxed her to the sofa. Imogen buried her face in Bernadette's shoulder whimpering quietly.

Into all of this chaos, Maneet appeared wearing a pair of pyjamas lent to her by Bernadette.

"Um... what's actually going on? I heard a hell of a lot of shouting," she asked sleepily looking at Bernadette and Imogen with interest.

"There have been a few relationship problems," said Bernadette, "which sort of came to a head this morning, sorry."

"Oh, don't be, don't be, to be honest, I don't mind, it's better than EastEnders." Maneet laughed at her own joke which was probably meant to diffuse things. "Anyway, I'll go and make some coffee, would you like some?"

"Yes, please," Bernadette nodded.

"Great, great."

"Help yourself if you're hungry I'm sure D'Arcy won't mind."

"Sure, thanks. I'll see if I can find some bread to make toast, or whatever or something."

Maneet left the room. Imogen raised her puffed and red face to look at Bernadette.

"How are you feeling now, darling?" Bernadette asked her gently, brushing the tears from her cheeks. Imogen regarded her like a frightened child.

"Like shit, like fucking shit. Tell me she didn't mean it, tell me, Bernadette. Please tell me, because I can't take it if she did." Tears sprung once more to Imogen's eyes as she said this.

"I don't think she can have, my darling, honestly, but if you can, tell me what happened?"

"I... I couldn't take it anymore, I'm sorry. I know you were supposed to talk to her, but it just came out. I asked her if there was someone else and she went crazy."

"Right, I see."

"It was a mistake, right? Asking that?" Imogen sniffed.

"Didn't you two make love last night?" Bernadette was reluctant to answer this directly, but she certainly thought to herself that Imogen had been hugely unwise.

"Yes, we did, she was so nice to me and loving."

"So? Why did you?"

"I couldn't help myself, I had to know. You saw the way she ignored me yesterday. It's not the first time. The way she says everything is hers and not ours anymore. You don't know how much it hurts me."

"I think I can imagine, really, I can, sweetheart." Bernadette smiled stroking Imogen's hair lightly.

"I've fucked it up now. I guess. I'll have to move out." Imogen's tone became bitter. The bitterness of someone who feels entirely and comprehensively rejected.

"No, Imogen..."

"You heard what she said, she hates me. She can't stand the sight of me. I may as well be dead. I may as well be fucking dead." Imogen buried her head in Bernadette's shoulder once more and started to cry.

This was not good, Bernadette prayed Eve was making some headway to resolve things soon.

Maneet reappeared with a tray with coffee, milk and sugar. There were some pieces of buttered toast too. She set it on the coffee table. Taking one look at Imogen, she put a finger to her lips and strategically withdrew. Bernadette absently continued to stroke Imogen's hair and wondered how they always got into these situations at D'Arcy's house. Now one of their client's had witnessed the chaos too. A fleeting thought sped through her mind that perhaps they were all better off without D'Arcy and then she squashed it. It wouldn't be better for Imogen, and somehow this had to be mended.

After another very long while, Imogen sat up, accepted the cup of coffee from Bernadette and sipped it gratefully. Bernadette decided not to talk about things any further and was just wondering what was happening when Eve appeared at the door.

"Is it OK if I just talk to Eve?" Bernadette asked Imogen.

"Sure, I'm not going anywhere." Imogen shrugged.

"No, no you're not! Don't you dare move from that sofa."

Imogen nodded and shot her a grateful look for her obvious concern.

Bernadette went to the door and pulled it to behind her.

"What's going on?" She said in hushed tones.

"I'm sort of getting to the bottom of this, and now I think D'Arcy needs to speak to Imogen."

"If you're sure?" Bernadette looked doubtful.

"It will be OK, I promise you."

"Alright then, I'll check if Imogen is willing."

"OK."

"Did you do what I think you did?" Bernadette asked her suddenly.

"I slapped her, yes, and I'll tell you later. I had to."

"OK. It seemed to work."

"Yes."

Bernadette returned to Imogen, she sat down beside her and took her hand.

"Darling, would it be OK if, if D'Arcy comes in to talk to you?" she said tentatively.

"OK," Imogen whispered, "but you have to be here, next to me, don't leave me alone."

"I won't, I promise. I will be here the whole time."

"Then, yes, OK."

Bernadette beckoned to Eve.

"She says yes, but I have to sit here next to her."

"Sure, of course, I'll go and get D'Arcy."

Eve disappeared. Imogen glanced at Imogen who looked apprehensive. They didn't have to wait long. Eve came back with D'Arcy who looked equally distressed. She had evidently been crying too. D'Arcy sat down on a sofa opposite and looked down at the floor. Eve sat next to her.

"Now," Eve said quietly, "I'm setting some ground rules here for both of you. There isn't going to be any shouting and each of you has to listen to what the other person has to say without interrupting. OK?"

"Yes," D'Arcy said in a small voice.

Imogen nodded dumbly looking at D'Arcy the pain in her eyes clearly visible.

"D'Arcy, tell Imogen what you told me just now," said Eve.

There was a long silence before D'Arcy said anything.

"OK..." said D'Arcy at length, and they waited a little more for her to pluck up the courage to speak. "Imogen... I... I didn't mean... those things I said... I'm sorry... I am so sorry." Her voice was very quiet, subdued, and she spoke in halting tones.

"When you said that thing, about me seeing someone else, I just lost it. I'm so sorry. I said some terrible things to you, and I didn't mean them... I didn't." D'Arcy's voice broke out in a sob and tears began to roll down her cheeks.

Imogen's eyes were glistening, and she was also on the verge of tears once more.

"And?" Eve prompted her.

"I've been very mean to you for weeks. I've been distant. I've been a real bitch at times. I behaved terribly badly towards you. I know that." D'Arcy sounded a little stronger now in the manner of someone who starts to get things off their chest.

Imogen nodded dumbly at her but said nothing.

"And why were you being like that, D'Arcy?" Eve said gently.

"I... I... well, it's not because I don't love you. It's not what you think or because of someone else. It's because... because... I do... I do love you... so much..." D'Arcy stopped again as she started to cry.

Tears began to roll down Imogen's face.

"And?" said Eve again.

"Imogen, there's something I haven't told you."

Imogen's expression became suddenly intent, as if this was going to be a hammer blow.

"I've been offered another part in a movie... I didn't know how to tell you... because it's going to be at least six months, away or longer... and I couldn't stand..."

"What..." said Imogen hoarsely. "All of this because of a movie?"

"No... that's part of it but it's not all of it." D'Arcy looked at her miserably.

"What else? What else is it?" Imogen demanded finding some strength herself from somewhere.

"Imogen. Let her speak," said Eve quietly but firmly.

"Sorry." Imogen sat back and took hold of Bernadette's hand for comfort.

"It's not just that. It's because I just want to be normal, a normal couple, do normal couple things together without you judging me," D'Arcy cried.

"But I don't..."

Eve held up a hand to stop Imogen from saying anything further.

"But you do, it feels like it. I've become afraid to tell you anything because you want to punish me and it's stopped being a game, Imogen. It was a game, and it's true I needed it sometimes, I even wanted it, and it perhaps did me some good, like I told you... but I'm not your submissive, I don't want to be that, and it seems it's what you want and... just to dominate me all the time and..."

"You started to withdraw from me," Imogen put in.

"Yes..." D'Arcy nodded.

"Why didn't you tell me?"

"Because I was afraid you would... spank me..." D'Arcy said quietly.

"Oh fuck!" Imogen wailed. "I'm a monster, I've become a monster. What have I done? What have I done? This is all my fault."

"Imogen, you need to stop it too, come on, that's not helpful," Eve cut in.

Imogen subsided though it was clear from her expression she was far from happy with herself.

"D'Arcy, have you said everything you want to say?" Eve asked her.

"Yes, Imogen, I don't mind the games. I want to play those games. But it's becoming more than that. It's becoming who we are and it's not... who I am. I just want to be your wife, your loving caring, wife. That's all."

D'Arcy stopped and when it seemed she wasn't going to say anything further at that point. Eve turned to Imogen.

"Now you can speak," she said.

Imogen paused trying to gather her thoughts, her feelings. This had hit her, perhaps even blindsided her in the way that things from partners often do. It was perhaps becoming clear to her she had really not considered D'Arcy in the way she had been acting, and this had rebounded on her in a most spectacular way.

"I don't know what to say. I mean, I'm truly sorry for making you feel that way. It was never my intention. I guess I just let my impulses get out of hand and I never wanted you to feel that you can't tell me things."

"And I want to tell you things, darling, and this is your house, not just mine, it's ours. I'm so sorry, so very, very sorry," D'Arcy said.

"I'm sorry too. I just want you to love me, how you used to, I want to be how we used to be," Imogen cried out.

"But I do love you, I do!" D'Arcy wailed.

"And I love you, can't you see that? I'm aching for your love, every moment, every single moment..." Imogen trailed off.

Bernadette decided perhaps now was a good time for some reconciliation and talking. She interrupted and decided to take charge. She glanced at Eve who nodded in assent.

"OK, now, D'Arcy, come over here and sit beside Imogen," she said firmly.

D'Arcy did as she was bid and sat facing Imogen on the sofa. The pair of them were crying wordlessly. Bernadette ignored this. She had decided what to do. Eve smiled at her with approval, she had probably guessed what Bernadette was intending.

"OK, Imogen, take D'Arcy's hands and hold them."

Imogen took D'Arcy's hands and held them gently.

"Now, you both need to talk, that much is clear, but first I want you both to make some vows to each other."

They both turned to Bernadette and looked at her in puzzlement.

"Yes, vows, I know what you are thinking. You don't just need to make vows at a wedding. Believe me, there's one thing I know, communication is the key. I've learnt it the hard way. So, I want you to make each other some promises here and now, OK?"

"OK," said D'Arcy in a small voice.

"Yes," said Imogen quietly.

"D'Arcy, do you promise to be honest and open with Imogen from now on? Do you promise to tell her everything and not hold back? Do you promise to listen to what Imogen has to say, treat her with respect and never withhold your love from her in the future no matter what?"

"Yes, yes I do, I promise," said D'Arcy catching on to what Bernadette was doing.

"And, Imogen, do you promise to be open and honest with D'Arcy from now on? Tell her everything and not hold back? Do you promise to listen to what D'Arcy has to say, treat her with respect and never to withhold your love from her in the future no matter what?"

"Yes," Imogen whispered.

Bernadette took a deep breath to lay some strictures on them, hoping they would comply.

"Furthermore, there is to be no more spanking or games like that of any sort for at least a month. You both have to learn to work out your problems in other ways by talking and communicating. Keep your games by all means but keep them for the bedroom and for sex. Don't let these spill over into the way you handle each other. OK?"

They both nodded. At the low ebb they were, they were likely to agree to anything which might help them. Bernadette played it to her advantage.

"If I find out there's been *any* spanking or chastisement or anything like it at all in the next month, I will be very cross with you both." Bernadette smiled at them, nevertheless.

Imogen smiled weakly at this and so did D'Arcy.

"If Eve and I leave you to talk, can you manage to keep to your promises? When I say talk, I mean talk. I don't mean anything else. We will come back and check on you shortly. You need to work things out and let out everything you've not been saying to each other, OK? Can you manage that?"

"Yes," said Imogen.

"Promise?"

"We promise," said D'Arcy.

Bernadette nodded in approval. "Fine, we'll leave you to it and go and sort out some breakfast."

"Am I allowed to kiss her?" D'Arcy asked.

"Kissing but nothing else, not yet."

"OK... mother." Imogen laughed.

Eve took Bernadette's hand and the two of them left the room, quietly closing the door behind them.

"Fuck, well done you," Eve whispered.

"I know, and thanks but you did wonders with D'Arcy," said Bernadette. "Let's go and find Maneet."

* * *

They discovered Maneet in the living room watching TV. There was an empty plate on the coffee table which looked as if it had contained curry and rice.

"Oh hi!" said Maneet turning around. "How's everything going?"

"I think we've made some headway," Bernadette told her. "We've left them to talk."

"Oh good, well, I've been watching TV as you can see, and I heated up a bit of the leftover curry, it was yummy."

"For breakfast?" Bernadette made a face.

"Oh yes, it was delicious."

"We're going to make some breakfast now, bacon, eggs, and so on, would you like some?" Eve asked her.

"I wouldn't say no." Maneet laughed. "That was only a snack I had."

"Fine, we'll pop into the kitchen."

"I'll join you." Maneet turned off the TV and picked up her plate.

When they arrived in the kitchen, Constantina was there tidying up and laying the table.

"Constantina," said Bernadette, "we're going to make breakfast, you can go and have a rest."

"But is my job!" Constantina protested.

"No, you can go have some time off, go on. Eve is going to make breakfast. You can leave it to us."

"But..."

"Constantina, we love you but let us do the breakfast, just this once, OK?" Eve said smiling sweetly whilst ushering her out.

"OK, OK! I go, I go," Constantina grumbled but she looked secretly pleased. "Is my princess...?" she asked anxiously at the door.

"Everything will be fine, darling," Eve told her. "Don't worry."

"Yes, well sometimes there is too much, this, you know." Constantina smacked her hand into her palm lightly.

"We know and there won't be for a while, we're sorting it out. Now go on, go and have a rest."

"OK, I go… I go…" Constantina left the room in dramatic style.

"What did she mean by too much?" Maneet asked curiously smacking one hand into the other.

Eve started to bustle around getting eggs from the fridge and finding the other ingredients she wanted.

"After what you've seen and heard, I guess you deserve to know," said Bernadette. She put the kettle on and then sat down at the table with Maneet while Eve began to put a pan on to make bacon.

"Ooh, sounds intriguing."

"Believe me, *that* is not the word I'd use…" Bernadette laughed and began to relate the potted history of D'Arcy and Imogen's relationship, how they had met, whilst judiciously leaving a few things out. However, Imogen's predilection for spanking had to be mentioned. As Bernadette suspected, Maneet did not bat an eye.

"Wow," she said. "It's quite a story. I didn't suspect Imogen was quite that naughty."

"This is just between us, right," Bernadette said anxiously.

"Of course, after all, you know a very big secret of mine."

"We're even then, I suppose."

"Yes, goodness, I never expected quite such an entertaining weekend." Maneet laughed.

"It wasn't our intention to give you one, to be honest, but this has been brewing for a while," said Bernadette with a shrug.

"It seems as though you've sorted it."

"She's quite the mediator," Eve added looking at her wife with admiration. "I've seen a new side to her."

"I have my moments." Bernadette smiled.

In the meantime, Eve had cooked up some sausages, bacon, mushrooms and tomatoes, topped off with creamy scrambled eggs which were her speciality. Bernadette helped her to distribute it all onto plates.

"I'll take these to them, and I'll be back in a jiffy."

"I'll make your coffee, darling." Eve smiled.

Maneet watched this exchange with interest.

Bernadette carried the two plates into the living room where she found D'Arcy and Imogen with their arms wrapped around each other.

"Here's some breakfast and I want you to eat it, you need it," she said setting the plates down.

"Oh, Bernadette, we've been talking and..." D'Arcy began.

"That' great, and I do want to hear, darling. Eve and I will come after breakfast and you can tell us both what you've discussed. In the meantime, just eat, OK?"

"OK," said D'Arcy meekly, picking up a plate and handing it to Imogen along with some cutlery.

"Very good," said Bernadette leaving them to it. She returned to the kitchen and took her place. Eve had put her plate on the table alongside a cup of coffee.

"Your wife is an amazing cook, these eggs are to die for," said Maneet who had made some headway in her own repast.

"She's amazing all round and she looks after me as if I was a queen."

"You are, you are my queen." Eve smiled.

"You are my witch," Bernadette shot back.

"You two seem to get on so well," Maneet observed pushing her plate away and picking up her drink. "What's your secret?"

"Oh, we've had our ups and downs, believe me. Some blow ups. But I think we allow each other to express ourselves, and how we are. We see to each other's needs very well. We take care of each other, although, Eve takes care of me in almost every way imaginable."

"And you take care of *me*, you just don't know it," Eve replied at once.

"I suppose I do, I work, and I bring in the main income, although Eve's art is fast becoming a big seller."

"You do far more than just that and you know it. You fulfil my desires, you love me, you care for me, you cherish me. It's not just about material things."

"Wow, amazing," Maneet said, taking this all in. "I can't imagine having such a relationship with Akshay."

"Can't you?" Bernadette asked her, between mouthfuls of egg, bacon and toast.

"No..."

"Could you imagine it with Lunara?"

"Well... yes... I suppose." Maneet shrugged.

"Doesn't that tell you something?"

Maneet sighed. "I know what you're thinking."

"What am I thinking?" Bernadette looked at her with interest.

"That I'm an idiot, a total fucking idiot to be going and marrying a man who I don't even really love because of my parents' expectations. I'm consigning my beautiful love of my life to live in obscurity while I carry on an affair with her and live a sham marriage with my husband."

"You said it, not me." Bernadette smiled.

"Yes, but you thought it."

"Actually, I didn't think precisely *that* no, you're wrong about it." Bernadette laid down her fork, after consuming the last piece of bacon.

"What did you think?"

"I just wonder why you are willing to compromise your happiness, and that of your lover, for a whole bunch of other people including your parents?"

"My culture..." Maneet began.

"So, you say, but is it just *that*? Sometimes it takes courage to do the right thing."

"I'm a coward, is it what you're saying?"

"No, you're human. But just for a moment put yourself twenty years down the line, pursuing the course of action you intend to take. Imagine how you could have lived those twenty years so differently in true happiness with someone you really love. How will you feel then?" Bernadette picked up her coffee and sipped it.

"You're a hard bitch, do you know that?" Maneet said ruefully, but she was smiling.

"You asked me." Bernadette shrugged.

"I can see why they say you're so tough in the courtroom."

"Actually, she's a pussycat at home." Eve laughed.

"You could have fooled me."

"Oh, she can be very assertive, when she wants to be, and when I want her to be." Eve shot Maneet a sly look which wasn't lost on her.

"I hear what you're saying, and I know you're right." Maneet let out a big sigh. "But I just can't."

"Then you've answered your own question." Bernadette raised an eyebrow.

"I wish I was more like you."

"Believe me." Bernadette laughed. "It's been a long road to get to be me, so I'm not judging you."

"Anyway, we just carry on, don't we, because sometimes we have to, or at least, I have to. That is what I feel. Aren't you worried about the stuff which has happened recently, your safety and so on?" Maneet moved on to another topic.

"Yes, I am but I'm trying to leave the worry until Monday. We are safe enough here. D'Arcy has personal security. They will just step it up, if they haven't already."

"Oh? I didn't see them?"

"When we are here, her personal bodyguard is discreet. His name is Carragh, he goes with her everywhere although he's not armed. He normally sleeps just down the hall from her. Also, he's pretty hot, if you like that sort of thing."

They all laughed.

"I'd like to meet him, just to check for myself you understand." Maneet giggled.

"I'm sure it can be arranged." Bernadette set down her cup. "I think it's time for me and Eve to go and see how those two are getting on, apparently there are things they want to tell us."

"Can I come?" Maneet asked.

"Well, you're practically family I guess, so unless they object."

✳ ✳ ✳

The three of them returned to the living room, as the door opened, D'Arcy broke apart from Imogen and shot a guilty look at Bernadette.

"We were only kissing I promise," she said.

"It's OK, D'Arcy." Bernadette laughed. "Anyway, do you mind if Maneet is here, I mean, we had to sort of explain it all to her anyway."

"Sure, why not. Half the neighbourhood must have heard us," D'Arcy said self-deprecatingly.

Bernadette and Eve sat down opposite D'Arcy and Imogen. Maneet separated herself a little as a spectator to the scene being played out.

"You wanted to tell me what you've talked about?" Bernadette asked them.

"Yes, we've talked, a lot and we both realise we've not been totally honest with each other about things. I mean, I've been worse than Imogen in that respect," D'Arcy began.

"No, I was definitely worse in being so selfish and thinking only of my feelings," Imogen objected.

"Don't start another argument, you two!" Bernadette admonished them, and they all laughed.

"I think we understand each other better now, thanks to you, both you and Eve," said D'Arcy.

"We are going to be more considerate towards each other," Imogen chimed in. "I am going to stop being so dominating, it's going to be hard, but I am going to do it. D'Arcy wants me to change, and I am determined to do so."

"I didn't say I want you to change, but you know, let's keep those things for sex like we did when we started."

"You're right, and I'm so very sorry, my darling." Imogen lowered her eyes shyly with a look of contrition.

D'Arcy however, seemed determined to compete in the sackcloth and ashes stakes.

"I'm sorry too. I said the most terrible things to you. I don't know what possessed me. I want everyone to know here and now that this isn't just my house, it's ours, when we are married, I am putting it all into our joint names. I've been selfish too. I stopped considering us as a couple. It was very, very wrong of me."

Imogen smiled and took hold of her fiancée's hand.

"She's going to do her movie and I'm OK with it. I know it's going to be hard for us, but I'll try to go and see her and she'll try to fly home sometimes. She needs to have her career and I know that. We've always got the video calls like we did before."

D'Arcy sighed. "This is a new beginning for us. We're going to do normal couple things together. We're going to cook together, and stuff, go out a bit more. You know, obviously, with Carragh as security and stuff."

"That's good, very good, from both of you. I'm glad," Bernadette told them.

"Thank you, and Eve, for getting us to this point."

"I couldn't lose you, my darling, I could never lose you," said Imogen suddenly and passionately to D'Arcy.

"Nor I you." D'Arcy's eyes filled with tears.

"I was so sad when you..."

"I know, but hush now, I promise never to say those things again."

"Thank you."

The two of them moved in for a kiss.

Watching this indulgently, Bernadette decided perhaps they needed to go and make it up in a much more physical fashion.

"You've made such great progress, the two of you can go to your room and do whatever you need to do," she said.

"Really?" said D'Arcy getting up and pulling Imogen up after her.

"Yes, children." Bernadette giggled. "But remember your promise to me."

"We will, not for a month."

"Good, now go on, we can take care of ourselves." Bernadette made shooing signs with her hands.

Needing no second bidding the two of them skipped from the room.

"It *is* just like having kids," said Bernadette to Maneet.

"You handled it very well though. My mother would have taken her sandal to my arse."

"Yes, well, the less said about it that under the present circumstances..."

"Sure. I never understood the attraction really for *that* particular fetish. My mother spanked any such potential ideas out of me, and I can assure you it was very painful."

"We're all different." Bernadette laughed. "But I gather you had a bit of a strict upbringing."

"Oh, in lots of ways, yes, but it's the Indian way. Indian mothers have a reputation and mine was no exception. She loved us deeply in lots of ways as did my dad. She was the disciplinarian, he the indulgent one."

"Will you do the same to your children?" Eve wondered.

"I don't know." Maneet pondered this for a moment. "I hope I would not. Assuming I have children, of course. I mean, it's expected of me."

"Don't you want them?"

"I don't know."

"What if it was you and Lunara?" Bernadette asked her, sliding in the awkward question.

"Then, it would be different." Maneet grew misty eyed.

"Think carefully, darling, about your actions. That's all I'm saying. Anyway, we should shower, get changed and there's the pool." Bernadette got up and held her hand up for Eve.

Maneet watched them enviously. "I wish Lunara was here," she said suddenly.

"I'm sure D'Arcy would let you bring her, sometime." Bernadette smiled.

"Really? Would she invite me again?"

"I'm pretty sure you've made the friend list under the circumstances."

"God, how lovely. Anyway, I've seen the pool and I can't wait to swim in it."

"Not to mention the jacuzzi." Eve laughed.

"Come on, darling." Bernadette pulled her towards the door.

"See what I mean?" Eve winked at Maneet. "So assertive."

* * *

The weekend seemed to go quite swimmingly after that. Nothing much of great importance was done and

Bernadette enjoyed the opportunity to simply relax with Eve. They used the pool, the gym, walked in the garden, and ate delicious meals prepared by D'Arcy's chef. Eve gave them all a massage, as she said it was good practice for her course. They pronounced her to be excellent at it.

D'Arcy and Imogen seemed to have taken on a new lease of life. Their romance was blooming once more, and they spent a lot of the weekend holding hands or entwined around each other.

On Sunday morning, Bernadette received a call from Olivia.

"Hi," she said answering her mobile and drawing a little apart from the others.

"How's it all going up at the mansion?" Olivia asked her.

"It has been somewhat eventful, and I'll tell you about it sometime. Nothing to do with any security threats though."

"Eventful?" Bernadette heard the curiosity in Olivia's voice.

"Let's just say we helped Imogen and D'Arcy smooth out some relationship issues."

"Ah! Say no more." Olivia chuckled. "I didn't know you were a relationship counsellor too."

"Perforce, yes, and Eve too."

"I'll remember that, if Carole and I ever need your services." Olivia laughed at her own joke before continuing. "Anyway, I managed to track down the CCTV of the that four by four."

"Oh?"

"I'm afraid it wasn't so helpful. The car has stolen plates. It will probably turn up as a burned-out wreck soon in some abandoned warehouse. I'll keep an eye on the daily bulletins. We might get forensics off it. In the meantime, I checked out Maneet's place, and I swung by yours but nothing untoward as far as I can see."

"Oh." Bernadette tried to keep the disappointment out of her voice.

"It's as much as I can do without an official investigation and, of course, as you know, that could get messy right now. I'm trying to do all this under the radar, sorry."

"Don't be, we appreciate everything you are doing."

"The question is what do you want to do. Do you want to go back home tonight, all of you?"

Bernadette paused for a moment, she had planned on doing so, and they would have to go home at some point. She hadn't any work clothes either. They could stay another night and go home early, drop off Maneet or take her to work.

"Can I let you know? I'll talk to everyone. I'm thinking we could stay one more night and drive home in the morning instead."

"Sure, ring me back, I just need to know so I can give you an escort."

"Thanks."

Bernadette disconnected and joined the others.

"That was Olivia," she announced. "She found the four by four on CCTV, but it wasn't helpful..." She went on to outline the discussion she had just had, and the options.

"Of course, you must stay here the night," said D'Arcy at once. "I won't hear of you going back today, it's obviously not safe. You need security, I can get my firm to sort it out."

"I don't think we need to quite go down that route, yet," Bernadette demurred. "Although I think you should beef up your own security."

"Yes, you're right." D'Arcy sighed. "But if you're sure? I'm worried about all of you, and that includes Maneet."

"Really?" Maneet looked surprised.

"Yes, of course, you're my friend now, of course, I would worry about you!" D'Arcy shot her an earnest look.

"Really? Oh, well."

"Look, I promise you if things change, we'll take you up on your offer," said Bernadette soothingly.

"OK, well, anyway, I'm going to send a security man with Imogen!" said D'Arcy firmly. "And don't you dare disagree with me, darling." Her chin came up with a determined look.

"Far be it from me." Imogen held up her hands in supplication.

"Right, it's settled, I will talk to Carragh. You can all stay tonight, and then go home in the morning."

"Fine, that's good. I'll phone Olivia back," said Bernadette dialling the number.

D'Arcy was more than pleased to have them for a bit longer, and she celebrated by having the Chef make steak, chips and salad for dinner which pleased them all. They watched one of her movies together and went to bed.

"Do you think everything will be OK?" said Eve as they cuddled up close under the blankets.

"I don't know, darling, but it's probably a good thing the conservatory is put off. I want you to stay indoors locked up, OK?"

"Yes, yes I will." Eve kissed her softly.

"I love you, you're everything to me."

"And you to me, you need to take care too."

"I will, I promise you."

"At least we sorted out Imogen and D'Arcy."

"Yes, thank God!"

"OK, Kiss me..."

Bernadette moved her lips closer to Eve's.

"And then?"

"You know what happens then... don't you?"

"Mmm... hmm..."

CHAPTER SEVEN

The next morning was quite a bustle. Eve and Bernadette woke early, showered and changed. Eve packed the bags after they had dressed. When they arrived in the kitchen, D'Arcy was cooking breakfast, standing in a robe with bare feet and her hair hanging loose at the back. Bernadette thought privately she looked utterly ravishing, and it was easy to see how Imogen loved her and was so physically attracted to her. There was no denying D'Arcy was a catch in that respect and if Imogen wanted a trophy wife, D'Arcy was it. However, this was not Imogen's motivation and Bernadette knew they were actually besotted with each other. She was happy for them both.

"Oh, hi," said D'Arcy breezily. "Sit down, breakfast will only be a moment, darlings."

They were shortly joined by Imogen, and Maneet. D'Arcy soon placed a plate of toast, on the table with coffee. Then she doled out plates of fried eggs, bacon, sausages and tomatoes.

"Oh God, this is glorious," said Maneet cutting into her eggs after placing them onto a slice of toast. "I normally just have a bowl of cereal."

"Eve says that a good breakfast is the key to a good day," Bernadette told her.

"And I completely agree!" D'Arcy sat down with her own plate containing a hearty portion. It was amazing to Bernadette how D'Arcy could maintain her figure with such a healthy appetite, but she seemed to run on rocket fuel.

"She does," Imogen added. "She feeds me like this every day."

"And when I'm away Cheffie will make sure you get a good breakfast too, darling."

"Wow, well, I didn't know that!" said Bernadette impressed.

"Oh, well, I got the idea from Eve and when I told D'Arcy, she completely agreed."

"I did, darling, you're such a wise one, Eve," D'Arcy trilled.

"She's a little witch!" Bernadette said affectionately.

"Oh, don't say so."

"Oh, but I am D'Arcy, I am Bernadette's little witch." Eve winked at her.

D'Arcy looked from one to the other and then they all burst out laughing.

"Carragh will drive Imogen to the office," said D'Arcy. "I've got a bodyguard for her who will arrive this morning."

"OK," Bernadette replied. It seemed a sensible move. "We'll drive out together, Olivia will arrive soon, and she can escort us most of the way."

"Good!" D'Arcy said approvingly.

"Could I go with Imogen, perhaps? I can get picked up from your offices," said Maneet.

"Sure, why not," Imogen agreed.

"Anyway," D'Arcy announced putting down her cup. "I've been thinking about the wedding, darlings. And, Imogen, I don't know if you are going to like my idea, but Maneet has inspired me so much, I think we should have an Indian wedding instead of a normal old boring one."

There was silence at the table for a moment and then they all burst out laughing.

"What? What's so funny?" D'Arcy protested.

"Oh, you are, darling, you're adorable." Imogen took her hand and squeezed it affectionately.

"But Imogen, don't you see what fun it would be?"

"Darling, I think you really have to be Indian, and probably Hindu, to have an Indian wedding, even though I think it would be incredibly entertaining I'm sure," said Bernadette diplomatically.

"Oh? Oh!" D'Arcy looked disappointed.

Maneet caught Bernadette's look and chimed in, "She's right really, D'Arcy. I mean, you know some people could be offended you know, these days and stuff."

"Oh, really? That's a shame, it seemed such a good idea." D'Arcy was quiet for a moment, and then brightened up, "Oh well, it can't be helped. I suppose we'll go for a normal one then."

"Will you both wear wedding dresses?" Maneet asked politely.

"Oh yes, we will, won't we, darling?" D'Arcy looked at Imogen.

"Of course!"

Breakfast having been consumed, a tearful D'Arcy waved them all goodbye from the front door. Bernadette looked back at her and thought about how D'Arcy always cried when they left after staying the weekend. It was touching in some ways. D'Arcy wore her emotions on her sleeve and was still very much a child in many ways. The woman who had never had to really grow up, that was D'Arcy. Imogen had brought some measure of maturity to her life, and although it had gone off the rails somewhat, Bernadette hoped it was all now back on track.

"That was a weekend and a half," said Eve, as she slipped into the passenger seat.

"Yes, I need a weekend to recover," Bernadette agreed, gunning the motor into life.

They eased out of the driveway with Carragh following in the black Merc, and Olivia was waiting in a squad car just outside the gate. They drove in convoy to Dublin, past Bernadette's offices, where Imogen and Maneet were dropped off, before heading for Bernadette's house. Olivia came in for a cup of tea while Bernadette went upstairs to change.

"Darling, you need to wear that grey skirt suit, a nice sky-blue blouse, and the pink mules," Eve called after her.

"OK."

"I always dress her in the mornings," said Eve to Olivia who had listened to this exchange with interest.

Olivia said nothing and went back to stirring her tea.

Bernadette returned downstairs and did a twirl for Eve.

"Beautiful," said her wife. She had already arranged Bernadette's hair and makeup at D'Arcy's.

"We can go when you finish your tea," Bernadette told Olivia.

"Thanks, and this tea is almost as good as your office tea," Olivia observed.

"A compliment indeed." Bernadette laughed.

"I've been to a real Japanese tea ceremony," Eve told them.

"Have you? I'd love that!" said Olivia.

"You should go with Carole," said Bernadette.

"Yes, it would be nice. Maybe one day." Olivia sighed leaving them with the impression she was very unlikely to actually carry out such a plan. She consumed the tea and Bernadette said goodbye in her usual fashion to Eve.

"Wow, *that* was hot!" Olivia said impressed.

"I can vouch for it," Bernadette agreed.

She drove to the office with Olivia in tow, parked the car and went inside. Olivia waved as she eased her squad car past and headed back to the Garda station. Bernadette dropped her keys as usual with Juanita, although the thought did cross her mind that perhaps she shouldn't be asking Juanita to move her car. She quashed it. These incidents shouldn't stop them from living their lives.

Once in her office, she was joined by Imogen.

"Is your, err, bodyguard here?" she asked.

"No, but he will be soon."

Imogen accepted the coffee from Bernadette and sipped it.

"I want to thank you, and Eve, so much, for what you did. You really saved our relationship!"

"We were glad to help, darling, but you saved it yourself with communication."

"But without you, we would never have got there."

"Well, I just comforted you, Eve did the groundwork with D'Arcy." Bernadette shrugged unwilling to be made the heroine of the hour.

"What, happened, you know between Eve and D'Arcy, did she?"

"She slapped D'Arcy, yes. Eve said D'Arcy was becoming hysterical and it was all she could think of. She gave her a hard slap across her cheek and D'Arcy stopped. Then after a while, she was able to talk to her properly."

"Goodness," said Imogen, "I never thought Eve would..."

"Do such a thing?"

"Not that D'Arcy didn't deserve it," Imogen reflected.

"We're not going down that road, darling, are we!" Bernadette stated this in firm tones.

"I know and I made a promise and I'm going to keep it," Imogen said meekly.

"Good! Anyway, Eve's not like that, well, not really. She said it was a last resort."

"Of course." Imogen shrugged.

"Anyway, I'm glad things are mended, and if I was you, I'd get on with the wedding, my sweet."

"Yes, you're right, we need to. I need to stop pussyfooting around."

"Absolutely, but for now, let's make sure we are prepped for court tomorrow."

"Sure. What are we going to do about going home?" Imogen wondered.

"We'll go as normal. We can't live our lives expecting Olivia to escort us everywhere, anyway, you've got Carragh and the new bodyguard."

"Yes, but what about you?" Imogen's face took on a worried expression.

"I'm sure everything will be OK. I mean, letting tyres down is a bit childish. Perhaps they'll stop now, and we can all just get back to normal."

"If you say so." Imogen didn't appear convinced.

In truth, Bernadette was trying to convince herself. She did not know the answer to Imogen's question and was trying to put it out of her mind.

*　*　*

It was just after lunch when the door of Bernadette's office flew open and pinged hard against the doorstop, making her jump.

"What on earth?" Bernadette exclaimed looking up from her computer.

"Bernadette, you must come, you must come now, quick!" Juanita was breathless from apparently running up the stairs, an exertion she would undoubtedly not have indulged in were it not important.

"Whatever is wrong, darling?" said Bernadette getting up.

"Come, just come and look... you must look!" Juanita exclaimed waving her hands wildly to emphasise the importance.

"Alright, alright I'm coming."

They were met at the top of the stairs by Imogen and Alison who had heard the door bang open and had come to see what the fuss was about.

"What's happening?" Imogen enquired with interest.

"Come on!" urged Juanita. "We can't stand talking here, we must go!"

Bernadette shrugged at Imogen and followed Juanita downstairs. With what was now an entourage in tow Juanita led them out of the office and onto the road outside. Bernadette's car was parked just one space up from the front door. Juanita took them down the steps to the car and pointed dramatically at it.

"Look!" she commanded.

"It's my car," said Bernadette nonplussed.

"No! LOOK!" Juanita directed their attention to the nearside tyre at the front.

There unmistakably was an ugly looking knife sticking out of the tyre wall with a note tied to it.

"Fuck!" said Bernadette tears springing to her eyes.

"What does the note say?" Alison asked going down to examine it. She bent down and looked up at them her expression very serious.

"What does it say?" Bernadette asked her.

"It says, 'you are next you immigrant loving bitch.'"

"Fuck, oh shit!" Bernadette said with a crack in her voice. It's one thing to be brave but another to be faced with something like this.

"Just what I did say when I saw this," Juanita announced. "I said fuck and also the shit, many times."

"It's OK," said Imogen putting her arm protectively around Bernadette's shoulders.

"No, it's not, it's fucking not," said Bernadette tears coursing down her cheeks.

"Right, no, of course not, but let's get organised," said Imogen practically. "Alison and Juanita, you need to take some photos of this with your phones, but don't touch it. I'm going to take Bernadette inside, and then you two come inside also. I'm going to call Olivia."

"The Garda?" said Alison.

"Yes, things are getting out of hand, we need to take some action."

Imogen hurried Bernadette indoors, she was still crying and unable to think straight. They bumped into Andrew who was leaning out of his office doorway.

"Oh, my goodness what's happened?" he asked at once very concerned. "What is going on, come into my office, come in, come in."

For all his seeming concerns about details, and their jokes, Andrew was very quick to act when there was a crisis. He certainly perceived there to be one brewing.

Imogen sat Bernadette down at the meeting table in Andrew's office and began to explain what had been happening. While she was doing so, Alison and Juanita joined them having taken the photos, and showed them to Andrew. He tutted over these in some alarm.

"Why didn't you tell me about the tyres and so forth?" he demanded at the end of the explanation.

"We didn't think it was as serious as this!" Bernadette said suddenly having found her voice and recovered enough to think.

"It evidently is serious. I mean, I'm one of the senior partners here, I have a right to know about security issues for everyone's sake."

"Well, we are telling you now aren't we!" Imogen said in admonishing tones.

"Yes, I'm sorry, of course. I was just a bit shocked myself that's all. Goodness, what a to do and what *are* we to do?"

"One thing we're not doing is getting off this case," said Bernadette with sudden anger.

"Well, now, Bernadette, have you considered, I mean..." Andrew began but seeing the martial light in her eyes he trailed off.

"I'm calling Olivia," said Imogen getting up and dialling her number.

"That's great, but what about the other staff, safety and so on?" Andrew wondered out loud. "I'm not worried for myself of course, but the others, I mean it's very alarming."

"For a start, it's targeted at me and probably Imogen," said Bernadette. "But in any case, I think it's time to bring in the big guns."

"What?" Andrew paled at this reference.

"Not literally, Andrew," said Bernadette. "It's time to use my contact in the Garda."

"Alright, fine, but I want to be kept in the loop," Andrew said firmly.

"We will convene again this afternoon, just let me get things in motion." Bernadette turned to Juanita and Alison. "I'm sorry about all this and that you had to see the knife in the tyre. If you're worried for your safety just let me know, I'll do whatever is needed to ensure you feel safe."

"Ach, I don't care about these knives, in Spain we have much bigger knives," said Juanita dismissively heading back to her desk.

"Just let me know what's happening on it," said Alison leaving the room also.

"Yes of course," Bernadette replied. "OK, I'm going to call DCS Brogan."

∗ ∗ ∗

Within the space of less than an hour, Olivia and DCS Brogan were in the meeting room with Bernadette and Imogen. Tea and coffee had been provided although by the time the tale was told Brogan looked as if he wanted something much stronger.

Olivia had been re-introduced to him, as he had met her briefly at the wedding, and he acknowledged her part in assisting them with a gruff but friendly smile.

After a few moments of silence, Brogan spoke. "I'm very saddened by this news, very saddened indeed," he said to Bernadette. Then he scowled and got up pacing the room like a caged animal.

"What am I talking about? I am fucking incandescent, fucking incandescent with rage that this, this has been happening in the fucking Garda! I am fucking furious some fucking tossbag white supremacists are in our organisation. One thing I cannot stand is racism in any form, or anything else like that in the Garda. Motherfucking turdballs, I will have their fucking balls on a fucking platter if I can find out who they are. Sticking knives into people's tyres, whatever fucking next. Fucking dirtballs. I will find these people or my names, not Jim O'Shanter, which of course it's not, but never mind about that."

He came to a stop glaring and nobody in particular before resuming his seat. Bernadette and Imogen were by now starting to be used to his sudden fits of temper, and any of his Foxcatchers would have told them this was entirely normal for Brogan. Olivia, never having witnessed it before seemed spectacularly impressed by this performance. Having got things off his chest, Brogan calmed down.

"Right," he said. "This is going to get sorted and no mistake. Fortunately, my Foxcatchers unit is not busy at the moment and so I'm going to be getting them involved in the investigation and protection. This doesn't happen on my watch, not on your Nelly or I'm a monkey's uncle." After this somewhat esoteric pronouncement, he turned to Olivia. "You are seconded with immediate effect to this investigation, and I'll let your superintendent know."

Olivia flushed with pride. "Thank you, sir," she stammered.

"Yes, well, you've obviously got your head in the right place so it's only fair. Now, first things first. Obviously, the targets here are you, Bernadette, and possibly your wife, and Imogen, and I guess your fiancé."

"I have got a bodyguard and so does D'Arcy," Imogen ventured.

"Not armed, dear girl, not armed," said Brogan. "No, this calls for proper armed protection. I will assign an officer each to you four from my own units. I'll also put a twenty-four-hour armed guard at your office for the moment. Olivia, you'll start investigating these fuckers right away with my blessing, you can liaise with DI Gallway on getting things underway, alright?"

"You've got it," said Olivia impressed.

"Good, well now that's sorted. What about this court case you're involved in?" Brogan asked Bernadette.

"Well, as we've said, it seems very odd how it's turned out, and we believe our client was provoked," said Bernadette.

"Yes, it is very odd, I grant you. I am, naturally, not supposed to get involved in these things. At least not overtly. However, I'm not happy at the way things are turning out and if this Maguire character did provoke her then he's going to find himself in very hot water indeed."

"There is something more, Jack," said Bernadette, "we've discovered about Maguire."

"Oh?"

"I didn't want to say as it's evidence but under the circumstances."

"Go on spit it out, my lips are sealed, as you should very well know!" he replied with a smile.

"Yes, sorry, well. We discovered that before he joined the Garda, he was a member of *White Knights of Ireland* a white supremacist group."

"Was he, was he indeed," said Brogan his brow clouding over and once more he looked thunderous. "Well, Olivia, I want you to investigate this character, discreetly and see what else you can find out."

"Yes, sir."

"This is all hush hush, OK? I don't want this leaking out generally to the force, exactly what you're doing. We can't keep the tyre thing under wraps, nor what my team is up to, but we don't want people thinking we're investigating Garda officers, no. We can say we're looking at white supremacist organisations. I can trust the Foxcatchers, and I need to trust you, can I?"

"Yes, completely, sir."

"Good because if there is any hint that this fucker is involved in anything like this, I'll be personally nailing his fucking bollocks to the ceiling."

"Sir." Olivia shot a glance at the others and they were all undoubtedly pondering on the image of Brogan doing exactly that to the unsuspecting Maguire.

"Right, good. Now justice must naturally run its course, but I'm not having these fuckers impeding it. Anything we find out, we'll let you know. But I've got to go and see the AC and inform him of what I'm doing. I can assure you he will be as furious as I am."

"Thank you, Jack, thanks so much," said Bernadette. "And Olivia too."

"Yes, well it's the least I can do. Now I'll be off, the Foxcatchers will be in touch, I'm sure, and your protection officers will turn up shortly. If any other member of your staff gets threatened let me know, but in the meantime hopefully, the armed presence will put these people off. If it does at least that, then we've done our job."

"Thanks again," said Bernadette.

"Thanks," said Imogen accompanying Brogan out.

"Well," said Bernadette smiling at Olivia. "You've got your wish, to work with the Foxcatchers."

"I know. The world moves in mysterious ways indeed."

"Yes. It certainly does, I didn't expect this when I got involved with Maneet's case for starters."

"What about Maneet?" Imogen said suddenly.

"She probably needs a protection officer," said Olivia. "I'll speak to Brogan right away."

"Good, then I guess we just need to wait."

"Absolutely," Olivia said, and then her phone began to ring, she picked it up. "Oh, right, yes, sir, well, sure, thanks, yes, sure, Seamus it is. There are a few things to discuss, can I call you back in five. Sure. OK." She disconnected. "That was…"

"Seamus Gallway?" Bernadette smiled.

"Yes, yes indeed, anyway I'd better get on. His team are on the way. You just need to wait. Can I use this meeting room for the moment?"

"Sure, of course. I need to phone Eve and tell her to expect guests."

"I'll speak to D'Arcy," said Imogen. "What about court tomorrow?"

"We go ahead with it, I guess." Bernadette shrugged. "We can take our armed protection officers with us. We will also need to brief the rest of the staff, so let's do so before the Foxcatchers arrive."

✳ ✳ ✳

After some time had passed, several Garda detectives arrived at the offices, along with a forensics team. Bernadette was unable to use her car and needed to remain at the office to greet the newcomers. Two armed protection officers with SMG's were positioned at the entrance to their offices and would remain in place twenty-four-seven for the moment. Olivia had set up a temporary HQ in the meeting room where the Foxcatchers team was currently assembled. DI Seamus Gallway had not accompanied his team, but instead sent DS O'Flynn to oversee the investigation. Once they'd completed their work there, they would move back to Ballysruth or take a temporary office at the HQ in Dublin.

Imogen and Bernadette were ushered into the meeting room by Olivia. Bernadette looked around at the faces while she and Imogen were introduced.

"This is Bernadette Mackenna, I'm sure you probably know, and her junior counsel Imogen Stewart," Olivia was saying. "Now this is DS Kathy O'Flynn who is running the investigation."

"Hi," said Bernadette holding out her hand to shake O'Flynn's. O'Flynn was of medium height, with blonde hair, brown eyes and was quite curvaceous Bernadette noted. O'Flynn was wearing a black suit with a light blue blouse, and court shoes.

"Hi, nice to meet you." O'Flynn smiled. "Let me introduce the rest of the team. Here is DS Aileen Hughes, DS Iona Healy, DS Nikki Kruger, DS May Zhang, and protection officer Matelda Ossani."

It was interesting that Seamus had sent an all-woman team, but Bernadette was not to know that the Foxcatcher unit was predominantly staffed by female officers. He had remained behind at their HQ in Ballysruth, along with his number two DS Connor O'Rorden and DS Brendan Duffy to continue with other work.

Bernadette and Imogen nodded to each of them, and they all smiled back.

"Right, so Aileen and Iona are assigned as protection officers to you Bernadette and your wife, Eve, is it? Nikki and May are assigned to Imogen and D'Arcy, and Matelda will be assigned to Maneet. Olivia and I will manage the investigation between us for the moment, unless we need anyone else, and we can get them up from our unit."

"Great," said Bernadette. "Look, you can use this meeting room for as long as you need. Imogen will arrange for security passes for all of you for the front door. Also, for the armed officers out the front so they can come inside for the loo or get coffees and stuff. The same goes for you all, help yourselves to the refreshments in the kitchen."

"Thanks. We are grateful for your cooperation." O'Flynn smiled.

"On the contrary, we're grateful for everything you're doing for us," Bernadette demurred.

"We're doing our duty. Brogan has briefed us, and I have to say none of us is happy to hear about this kind of thing in the Garda."

"No, indeed."

O'Flynn became a little more business like now the pleasantries were out of the way. "Anyway, you probably all want to get home. Bernadette, we need you to leave your car here until we are done with it. Once we have then you can get the tyre replaced."

"Thanks, yes it would be nice, it's been a long and quite exhausting day one way or another."

"I'll let you go then, leave things to us."

"Look, erm, if you need an extra pair of hands, my lead investigator Micky is available," Bernadette said after a moment's thought. "He's good at researching things."

"Sure," said O'Flynn. "Send him to us, I'm sure we could very likely use his help."

"I'll let him know," said Imogen leaving the room at once. Both she and Bernadette knew Micky would be thrilled to be working with the Garda.

O'Flynn turned away and Bernadette found Aileen Hughes, a sparky blonde standing next to her with grey eyes, a grey skirt suit but natty red shirt under it and high heels. Beside her was her slightly taller counterpart, Iona Healy, who had her dark hair cut in a bob. Her eyes were greeny-blue, she had sensuous lips, and wore a navy blue skirt suit with lower heels than her colleague.

"Hi, I'm Aileen, in case you forgot, and this is Iona, we'll drive you home, and be with you twenty-four hours a day. Well, not literally of course." Hughes laughed at her own joke.

"OK, great, I'll just get my stuff, and we can go."

"Good, good."

Imogen came back into the meeting room with Micky in tow. He was introduced to O'Flynn and Imogen was reintroduced to Nikki Kruger who was thin, tall with shortish blonde hair and blue eyes. She was wearing a black suit and white shirt and spoke with a broad South African drawl. Beside Kruger was May Zhang, shorter with oval brown eyes, a rosebud pair of lips, and Bernadette thought she was very beautiful. Zhang's hair which she had recently grown longer, was braided into a single ponytail and curled up behind her head. She looked very smart in a black suit and crisp white shirt.

Imogen gave Bernadette a hug. "See you tomorrow, darling. You go on home. I'll sort the passes out and then I'll go too."

"Thanks, darling, see you tomorrow then, all ready for court."

"Yes."

Bernadette left the office accompanied by Hughes and Healy.

* * *

On the short drive home, Hughes kept up a stream of amiable chatter. Bernadette responded in kind although her thoughts were very much on the events of the day and what they had got themselves into. She was grateful for Brogan's intervention, however. Hughes pulled the car into Bernadette's driveway and once the gate was closed, they got out and followed Bernadette to the front door.

The door was opened by Eve, who stood there in bare feet smiling wearing jeans, a t-shirt.

"Hi," she said. "Come in, come in."

"Hi, darling," said Bernadette moving up to kiss her. She turned and introduced Eve to Hughes and Healy.

Once inside Bernadette kicked off her shoes and hung up her jacket.

"Do you mind if we take our shoes off too?" Hughes asked politely.

"Sure, please, make yourselves at home," said Bernadette. "And welcome to our house."

"Yes," said Eve. "Welcome, come in the living room, I'll put the kettle on. Dinner won't be long. We can get to know each other in the meantime."

"Sure," said Hughes and she removed her heels with a noticeable sigh of relief. "I love these shoes, but I love being barefoot."

"Me too," said Healy removing her own shoes.

They followed Bernadette into the living room. Hughes and Healy sat next to each other on one sofa, and once the tea and coffee were made, Bernadette sat with Eve on the other.

"So," said Hughes smiling and sipping her drink.

"Look," said Bernadette, "you can see we're gay and a couple and I hope that doesn't..."

"Make us uncomfortable?" Hughes let out a crack of laughter.

Bernadette regarded her slightly puzzled.

"We are gay too," Healy explained with a twinkle in her eye. "In fact, we're engaged."

"Oh? Oh!"

"So, we are far from uncomfortable, we've never felt more comfortable in our lives," said Hughes.

So saying, she and Healy moved closer together, and Hughes slipped her hand into Healy's.

"Then that sorts out the next question, as we've only got one guest bedroom," Eve laughed.

"We will be very happy to occupy it," said Healy.

"Anyway, let's get the formalities over so you understand what close protection means for you," said Hughes.

"OK." Bernadette picked up her coffee and took a sip.

"We need to see the layout of the property here, and also know all the alarm codes, etc. I will be your close protection officer," Hughes said, "if that's OK."

"Of course," said Bernadette.

"Trust you to get the blonde one." Eve laughed.

"You can change if you like," said Healy.

"No, it's fine," said Bernadette.

"Great," Hughes continued. "So, I will accompany you everywhere you go, and Iona will stay with Eve. We are armed of course." She opened her jacket to reveal her Glock pistol. "We also have submachine guns in the car. Iona will keep one inside handy just in case. Obviously, I won't come into the loo with you when you are at court and stuff, but if you do go then, I'll be outside, and at home, we'll be here with you and in the next room at night. If anything happens or goes down, then you need to follow our instructions to the letter. Does that make sense?"

"Perfectly," said Bernadette. "And just once again, we're so grateful—"

"It's fine," Hughes cut her off with a smile. "We were kicking our heels down in HQ and this is a welcome change from church crimes I can tell you."

"Really, I'd love to hear more about your work."

"Oh well, we can tell you over dinner, but we certainly remember you from the Diana case."

"Yes, that was something," Bernadette replied recalling it.

"Anyway," said Eve, "we should have dinner. I've made *beef bourguignon* I hope that you'll like it."

"Oh God, it sounds delicious already," said Healy.

"Eve is the cook in our relationship, and she's fantastic at it."

"I can hardly wait, I can smell it and it's making my mouth water," said Hughes.

"Let's eat." Eve smiled getting up. "We can talk over dinner."

* * *

Over the meal, which Hughes and Healy pronounced to be delicious, the formal atmosphere became quickly informal. Wine was declined by the detectives as they were now on duty around the clock, so Eve put a bottle of sparkling water on the table instead. Eve had shown Hughes and Healy the layout of the house, and the gym. She said they were more than welcome to use it.

"Eve was a personal trainer," said Bernadette. "And she still trains me to the point of exhaustion."

Hughes laughed at this and said perhaps they could join in the training sessions if they had any.

"For sure," said Eve.

"You should just continue as normal," said Healy. "Don't mind us."

"Thanks, we feel as though you are our guests though, so we want you to feel comfortable. You don't have to dress formally and so on, if don't want to," said Bernadette, "we don't."

"Thanks, we already feel at home, and I must get the recipe off you, Eve," said Hughes.

"She's the cook and she looks after me very well," Healy added.

"When do you two plan to marry then?" Bernadette enquired.

"Oh, as soon as we can really, cases permitting and so on."

"Don't leave it too long."

"No," Eve agreed. "Besides it's a lot of fun, the wedding."

"I'm sure." Hughes laughed.

The conversation turned to other topics, and after a discussion about the arrangements for the next day, the dishes were cleared away and they all turned in for the night.

"I guess that curtails our activities for a while," Eve whispered, as she and Bernadette lay together in bed.

"When this is all over, I'll give you the best Shibari session you ever had." Bernadette kissed her softly.

"Ooo, sounds exciting. I'd better make sure it's a very long list then."

"I bet you will." They kissed more urgently, and Bernadette pulled in closer. "Anyway, I'm sure if we're quiet, we can do most things."

"Oh, like what?" Eve's eyes were teasing her in the half light.

"Like fucking you the way I want to right now."

"You mean like this?" Eve's hand ran lightly down Bernadette's body and arrived between her legs.

"Oh fuck, yes... oh yes... I want it... and God do I need it..." Bernadette whispered gasping at the touch.

"And you are going to get it..."

"Oh... yes... fuck... yes... please... oh... yes..."

CHAPTER EIGHT

The morning light crept under the blinds, and Bernadette stirred. She was spooned up with Eve who had her arms around her. The alarm would go off soon. Bernadette began to turn around to face Eve who woke up sleepily.

"Hi, darling." Eve smiled.

"Hi." Bernadette kissed her and then began to slide out from the bedclothes.

"Where are you going?" Eve pouted.

"I've got court, and we've got guests who will want to use the bathroom."

Eve came fully awake at this.

"Yes, you're right, go on then, get your shower. I'll sort your clothes out."

"Thank you, my love."

Bernadette eased out of the bed, put on a robe and disappeared to the bathroom. She returned shortly and sat while Eve arranged her hair. She had laid out a black skirt suit, black high heels and a cream blouse. The first day of court always needed to be formal. They could never tell who the judge might be, and it behoved them to look very smart.

Once the lay of the land was discovered, it might be possible to dress a little softer depending on the case, and the witness. It was all part of the game, to dress for a power play or to seem more conciliatory. In any case, they would wear their gowns over the top of their normal clothes. Wigs were no longer the fashion in the Irish courts, judges and barristers had for the most part dispensed with these.

"Thanks, darling," said Bernadette when Eve had finished. Eve dropped a kiss on her lips and went downstairs after completing Bernadette's makeup. Once Bernadette was dressed, she followed and found Eve serving up Hughes and Healy in the dining room where she joined them.

"Wow," said Hughes admiringly, "You look every inch the barrister, I'd certainly be intimidated."

Bernadette laughed, shrugging it off and took a seat. Eve slid a plate of scrambled eggs, bacon, toast and mushrooms in front of her and then gave her a cup of coffee. Eve took a place herself next to Bernadette.

"Oh, she can be very assertive when she wants to be." Eve giggled.

"Can she now?" Hughes grinned slyly catching the undertone.

"So, Eve does this for you every day, she says," Healy said.

"Yes, she's a treasure, she pampers me and takes care of me in every way, I'm so lucky." Bernadette smiled before consuming a forkful of eggs and toast.

"Must be nice." Healy sighed dramatically.

"Oh! I take care of you very well and you know it." Hughes said but her eyes were twinkling.

"But do you lay out my clothes, do my hair and makeup?"

"Behave!" Hughes said playfully.

"Now who's being assertive."

Eve and Bernadette observed this exchange with interest. It was clear these two were very much in love and also in tune. Bernadette wondered about their relationship with the natural curiosity one has, but it wasn't her place to ask. No doubt such things might emerge in time depending upon how close they got.

"These eggs are delicious," said Hughes, "meltingly so."

"Kind of you to say so," Eve replied.

The rest of breakfast centred around the day ahead. Eve was wearing her robe and nothing else, whilst the others were fully dressed. Bernadette wondered how long Healy would keep that up, given she was staying at home with Eve. On the other hand, Healy was on duty and so perhaps this was the protocol. Eve, however, was quite persuasive in her way and she hoped her wife would not be a bad influence on Healy. She had said nothing to Eve, however, as they had no idea how long this situation would pertain. It may well go until the trial which under the circumstances might be hurried along somewhat, it would be helpful if so.

With breakfast over, Eve accompanied them to the door, and put her arms around Bernadette's neck for the customary goodbye kiss. The kiss was every bit as mind blowing as it ever was to Bernadette, and Hughes, and Healy looked on with interest.

"Does she do that every day too?" Healy asked, while Eve touched up Bernadette's lip gloss.

"Every day, without fail," Bernadette replied.

"I want to leave my lips on hers, so she doesn't forget me during the day," said Eve.

"You should kiss me goodbye like that," Healy said to Hughes. Her expression was quite serious and Hughes reading it, kissed her lovingly without hesitation for a few long moments.

"Oh fuck!" said Healy.

"Was it not to your liking?" Hughes cocked an eyebrow.

"Far from it, it was absolutely to my liking please do it again tomorrow."

"If it's what you want, honey." Hughes squeezed Healy's hand.

"Shall we go?" said Bernadette.

"Yes, for sure."

"Oh, I forgot to tell you, Iona, my wife is a bit of a witch... so..."

"What?" said Healy her eyes widening.

Bernadette laughed, and so did Hughes, as they left the house.

"What did she mean by that?" Healy said to Eve as they were getting into the car.

"What she said."

"What spells and stuff?"

Eve giggled like a schoolgirl. She stood with Healy and waved goodbye until the car disappeared from view, then went back inside with Healy.

*　*　*

Hughes drove them to the office, and parked. They were due to pick up Zhang and Imogen before heading for court. Bernadette picked up a coffee for her and Imogen, she made one for Hughes.

"I can do that," said Hughes, "You don't have to."

"We're all in this together, aren't we?"

"You're so different to how I imagined you from seeing you in court." Hughes followed her up the stairs.

"How so?"

"I thought you were a hard bitch, to be honest, though sympathetic too and caring."

"And now?" Bernadette paused at the top, interested in the answer.

"You're softer, and so much nicer."

"Well, thanks!" Bernadette laughed.

"I mean it in the nicest possible way."

"I know, and thanks, for the compliment."

Hughes smiled and said, "I'm going to check up with the team, let me know when you're ready to go."

"Sure." Bernadette went into her office and was just sitting on the sofa when Imogen arrived.

"Hi, darling, coffee?" said Bernadette handing her a cup.

"Thanks, I've just been making sure we've everything for court."

"Great." Bernadette sipped her drink knowing they had some time before they needed to leave. "How's your new armed protection?"

"Oh, well I've got the gorgeous May and I've left Nikki at home with D'Arcy. They hit it off right away and I can see they'll get along like a house on fire."

"Great, and how did your new bodyguard and Carragh take it?"

"Oh, he's happy enough, I don't need the bodyguard now I've got May. She's gone to check in with her team in the meeting room."

"Yes, Aileen did too."

"Isn't it a bit weird though, having these extra people around?" Imogen set down her half empty cup.

"Yes, but apparently Aileen and Iona are a couple, so that suits us very well."

"Lucky," said Imogen.

"Everything else OK?" Bernadette raised an eyebrow.

"Yes, and I'm keeping my promise. The paddle and stuff have been put away in the cupboard. We're being normal, as much as we can be, but things are good. D'Arcy is very loving to me, and I think we are definitely on the mend."

"That's what I like to hear." Bernadette smiled. "Have you discussed wedding plans?"

"We have, and I'm thinking we might go for a small wedding under the circumstances. Just a few guests."

"I think you are wise, what does D'Arcy think?"

"She doesn't want to argue but I can see she is torn. She wants the whole nine yards."

"Maybe you can compromise?"

"Yes. We have to compromise, that's the name of the new game. Not just what Imogen wants. That was wrong of me and selfish."

"Your relationship is maturing, my love."

"I suppose." Imogen sighed. She reached out and held Bernadette's hand briefly. "You helped us so much, both of you. I can't thank you enough."

"Was D'Arcy OK, about, you know... Eve?"

"Slapping her? Don't give it another thought. D'Arcy was fine with it."

"That's good."

"D'Arcy is grateful too, because she didn't know how to tell me things. Now she's no longer afraid to do so."

"Is she going to do this movie?" Bernadette floated the question.

"Yes, she will, and it will be at least six months."

"If you want to take six months, go and be with her then..."

"What?" Imogen cut in with a laugh. "And let some other junior counsel get their feet under my desk."

"I could get a locum or something."

"No, I was born to do this job and I want to do it. Besides, what would I do, kicking my heels on a movie set? I'd be bored shitless."

"The offer's there."

"Thanks, I know you mean well, but no. My place is here, with you!" Imogen said it so emphatically, Bernadette resolved not to mention it again.

If truth be told she didn't want Imogen to go away for six months or any months.

"OK, but you can take a couple of weeks holiday perhaps."

"I'll think about it, when the time comes." Imogen smiled.

"Yes, well, the time has come for court I think, shall we?"

* * *

Hughes drove them to the Criminal Courts of Justice. She parked nearby and they headed for the building and walked up the long sweeping steps. The courthouse was a massive building with a curved fascia of windows. Bernadette and

Imogen had spent many hours at the court and it was equally familiar to the two detectives.

They found a meeting room and Imogen went with Zhang to procure some coffee. Shortly afterwards they returned, and they all sat sipping their drinks. Bernadette liked to do this so that they could relax before court began.

"This is fascinating for me," said Zhang. "I never get to see things from this side of the fence."

"Hopefully you can enjoy the show then," said Bernadette. "Anyway, today is just a formality though slightly unusual since we've got an armed escort."

"Do you think the judge will mention it?" Imogen wondered.

"Most probably, anyway have you a photograph of the tyre?"

"Yes, on my phone."

"We might need it."

"Don't you get nervous?" Hughes asked Bernadette. "I always do when I have to be a witness."

"I get very nervous, but I try not to show it."

"No weakness?"

"Something like that."

"She has a routine," said Imogen, "to calm her and prepare herself to speak, I'm learning it too."

"Ooh, can you teach me?" Zhang said at once.

"Sure, if you like."

"Look at us taking lessons from a defence counsel, traditionally you're the enemy." Hughes laughed taking a sip of her drink.

"I don't like to think of it that way. Of course, court is adversarial, but I don't regard the Garda as our enemy.

Olivia, for example, has been particularly helpful." Bernadette set down her empty cup.

"You're different to other lawyers, more approachable."

"I try to be." Bernadette smiled.

"Don't let it fool you, she's an utter bitch in the courtroom," Imogen said with a smirk.

"When I need to. It's all part of the... persona I suppose. I do what's needed to get the result I'm trying to get."

"I've seen you in action and I'm glad I'm not the one facing you in court," said Hughes.

Imogen's phone buzzed. "Maneet is here and looking for us."

"It's time we got to court anyway," said Bernadette.

They got up, disposed of the empty cups in the bin, and Imogen wheeled the suitcase containing their papers. They had removed the gowns from the case and put them on and suddenly everything seemed a lot more formal. Maneet was waiting for them outside the court with Matelda Ossani. Matelda was Italian and had been attached to the Foxcatchers while on a case in Rome. By accident or design, she had returned to the UK and was now very much part of the team. She was an interpreter by trade with a penchant for something more adventurous. She was trained now as a personal protection officer. Matelda was middle aged, quite toned since recently using the gym, she had short brown hair. Bernadette thought she was good looking and certainly well dressed in a blue skirt suit, white blouse and black court shoes.

"Hi, sorry I meant to be here sooner, this is Matelda, who I'm sure you've met," said Maneet giving Bernadette a hug and then Imogen too.

"Hi," said Matelda with a brief smile.

"Shall we go in?" said Bernadette.

They entered the courtroom en masse, and Imogen showed Maneet to the dock where she took a seat with Matelda. Matelda's presence was explained to the court officer who was to have normally sat with Maneet, and the officer withdrew. Bernadette and the others made their way to their lawyer's station. Imogen began to arrange the papers. Hughes and Zhang stood looking around protectively while this was going on.

The courtroom was like all of the those in the building, of a reasonable size, with public benches at the back. The judge's bench sat up high giving the judge a good view, and behind it were large windows letting in daylight. The walls were wainscoted with a light wood, and there were benches for the lawyer, clerk of the court, and the jury, as well as the witness stand, up near the judge.

Shortly after they were ready and about to be seated, the door opened, and two barristers entered. One of whom, Bernadette presumed was the junior of the other. The first was a woman of Indian descent, who was quite striking though rather severe in demeanour. She carried herself well wearing a blue jacket, trousers, white skirt and very high shiny black heels. Her silky black hair was tied up neatly and business like. Behind her, Bernadette recognised Carole Cooperson, who was a junior barrister for the prosecution service. She was a young blonde with a pretty face, black suit and white shirt, pulling a suitcase.

Bernadette knew Carole very well since she had managed to hook her up with Olivia. Carole flicked her a smile behind her senior's back and then averted her eyes.

Bernadette did not betray that she knew Carole and turned back to her bench. Imogen had not missed the smile either.

While Carole was getting ready, the other barrister came over to them.

"Hi," she said crisply, "I'm Priteshi Patel prosecuting counsel."

"Hi, Bernadette Mackenna," said Bernadette. "This is Imogen Stewart my junior partner."

Priteshi flicked a glance at Imogen but didn't deign to acknowledge her particularly otherwise. Bernadette winced inwardly. She could already tell what sort of barrister Priteshi was and her thoughts about it were not pleasant.

"You're new to the prosecution service, are you not?" she said amiably enough.

"Yes, I am. I replaced Shane Wilson. He went back to England. Now they've got me. I intend to shake things up a bit."

"Indeed." Bernadette kept her voice entirely neutral.

"Anyway, we would all avoid costly proceedings if your client was to plead guilty," said Priteshi.

"We could, but my client isn't going to." There was a hint of steel in Bernadette's tone.

Priteshi didn't bat an eye, this was obviously her opening gambit. "As you wish," she replied with an air of one who had done her duty and was now going to win anyway.

"I do wish it and so does my client."

"OK, well, nice talk." Priteshi turned her back and returned to her bench.

"Nice talk!" Imogen whispered furiously.

"Calm yourself, it's all part of the game." Bernadette was unfazed.

"I'll give her a game!"

"Easy tiger," said Hughes settling in beside her.

"You're right." Imogen sighed and subsided.

Bernadette glanced at Maneet and could see she was staring daggers at Priteshi. Since the judge had not arrived, she wandered over to talk to her.

"Fucking typical, they've put an Indian lawyer up to show they aren't prejudiced!" said Maneet in an infuriated undertone.

"I wouldn't worry about it. I know her sort. Thinks she's won before the game's started."

"Is it a game?" Maneet wondered.

"Oh yes, but a deadly serious one at that." Bernadette winked and returned to her station. As she did so the Tipstaff arrived to announce the judge. The court rose as one and Justice Samuel Buckley entered the room. It was some time since Bernadette had been in a courtroom with this particular judge, and in fact, it was on a very notable murder case. Justice Buckley was around fifty years of age and greying around the temples. He had a kindly face, and a pleasant demeanour. He took his seat and surveyed the courtroom for a few moments.

"So, this is the pre-trial hearing for the case of the DPP versus Maneet Johal-Lynch, am I right?"

"Yes, Judge," said Priteshi rising at once to her feet.

"And you are?" Justice Buckley fixed her with a beady stare.

"Priteshi Patel, Judge, prosecuting counsel, and this is Carole Cooperson, my junior counsel."

"I see," he responded writing something this down in his notes. "Thank you, Ms Patel."

"It's Mrs," said Priteshi.

"Is it?" His tone was sardonic.

"Yes, Judge."

"Very well, thank you, Mrs Patel."

"Thank you, Judge," she said resuming her seat.

He turned his attention to the defence counsel's bench, looking slightly askance at the number of people sitting there.

"Who is the defending counsel?" he asked.

Bernadette stood up, this being her cue.

"Bernadette Mackenna, Mrs," she said at once, learning a lesson from Priteshi's experience.

"I see." Justice Buckley thought for a moment. "I recognise you! You've been in front of me before."

"Yes, Judge, I was, the DPP versus Diana O'Malley." She smiled.

"Ah yes, sad but memorable case. Very good, very good." He paused. "Now, who are all these other people?"

"Judge, if I may, this is Imogen Stewart, my junior counsel. This is DS Hughes and DS Zhang who are armed protection officers assigned to us. Over on the bench, my client Ms Johal-Lynch also has an armed protection officer, Mrs Ossani, beside her."

Justice Buckley blinked rapidly at this intelligence and looked a little nonplussed. Priteshi's head jerked up and she looked over with renewed interest at the defence entourage.

"And exactly why do you need armed protection officers in my courtroom?" Justice Buckley demanded.

"Judge, I am sorry to inform you but a number of unfortunate occurrences culminating with a death threat against myself have arisen since I took on this case. The

Garda have therefore assigned armed officers for the duration of this case."

"Unfortunate events? What kind of unfortunate events?"

"Judge, in the past week, my tyres were deliberately deflated on two occasions, my client was followed by an unknown party in a large black four by four. On Monday a knife was stuck into my car tyre with the words 'you are next, you immigrant loving bitch' written on a note attached to the knife. I think there was no mistaking the intent. We have a photograph of the knife in question if it pleases the court."

Justice Buckley blinked rapidly at this and looked extremely perturbed. He beckoned to Bernadette, and Imogen approached the bench where the clerk of the court took her phone to show it to the judge. He examined the photograph for a few moments and handed it back.

"I see," he said evidently not at all pleased. "Mrs Patel, do you have any knowledge of these events?"

"Judge, no I... I'm sorry... I was not aware." Priteshi stood up. She looked slightly taken aback herself. Bernadette noted this and was happy since it meant Priteshi, or the prosecution service was not part of it.

"Right, well. I'm sorry to hear about this, Mrs Mackenna. Naturally, under the circumstances, I will allow your protection officers to remain. I will have to consider the implications of this quite seriously, however, and perhaps we need to speed up the course of justice as regards this case. Anyway, let us get on with the events of the day. So firstly, Mrs Patel, has the prosecution service provided all of the necessary documents and evidence to the defence?"

"Judge, we have," said Priteshi standing up.

"Good, and, Mrs Mackenna, have the documents been received?"

"They have, Judge," said Bernadette.

"Excellent then that's one thing to tick off the list. I'm glad to see the prosecution service isn't being tardy for a change."

This statement wasn't met with equanimity by Priteshi who looked most put out by this criticism, however, it didn't do to argue with a judge, so she held her peace. All barristers who had attempted this and most had, at one time or another, came unstuck, and usually never did it again.

"Now then, is that your client over there you said, Mrs Mackenna?" The judge glanced at Maneet.

"Yes, Judge. Ms Johal-Lynch."

"Right, Ms Johal-Lynch, kindly stand up."

Maneet did so and waited for his next instruction.

"What is your intention in this case? How are you planning to plead?"

"Not guilty, Judge," she said quietly.

"Very well, we know where we stand, you may be seated." He smiled amiably at her. "Now, Mrs Mackenna, does your client require a jury trial, as in this case it can be dealt with summarily by a judge?"

"My client requests a jury trial," Bernadette replied standing up.

"Fair enough, fair enough."

Priteshi stood up. "Judge, is a jury trial really necessary in this case?"

The question hung in the air like something with a bad odour, while Justice Buckley regarded her as if he could not believe his ears.

Bernadette flicked a quick look down at Imogen. It would be unthinkable for a prosecution lawyer to question the defendant's right to trial by jury.

"It is her legal right," said the judge in a mild tone which was at odds with his expression.

"Judge, I don't like to be forward, but the evidence is overwhelming in this case, I have multiple witnesses and it's pretty much a foregone conclusion from where we sit. Why waste the court's time and money on a jury trial for such an offence and also a trivial one at that."

The judge looked at Priteshi and Priteshi looked at the judge tilting her chin in defiance. Imogen barely managed to stifle a snort of derision. Both she and Bernadette knew Priteshi was skating on thin ice.

"That's what you think, is it, Mrs Patel? Perhaps in your view, I should dispense with a trial altogether, take your word for it and hand out summary justice instead? To avoid wasting the court's time and money." Justice Buckley's tone had become quite sarcastic at this point and the affability had vanished from his face.

"I... well... I wasn't exactly saying that..." Priteshi began to backpedal a little realising she might be getting into hot water.

Justice Buckley, however, wasn't finished. "And then as you said it's a trivial matter, although I see on here a long list of witnesses, and by the same token your department has elected to bring a prosecution and were it to be so trivial you might, for example, have elected *not* to do so..."

"Well, Judge... I..."

She got no further as he was now in full flow. "Also, it's so trivial apparently, that death threats have been made against the defending counsel and I have three, not one, but three, armed protection officers in the courtroom. And in the context of what I've said I would like you to explain to me what is so trivial about these proceedings!" Justice Buckley had raised his voice at the end, and it was clear he was more than just displeased.

"Judge, I apologise, I meant no disrespect to the court," said Priteshi when she could get a word in edgeways.

"Indeed, and apology accepted," snapped the judge by no means mollified. "Now, can you elaborate any further objections to the defendant's legal right to a jury trial? If indeed you now have any."

He left her some room to back out and she took it.

"The prosecution has no objection to a jury trial, Judge." She phrased it this way to make it seem as if it wasn't just her personally having objected, to perhaps save face, Bernadette mused.

"Excellent, then a jury trial it is." The judge smiled once more, and it seemed as if he was able to shrug off his ire as quickly as it had arrived. "Now, Mrs Mackenna, have you sent the necessary papers to the prosecution counsel?"

"Judge, we are still in preparation, and we will be sending them in due course."

"Very well, all filings to be completed no later than two days before the trial." He turned back to his list. "Now I see there are several names of Garda officers on here as witnesses, Mrs Patel, are you sure these are *all* necessary?"

Priteshi stood up. "Judge, all of these were witnesses to the assault including the officer who was assaulted, and we feel it's necessary for their statements to be heard in open court."

"Very well." Justice Buckley inclined his head. "Mrs Mackenna, you've only two witnesses here as I can see."

"Currently, yes, Judge, although it's possible we may want to include further witnesses should something of material importance come to light, if it please the court."

"Fair enough, but these names must be lodged two days before if needed."

"Thank you, Judge."

So far Justice Buckley had been accommodating and she hoped it would continue.

"Right, any special technical requirements, over and above say video or photographic evidence that sort of thing. Otherwise, liaise with the clerk of the court for the recordings and videos."

"No other requirements, no, Judge," said Priteshi.

"We have no special requirements either, Judge," said Bernadette.

"Good," said Justice Buckley happy things appeared to be on track once more. "So, any other matters I need to be aware of at this time?"

"No, Judge," said Priteshi.

"No, Judge," said Bernadette.

"Excellent, then hold on for a moment." Justice Buckley beckoned to the clerk of the court, and they held a whispered conversation during which the clerk consulted her computer several times. After a few more moments, the judge said, "Is two weeks too short a time for you to prepare for trial? Apparently, we can slot you in and given the issue of armed protection, it seems expediency would be paramount."

"We are happy to proceed as soon as possible," said Priteshi. This was predictable since they would want this swept under the carpet sooner rather than later.

"Mrs Mackenna?" Justice Buckley looked at her with interest when she didn't speak immediately.

"If I may confer with my junior counsel, Judge?" she said.

"Certainly, certainly."

Bernadette squatted beside Imogen for a whispered exchange.

"Is it enough time for the investigation?" she said to Imogen.

"I don't know but it's better to just get it done if we can, isn't it?"

"I think so but I'm a bit worried we might miss something."

"We'll get it done, don't fret, I'll talk to Kathy," Hughes murmured.

"Fine, let's go for it then." Bernadette smiled and stood up. "Judge, we are happy to proceed with that schedule."

"Splendid!" said Justice Buckley. "In that case assuming there are no further questions, I will see you all in two weeks."

He stood up and the Tipstaff entered the courtroom and bade all to rise. As they did so, Justice Buckley left the room.

Priteshi spoke briefly to her junior, and then with a brief nod in Bernadette's direction strode from the courtroom giving the impression of a woman who had no time to waste. Carole was left to pack up the papers.

"Well, la di dah!" Hughes exclaimed watching her leave.

Zhang and Imogen giggled. Carole came rushing over to Bernadette.

"I'm sorry, so sorry about that. I couldn't stop her, she's well, very overbearing."

"It's OK, darling," said Bernadette with a smile.

"You two know each other?" said Hughes in surprise.

"She's dating Olivia, and in fact, Bernadette got them together," Imogen explained.

Carole blushed rosy pink at this.

"Wheels within wheels." Zhang laughed.

Although Bernadette was dying to quiz Carole about the case and if there was more to it than the prosecution was letting on, she felt it unethical to do so.

"Don't worry, darling," she said instead, "I can handle her sort."

"She's very dictatorial," Carole told them. "She treats me like her PA, not a junior counsel at all."

"I'm sorry," said Bernadette.

"It's OK, I just have to grin and bear it until I've served my time."

"You make it sound like a prison sentence."

"It feels like it sometimes. Anyway, I must go, she'll be wondering where I've got to."

With that, Carole scurried away with her suitcase in tow.

"Poor girl, I bet she's a tartar," said Hughes.

Maneet had joined them by now.

"What a dreadful bitch!" she said.

The others burst out laughing.

"Let's go and have lunch," said Bernadette.

"We can go to Chapter One," said Imogen, "I'll pay, or rather D'Arcy will."

"Oh. I think the firm can stand this one," said Bernadette.

"No, I'll pay again, actually Akshay will," said Maneet.

"Fine." Bernadette laughed. "Let's not argue about the bill and let's get going."

* * *

Since they were quite a large party, they were shown into the Jameson Room for private dining. This secluded room contained a dark wood long dining table, with leather upholstered chairs. The wallpaper resembled cladding with very thin slices of wood. A plush grey carpet completed the subdued opulence of the setting. There was a window with a blind, but it was hard to tell if it was a false window since this was a basement restaurant.

"Wow," said Hughes, looking around as they took their seats. "This is not our usual style in the Foxcatchers, is it, May?"

"Very posh," her colleague agreed.

"The food here is wonderful," said Maneet. "I loved it last time."

The waiter arrived and distributed menus along with sparkling water and bread rolls.

"So, that seemed to go alright," Hughes said, buttering a roll.

"It's just the opening gambit, really, always straightforward," said Bernadette.

"Apart from the judge getting annoying with that bitch," said Maneet.

"Do you know her by any chance?" Imogen asked, since it appeared Maneet had taken Priteshi in some dislike.

"I don't but I know her type. Arrogant shits brought up with a rich family, think they own the place. She probably believes in harsh punishments and the death penalty. I hated her on sight."

"You realise you'll have to face her on the stand," Bernadette said mildly.

"Shit." Maneet made a face.

"You're going have to put your animosity aside for that."

"Fuck!"

The others laughed at her expletive.

"This kinds of bitches don't belong in the courtrooms!" Matelda said scowling.

"Unfortunately, we've no choice in the prosecution's choice of barrister," said Bernadette.

"Lots of people think Bernadette's a bitch when she gets going," Imogen observed.

"Ah, but I can she is a nice person, not like that other one," Matelda retorted.

The waiter returned to take the orders. With a recent chef change, there had been a menu revision and the starter choice for lunch was *Steamed Souffle of Aged Mossfield, Gouda, Truffle, Vin Jaune, Nutmeg* or *Heirloom Tomatoes, Donegal Lobster, Artichokes*. This was to be followed by *BBQ Anjou Pigeon Glazed in Timiz Sambal, Carrot, Pomelo, Satay Jus Gras* or *Sole Viennoise, Violin Courgette, Watercress, Lemon, Razor clams, with Parsley and Buckwheat*. Bernadette bemoaned the loss of a beef dish but opted for the lobster and the pigeon. Most of the others followed suit, apart from Matelda who opted for the souffle and sole. She told them she preferred fish when it was available.

The orders being taken, the talk turned to other topics than the court case. Hughes and Healy regaled them with a few tales from recent cases including the murders of several nuns at a convent. The ending to this tale was quite unexpected leading to several exclamations.

"The murderer was into some very kinky habits," said Zhang, "including a fair bit of sexual spanking."

"Really?" said Imogen with interest.

Bernadette, who was sitting next to her, squeezed Imogen's hand under the table encouraging her to be circumspect about her own predilections. Imogen returned the squeeze, glanced at her boss and smiled.

"We encounter all sorts," said Hughes. "Take for example the investigations in Rome."

"Now that was quite an adventure," said Zhang.

"Tell us more," Maneet said as the food arrived.

Conversation flowed freely and the story about the Rome case took up most of the lunch. Everyone pronounced the food to be outstanding, and elected to partake of either the *Strawberry, Violet, Chartreuse, Aniseed Herbs* or *Chocolate, Sobacha, Coffee, Salted Milk Sorbet* for dessert. This was followed by coffee and *Petit Fours*.

All of this having been consumed, there was a final discussion about the bill. In the end, Maneet insisted on paying for it and Akshay's credit card was hit once again.

Bernadette and Imogen exchanged a look which indicated they both thought perhaps Maneet was taking the piss, however, she was the client, and they were not disposed to argue too much.

Hughes, Healy and Matelda said it was one of the best meals they had ever had. The party broke up, Maneet returned with Matelda to her offices, while Hughes drove the others back to Bernadette's office.

CHAPTER NINE

The two weeks between the pre-hearing and the trial seemed to pass quite quickly. At Eve and Bernadette's house, Hughes and Healy began to relax into living there. Healy in particular was often found wandering around in a robe, like Eve, and little else, apart from her Glock in a holster, her SMG was always somewhere within easy reach too. It was an incongruous look and one which amused her fiancée, Hughes.

"I've been posing for Eve," Healy announced one day towards the end of the second week when Bernadette returned home with Hughes from the office.

"Have you indeed?" Hughes said a little sardonically.

"Yes, naked, she loves my body, she says it's great for drawing."

"I love your body too."

"You don't mind, do you?" Healy asked her.

"Does it matter if I do?"

"Are you upset? Tell me if you're upset."

"I'm teasing," said Hughes, and wrapped Healy in an embrace kissing her softly.

"It was my idea, I persuaded her," Eve said interrupting.

"She is very persuasive." Bernadette laughed.

"It's OK, I don't mind, but I would like one of the drawings for our house," said Hughes.

"Sure, you can have whatever ones you want."

Hughes looked at her shyly. "Can you draw me for Iona?"

"Sure, of course, this weekend, with pleasure."

Bernadette had taken in some of the dynamics of Hughes and Healy's relationship. She divined that perhaps Hughes was a little more dominant and Healy liked it that way. She wasn't to know initially about their bedroom antics, as they had been very discreet although Bernadette was sure they made love every night. Neither she nor Eve heard them, they were somewhat preoccupied themselves.

The four of them did indulge in gym sessions together, however, and although Hughes had accidentally opened the cupboard containing Eve and Bernadette's Shibari gear and sex toys, she never said a word. There was an unspoken agreement by which they all knew things about each other but didn't articulate them.

The four of them were becoming good friends and soon they were more like a family than strangers.

* * *

One night as Bernadette and Eve lay in bed together, Eve confessed she and Healy had been talking about sex.

"Have you? Well, I'm hardly surprised, although I hope talking was all you have been doing," Bernadette whispered.

"Oh, honestly. Of course! I've been very good. I haven't used any toys and I've been very discreet. I used my fingers a fair bit though. Going to bed to do it, I say I'm just having a nap."

"You're a naughty girl." Bernadette smiled. "But I love you so much."

"Iona told me something."

"Oh?" Bernadette propped herself up on her elbow with interest.

"She and Aileen are a bit like Imogen and D'Arcy, in the bedroom."

"No!"

"Shh, not so loud, yes, except it's because Iona wanted Aileen to dominate her. She craved it. She goaded her into it."

Bernadette absorbed this information.

"Did she indeed?"

"Yes, and now it's part of their sex lives."

"Who would have thought it?" In fact, Bernadette had begun to suspect something of this nature.

"Iona's looking forward to getting back home, she said Aileen is compiling a list. Iona can hardly wait for her consequences."

"She sounds like you." Bernadette giggled.

"Yes."

Bernadette lay down and pulled Eve closer, kissing her on the lips.

"I'm making a list too. When this is over, you will find yourself truly tied up, my girl."

"Oh, God, yes."

Bernadette paused, between kisses, to ask something else which occurred to her.

"Did you tell her about us?"

"Maybe…"

"You did, didn't you! Another one for the list, you little witch."

In a way, it was a relief. Somehow the knowledge of each other's secrets, though it was never mentioned removed any barriers between the four women and they became more relaxed than ever. None of them worried if say they bumped into each other naked heading for the bathroom, or if perhaps there was some bedroom noise after all. All of them knew they would remain friends after Hughes and Healy returned to their unit.

✳ ✳ ✳

On Friday, at work, Hughes came into Bernadette's own office and said, "We've got a bit of news."

"Oh?" Bernadette looked up.

"We found the four by four."

"Really? Wait, Imogen needs to hear this."

They repaired to Imogen's office and sat on the sofa while Hughes enlightened them.

"The car was discovered on some abandoned wasteland. We've been keeping a marker on the system in case it came up. Forensics have been over it and there are some preliminary discoveries."

"Do tell!" said Imogen eagerly.

"The fingerprints belong to known members of a white supremacist and designated terrorist organisation. It's on the watch list. These people have been under surveillance by a special unit in the Garda. However, the bad news is they've fled across the border to Northern Ireland and now of course we've got the British police to deal with. If they are caught, then we'll have to try and extradite them."

"Damn," said Bernadette.

"Yes, because we can't interrogate them directly, obviously, unless they are in our custody. We can't extradite them into our custody without being able to charge them. So, it's a bit of a chicken and egg situation I'm afraid."

"I'm very familiar with the issue." Bernadette had recently defended Callum Jenkins on an extradition request from the UK.

"Sorry." Hughes sighed.

"Does this mean you are all going to stand down?" Imogen looked worried.

"Oh, no, we're with you all the way to the trial. Brogan has seen to *that*. The investigation continues." Hughes gave her a reassuring smile.

"Phew!"

"The other bit of not good news is so far we've been unable to link these people to Maguire. So, it doesn't really help your case, I'm afraid. If the fugitives have connections to Maguire, we can't get those without being able to talk to them. We are still trying but he's dug himself in deep, assuming he's involved." Hughes' expression was apologetic on imparting this news.

"If we bring this up based on what you've told us, the prosecution will claim it is still nothing to do with him," said Bernadette.

Imogen said, "Yes, it's still Maneet's word against his and several other officers. They all claim he did not say what she said he said, and who is the jury going to believe?"

Bernadette had received all the statements corroborating Maguire's story from the prosecution, and although Bernadette would try to get them to retract what they said, if they were adamantly going to stand fast in court it put her in an impossible situation.

"I'm sorry," said Hughes. "I believe very much Maguire did provoke her, because it just doesn't make sense otherwise. I've met her and I can't see it really."

Bernadette exchanged a glance with Imogen.

"Well, she does have a temper. We know that, but we're not bringing that up," said Bernadette.

"Oh? Well, even so, I still can't see it. I've watched the footage myself. The angles were all wrong, but I swear he did say it," Hughes replied with a smile.

"I wish there was a way to prove it."

"We are trying to help you, believe me. We don't like people like that in the Garda. It pisses me off no end, and all the others in the team."

"How's Micky doing?" Bernadette asked, moving on as there seemed nothing more to be said.

"Well, he seems to be fitting in. He's been helping us on the Dark Web, trying to track down Maguire."

"Is it safe?" Imogen asked anxiously, after their previous discussion with Micky about the Dark Web.

"He's using our access and fake profiles, so don't worry, he's well protected. A nice lad too."

"Thanks, I'm pleased. He's done some great work for us in the past," Bernadette said.

"He'd make a good Garda detective," Hughes quipped.

"Don't you dare suggest it to him!"

"I won't, I won't, I promise." Hughes laughed.

"Thanks for the update, anyway."

"You are welcome, I'll get back to it until you're ready to go out or something." Hughes got up and left the office.

Bernadette turned to Imogen. There had been some interviews for the new PA during the week and Imogen had been conducting them with Alison. "How's the recruitment going?"

"We've pretty much decided on someone. Lucy Ferguson, she's young, eager, seems very capable, Scottish. She's got a pretty good sense of humour. I reckon she fits the bill."

"OK, great. Should I see her before we make her an offer?"

"If you want to, of course."

Bernadette thought for a moment. "I probably should, after all, it's my firm, and I should know who I'm hiring."

"Yes, I'll arrange it for next week."

"Sure."

"You will like her though I'm certain."

Another thought occurred to Bernadette.

"How's D'Arcy getting on with Nikki?" Not much had been said lately about D'Arcy and Imogen, or her armed protection officer Nikki Kruger.

"Oh, well firstly, we've kept our promise," Imogen began.

"I wasn't asking." Bernadette raised an eyebrow.

"But you were thinking it."

Bernadette laughed. "OK, true, but I believe you two will keep to the agreement, though I can imagine what's going to happen afterwards."

"Of course, but we'll be keeping it in the bedroom, though we will still make a game of it."

"Just like me and Eve?"

"Exactly."

"And Nikki?"

"Oh, well she D'Arcy are now best buddies." Imogen laughed.

"Really?"

"Oh, yeah, they do cooking together, everything. I think D'Arcy has enjoyed having her around. She has also been teaching D'Arcy to swear in Afrikaans."

Bernadette laid her head back and laughed at this. "I can just picture it, honestly."

"I know," said Imogen with a fond expression, thinking of her fiancée.

"You're not jealous?" Bernadette wondered.

"Amazingly enough, no. I can't explain it. Whatever happened on that weekend seems to have changed some things for me."

"In a good way by the sound of it."

"Yes. Thanks to you."

"Oh, I'm just so happy things are working out." Bernadette squeezed her hand affectionately.

"Me too."

"Anyway, Eve and Iona are getting on well. Neither of them seems to get dressed most of the time and wander around in robes. Eve's drawn both her and Aileen naked." Bernadette shook her head.

"Funny isn't it. I mean, weird having people in your home, though I think we're lucky with who we got assigned."

"Yes, very much so. Though we can't have noisy sex."

"A downside."

"We still have sex though..." Bernadette's eyes twinkled.

"But of course."

The two of them giggled at this.

Bernadette lowered her voice a little more, confidingly. "I also think Iona likes to be spanked, and Aileen obliges her. From what Eve tells me."

"Really? Oh, my goodness, who would have thought it," Imogen whispered.

"Don't say anything though."

"I won't but how funny." Imogen winked at Bernadette.

"I thought you'd like that part."

"Indeed. I'm glad I'm not the only one. Shame I can't swap stories with Aileen."

"Don't you dare."

"I'm joking, I'm joking!" Imogen held her hands up in supplication. "After all, I don't want to end up over *your* knee."

"Oh you! Stop it at once."

The two of them chuckle at what had now become a standing joke. Bernadette didn't feel close enough to Hughes to talk about personal stuff. There was still a little bit of professional reserve. That had clearly gone out of the window as far as Eve and Healy were concerned. However, she was entirely indulgent of her wife and would never censure her for it. She would, however, be adding it to the Shibari list, as part of the game.

"Anyway, enough gossip, let's get back to work. We've got to get those affidavits in by Wednesday next week, and we've got nothing more in the tank." Bernadette sighed.

"Maybe something will come up?" Imogen said hopefully.

"Fingers crossed, it's not over until it's over."

On which note, she gave her junior and friend a peck on the lips and headed back to her own office. She was pensive, wondering exactly how the trial was going to turn out. She didn't like going into it what she considered empty handed. She wasn't happy but there was nothing to be done. Unless she could break the witnesses on the stand, or Maguire, it seemed almost impossible to defend. Bernadette did not like leaving things to providence, but this time it appeared she was perhaps having to rely on fate. It was not a good place to be.

* * *

Lucy Ferguson was not tall. She had platinum blonde hair set in a bob, blue eyes, and a nice smile, sweet lips too. Bernadette mused on these features as the prospective PA sat demurely next to her on the sofa in Bernadette's office. Lucy had dressed up in a smart black suit, high heels and white blouse. She sipped her coffee delicately and waited for Bernadette to speak. Bernadette had decided to be informal which is why she chose the sofa rather than interview Lucy with a desk between them.

"So," said Bernadette smiling, "my colleagues seem to feel you're the right person for the job."

"Well, it's kind o' them tee say so," said Lucy.

"How do *you* feel about it?"

"Ah wud love te work here, it seems ideal." Lucy smiled at her disarmingly.

Bernadette probed a little further, to make sure it wasn't a pat answer. "Why do you want to work for my firm? I mean, why did you choose this job particularly?"

Lucy looked at her and Bernadette could tell there was something going through her head. She waited patiently.

"Can I be honest wi' ya?"

Perhaps there was something about Bernadette which made Lucy feel she could be open. After all, normally people did not want to jeopardise their chances by saying the wrong thing.

"Sure, of course, honesty is everything in my book."

"Well." Lucy made a face. "I dinnae precisely choose this as my favourite ever company, you know, I mean, ah need a job, ya ken, so I applied te' quite a few. Sorry... that sounds terrible."

Bernadette laughed. "Thank you, that was... very honest indeed."

"Look, ah ken go, I mean, thanks fer your time an' all that." Lucy set down her cup.

"No, wait. That's good, what you said. Of course, you applied for many jobs, everyone does. You're the first person, to be honest about it though, I love it."

"You do?" Lucy regarded her strangely and received a reassuring smile in return.

"Yes, it's refreshing, for sure. But, so now you've got this far, why do you still want the job?"

"Ach, well, I like the place, it's nice, nice people, ye know." Lucy gave an answer straight away which was a good sign.

"Your CV says you've done legal work before, you were working for a solicitor's firm or something, so you must have heard of my firm, or me?" Bernadette cocked her head onto one side.

"Sure, I have of course, who hasn't. Ye've quite a reputation for sure. But now I've met you..."

"Now you've met me what?"

"You're nothing like the bitch they said you were. Sorry, sorry, I mean, look I've said too much, I'd better..." Lucy put her hand to her mouth and blushed.

"No, really, stay, I'm intrigued. What else did they say about me at this firm, what was it? Morgan Fergal and Partners?"

"Um... you don't want te' know really... do you?" Lucy regarded her in surprise.

"Oh, but I do, I do..."

"Well, I mean, don't hate me, will ye. They said you and well, Imogen, were a pair of fucking lesbian bitches who they'd never want to seen wi' in broad daylight, in fact, they said you only come oot at night like the vampires you are..." Lucy trailed off as Bernadette laid back her head and roared with laughter.

"Now, *that*! That was funny," she said at length.

"It was?"

"Oh, yes, it's precisely what I always thought and now you've confirmed it. It's priceless, wait until I tell Imogen."

"You're going *tell* her?" Lucy said surprised.

"For sure, she'll have a good laugh about it."

"Oh." Lucy wasn't yet aware of the dynamics of the firm, but she would soon learn.

"Anyway, in spite of me being a fucking lesbian bitch, you're still here and you still applied for the job."

"Ah did, yes, 'cos I don't believe somethin' just 'cos I was told it. I want te see for maself, d'ya ken?"

Bernadette nodded. "I do indeed, and now you've seen, you'd like the job?"

"I wud, very much. I know it dinnae sound like it at the beginning of this talk, but I really wud like the job. I really love it here, to be honest. It's just wit ah wus lookin' fer." Lucy almost gushed this last part out and Bernadette could tell it was completely genuine.

Bernadette smiled at Lucy. She'd heard enough. She decided she liked Lucy very much. A straightforward lass who spoke her mind. She would fit in very nicely. Bernadette stood up and held out her hand.

"Welcome to the firm."

"Really? You're really gonne give me the job?"

"For sure, you're hired, I'll take you to Alison, you can sign the paperwork and arrange a start date."

"God, thanks, I mean really, thanks. I won't let ye' doon." Lucy shook her hand with a grateful smile.

"I know you won't. I just wanted to meet you, I trust my colleagues, but it is my firm after all, and you might have hated me or something," Bernadette raised an eyebrow.

"Noo, oh no! Dinnae say that! I really liked you... I mean, from the moment I met ye'. It wud be a privilege to work for you, and Imogen."

"Thank you, and I like you too, Lucy. Shall we go?

Bernadette led Lucy to Alison's office. She was chatting with Micky when they walked in.

"Alison, hi." Bernadette smiled.

"Bernadette."

"So, I'm happy to offer Lucy the position. If you can sort out the paperwork and her start date. I'll leave it all to you to organise when she starts, and so on."

"Sure, of course," said Alison standing up.

"Hi, I'm Micky by the way," said Micky introducing himself without ceremony.

"Hi!" Lucy furnished him with a broad smile.

Alison looked at him sharply and Bernadette did not miss the hint of jealousy in her expression. It was gone as quickly as it appeared.

"I'll leave you to it," said Bernadette. "I'll look forward to you joining us, Lucy."

"Bye, and thanks again," Lucy replied.

"You're welcome." As Bernadette left, she could hear Lucy remarking on the number of stuffed animals residing on Alison's desk, and Alison pointedly informing her that Micky had bought them for her. All of which confirmed that the relationship between Micky and Alison was more than just a professional one.

Chuckling to herself, Bernadette made her way to Imogen's office.

"Well?" said Imogen at once, when Bernadette entered and sat down on the sofa.

"I like her, and I've hired her."

"Oh good, I'm glad." Imogen came around and sat down beside her.

"She did say something interesting though."

"Oh?"

"Apparently where she worked before, we are known as the lesbian bitches, vampires who only come out at night."

"Really?" Imogen laughed heartily at this.

"All of our suspicions are confirmed."

"We are such terrible people and she still wants to work for us."

"Yes, she likes it here.

"I liked her from the outset," Imogen agreed. "She's just the sort we need, and her references are fabulous, she'll be a real asset."

"I'm sure. You and Alison did a great job."

"We did, we did." Imogen pretended preen herself.

"So, the affidavits going in today?" Bernadette wanted to check.

"Yes, they will be alongside any other evidence we have. Which is unfortunately not much."

"No." Bernadette sighed.

"Can we win?"

"I don't know. I feel like our chances are very slim at this moment, unless something turns up."

"Well then, I suggest you get your wife to cast a few of her witchy spells." Imogen laughed.

"Good idea."

The two of them smiled at each other. They were joking, although only half. Bernadette really did wonder sometimes if her wife really was a witch. Eve was so incredibly perceptive, and things seemed to go right around her too.

"You know, things have a way of turning out, so let's not give up hope yet," Imogen said sagely.

"They do sometimes." Bernadette pursed her lips. "I still don't like the odds this time. They really have stacked the deck."

"Win or lose, I still love you." Imogen took her hand and held it.

"I know, darling, and I love you."

✳ ✳ ✳

Patrick Kelly sat in Bernadette's officer with Bernadette and Imogen. He was handsome with black hair, green eyes and clean shaven. He wore a beige linen jacket, cream shirt, jeans and blue suede boots which were his trademark. Patrick was a psychologist and Bernadette had called him in on the off chance he might be able to give his expert opinion on Maneet's behaviour at the rally.

He had watched the footage on her computer with great interest and Bernadette had filled him in on what Maneet alleged was said to her. He sipped his coffee and listened attentively as was his won't. When she had finished Bernadette asked him, "Well, what do you think?"

"What do I think?" He looked amused. Bernadette let this pass, she had known Patrick a long time and been friends with him at university. He continued, "I mean, if he did say that then she would have been upset, anyone would."

"Yes, sure, but in your professional opinion could you say it was out of character?"

"I don't know her at all, to start with, so I can't say *that*." Patrick shrugged. "For me to even have a chance of saying it, would require me doing a full psychological assessment and even then, not knowing her on a long-term basis, I still couldn't do it in all conscience. I mean, I could, but it could easily be challenged."

"Bugger," said Bernadette, although in the back of her mind she probably knew this was going to be his answer all along.

"Had she been a long-term patient of mine and willing to consent to my giving evidence then I would be able to say with some degree of certainty as a professional. But she's not, I don't know her from Adam, and I can't make a claim like that under oath."

He put his fingers into a steeple and furnished Bernadette with a smile.

"Oh you, why do you have to be so… right about it!" she said in frustration.

He laughed at this, as old friends they were quite informal.

"Yes, why did you come here if you knew this already?" Imogen chimed in crossly.

"Oh, as to that, I hadn't seen Bernadette in a long time so…"

Bernadette made an exasperated noise.

"It almost feels as if you're not pleased to see me," he said with his eyes twinkling.

"I'm pleased to see you but not with what you've told me. We're up against it as it is, and this was possibly just another way we could bolster the case."

"I'm sorry, honestly I'd help if I could, but you can see it can't work."

"No, I can see. It was a longshot I suppose." Bernadette sighed.

"Anyway, how have you been, how's married life?" he said, dismissing the topic out of hand. He had, naturally, been a guest at the wedding.

"It's very good, amazingly so…" said Bernadette and they talked for a while about Eve's art, the gym and plans for a conservatory among other things.

When she'd finished, he said to Imogen, "I gather you are to be married too?"

"Yes, to D'Arcy."

"Sure, I'm sure you make a great couple."

Imogen eyed him suspiciously in case he was being sarcastic, but the remark seemed to be genuine. However, she had a bone to pick with him.

"I wanted to get you out on a date, you know that don't you, I mean, before…"

"Ah, yes." He laughed in a self-deprecating manner. "The thing is, and I'm really sorry, but my gaydar is pretty good you know."

"So, you avoided me because you thought I was gay?"

"*Knew* you were gay," he corrected her.

"I could have been bisexual."

"You're not though." He was too perceptive for her. She sighed.

"Fine, you're right."

"In spite of my reputation which I'm sure Bernadette furnished you quite an account of, I'm not really one for being a notch on someone's bedpost."

"You were perfectly happy to put some notches on your own," Bernadette countered.

He held up his hands in surrender. "Touché. A palpable hit. Yes, I'm a hypocrite and all those things you've told me on several occasions."

"Ha! So, she has called you out?" Imogen regarded Bernadette with renewed respect.

"Oh, yes, frequently and comprehensively. I've had my character shredded in no uncertain terms more than once. I swear she was using me as target practice for her court cases."

Bernadette burst out laughing at this.

"It made not one blind bit of difference to your thoroughly reprobate behaviour. You were a Lothario of no mean order at uni. His reputation was dreadful absolutely dreadful but still, all the girls wanted to open their fucking legs for him, more fool them!"

"You see?" Patrick said to Imogen, not in the last abashed by what Bernadette had said.

"It's probably just as well we didn't go out," said Imogen. "Although, you missed out on some mighty good sex, just so you know."

"Be glad you didn't do it, really. He doesn't need your knickers in his trophy drawer!" Bernadette said firmly.

"What can I say?" Patrick laughed. "You've floored me as usual. I'm sure the sex would have been wonderful, red heads usually are most passionate. And how did you know about my drawer?"

"You showed it to me, remember, at uni."

"You really had a collection of women's knickers?" Imogen stared in surprise.

"I was young, foolish."

"Old and still foolish," Bernadette said acerbically.

He held up a finger.

"Ah, not quite. I'm actually going steady with someone, as it goes. I know you'll be amazed."

"I'm amazed they'll have stayed with you considered your past record."

"Well, they have. I know it's surprising but it's true."

"They must be a saint in which case. Don't tell me you're falling in love?" Bernadette regarded him with interest.

"I might be, I might indeed." His smile was, however, a dead giveaway.

"Good God, they must be a paragon indeed, who is this superwoman?"

"A childhood sweetheart actually. I ran into her quite by accident and by some good stroke of fortune the flame was still there, for us both."

"Wonders will never cease."

"You should be glad for me," he said pretending to sound offended.

"Oh, I am and for the legions of women whose hearts you will no longer break."

"There is that." He lifted up his cup in a toast and drained it. It seemed he was ready to depart. "Anyway, I've another meeting so..."

"We must meet her then, sometime." Bernadette softened her tone.

"For sure, when you're not quite so busy, by all means."

Bernadette finished her cup too.

"I'll ring you. It's been nice to see you."

"Sorry, I couldn't be more help."

"I'll see you out," said Imogen getting up.

"As long as you're not throwing me out," he quipped.

"Oh, you'd know if I was throwing you out."

He laughed, bent down to furnish Bernadette with a kiss on the cheek and followed Imogen out of the room. Shortly she returned.

"You're better off for never having been where many women have been before," said Bernadette when Imogen handed her another cup of coffee.

"I know. I was a bit infatuated at the time. Well, briefly and then there was Shane. What a disaster that was, and I was."

"But you're not now!" Bernadette took hold of her hand.

"No, thanks to you, and Eve, and D'Arcy."

"Exactly. Don't miss what you never had. He wasn't worth it."

"I thought he was your friend?"

"He is, but I'm not blind to his multitude of faults."

"What about my faults?" Imogen pouted.

"Darling, that's entirely different. You probably have faults, I certainly do, but I love you to bits and so they are nothing to me."

"Oh fuck, you say the nicest things." Imogen teared up.

"You know you hold a very special place in my heart, dearest. Patrick could never be *that*. There are friends, and there are family. It's not the same at all."

"Oh fuck, fuck! Stop or I'll be in floods." Imogen's eyes were bright.

"Anyway, don't forget it."

"As if I would," said Imogen recovering. "I feel the same about you."

"I know." Bernadette smiled.

"Lesbian bitch lawyers, sisters under the skin." Imogen raised her coffee cup in salute.

"Exactly." Bernadette clinked her own cup against it.

"I can't really imagine Patrick settling down, that's a turnup for the books," Bernadette mused, returning to the original topic.

"Perhaps he's met his match?"

"Perhaps he has. He needs taking in hand... by someone."

Imogen started to laugh.

"I know what you're thinking," said Bernadette with a smile.

"Yes, oh yes... you can read me like a book." Imogen's eyes twinkled mendaciously.

"Usually and certainly regarding sex, and kinks, yes, I can."

They laughed, and Imogen squeezed her hand enjoying the moment of camaraderie.

* * *

Friday arrived, the weekend before the impending trial. No more current links between white supremacist groups and Maguire had been found. The affidavits had been filed. Bernadette and Imogen had discussed the line of attack on the witnesses, and particularly Maguire. The Foxcatcher team was still working on the investigation. However, Bernadette was going into the trial without the confidence she had enough to get Maneet off the charge. It did not mean she wasn't giving it her all to try.

"You seem quiet," said Hughes as they made their way back to Bernadette's house.

Bernadette had finally got her car back, and the tyre had been replaced by a mobile tyre firm. She was happy to be driving once more with Hughes sat in the passenger seat. In the last two weeks, they had come to know each other quite well.

"I just don't like going into court without a decent shot at winning." Bernadette sighed.

"Don't you think you have a chance?"

"There is always a chance, but playing the odds on this, it's not a very good one."

"I'm sorry." Hughes smiled reassuringly. "We're doing our best. It's disappointing for us because I would dearly love to nail that fucker. We're laying off him for the moment, but after the case is over, we'll be pulling him in to question him. Win or lose."

"That will be something at least."

"What will Maneet get if she loses?"

"She could get a fine probably of around fifteen hundred Euros, and she would be liable to prison for up to five years. I don't think it would come to prison though."

"No, I can't see it myself," Hughes agreed.

"The damage to her reputation is the problem. If not for that she would probably take it and become a protest hero." Bernadette laughed.

"I imagine she is to some," Hughes mused.

"Watch this space. There will likely be protests organised for the court case on Monday."

"Her colleagues?"

"Yes, for sure. I'd almost guarantee it."

They arrived home, and Bernadette pulled the car into her driveway and waited for the gate to shut behind them. Eve had managed to put the building work off for a while longer, and the conservatory company seemed happy enough as they were very busy. Eve felt having workmen around was probably a bad idea while a threat against Bernadette existed.

Once inside, Bernadette shut and locked the door. She and Hughes gratefully shed their shoes. They hung up their jackets, but Hughes' holster and Glock remained firmly by her side. In the living room, Eve and Healy were sitting on the sofa talking. When Bernadette and Hughes walked in, Eve jumped up to greet her wearing a satin short robe and nothing else as usual. As this was often how Eve dressed at home, and greeted her, Bernadette didn't bat an eyelid. In fact, were it not for having company she would be removing Eve's robe in short order. The sight of her wife with the fabric moulded to her curves was almost always arousing, she suspected it was why Eve didn't wear many clothes. Also, Eve, just seemed to like being almost naked, which went along with her free spirit. Bernadette thought it must be the artist in her. Eve kissed her softly and gently, nuzzling her lips provocatively.

Healy stood up. She was also wearing a robe, and notably, her pistol was missing. Bernadette noticed it on the table nearby.

"Hey," said Hughes going up to her with a smile. "How was your day?"

"It was good, but what's it to you?" Healy suddenly shot her a petulant look.

Bernadette glanced at Eve who looked nonplussed.

"OK. So, where's your firearm?" Hughes with a sigh, ignoring this.

"It's there, can't you see!" Healy snapped.

"Why aren't you wearing it?" Hughes asked her with infinite patience.

"I could easily get it, so what's the big deal?" The manner in which Healy has addressed Hughes seem quite outrageous to Bernadette.

Hughes was unperturbed. "Come with me and I'll explain it to you."

"No, I want to stay here!" Healy sounded like a petulant child.

"I said come and when I say come, you come!" Hughes told her firmly, taking Healy's hand she led her out unresisting.

"Well!" Bernadette whispered.

"I can't understand it," said Eve. "She wasn't like this before."

They fell silent, as they could hear some fierce whispers from the dining room.

"What are you playing at?" Hughes was saying.

"Nothing."

"No, I know what you're angling for and if we were at home then you'd certainly be getting it."

"Oh, shut up, you silly bitch!" Healy said, almost not caring if she could be overheard.

"Oh, you little brat, I didn't think you'd do this here. Fine, get upstairs *now*. I'm going to deal with you very shortly."

Hurried footsteps were heard, while Hughes returned to the living room. Bernadette and Eve regarded her with interest.

"Erm, I don't know how to ask this but..."

"You want some privacy?" Bernadette ventured.

"Yes, I mean if you don't mind, it's just, well, something I have to do. Sometimes Iona just needs..." she trailed off and looked a little beseechingly at Bernadette.

"It's OK, we don't need to know." Bernadette smiled. "We'll go to the gym for a while, how long do you want?"

"About half an hour or so, is that OK? If you can lock the door to the gym and the patio door. Take your phone, call me if you need."

"There's a panic button in the gym," said Eve practically.

"What about our gym gear?" Bernadette wondered.

"Also, a set in the gym."

"You think of everything." Bernadette kissed her lightly. "We'll get going and leave you to it, we might be longer than thirty minutes depending on the workout."

"That's fine, and thank you, I appreciate it. Iona... has... well... needs and when she gets like this, it's because she... well... I have to fulfil them. I'm sorry." Hughes seemed genuinely contrite.

"It's fine, darling," said Bernadette giving her a hug. "We understand, we really do."

"Thanks."

Hughes watched them go and checked they locked the door behind them. She watched them all the way to the gym until they were inside, and the door closed. Eve locked the gym door.

"Goodness, I wasn't expecting *that*!" Eve said. "Iona must get similar cravings to me."

"Yes, indeed."

"We could... you know... Shibari..." Eve suggested.

"No," said Bernadette firmly. "Shibari happens when I say and that is not today."

"Oh... so strict." Eve made a mock pout and then she laughed. "OK, let's workout then."

They put on their gym gear and settled into an exercise session. In a way Bernadette was glad as she was getting used to regular workouts, particularly now they had their own gym at home. She missed them if they didn't have them. She knew how privileged she was to have such a good life. It was important never to take it for granted.

They did a few circuits and finished off with some kickboxing practice. Bernadette was getting good at it with her right hand particularly, and felt if she was ever threatened physically, she wouldn't be intimidated. Eve also trained her in some takedowns and Eve had studied martial arts quite extensively.

After forty-five minutes they finished, they showered, and changed into robes themselves. The gym gear went into a wash basket, and they returned to the house. Hughes and Healy were downstairs, sitting together entwined on the sofa and both also wearing robes. It was noticeable both were wearing their holsters and sidearms. The two of them seemed to now be in perfect accord and if anything, Healy was acting in a very loving fashion towards her fiancée.

"Hi." Hughes smiled as they came in. "Thanks so much for being so accommodating."

"It's our pleasure," Bernadette replied. "The least we can do."

"Iona and I would like to get all of us a takeaway, on us."

"You don't have to," said Bernadette at once.

"Oh, but we want to. You've been feeding us all this time and everything. It's only fair," Healy said.

She looked much calmer, and relaxed, even smiling.

"We won't say no, of course, it would be lovely," said Bernadette.

"Yes, thanks so much," said Eve.

"Come and choose something with me then, and show me the best takeaway to order from," said Hughes getting up.

"Sure, we've got some menus in the kitchen." Bernadette walked towards the door. "Our favourite is an Indian called Spice Guru."

"Sounds great."

They poured briefly over the menu, and ordered some mains, rice, naan and sides. While Hughes got onto the phone, Bernadette returned to the living room.

"Where's Eve?" she asked Healy.

"She went upstairs I think," said Healy who was idly flicking through her phone.

"Oh, well, I'll go and check up on her while you wait for the food."

"Sure, OK." Healy gave her a sly grin.

Wondering what the grin was for, Bernadette wandered upstairs and quietly opened the bedroom door. She quickly shut it behind her and stared in surprise. Eve was on the bed, on all fours naked with her arse in the air. Her fingers were between her legs and she was letting her breath out in little gasps.

Bernadette lay down beside her. "What on earth are you doing?" The question was superfluous as it was perfectly obvious.

Eve spoke in urgent quick breaths. "I'm sorry, I had to... oh fuck... oh... it's just Iona... she told me about the spanking... with a paddle and then... oh God... she showed me her arse... it was so red... oh fuck... oh my God... oh..." Eve didn't stop.

Bernadette at once understood exactly why Eve was so turned on. Eve found the idea of such chastisement extremely arousing. Nevertheless, the brazen and wanton behaviour of her wife took her slightly aback.

"Oh my God!" Bernadette's eyes widened. "Why you little witch!" She sat up and pursed her lips. For some reason she was quite cross, particularly as they had guests and Eve's naked backside was suddenly so inviting.

Without thinking she planted a sound smack on Eve's buttock.

"Oh! Oh fuck... oh God..." Eve gasped without stopping what she was doing.

"You horny little witch, you are completely outrageous, maybe this is what you want is it, is it?" Bernadette punctuated the sentence with half a dozen well aimed and hard smacks.

"Oh... oh... oh... fuck... oh... yes... yes... oh... fuck..." Eve cried out going even faster.

"My God you even like it, I cannot believe you, honestly." Bernadette slapped Eve's arse another three or four times but then she stopped, as it seemed to have the desired effect.

"Oh... fuck... fuck... oh... God... oh my God... ohh!" Eve screamed out as she climaxed.

Bernadette watched her and was unable to prevent herself from being thoroughly aroused.

As Eve's orgasm began to subside. Bernadette pushed Eve gently down onto her back and straddled her. She manoeuvred into position so that Eve could use her tongue.

"You know what to do, you little witch, hmm, don't you?" she whispered.

Without further prompting, Eve began to flick her tongue gently and then faster. Bernadette moved her pelvis against Eve's mouth, being very close to finishing already.

"Oh fuck... Eve, you're so bad... you're a little bitch... you're so naughty... so fucking naughty... fuck... oh my God... fuck... you make me... oh God... fuck... I'm going to... ohh!"

Bernadette's orgasm overtook her and her whole frame shuddered. Eve's arms wrapped around her thighs holding her tight. She looked down and Eve was smiling like a Cheshire cat.

A little while afterwards they lay together on the bed, holding each other close.

"You're bad, do you know that?" Bernadette whispered. "Look what you made me do."

"But I liked it." Eve kissed her.

"I know and that's what worries me."

"Why?"

"Because I'm not Imogen and I don't want to be."

Eve turned to her and looked at her with a serious expression. "But the thing is, I might want you to smack my arse sometimes, after all."

"Oh."

"What do you think? Would you?" Eve said softly.

"I'll have to think about it. I don't want to become like Imogen."

"No, but maybe like you did then? Just before?"

"Maybe."

"OK." Eve kissed her and Bernadette could see from her eyes she was a little disappointed. Bernadette did not mind the Shibari, in fact, she quite liked it, but she didn't want to go into discipline too. Although she admitted to herself that there had been some sexual arousal and even satisfaction in planting a few well-placed smacks on her wife's arse.

Seeing Eve's expression, she at once relented because she loved Eve more than anything and couldn't bear her disappointment.

"If it was just like *that*, then maybe I will, but not too often..." she said.

Eve smiled. "OK, thank you. Thank you so much."

"You don't have to thank me, I love you, I will always try to please you, if I can."

"I know and I love you for it. I appreciate it more than you know putting up with my horny behaviour."

Eve kissed her then, a full-on dynamite fireworks kiss. Bernadette felt as if the world was spinning before she came back down to earth.

"Shall we go and eat? The food is probably here by now," Bernadette said at length.

"Yes, let's."

* * *

The rest of the weekend passed without any further incident. It seemed evident that Healy needed what she had craved, and once Hughes had given it to her she was almost a different person. She was attentive and loving to Hughes, getting her cups of coffee and generally twining herself around her fiancée at every opportunity.

Bernadette understood this completely, since Eve was just the same with the Shibari. When she became petulant, tetchy and deliberately bratty, Bernadette knew it was past time to give her a session. For Eve it was something almost like an endorphin hit, a drug of sorts, a longing which had to be fulfilled. Bernadette had sufficient experience of Eve's ways to understand her almost completely. She was sure the same thing could equally apply to someone like Healy. Perhaps one day, she and Hughes might know each other well enough to compare notes. Within a few days, the trial would be over and the Foxcatchers would probably be wrapping up. It's unlikely the death threats would hold once the proceedings were dealt with. It had been an attempt to persuade Bernadette to give up as Maneet's barrister. At this rate Maneet may get convicted in any case, Bernadette mused. However, she was very grateful for the protection while it lasted.

They spend a lazy Saturday at home while Eve painted, and the others chatted or watched TV. They took one or two spells in the hot tub. Hughes and Healy kept their guns in easy reach. On Sunday Bernadette took them all to her and Eve's favourite beach Killiney Bay, a long stretch of sand a little to the south of where she lived. They all walked together barefoot on the sand and paddled in the warm water. They ate fish and chips at a pub nearby. Then they spent a pleasant evening playing cards and eating Beef Stroganoff which Healy and Eve had made.

Monday's alarm penetrated Bernadette's consciousness. She had her arms wrapped around Eve. They had made love, gently and softly at bedtime covering each other with sweet kisses. Eve opened her eyes, kissed Bernadette lightly.

"Haven't you got court today?" she said.

"Yes, I have."

"Have your shower then. But before you do, thank you for a wonderful weekend."

Bernadette smiled.

"Was it really wonderful?"

"Of course, because I spent it with you."

"I love you."

"I love you too."

After her shower, Eve braided Bernadette's hair into a French plait which was one of her favourite styles. She did Bernadette's makeup and then left her to get dressed. Eve had laid out a black jacket with black wide trousers, a white blouse and black stilettoes. This was typical first court day dress to impress. As the trial progressed, she might dress Bernadette a little more softly depending on the circumstance. However, today would have the jury selection, followed by the prosecution witnesses. Maguire was first up and if Bernadette seemed a little intimidating this was all to the good. She knew Imogen would be doing the same dress wise.

After a swift glance in the mirror, Bernadette went downstairs. Eve was serving up breakfast in the dining room, she put a plate of scrambled eggs and bacon in front of Bernadette. Healy did likewise for Hughes. Healy had been very attentive to her fiancée for the last two days. Eve and Healy took their own seats, and they started to eat in companionable silence.

After a while, Hughes said, "So did you make this, Iona?"

"Of course, I did, Eve has been teaching me. I'm going to do more cooking at home when we get back there."

"That will be nice." Hughes smiled at her. Hughes had been traditionally the better cook and the one to keep house.

She seemed genuinely pleased her fiancée was going to share the load.

"Yes, because I am nice. Well, most of the time."

Bernadette and Eve suppressed a snigger at this slightly ironic statement.

"I love you, darling," was all Hughes said, declining to comment further.

"How do you think it will go today?" Eve asked Bernadette. She was sitting on Bernadette's left, as she always placed Bernadette at the head of the table. Her foot slid up under Bernadette's trouser leg and provocatively up her calf.

"I don't know. I hope I'll be able to get some good hits in on their star witness, Maguire, but other than that it's hard to tell." Bernadette's voice didn't betray a hint of the pleasant sensation of bare toes running up and down her skin.

"I'm sure you'll be fine. It will go well."

"I hope so." Bernadette's hand stilled Eve's leg under the table. Eve made a pout and then smiled mischievously.

Bernadette drained her coffee cup, and noting the others had finished, she got up to go. Eve accompanied her to the front door and kissed her soundly as always. Through the corner of her eye, Bernadette noticed Healy doing the same to Hughes.

Eve touched up Bernadette's lipstick. "I'll see you later, darling, hope it goes well."

In the car, Bernadette watched both Eve and Healy waving goodbye as she drove away.

"Thanks, by the way," said Hughes.

"For what?" Bernadette pulled the car into the main drag and turned in the direction of the office.

"For everything." Hughes shrugged. "Taking us into your home, looking after us so well, and showing us both how a loving couple should act."

"Well, we're just being us."

"That's my point."

"Iona does seem to love you very much," Bernadette observed.

"And I love her, to distraction. I'll do anything for her. She's my life." This heartfelt sentiment was delivered with a lot of emotion.

"I'm sure she feels the same."

"Yes." Hughes smiled.

"You two should get married, tie the knot finally."

"We will when we get half a break. I want to invite you and Eve, if you'll come." This was expressed quite shyly.

"Of course, why would we not? I'm flattered."

"I consider you a good friend, I hope you feel the same. I mean, I know we've not known each other long." Hughes shot a glance at her.

"I do, I really do."

"Thanks."

They arrived at the office, to collect Imogen and Zhang. There was some time before they had to leave, so Bernadette parked the car and went up to see Imogen, while Hughes went to check in with O'Flynn.

"Are we ready?" Bernadette asked passing a cup of coffee to her junior.

"Sure, we should leave in around fifteen minutes."

Bernadette took a seat on the sofa and related the events of the weekend. Imogen listened with fascination.

"So, you think, Aileen... she..."

"Yes, I'm sure of it, because of what Eve said."

"That's the second time you've slapped Eve's arse." Imogen laughed.

"And I'm not intending to make a habit of it," Bernadette said severely.

"You never know you might like it."

"I'm not you, Imogen, at least not that way."

"Believe me, darling, you don't want to be me, these kinds of needs... cravings... are hard to resist. We're both doing well on your strictures though."

"As you keep reminding me."

"I don't want to disappoint you. *We* don't want to."

Bernadette smiled. "Well, you haven't, and you won't. Now stop teasing me."

Imogen laughed. "Perhaps I should get some tips from Aileen."

"No!"

"Ow, so assertive... OK... OK... Mrs Mackenna." Imogen held up her hands in mock surrender.

"You and Eve, as bad as each other the pair of you."

"I'll take that as a compliment."

"Oh you!"

Imogen glanced at her watch, becoming business like all of a sudden. "Time to go."

"Great."

Bernadette stood up, while Imogen picked up the suitcase containing their files and robes."

"Ready?" she said.

"Ready!" Bernadette replied.

✳ ✳ ✳

They swept up the long curving steps to the Criminal Courts of Justice with Hughes on one side, and Zhang on the other. The two detectives were on high alert scanning left and right, looking for any clue of potential trouble. Maneet would meet them inside in a meeting room with Matelda.

"I told you," said Bernadette to Imogen. On the right and being kept at bay by Garda officers was a large contingent of protesters. They were waving banners with "Free Maneet", "It's a conspiracy", "No justice for racists", and various other slogans. Bernadette could make out Judd, Lucy and Lunara in amongst them. Lucy was their witness but wouldn't be needed for at least a day.

"Who can blame them," Imogen replied.

They continued until they hit the press contingent who were, as usual, hanging around near the top of the steps hoping for a snippet of something. Bernadette didn't always talk to the press at the beginning of the trial, but she decided to stop and make a short statement. As she did so, a semi-circle of reporters gathered around, and Hughes and Zhang moved in closer watching the crowd.

"Bernadette, what do you reckon? Is this a trial about racism?" shouted one hopeful hack.

She held up her hand in her customary way, indicating she would speak. Microphones were shoved towards her while the press jockeyed for position.

"You know what I'm going to say, because I always do," she began smiling. "This is first and foremost about justice.

You also know very well I can't say much at this point, I can say this. We believe Maneet is not guilty, and we shall do our best to show the court why that is!"

"But she was shown on film assaulting the officer, how can she not be guilty?" It was a provocative question, and one which Bernadette chose to ignore.

"My answer to that is, see you in court."

She turned her back to the raucous sound of shouts which faded as they entered the doors and arrived in the large open atrium. Hughes and Zhang visibly relaxed as they made their way to a prearranged meeting room. Maneet was already there with Matelda.

"Hi, darling," said Bernadette giving her a hug. "Are you ready for today?"

"Yes, for sure, though I'm nervous as hell."

"Don't be. We've got jury selection first and then prosecution witnesses, so you don't need to start worrying really until it's your turn."

"OK." Maneet did not look any less concerned.

Imogen disappeared with Zhang to get some coffee, and soon returned. Once everyone was seated. Bernadette sipped her coffee for a moment.

"We've got extra armed security for the trial," said Hughes. "An armed officer on each door from the Special Tactics Unit. Brogan is now in charge of that too, so it makes it easier for us. It has all been cleared with the court."

"Do you really think there's still a risk?" Imogen asked her.

"There's always a risk," said Hughes. "Once that threat was given, we knew there was a credible threat. Our security services have also indicated high threat levels from their intelligence which we cannot share. We feel once the trial is over then the threat should subside."

"I suppose this should make me feel better, but it really doesn't." Bernadette laughed lightly setting down her cup.

"We are here to keep you safe, and Matelda is the best markswoman on the Foxcatcher's team," said Hughes.

"Oh, Aileen, I'm not that great." Matelda blushed.

"Yes, yes you are!" Zhang said. "Who was it, took down the sniper from a helicopter in one shot?"

"Oh, well, you know."

"She's one of our best, as is Iona," said Hughes. "So don't worry, we've got your backs."

"I, for one, am grateful," said Imogen.

"I am too, don't get me wrong," Bernadette added.

"Anyway." Imogen finished her drink. "Looks like it's that time. I need the loo first."

"We'll all go," said Bernadette to general laughter.

The courtroom was already packed with press and interested public. Some of the main people from Maneet's organisation had managed to get in too. Bernadette gave Maneet a brief hug as she made her way to the lawyer station. Matelda accompanied Maneet to the dock and they both took a seat. Matelda examined the people in the courtroom looking for potential threats.

While Imogen set out their papers, Bernadette noted there was an armed officer at the main entrance and also at the witness and judge's entrance. It seemed they were well covered. Hughes and Zhang took their seats alongside Bernadette and Imogen.

While they waited Priteshi Patel swept in with Carole behind her. Priteshi looked very inch and imperious as before, with a severe cut black skirt suit, white blouse, red nail polish and lipstick. She glanced briefly in Bernadette's direction and gave her a brief nod. Carole set about arranging the papers.

In a short space of time, the Tipstaff entered the courtroom and announced the arrival of the judge. Everybody stood up as one, and Justice Buckley entered the room. He looked no less benign than at the pre-trial hearing and looked about the courtroom before taking a seat.

After shuffling a few things around on his desk, he said, "Aha, so here we are at last and within a short space of time, it seems, at the trial involving the DPP versus Maneet Johal-Lynch."

Having said this, he thought for a few moments before speaking again. "Well, first things first, we'll get the jury sorted shall we, hopefully, that won't take too long." He shot a meaningful glance at both counsels. Bernadette knew that jury selection could be quite drawn out if one wanted to. There were objections and questions, and each barrister was going for the type of jury they wanted. The final result was usually a compromise.

Bernadette was pushing for a mix of ethnicities and gender, hoping for more women, who would generally be more sympathetic to a woman. No doubt Priteshi would go for a more Irish oriented male mix if she could. As it happened, Bernadette was wrong. Priteshi raised few objections and seemed quite content to have the jury almost as Bernadette had wanted. Bernadette could only conclude Priteshi was so sure of her case, she didn't feel the need to make a big thing of getting a sympathetic jury. Also, this would indicate the lack of any racism in the prosecution's case. They would know by now from the evidence presented by the defence that racism was going to be brought up. They would have tried to work a strategy to defend their own case against it.

Once this part was over, Maneet was asked to enter her plea to the court, which she did in strident tones, pronouncing "Not Guilty" in a clear calm voice. Bernadette was proud of her, and although it was a small thing, it was also a signal to the jury that the defendant was confident in their position.

Since the jury was selected and duly sworn in before the morning break, Justice Buckley evidently decided to cut the prosecution loose and have the opening remarks.

"Mrs Patel, you may address the court with your opening statement before we break for tea," he said affably.

"Thank you, Judge," said Priteshi and stood up with her hands on her podium preparing to give her speech. After a minute or, she began. "Judge, members of the jury. This case you have before you is rather a simple case. No matter how the defence may try to obfuscate the issues, there is no doubt that the defendant, Ms Johal-Lynch did assault Sergeant Maguire in the performance of his duty."

She paused and stared momentarily at Maneet in order to try to psych her out, but this did not work. Maneet stared back at her implacably unabashed.

"We will show you footage which clearly and irrevocably shows the assault was carried out unprovoked by Ms Johal-

Lynch. Not only that, but we will also bring the testimony of Sergeant Maguire's fellow officers to bear witness to this fact. And it is, members of the jury, a *fact!*"

She wrung out the word 'fact' as if this in itself proved the case and no more was needed. Bernadette smiled to herself, it was not a bad performance at all overall, but she felt she could do better even so.

"A fact, no matter how the defence may attempt to divert your attention from the evidence, you will see and hear this case is proven and will be proven beyond reasonable doubt. A test no doubt the defence will remind you of. Well, I am doing them a favour by reminding you of it now, and I have no hesitation in saying you will see there is no doubt, *none*, that Ms Johal-Lynch is guilty. And by that token, I am sure you will return a verdict of guilty in this case."

Priteshi paused, and Bernadette thought this would be a great place to end such an impactful speech, but it seemed Priteshi had other ideas.

"The Garda," Priteshi continued, "has a difficult job. A job which often puts their lives on the line every day. Law and order is something which all good and law abiding citizens applaud. They want it, they need it and as such, it is the Garda who helps to offer safety, security and order in these troubled times."

Bernadette glanced at Imogen, this seemed to sound more political than legal. The judge shifted in his seat but said nothing. However, a quick scan of the jury told Bernadette their attention had begun to wander.

"When the Garda, our very institution which protects us is threatened, then it is a threat to all of us. Where would we be if citizens are allowed to attack the Garda, without any kind of consequence? Where would we be, members of the jury? In a very bad place indeed!"

The judge coughed discreetly as if to make a subtle commentary on this speech. Some of the jury were now staring at the ceiling.

"Yes, a very bad place, and that's why it's not only your duty as a juror but your civic duty as a citizen of this great country, to make sure that justice is served. Justice must be done. Those who assault the Garda must not be tolerated. It is an affront to decent citizens. So, I say again. The evidence will show that Ms Johal-Lynch is guilty, guilty and guilty again! And so, I am sure you will find her!"

As she said the words 'guilty', Priteshi pounded her fist on the podium for emphasis which startled the judge and some of the jurors. Overall, Bernadette did not think it had done her any favours.

"Right," said Justice Buckley when it became apparent Priteshi had really finished. Not being sure, he had waited a moment in case there was more. However, reading his expression, Bernadette imagined he was somewhat thankful there wasn't.

"Yes, well, moving on," he continued. "We will take our morning break, and then you may call your first witness."

* * *

"Well," said Imogen once they were all ensconced in a meeting room with coffee, "what was that speech?"

"I think it wasn't the kind of speech a barrister would normally make," Bernadette said wryly.

"Perhaps she has her sights set on bigger things," said Hughes.

"I think that sort of grandstanding won't go well with some judges, and she'll be taken down a peg or two."

"I'd like to take her down some pegs," muttered Maneet darkly sipping her drink.

"Cool your jets, missy," Bernadette told her. "You can't be showing any kind of temper in the courtroom or you're simply playing into their hands."

"Fuck, I know, but she annoys the hell out of me already!"

"Me too," said Imogen. "But the best revenge is when Bernadette gets stuck into her witnesses."

"What about when she gets stuck into me?"

"Then you will keep a level head, understood!" Bernadette replied firmly.

"God, she's so assertive. Have you noticed?" Hughes said chuckling.

"She is, for sure." Imogen winked.

"Stop it!" said Bernadette and picked up her coffee.

"See what I mean? I need to ask her for some tips." Hughes was grinning.

They laughed and it eased the tension. The start of a court case did generate its own atmosphere and it was easy for emotions to surface. Once things were underway, things felt a little smoother because the momentum carried everyone with it. Initially, even Bernadette would be anxious.

"Anyway, it's early days, let's keep cool, calm and collected," she said as she drained her cup.

"Amen!" Imogen replied, following suit.

As a group, they headed for the ladies room, before returning for the second half of the morning session.

✳ ✳ ✳

Once the court was settled in again, and Justice Buckley was seated, he told Priteshi to proceed. This was the moment Bernadette was really waiting for, a chance to tackle their main witness.

"I call Sergeant Franklin Maguire," said Priteshi.

Maguire duly appeared, in full dress uniform and took his place on the witness stand. He was around thirty-five years of age, with a shaved head. He had a slightly bulldog-like appearance and Bernadette felt he probably resembled a stereotypical thug when out of uniform. This was to his detriment. Many such types appeared in footage of white supremacist groups. He was sworn in by the clerk opting to take an oath on the bible. Bernadette thought this was probably a considered act since he might be thought of as a godly person, or some such, by the jury. When he had finished, he was asked to state his name and occupation before Priteshi began her questions.

"Sergeant," she said, "can you take us through the events of the day of the rally in question, both prior, during and after?"

"Yes, I can," said Maguire, pausing for a second. Priteshi gave him a nod and he began. "I was on duty when we received information there was a rally being held in Phoenix Park."

"Has this rally been notified beforehand to the Garda?"

"No, it had not."

"Did this strike you as strange?"

"Yes." He nodded. "Usually we are told of any event like this. So that in itself aroused my suspicion."

"Suspicion of what?" Priteshi prompted him. She would do so from time to time, as counsel did with their witness to ensure that the jury heard all of the information. She wasn't allowed to lead him or really cross examine him, as it was her own witness.

"There might be trouble, something like that, I don't know." He shrugged in a non-committal way.

"So, what did you do?"

He paused before answering, perhaps deliberating and then said, "I decided to assemble a force and go out to the site of the rally to assess the situation."

"What happened then?"

"We went to the site, and I formed up the squad in a line, and we advanced on the rally."

Priteshi nodded as if in approval. "Why did you do that?"

"As a show of force and to deter any wrongdoing."

Bernadette grimaced at this pat answer, it just sounded incredibly trite.

"I see, and then?"

"The woman who was speaking." He pointed to Maneet. "That woman, the defendant, came towards us. So myself and five other officers went forward to meet her."

"What happened then?"

"Without warning, she attacked me, punched and kicked me. She was restrained and cooperated. We took her into custody, and she was charged with assault. She was later released pending prosecution."

"What happened to the rally?"

"I believe they dispersed."

Priteshi then posed what would be her key question having established the background. "So, did you or any other officer at the time say anything to provoke this attack?"

"Nothing, no."

"How bad were your injuries?" Priteshi asked him.

"Oh well, I got a bruise or something on my lip I think but nothing too serious thankfully."

"Thank you, Sergeant." Priteshi looked over at the clerk. "If it please the court, I will now show the video of the assault while Sergeant Maguire is present."

"By all means, continue," said Justice Buckley.

The clerk ran the video clip, and this was played while Maguire talked through it, repeating pretty much what he already said in answer to Priteshi's questions. This time he added the date and times referring to his notebook when things had taken place.

"Thank you again, Sergeant." Priteshi furnished him with a big smile. "No further questions, Judge."

Justice Buckley shifted his attention to Bernadette. "I assume you have questions for this witness?"

"Yes, Judge."

"Very well, carry on, carry on."

He sat back and put his palms together, no doubt in anticipation of a bit of a show. Bernadette stood up and surveyed the Sergeant coolly. He returned her with a slightly defiant stare as if he was waiting and expecting him to do her worst. She smiled at him a little disarmingly and the court waited in expectation.

"Sergeant," she began, "you said you had not been notified of the rally, am I right?"

This was a mild beginning though he would doubtless suspect everything she did, since he would have appeared before defence lawyers before.

"No."

"Is there a legal requirement to do so, inform the Garda about the rally?"

He hesitated. She knew he knew the law perfectly well, however.

"No." It seemed he was going to try and keep his answers short.

"So, then they were within their rights not to do so, am I right?" she said with another smile.

"Yes."

"But you stated under oath 'Usually we are told of any event like this. So that in itself aroused my suspicion.' Is that not so?"

He regarded her more warily, she was, he knew, manoeuvring for a point.

"It did, yes."

"Has this particular group a history of trouble at rallies or something like that?" She kept her tone mild, like a cat toying with an intended prey. She would reserve the tougher tones for the hard questions.

"No, not to my knowledge."

"Then why this time, why did it, as you said, arouse your suspicion?"

A small twitch of his mouth showed her he didn't like this line of questioning.

"I can't precisely say, you know it's just in police work you get a nose for trouble, and this seemed like it could be trouble."

This was a flannel answer, and he knew it. He looked around but there was nobody to rescue him, and nor would there be.

"Let me get this straight. You just said there was no history of problems with this group, you had no evidence to suggest trouble but that your nose, apparently informed you there might be, is that correct?"

"Yes, yes, it is."

"Is that something you learnt at the college is it? Nose based policing?" It was a dig and as she predicted Priteshi did not miss it.

"Objection!" Priteshi was on her feet at once.

"Mrs Mackenna, perhaps it was a little out of line," said Justice Buckley, with a smile. Bernadette had noticed his amusement at her crack.

"I withdraw the question, Judge," she said. Maguire was, however, nettled, and she'd taken a small liberty to get in a sarcastic barb and try to get under his skin. He might, if pushed, reveal something when she got to the really hard questions. She decided it was time to subtly shift gears.

"We'll leave it for the moment and let me ask you this. Why did you decide to turn out in force for the rally, with riot gear no less?"

"I've already told you, I thought there might be trouble," he said a trifle tetchy.

"Yes, but why, why such a large Garda presence?"

"It's our practice to ensure public order, it's not unusual to go out to a rally in force."

"Yes, but I have to come back to this, as to why this particular rally?"

"I told you that I thought there might be trouble."

"Yes, yes you have told us that you acted on what appears to have been a hunch. You said you had a nose for it, but the thing is I'm not buying it, Sergeant. I'm not buying it because in my experience the Garda doesn't act on hunches, it acts on evidence or intelligence, because otherwise, they would be going out for every possible occasion an officer thought something might be up because their nose told them. I put it to you that you aren't being straight with me or the court. You aren't, are you?"

The change of tone took Maguire by surprise. Bernadette was an expert at the sudden attack, and it was often effective, particularly when the witness was not expecting it.

He evidently considered things for a moment and then, at length, he said, "We were informed there might be trouble."

Bernadette pounced on this. "What kind of trouble?"

He shrugged. "Disorder that kind of thing."

This made more sense to Bernadette, but she was not finished.

"And who informed you?"

"I'm not at liberty to say." He shot back a retort.

"But you are under oath."

Priteshi was on her feet. "Objection, Judge, the Sergeant is not on trial here."

Justice Buckley, who had betrayed no sign of having a problem with the questions thus far, said, "What *is* your point, Mrs Mackenna?"

If challenged she had to explain herself.

Bernadette was ready for it, however. "I want to understand what prompted the presence of the Garda at this rally. I believe it is a relevant point, Judge, on the basis of the events which unfolded. It could be seen, in itself, as a provocation to arrive in the fashion they did to a peaceful rally in full riot gear."

The judge nodded in assent at the cogent response. "Very well, proceed."

Priteshi made a face and resumed her seat. She would have done the job for long enough to know that you win some and you lose some.

"Thank you, Judge," said Bernadette. "Who informed you, Sergeant?"

Maguire sighed, as if this was becoming tiresome. Justice Buckley looked at him sharply.

"A credible source."

"Who said what?"

Still appearing reluctant to answer, Maguire continued, "That there might be some kind of trouble or unrest at this rally, so we took serious precautions as a result."

Bernadette knew she wouldn't get the source. The Garda had their sources and informants, and they couldn't be made to reveal these in court. It also would not be politic to try.

"By which you mean you turned up in full riot gear?"

"Yes."

She began to move closer to her objective now. "Why were you not in riot gear?"

"I was directing operations."

"But not in riot gear, if you felt that there was a threat, why were you not in riot gear?" She persisted pushing towards her point.

"I felt I might be less provocative that way."

This was an unexpected gift, and she took it. "Oh, so you think that there could be provocation by arriving in full riot gear as your other officers did?"

"Some people might find it so, yes. We have to be sensitive to that." He evidently did not see the dichotomy in what he'd just said, and which she may well return to later, however, she wanted to hit the nub of her questioning.

"OK, so after your force disembarked and arrived on the scene. Ms Johal-Lynch came to speak to you?"

"Yes, yes she did."

"Why did you come from behind the shield line with *five* other officers?" This was a key question and what she asked next would depend upon how he answered it.

"In case."

"In case of what?"

"In case of trouble."

She hit back at this immediately. "But you said you didn't want to provoke anything and now you're saying you were concerned about trouble. Don't you feel that six officers approaching one person might be provocative?"

"It could be seen that way, but it could also give someone pause for thought about starting something."

He didn't seem to think there was something incongruous about this at all. She pursued it with vigour.

"Give *who* exactly?"

"Well, anyone who wanted to start it." This sounded lame and she wasn't going to allow him to get away with that.

"But who? Who was there but Ms Johal-Lynch in front of you, one woman against six officers do you really think she would start trouble as you make out?"

He looked cocky and said, "Well, she did, didn't she?"

The judge who wasn't looking too impressed overall with his demeanour said, "Sergeant, it's not for you to pass observations, just answer the question, if you please!"

Maguire looked up, a little contrite. It didn't do to annoy the judge. "Sorry, Judge. Well no, I didn't think she would, to be honest."

Bernadette still wasn't done. "But you still took several officers with you, why? I should have thought a one-to-one situation would have been less intimidating surely?"

"It might but if some others joined her then we were ready for it."

Her voice became incredulous. This was a great tone to use when the witness, had tied themselves in knots as Maguire had just done. "Ready for it? You had a large contingent of officers in full riot gear at your back, how could you say you were not ready for anything, including more people approaching you?"

He had trapped himself, and he knew it. "Yes, I see what you mean."

"Then why did you do it?"

"As I said, to avoid trouble."

She decided to go for the throat. She began softly.

"Is it not really the case that you were trying to provoke trouble rather than avoid it and thus your motivation for approaching Ms Johal-Lynch mobhanded?"

"No, it's not." His answer was emphatic.

"You would put her in a situation where she felt intimidated and perhaps not thinking clearly, wouldn't you say?" Her tone went up a notch.

"No, I would not." He was becoming defensive.

"You wanted to provoke her, yes or no?" She tried it once more.

"No, I did not."

Three goes at it had not rattled him. Bernadette decided to leave it but not without one final attempt to get something from it.

"I put it to you that what you did could nevertheless be seen or taken as a provocation, you can admit that, can't you?"

"Yes, I suppose you are right, it could."

She had some kind of admission which she might be able to use.

"We may well return to this but now let's take up the exchange between you and Ms Johal-Lynch."

"There was no exchange," he replied.

"Well, she says there was."

"There wasn't!"

Justice Buckley wasn't having any of it. "Sergeant, please confine yourself to answering questions. The jury will disregard the witness' last two statements."

Bernadette continued. "Sergeant, please turn to page three six one in the evidence book, paragraph two."

Maguire reached down and flipped the pages until he got to the requisite part.

"What does it say, can you please read it out?"

Maguire looked very much as if he didn't want to do so but he had to. "I went forward to talk to the Garda when the leader, Sergeant Maguire said, 'fuck your fucking rally, you Indian bitch. Why are you in this fucking country anyway? You fucking Paki whore. Go back to Paki land where you belong, you fucking little black slut, back to the gutter where your kind belong. We don't need people like you in this country. Fuck off, you cocksucking black piece of shit Indian dog.'"

His mouth had turned down in distaste as he read the words. Bernadette and others had watched him closely. It was very hard to tell whether the words were familiar to him or not. Several jurors were looking quite shocked. Justice Buckley remained impassive. He would have heard much worse in his time, so was unlikely to be fazed. Bernadette allowed the effect of the words to register on the jury before continuing.

"Did you say those words?" she asked at length.

"I did not."

"You never said anything in that paragraph to the defendant, yes or no?"

"No." His eyes shifted imperceptibly to the left as he replied. Nobody else would notice, but Bernadette did not miss it. The body language gave her cause to think he was lying. However, jurors were not likely to be experts in reading body language or see what she has just seen.

Bernadette was undeterred. "I put it to you that you did say those words, and I'll tell you why. Please turn to page four seven five."

Maguire did so, his eyes widened slightly. The judge and jurors would be doing the same.

"What do you see there?"

"Well, it's a screenshot of a website of the *White Knights of Ireland.*"

"And who are the *White Nights of Ireland*?" she said mildly.

"A white supremacist group," he said quietly.

"I'm sorry I did not hear you, who are they?" This was a tactic, it was to wrongfoot him and make him say it again but louder.

"They are, were... a white supremacist group." He spoke up but it was clear he was very uncomfortable.

"Of which you were a member and I right?"

"Yes."

"If you could turn to the next page."

He complied.

"That's your picture there is it not, on a website called *Irish Racewatch*, am I right?"

"Yes." He put his head down.

"It confirms what you said, am I right, you were a member of the group, yes?"

"Yes, yes it does, but I'm not a member now!" he added.

She let it pass, this was not a question she had asked him. She continued to pursue her objective.

"There were incidents of racial harassment and other similar crimes, culminating in a conspiracy to attack a Sikh temple with a homemade bomb. The perpetrators were sent to prison, is that correct?"

"Yes, yes that's correct."

"The group was disbanded after that, yes?"

"Yes."

"So, although you're not a member, when you were a member, were you involved in incidents of racial harassment and other crimes?"

He didn't answer.

"Were you or were you not? Answer the question."

"OK, so I did go on some rallies and stuff, but I wasn't harassing anyone. I've never been arrested or anything. I wasn't involved in that bombing stuff," he blurted out.

"I see," she said in a tone which sounded just as if she did not see at all. "So why *did* you join the organisation?" Her voice changed again, more friendly, approachable.

He regarded her warily. "I don't know, I suppose at the time I was worried about immigrants coming into the country."

She took this and decided to take it further. "You suppose at the time? Were you or weren't you worried about immigrants?"

"Well, yes. I guess."

This was another admission and she wanted to examine this to see if there was another chink in his armour. "Why was that?"

He thought about this for a while before answering and she let him have the space, she was looking for another opening to attack but he may not guess her intention to do so. Witnesses were under pressure when on the stand and so they didn't always act as rationally or considered as they might. Lawyers knew this and exploited it ruthlessly.

He finally answered her. "I thought they were taking our jobs you know, that's what they were saying, anyway, in the organisation."

She raised an eyebrow slightly. "And what's your view of immigrants now."

"Well, I don't mind them." He shrugged.

"You don't mind them? That's nice. But perhaps you don't really like them?"

"I didn't say *that*."

"But you do dislike immigrants, am I right?" Bernadette wasn't prepared to let this go.

"I don't dislike them, no."

She went back on the offensive. "Are you a racist, Sergeant?"

"What?"

He wasn't expecting this at all. A direct assault on his beliefs.

"I said are you a racist, a simple enough question. Are you?"

"No, I'm not." He was trying to sound emphatic although it did not quite get across that way. She came back at him again.

"But perhaps you were when you joined the *White Knights of Ireland*, am I right?"

"I don't really feel that I was, no." This was a wishy-washy answer leaving her room to go again, a mistake on his part.

"Oh, you don't feel that you were. You nevertheless joined an organisation which was disbanded and was entirely racist. But you are saying you weren't a racist in a blatantly racist group, is that what you're trying to tell the court?

"Not exactly, no I mean..."

She cut him off. A lawyer trick which was used when you didn't want the witness to elaborate and it appeared, they had answered the question.

"What do you mean? That you were a racist then but now you're not one? Is that what you're saying?"

Priteshi who had been squirming a little over this question, attempted a rescue.

"Objection, Judge, why is my learned colleague asking these questions. The Sergeant has already said he's not a racist."

"Mrs Mackenna?" said Justice Buckley, although his expression indicated he wasn't well disposed towards this objection.

"Judge, I don't feel he has said he's not racist and, even so, I think we're entitled to know what his feelings are about race, since he denies making racist remarks. I should be allowed to test his views, as it is material to the case and whether his testimony is considered truthful or not," Bernadette said reasonably.

"I agree," Justice Buckley nodded his assent. "I can't see any issue with the line of questioning... continue."

Priteshi sat down, she didn't look happy.

Bernadette turned to Maguire. "Are you saying you were a racist but you're not one now?"

"I..." Again, hesitation which she exploited.

"Yes or no, Sergeant?"

"No, I'm not one now."

"But you were, yes or no?"

"I deny being a racist." He wouldn't quite give her an answer to her question, so she tried a different tack.

"When you joined that organisation, and you have admitted doing so, did you hold racially motivated views? Views which could be construed as racist against one or more ethnicities in this country?"

"Yes. Yes, I did, I was young and hot-headed and..."

She interrupted again, having got what she was after.

"So, you were a racist and you're not now, correct?"

"If you put it that way then yes." He was forced into an admission.

"I do put it that way, and I question as to whether you're telling the truth about your current views. Are you?"

"I am. I have nothing against coloured people or any other kinds of people." He was well on the defensive at the moment.

"Right, I see. Nothing against them but you don't really like them, am I right?"

"No." He became exasperated and raised his voice. "I don't dislike anyone. I have nothing against anyone of a different race or colour. I did something wrong, and can't a person be allowed to make a mistake?"

"Of course, a person can make a mistake, Sergeant. The issue is whether you had moved on from the mistake or whether in truth you have lied to the court and you did say those words to Ms Johal-Lynch, perhaps in the heat of the moment?"

"No, no it's not true. I never said it, I didn't." He was resorting to sounding like a victim now.

This was a fine line. If she really did press him too hard the jury might start to feel sympathetic towards him. She had failed to get an admission from him, however. He had remained solid on the subject of Maneet. She resolved to try one more thing.

"Are you a member of any racist organisation now?" she asked him.

"No," he replied.

"Did you leave the *White Nights of Ireland* because it was disbanded or because you decided it wasn't for you?"

"A bit of both, I suppose."

"A bit of both? Can you explain this further for the court?"

"Once it was disbanded, I reflected on things and realised maybe some of the things they were saying were wrong."

"So, to recap. You were a racist but you're not a racist now, or at least that's the story you are telling the court, am I right?"

She was treading a thin line and she knew it, but the judge might let her get away with it. It seems he was going to as he said nothing, and Priteshi did not attempt another objection.

"It's not a story, it's the truth," he shot back.

"And the truth, is a moveable feast, is it not, Sergeant?" she observed wryly. She had come to the end of her questions. There was material for her speech but nothing else to attack him on. "No further questions, Judge."

Justice Buckley smiled at her. "Thank you, Mrs Mackenna. Mrs Patel, do you have any more questions for the witness?"

"No, Judge, I do not, thank you." Priteshi stood up briefly and resumed her seat.

"Excellent, very good. It's certainly time and past for lunch, but I wanted to let Mrs Mackenna finish with the witness," said the judge by way of explanation. "In any case, we'll take our lunch now and resume in an hour."

The Tipstaff who had been hovering in expectation of this, bade the court to rise and Justice Buckley wandered leisurely out of the room.

* * *

In the meeting room, Imogen opened a large box containing a sandwich delivery and packets of crisps. There was also coffee and bottles of too. Bernadette let the others help themselves and then took a salad, cheese and salami roll for herself.

"He was a slippery customer," Hughes observed biting into a cheese, ham and salad roll.

"Yes, he was, but I didn't have him quite on the ropes. I had hoped to get an admission out of him, it would have made things easier," said Bernadette.

"I thought you did really well," said Maneet. "I was very impressed, you made him sweat for sure."

"He was lying, there's no two ways about it." Imogen picked up a salami roll too.

"I got that impression, I must say," said Zhang sipping her coffee.

"He was a fucking liar, a fucking bastard liar. I would like to squeeze his balls like a fucking pig that he is!" Matelda growled.

"Oh Matelda!" said Maneet and everyone went off into peals of laughter.

Hughes explained that Matelda had a penchant for squeezing testicles and told a recent story involving a particular offender they had arrested who came to grief in that way. Imogen then also explained how Constantina had demonstrated such a manoeuvre on a lawyer in court, during a court case much to everyone's amusement.

"So, Matelda, you're quite the tartar, aren't you?" Bernadette observed.

"Ach, what is this tartar?" Matelda said crossly.

There was more laughter while it was explained to Matelda that a tartar was a fierce person.

"Ah yes, well this is true, this is very true." She smiled biting into a salami roll herself.

"We've got the rest of the officers this afternoon," said Imogen. "I can guess what's that is going to be. It will be 'no he didn't say it' five times over."

"We can but try," said Bernadette. "If they are going to stick to that story it's going to be hard to make any headway."

"Yes."

They finished their rolls talking of this and that, wanting to put the court case to one side at least for a little while.

All too soon, Bernadette checked her watch and announced it was time to return. They did so, and Hughes made sure the armed officers at the doors were OK. Their shift had changed at lunch and a different set had taken over. They all took their seats and waited for the judge.

The Tipstaff announced Justice Buckley who entered the room and sat down at his bench. He shuffled his notes, just as he usually did, and then spoke to Priteshi.

"Mrs Patel, your next witness please, I see there are five, perhaps we can get through them all today, depending..." he let it hang. It was a hopeful statement as the judge could not dictate to lawyers how many questions they could ask or how long they could take. As long as the questions were relevant, they had to be allowed.

"I call Garda John Gorman to the stand," said Priteshi without commenting on the time it might take.

A young twenty-five-year-old officer arrived, with short tidy black hair, a youthful face and complexion and brown eyes. He looked smart in his uniform which must have been well pressed for his court appearance. He took the oath, stated his name and occupation and Priteshi began her questions.

"Garda Gorman, you were part of the team which attended the rally on the day in question, am I right?"

"Yes, yes I was," he replied nodding.

"You were not in riot gear, correct?"

"Yes, that's right."

"And can you take us through what happened when the defendant Ms Johal-Lynch approached the Garda line?"

She waited expectantly while he retrieved his notebook. He consulted it for a moment and then said, "The defendant, who you see over there, approached us. Sergeant Maguire told us five to accompany him to meet her. So, we went to the front of the line with him. I was on his right-hand side."

"And then what happened?"

"When she got up to us, she suddenly snapped or something like that, and she punched Sergeant Maguire. It seems like she just lost it for no reason."

"I see." Priteshi drew herself up as if in condemnation of such behaviour.

"We restrained her, she was arrested and then brought to the Garda station. She was charged with assault."

"Thank you, Garda Gorman. Did Sergeant Maguire say anything to the defendant to perhaps provoke her in any way?"

This was a key question. It would be asked four more times Bernadette knew.

"No, he did not."

"So, he said nothing, he did not insult her in any way, make any kind of racial remarks at all?"

The Garda looked shocked at this suggestion, however, Bernadette felt he was faking it. She was resolved to test him.

"No, absolutely not."

"To conclude, you can see no reason at all for the defendant's actions?"

"No, none at all."

"Thank you, Garda Gorman," said Priteshi. "No further questions, Judge."

Justice Buckley looked at her with satisfaction. He was no doubt happy this had been quite short and was probably calculating how long another four witnesses might go for.

"Mrs Mackenna," he said, prompting Bernadette to stand up.

"Yes, Judge. I have questions for the witness."

"Proceed, proceed," said Justice Buckley airily.

Bernadette shifted her gaze to Gorman and fixed him with a penetrating stare, which made him visibly uncomfortable.

"Garda Gorman," she began, "you said Sergeant Maguire did nothing at all to provoke Ms Johal-Lynch into attacking him, am I right?"

"Absolutely," he nodded in affirmation.

Bernadette had already decided upon a tactic. It would be to make him confront the words which Maguire had said and test his reaction. This would be the same for each of them. "Garda Gorman, please turn to page three six one in the evidence book, paragraph two."

Gorman reached down and found the part she was referring to.

"Please read it out."

Gorman, like Maguire, was reluctant but did as he was asked. "I went forward to talk to the Garda when the leader, Sergeant Maguire said, 'fuck your fucking rally, you Indian bitch. Why are you in this fucking country anyway? You fucking Paki whore. Go back to Paki land where you belong, you fucking little black slut, back to the gutter where your kind belong. We don't need people like you in this country. Fuck off, you cocksucking black piece of shit Indian dog.'"

He flinched as he read the words and did so slowly. Bernadette noted the expression on his face and his embarrassment. This was all to the good.

"Have you heard those words before?" Bernadette cocked an eyebrow.

"No."

"You deny Sergeant Maguire said those words?"

"Yes."

She paused giving him a moment to think perhaps she was finished before coming at him from another angle.

"You would naturally be protective to your colleagues, would you not?"

"Yes, I suppose..." His expression became wary.

"So protective perhaps you might lie on their behalf?"

"What? No!" He sounded outraged.

"A friend of yours, is he, Sergeant Maguire?" she floated the question.

"He... well, not exactly. Not a friend."

"But nevertheless, you would still protect him, as a fellow officer, wouldn't you?" She was pushing it a little asking this again but Priteshi did not register an objection.

"Yes, but he didn't say it."

"So, you agree you would protect him. I think you're doing exactly that, and you are lying. I think you're lying for Sergeant Maguire, are you not?"

"No, I'm not lying." The tone was one of protest. Gorman didn't like the accusation.

"You know, you are under oath, and I'm sure you understand the penalties for perjury. Isn't it better to do what's right? So, I'm asking you one more time, is it not the truth that Sergeant Maguire said those words? Now is the time to do the right thing, isn't it, Garda Gorman?"

Garda Gorman looked at her, he hesitated. The idea of lying under oath and perjury might not have occurred to him before now. As a Garda officer, he would have sworn to be truthful, honest and uphold the law. If he wasn't doing that, then he was going against the very thing he'd pledged to do. He hesitated just a fraction too long before he answered. It was as if he had to think about it, weigh it up.

If it had been the truth he would have come back straight away. She knew then for certain he was lying.

However, Gorman, it seemed wasn't minded, to tell the truth.

"I am doing what's right," he said. "He didn't say those words."

"Right." Bernadette's expression told him she did not believe him. "No further questions, Judge."

From the corner of her eye, she saw a look of triumph on Priteshi's face. Perhaps Priteshi did not know her own witnesses were not telling the truth. It was hard to say. Bernadette sat down, and Imogen reached across and gave her hand a consoling squeeze.

"Excellent, Garda Gorman, you can stand down," said Justice Buckley. As Gorman left the stand, he spoke to Priteshi, "Mrs Patel, you may call your next witness."

The next Garda officer was, Paddy Bannock, a thirty-year-old Scot, followed by Erin Lawson, an Irish woman of around twenty eight years old. Bernadette questioned them in the same fashion and hoped she might make some headway with Lawson. It should not make a difference that Lawson was female but sometimes Bernadette could get through to female witnesses better. However, in this case, they stuck to their story which was disappointing.

Gavin Amerson, a thirty-five-year-old proved a similar result, and then came Richard Hamble, the final witness. He was around twenty years old, and fresh faced like Gorman. He probably had not been on the force that long. He was a good looking blonde, with an attractive face with blue eyes. After Priteshi had finished Bernadette tried one last time.

"Garda Hamble," she said, "you know that if you lie, that is perjury do you not?"

"Yes," he replied.

"I am assuming you've not been long a Garda is that true?"

"About two or so years, yes."

She smiled at him disarmingly. He smiled back nervously. He had perhaps not been in court much before now.

"It would be a shame to ruin a promising career if you did bear false witness, wouldn't you say?"

He was definitely looking a little alarmed at this. She pushed harder.

"I want you to turn to three six one in the evidence book, paragraph two."

He did so and became a little agitated when he saw the words.

"Would you please read it out to the court?"

He looked at her unhappily. "Must I?"

"You must," Justice Buckley told him, though not unkindly.

Bernadette waited while he did so, haltingly and blushing furiously.

"Was that difficult?" she asked him mildly when he'd finished.

"I... I didn't like it no," he said with feeling.

"How did you feel when your Sergeant said that to Ms Johal-Lynch?" she floated this in catching him unawares and he started to answer without thinking.

"I don't think a Garda officer should say..." he trailed off with a slightly stricken look.

"You don't think a Garda officer should say that, like your Sergeant did, is that what you were going to tell the court?" she supplied helpfully.

"No... I mean, no, he didn't say it, that's not what I meant. I meant a Garda officer shouldn't say something like that, and he didn't, no he didn't," he blurted out trying to undo the slip he had made.

Bernadette calculated her next move. If she pressed him, he would probably deny it further. She could leave it hanging in doubt, reasonable doubt. She decided to risk it.

"Thank you, Garda Hamble. No further questions, Judge." She sat down.

Imogen shot her a puzzled look. Bernadette shrugged.

"Very good," said Justice Buckley. "Well, I let the tea break go by to see if we could finish, and we have. We'll adjourn for today and tomorrow I assume it will be the case for the defence. Am I right?"

"Yes, Judge," said Priteshi taking the lead. "The prosecution has no further witnesses."

The Tipstaff came in and bade the court to rise. Justice Buckley left the room, and the press made a dash for the door in order to try and be ready for any statements.

Priteshi marched out looking well satisfied with herself, leaving Carole to clear up.

"You had him on the ropes, why did you let him go?" Imogen said as soon as Priteshi was out of earshot.

"I thought about it, and if I pushed him, he would have dug into his position thus convincing the jury further that he hadn't heard it. The way I've left it now, I can use that in my closing remarks because it's ambiguous and they will remember it."

"I guess," Imogen replied. "I suppose I'd have tried to crucify him and get him to change his testimony."

"Yes, ordinarily I might have gone that route, but I'd already failed four times. This is now all about reasonable doubt barring a miracle. I managed to catch him out but not enough."

"She's right," Hughes put in, "I think he would have just denied it harder. I could tell."

"Well, OK. You're the boss anyway." Imogen smiled.

"I am and don't you forget it!" Bernadette joked.

"Oh, I won't. I just love it when she's so domineering," Imogen said to Hughes.

"It's pretty sexy, to be honest, I agree." Hughes laughed.

"Oh stop!" Bernadette shook her head in mock resignation.

Maneet had by this time come up to them.

"I guess that didn't go too well, did it," she said.

"I'm sorry, darling, I did my best, but these guys are solid with each other," Bernadette said a little contritely.

"Fuckers is what they are. Fucking liars too," said Maneet.

"They are bastards, lying fucking bastards," Matelda added.

"I suppose they need your ball treatment." Zhang laughed.

"Ach I will make the mincemeat from these cowards!"

Bernadette noticed Carole was hovering nearby, she took a couple of steps towards her. "Carole, how are you?"

"I'm fine," said Carole, she looked around to check they were not being overheard and lowered her voice. "But they're lying, and she knows they are lying. You didn't hear that from me."

Without another word she turned and hurried off out of the courtroom.

"Well fuck," said Imogen, who had followed Bernadette and was standing beside her.

"Fuck indeed," said Bernadette. "Though I'm buggered what we can do about it."

"I have a notion, sorry to interrupt." Hughes had overheard.

"Yes?" Bernadette was open to any suggestions at this point.

"Let me talk to Brogan, someone needs to read the riot act to these reprobates."

"OK."

"Carole obviously wants a job," Imogen quipped.

"You think? Maybe she just likes us."

"That too."

"Well, we've no room for another junior just now," said Bernadette.

"Think about it, though, darling, maybe we could."

"But you're my junior," Bernadette protested.

"Perhaps you need two."

"But..."

"I'll always be there. You know I will. I promise."

"Are you two married or what?" Hughes said having listened in on the conversation.

"I'm her work wife, and Eve is her home wife." Imogen laughed.

"Imogen is like family to me and Eve, that's all."

"She loves me to bits." Imogen's eyes twinkled.

Bernadette just giggled.

"You lawyers are a strange bunch, but I do understand. I'm half in love with Bernadette myself but don't tell Iona for God's sake." Hughes chuckled.

"Stop it both of you, that's enough!" Bernadette said sternly.

Imogen and Hughes just laughed. Imogen gathered their things, and they made their way to the court exit.

"Are you giving a statement?" Imogen asked before they reached the main doors.

"Perhaps," Bernadette replied giving it some thought. "Don't say anything to the reporters Maneet, not today."

"God no, that's the last thing I want to do," said Maneet.

They reached the top of the steps and Bernadette paused briefly to talk to the press. Below the protestors were still there blowing airhorns and chanting slogans.

"Today you heard the prosecution, tomorrow you will hear our side of the story," she began.

"Do you think the Garda are lying?" shouted out a reporter.

"My client was provoked. If you were in court, you would have heard the words which provoked her. We intend to prove it and we believe she is innocent. That is all I have to say."

Thinking better of it, Bernadette decided to stop there. The problem was she couldn't prove it, however, bravado in front of the press was a different thing. She pushed through with the help of Hughes and Zhang who very ably carved a path for them. They headed for the car as quickly as they could, while Matelda whisked Maneet away to their own vehicle.

"You handle the press well I've noticed," said Hughes looking impressed.

"Lots of practice, even when it's all just words and we've got no way of proving it," Bernadette smiled as they got into the car.

"I'll get onto Brogan as soon as we get to the office." Hughes picked up on Bernadette's frustration.

"Thanks."

* * *

Bernadette and Imogen were seated in Bernadette's office drinking coffee and discussing the case, before heading for home.

"What do you think, darling, about tomorrow?" Imogen said sipping her drink.

"I think we're fucked, if you want the honest truth. I can put Maneet up there but who are the jury going to believe? Maneet or six Garda officers? We have absolutely nothing to prove that Maguire said what he said. No footage or anything else. It's his and five colleagues' word against hers."

"Oh." Imogen wasn't used to Bernadette being quite so pessimistic about a case. Usually, Bernadette would still see light at the end of the tunnel even against all odds.

"I'm sorry, it must sound terribly unlike me. But I can't see any way out of it. It doesn't mean I won't do my best, but I don't see a case for reasonable doubt."

"Fuck," said Imogen putting out her hand to take Bernadette's.

"Fuck is right. I feel like we've done all this for nothing."

"Don't say that. Never say that. You can't possibly have predicted this outcome. You went in there and tried your best to break those witnesses. You nearly had the last one."

Imogen squeezed Bernadette's hand and Bernadette shot her a grateful look.

"I know, but maybe I should have pushed him." Bernadette's tone was regretful.

"You told me to never look back. Accept what you've done and move on. You should take your own advice, darling."

"You're right." Bernadette sighed. "I did what I thought was best at the time."

"Perhaps Aileen and Brogan can do something."

"Who knows, I can't rely on it. We'll just go in like we planned and do what we can."

"Exactly, so enough of this maudlin talk. Go home to your wife and fuck her brains out."

Bernadette let out a peal of laughter. "Oh, you're so funny. It's not quite so easy with our bodyguards around."

"Oh, we say we're going to take a nap, that's our new code word," said Imogen.

"Yes, and you live in a much larger house."

"You could always come and live with us too."

"Haha, that's a lovely thought, darling, but I don't think I could take D'Arcy twenty-four-seven," Bernadette chuckled. "We like our little house, anyway."

"I know, I'm teasing. You need your own space, but do come and stay with me sometimes when D'Arcy goes away filming, please?"

"Of course, we will, and you can come and stay with us too."

"Thank you."

"What about your wedding?" Bernadette changed the subject. Living with D'Arcy and Imogen was a nice fantasy, but it would drive both her and Eve crazy in a very short space of time.

"Oh." Imogen let out a long sigh.

"What does *that* mean?"

"It means we're getting nowhere. We've both still got different ideas. We're not arguing about it, but we're not finding any common ground either." Imogen gave a despairing shrug.

"Right, well, why can't you just do what we did? Have a private ceremony and then a wedding celebration in the garden. It's getting on for summer and still good weather for a marquee."

"Because D'Arcy always wants something fancier or different and she changes her mind from one day to the next!" Imogen's tone expressed her frustration.

"I see." Bernadette gave her a speaking look.

"Don't worry, I've not done anything, I've kept my promise." Imogen smiled. "But the month is up soon, and some days my hand itches for that paddle I can tell you."

"You've been very good."

"I've tried, but it's hard to learn new ways. I'm trying, I really am."

"Try not to go back to the old ways either, it's what got you into trouble before."

"I know," Imogen groaned. "Just sometimes I want to spank her arse so much..." she trailed off while Bernadette regarded her in amusement.

"What are you like, my darling?"

"I'm a hopeless case, I know it." Imogen shook her head.

"I'm not asking you to stop it altogether, just temper it. Temper it with other ways of dealing with each other."

"Yes, I know you're right."

"So then reach a compromise on your wedding for goodness sake, and get it done!"

"I remember telling you much the same thing." Imogen laughed.

"Yes and look what happened. It had to be taken out of my hands. Learn from my mistake if nothing else."

"Why is getting married so important?" Imogen said suddenly after finishing up her drink.

"It is and it isn't," was Bernadette's reply. "I didn't think it was important to me and Eve. I believe in the strength of the relationship. But somehow the public declaration of love was healing, it made us both feel more secure. I can't explain it to you. If you really don't believe in getting married, then you shouldn't but why did you get engaged?"

"I do, I do want to get married!" Imogen wailed. "I want to publicly bind that silly girl to me for life."

"Then you've answered your own question."

"Why do you have to be so damnably logical?"

"Isn't that your line?"

"Why do you have to use my own lines against me?"

Bernadette giggled.

"You're a hopeless case, darling, I love you dearly. You need to sort it out and you know it."

"Yes, yes I do."

"I think it's time to go home."

"Yes, for sure. I'll see if we can't so this wedding out once and for all. Talking is hard, the paddle is so much simpler."

"Imogen, no!"

"I'm teasing," Imogen's eyes were dancing.

* * *

That evening, Bernadette, Eve and their two bodyguards spent a happy hour in the gym, followed by a delicious lasagne and salad. Healy and Eve were doing all the cooking together, and Hughes said her fiancée was becoming such a great cook she'd never have to cook again. Healy naturally demurred and said she'd miss Hughes' cooking, and Hughes was suitably edified by that remark. Healy was rewarded with a long and lingering kiss. A dessert of Tiramisu rounded things off nicely.

"Delicious," said Bernadette.

"Iona made it, under my guidance," said Eve.

"You really are becoming a master chef." Hughes smiled.

"Oh, not quite *that* good." Healy blushed.

"How are things with court?" Eve asked Bernadette. They had not discussed it over dinner, but rather talked about other more frivolous things like tastes in cars, art and hot women in the movies. The four had become fast friends, and conversations often ranged over all sorts of topics, important and less so.

"Oh, well, I'm not hopeful of a good outcome. I wasn't able to break any of the witnesses, so we've got six against one and nothing to corroborate Maneet's version at all."

"Oh, that's not good." In sympathy, Eve's foot slid up the bare skin of Bernadette's calf. Bernadette smiled and squeezed Eve's hand under the table.

"Don't give up yet. I've spoken to Brogan and he's going to see what he can do," said Hughes.

"What can he do, though?" Bernadette said a little despondently.

"Oh, you don't know Brogan, he can do quite a bit when he sets his mind to it. He's got a lot of clout in the Garda. I wouldn't like to be anyone who he decides to turn the screws on."

Bernadette laughed lightly. "He seems quite a sweetheart to me."

"Oh, to you. But have you seen him in full flow?" Healy said.

"Yes, both Imogen and I have witnessed it, fortunately, directed at someone else."

"Yes, he's a force to be reckoned with," Hughes agreed.

"And Seamus, how does he cope?" Bernadette wondered.

"Oh, Seamus has Brogan's measure alright, he seems to deal very well with him. Besides Brogan has a soft spot for Seamus."

"Lucky Seamus."

"Not the same for poor old Connor." Hughes chuckled referring to O'Rorden, Seamus' long-suffering number two who had felt the acid end of Brogan's tongue more than once. "Did I ever tell you about the parrots?"

"Parrots?" Bernadette looked puzzled.

"Oh, yes, the Parrots, the bane of Connor's life, well..." Hughes proceeded to relate the long tale of parrots from the time one was taken into custody that belonged to a suspect on a case and ended up in Brogan's house. There were surprise appearances of the parrot in court, and other very funny episodes which had them all in stitches.

At the end of a mirthful meal, they had coffee and elected to retire to bed.

Bernadette snuggled into Eve and kissed her softly.

"I love you," said Eve nuzzling her lips.

"Imogen says I should fuck your brains out, what do *you* think about it?" Bernadette whispered.

"I think she's a very wise woman."

"Come closer then, my little witch."

Bernadette's fingers began to trace a trail down Eve's bare skin, and across her breasts.

"Oh, fuck!" Eve hissed in a breath. "God yes... I want... *that*! Oh... oh!"

Bernadette smiled as she felt her wife's body begin to arch and respond to the dexterous touch in all the right places.

CHAPTER TEN

orning arrived all too soon, Bernadette opened a sleepy eye and silenced the alarm. She looked at her wife's face which was relaxed and smiling. They had made love quite intensely that night. Reflecting on their sex drives, Bernadette mused that Eve was probably the hornier, judging from her daytime activities. However, perhaps this was a little curtailed by the presence of Healy. Bernadette doubted it very much but forbore to enquire too closely. Eve would tell her if she wanted to know, but she let it lie.

"Morning, my darling," Eve purred opening her eyes.

"Morning, my precious angel."

Eve kissed her and Bernadette returned the kiss quite passionately. Both flamed up at once.

"Fuck, I want you, have we... got time?" Eve looked lustfully into Bernadette's eyes.

Bernadette did not answer but her fingers slid quickly between Eve's legs.

"Oh... darling... fuck... oh yes... fuck... oh my God... oh... oh... oh... fuck... fuck... fuck... oh... oh... ohh!" Eve climaxed quickly and easily, kissing Bernadette hard while her own hand reached for Bernadette's very wet sweet spot.

"Oh... oh God..." Bernadette moaned pushing her pelvis into Eve's hand. "Oh my God... oh fuck... Jesus... fuck... fuck... oh... my God... fuck... oh... ah... ah... ah... ahh!" Her orgasm arrived just as rapidly, and she lay back panting slightly.

"That was a very quick quickie," Eve giggled.

"Yes, because sometimes you just make me so..."

"I know... oh believe me I know."

Recovering, Bernadette kissed her and slid out from the covers to take her shower. The hot water engulfed her and eased her mind, as she reflected upon the forthcoming day. She really felt, for once, she had nothing in the tank. No matter how she tried, she couldn't see the jury buying Maneet's version. Although she might hope for it, the chances of the cavalry coming over the hill to save the day at this point, seemed remote.

However, it would not stop Bernadette from giving it everything she'd got. She stepped out of the shower, pushing the thoughts to the back of her mind. Eve was waiting to do her hair and opted to brush it out and straighten it. It was a softer look reflected in some subtle understated makeup. Eve had laid out a grey skirt suit, grey mules and a pale pink blouse. Eve was very in tune with the day's events and as it was to be Bernadette's witnesses, she did not need to appear intimidating.

Bernadette went downstairs and took her seat at the head of the dining table. She accepted a plate of scrambled eggs on toast, with bacon and mushrooms. She smiled at her wife as Eve put a cup of coffee next to it and took a seat herself.

"Do you never get dressed in the day?" Hughes wondered cutting into her own eggs. Eve was, as usual, wearing a satin robe pulled tight which folded nicely around her frame. Bernadette was always appreciative of the effect it had on Eve.

"Oh, mainly when I go out," said Eve airily. "When I'm on my own I quite often wear nothing. I find it helps my painting and drawing."

"Don't let *me* stop you," said Healy with a laugh.

"Don't even think about it," said Hughes to her fiancée.

"I'll wear my pistol never fear." Healy poked her tongue out at Hughes.

Bernadette laughed. "Oh my God, what are the two of you like? What would Brogan say if he knew?"

"Just as well he doesn't," said Hughes wryly.

"What happens at home, stays at home," said Eve with a smile.

"Just as well," said Bernadette.

"You've a liberated wife, for sure," said Hughes.

"She's just my fancy-free hippy witch." Bernadette smiled at Eve, who smiled back.

"Leading my fiancée astray." Hughes chuckled.

"I'm just being myself, darling," said Healy.

"And I like you being yourself, so ignore my previous strictures. I mean, if you want to turn the place into a nudist colony, who am I to stop you?"

"Really?"

"Yes, yes and it's because I do love you, so much."

"I love you too." Healy smiled.

"Well, now that's settled, we'll leave the naturists at home and get going, shall we?" said Bernadette draining her cup.

"Naturists." Hughes snorted.

"I think we should wear things like this more at home, honey, when we do get back home?" said Healy indicating the robe she had donned, along with her sidearm.

"Yes, well we'll see," was all Hughes would say, although Bernadette suspected she was quite taken with the idea. From what she could tell Hughes and Healy were a highly sexed and somewhat kinky couple. "I'm not sure I want you distracting me all the time."

"Don't you? Don't you really?" Healy got up and stood with her arms around Hughes, nuzzling her gently with her lips.

"Oh God, you know what that does to me..."

"Well. You can save it for later, can't you... hmm?" Healy began to kiss her.

Bernadette took Eve's hand and she accompanied her to the front door, leaving the other two for a moment. Eve also pulled her in for a kiss.

"Have you really been wandering around the house naked?" Bernadette asked her.

"Oh yes, though sometimes I wear high heels."

"Oh God, stop... I've got to go to work!"

Eve kissed her and she closed her eyes. Her world became all sparkly and a heady mixture of love engulfed her for those few moments. When she opened them again, Hughes was waiting.

"Let's go." Bernadette sighed and reluctantly let go of her wife. She and Hughes drove away with Healy and Eve waving goodbye in the doorway.

"I'm really going to miss you two when this is over," said Bernadette as the car purred out and onto the main drag.

"Likewise," said Hughes. "We'll have to meet up sometimes, after all this is done."

"Definitely."

"It's an unlikely friendship, detectives and lawyers."

"Not forgetting my witchy artist wife."

"Her too."

They laughed. Bernadette turned on the radio and the two of them sang lustily to the latest tunes.

* * *

They arrived at the office, and after a quick coffee and chat with Imogen, they headed for the court. Arriving on the steps, the usual crowd of press were there, along with the demonstrators who seemed quite indefatigable. They had been whipping things up on social media and swelled their ranks significantly. There were now whistles and drums banging loudly, as well as airhorns. It seemed rather like a sporting occasion than a protest apart from the banners proclaiming that Maneet was innocent.

Bernadette led the way and pushed quickly through the throng declining to answer any questions about the case. There was nothing more to add at this point, in any case. With a night to think about it, she knew she was up against it. Talking to the press at this juncture would not help.

Imogen sensed her mood and slipped her hand into Bernadette's. Bernadette gave her a smile of gratitude.

They met with Maneet and Matelda in the meeting room. Imogen had been with Zhang to procure some coffee. Bernadette picked up hers and sipped it pensively before speaking to Maneet.

"This is your big moment," she said lightly.

"I know and I'm fucking nervous."

"Try not to be. I'm just going to walk you through the whole event but Priteshi will come on the attack for sure."

"That fucking bitch!" Maneet scowled.

"I know you don't like her, but just for me, please try not to lose your rag. If you do that isn't going to help us at all, OK?"

"I'm going to do my best to be on my best behaviour."

"I hope so, I really do." Bernadette's voice took on a tone of sincerity because she knew that Maneet losing it would simply reinforce the idea that she also lost it at the rally.

"I promise, honest, cross my heart." Maneet smiled.

"Anyway, at least I've got a speech to do first, to prime the jury."

"I'm looking forward to it, I've heard great things."

"She's amazing," said Imogen. "If I can ever be even half as good, I'll be happy."

"You will be just as good and maybe better," Bernadette said at once.

"You're too kind to me."

"You'll make a great barrister one day. I know you will."

The others watched this exchange with interest. It was unusual to see quite such a close relationship between two colleagues but at the same time, none of them felt it untoward.

"Thank you." Imogen finished her cup.

Maneet's phone rang and she picked it up. "It's Akshay," she said moving a little away from the others in the meeting room. Even so, everyone went silent, but Maneet turned her back and looked out of the meeting room window.

"What? You're not coming?" she said sounding a little upset. "Oh, it's a bad time for the market? What? Well, OK... why am I fighting it anyway? We've been over this. Don't you understand, I could go to fucking prison, Akshay, and at the very least I'll get a fine, my reputation is going to be fucking ruined, so of course I'm fighting it! You didn't realise? Really? What the fuck, Akshay, we've discussed this several times... no... I'm going now... I've got to be a witness and you're ringing me up like this upsetting me... well, I don't care if you don't mean to, you have... no fuck off... just fuck off... if you don't want to come fine, but you can fuck off, Akshay... yes... bye!"

She disconnected and her eyes filled with tears. Surprisingly Matelda went straight up to her and embraced her. Maneet burst into tears. Bernadette and Imogen exchanged concerned looks. This wasn't the time for Maneet's fiancé to be upsetting her like that. After a few moments, Maneet recovered and Matelda let her go.

"Are you going to be OK?" Bernadette asked standing up.

"Yes, yes, I will be, it's just I thought he'd come, the bastard. Fuck him anyway, we've got a job to do." Maneet put on a fierce expression.

"Alright, well then, I think it's probably time," said Bernadette.

They left the meeting room in a body and after the customary loo visit, they headed for the courtroom. Hughes checked the armed guards on the door and returned to the lawyer station where they were setting up.

"I don't know those two, do you?" she asked Zhang her brow a little furrowed.

"No, are they new?"

"I don't know." Hughes said no more but it was clear she wasn't happy about something. Since the court had not begun, she phoned Olivia and evidently, for reasons best known to herself, asked her to come to court.

Priteshi came in and while Carole was setting up, she came over to talk to Bernadette.

"Hi," said Bernadette surveying her coolly.

"Last chance to change your plea, and let's just get this put to bed." The arrogant tone was obvious. Bernadette could feel Imogen bristling beside her.

"We'll take our chances and let the jury decide, I think."

"Your choice." Priteshi shrugged as if to say, 'your funeral, mate'.

Bernadette could see Maneet scowling at Priteshi's back as she returned to her own station.

"What a fucking cheek!" Imogen said in a fierce whisper.

"She's only doing what I'd probably do in her position."

"Even so, you know exactly what she needs, and what I'd like to do!"

"I know..." Bernadette chuckled at the veiled reference to the paddling Imogen undoubtedly felt she wanted to dish out. You could take the paddle out of the girl, but you couldn't take the girl out of the paddle, she reflected with a wry smile. It was still Imogen's go-to solution and undoubtedly would remain so, no matter how much Bernadette tried to temper it.

Her thoughts were abruptly curtailed as the Tipstaff entered and announced the arrival of Justice Buckley. He came in looking remarkably cheerful as always and took a seat with some amiable glances all around to ensure all was well in his courtroom. Having assured himself it was, he addressed himself to Bernadette.

"Ah, Mrs Mackenna, I believe it is your turn, is it not?"

"Yes, Judge." She stood up.

"No doubt you have prepared some opening remarks?" He sounded almost hopeful. Bernadette's opening and closing addresses had something of a reputation in legal circles. He had heard one of hers before and at the time had appeared quite impressed by it.

"Yes, Judge, I have."

"Very well, then, in your own time, proceed." He sat back in expectation and waited.

Bernadette suppressed the natural nervousness she felt which always preceded her speeches. This was something she had never shaken even from her time acting on the stage at school. She gripped the sides of the podium lightly and imagined herself to be within a circle. Her circle of confidence. Allowing her mind to clear, she focused upon her breathing and then on the words she needed to say. Having readied herself, she raised her eyes to the jury and began.

"Judge, members of the Jury. It was the nurse in Romeo and Juliet by William Shakespeare who said 'There's no trust, No faith, no honesty in men. All perjured, All forsworn, all naught, all dissemblers.' And is this simply where we are today. A decision, members of the jury about honesty. About lying and about who is telling the truth and who is not."

She paused, checked the jury was attentive, and then continued.

"Officers of the Garda, sworn to trust! And I'll read you here the Garda oath which every officer must swear to when joining that organisation 'I hereby solemnly and sincerely declare before God that I will faithfully discharge the duties of a member of the Garda Síochána with fairness, integrity, regard for human rights, diligence and impartiality, upholding the Constitution and the laws and according equal respect to all people, while I continue to be a member, I will to the best of my skill and knowledge discharge all my duties according to law, and I do not belong to, and will not while I remain a member form, belong to or subscribe to, any political party or secret society whatsoever.'"

Once more she allowed this to settle before recommencing her speech.

"Regard for human rights. Is what it says. Will not belong to any political party or secret society whatsoever. Is what it says!"

Her voice rose for emphasis.

"And yet, here we had Sergeant Maguire who acknowledged before this court, membership of *The White Knights of Ireland*. A white supremacist group. A political group or even secret society with members convicted of conspiracy to murder. Yes, you can say it was many years ago, and yes you can say, as he did, that he is no longer a member. But I ask you this? Does a leopard change its spots? Did Sergeant Maguire change his views? Did he? That is for you to decide."

She looked around again, her voice had taken on a serious tone. The court was, however, silent.

"On the face of it, Sergeant Maguire did nothing wrong. On the face of it, he has five other officers who swore in this courtroom under oath that he said nothing to Ms Johal-Lynch. He claims she simply attacked him without due cause. For no apparent reason at all."

Bernadette took a long breath. She punctuated her speech with highs and lows of tone. Pauses were put in mainly for emphasis.

"Ask yourselves these questions and after you have heard Ms Johal-Lynch's testimony ask them again. Why would someone simply attack the Garda in superior force without provocation? Does it make any sense?"

She looked at the jury who were giving her their full attention.

"I can tell you that it does not make any sense to me. A rally which we were given to understand was peaceful was suddenly disturbed by the arrival of a large force of Garda officers in full riot gear. How would that seem to you in the same position? Threatening, intimidating? I think so, I very much think so."

Another pause, another check. She wanted to keep the jury with her.

"They begin to advance. What would *you* do? Ms Johal-Lynch goes forward to parlay. As she does so six officers, no less, appear from behind the line and advance on you. How would *you* feel? Ask yourself, exactly that question. I suggest at the very least you might feel a little anxious, if not worse. And then according to Sergeant Maguire, suddenly and out of the blue, she launches an unprovoked attack. Does it make any sense? I suggest to you it most assuredly does not!"

Bernadette punched out the last part for emphasis. To drive her point home.

"What does make more sense? I'll tell you. Sergeant Maguire lets fly a stream of racist invective which given the heat of the situation, the intimidation of the circumstances and the sensitivity and ethnicity of the defendant, sets forth a chain of events leading up to her assaulting the officer in question. This was a provoked assault. In fact, it was deliberate provocation. There was also duress. The duress of being subjected to racially motivated hate speech."

Bernadette glanced at the judge who seemed to be listening very carefully to her words.

"Ask yourselves another question. What possible reason could Ms Johal-Lynch a respected human rights lawyer have for committing an offence which would ruin her reputation and her standing? What possible reason? Now allow me to put to you another scenario altogether. Sergeant Maguire, for reasons which we do not fully know, assembles a force of Garda to attend a rally by the organisation, Irish against Discrimination. Yes, against discrimination, or in this case particularly racism. Sergeant Maguire who by his own admission has been a racist even though he denies he is one now."

She stopped raised one finger as if making a point.

"Doesn't this strike you as odd? He says he's acting on information received, though what information and from whom he doesn't disclose. The force in riot gear arrives at the rally and advances upon it. Ms Johal-Lynch comes out to speak to them, and Sergeant Maguire launches a stream of invective towards her. Under the circumstances, she is stressed, intimidated, and feels under duress. Then she is attacked by some extremely insulting invective and racial slurs. She loses her cool and attacks Maguire. She calms down immediately, does not resist arrest, and is later charged. Then, Sergeant Maguire assembles the six officers and by whatever means persuades them to lie to the court about what happened. To lie to the court!"

She paused again, her words were certainly hitting home, she could tell by the fleeting expressions.

"Lie to court, members of the jury, because loyalty to your Sergeant is more important than the oath you swore to the Garda. Yes, there's no trust, No faith, no honesty in men. All perjured, All forsworn, all naught, all dissemblers. I put it to you, members of the jury that this is exactly what we have here. No faith, no honesty in men, all perjured, all forsworn. You will get to decide, but when you do, after hearing all of the testimony, ask yourselves these questions. Unless you can say beyond reasonable doubt that the provocation did not take place, that there was no duress, then I would ask you to find Ms Johal-Lynch not guilty. Thank you."

Bernadette had softened the last part, but her words were strong, and so was her intonation. It was a good speech. She could tell from the smile Imogen gave her. She waited for the judge.

"Thank you, Mrs Mackenna," he said. "You may now call your first witness."

"Thank you, Judge," she replied. "I call Maneet Johal-Lynch to the stand."

Maneet came forward from the dock and took her place on the stand. She affirmed her oath and stated her name, and occupation for the court.

"Maneet," said Bernadette opting for informality. Apart from anything else, it made no sense to use her surname, and it also made the jury feel a little more connected. "You are a human rights lawyer, are you not?"

"Yes, yes I am," said Maneet.

"You're well known in international circles, you have spoken at the UN, in fact, you've quite a reputation?"

"Yes, yes I do."

It was important to establish this in order to assess the impact of a conviction on her.

"So, it's true to say that a conviction of assault on an officer of the Garda may be quite damaging, am I right?"

"Yes, it could be very damaging to me personally and to the NGO I work for."

"Thank you. In which case, I assume you would not lightly engage in the actions you did against Sergeant Maguire."

"No, no I would not." Maneet had kept her answers on an even tone but sincere.

"Have you ever done anything like that before?"

"No, I haven't."

Bernadette smiled.

"It's true to say then, this was quite out of character?"

"Yes."

"Why did you do it?"

"Because of what he said. I was completely shocked, stunned even. I've never been talked to like that before. I just... lost it. I saw red, and I hit out."

"So, you found it shocking?"

"Yes."

"Unusual even, to be insulted in that way?"

"Yes. Also, from a Garda officer. I wasn't expecting it."

"Understandably. So, can you take us through what you were thinking and what happened?"

Maneet paused for a moment to gather her thoughts, before recounting the events.

"Yes, sure. We had arranged the rally sort of quite informally. We weren't expecting a lot of people and we had not really promoted it."

"Is that why you did not inform the Garda?"

"Yes, we thought it might be a small gathering. Make a few speeches. Get some press perhaps."

"What was the point of it then?"

"To keep making our presence felt. We have noticed an uptick in racial crimes and if you don't keep putting it out there, it goes unnoticed. That would be a bad thing."

"What happened then?"

"There were perhaps more people than we had expected. Then out of the blue, the Garda turned up. Several vans, and they got out in riot gear. I mean, riot gear, I ask you? It just seemed ridiculous to me, after all, we were not doing anything wrong, we weren't causing trouble. They started advancing on us as if they wanted to start something."

Bernadette picked up this at once. Maneet had not mentioned it before but it often happened things came out in testimony.

"Sorry, you said they seemed as if they wanted to start something."

"Yes, just they seemed a little aggressive. It felt that way. I thought I had better do something to diffuse the situation. So, I decided to approach them, talk to them."

"What was your intention in doing so?"

"To get them to see, we were not a threat, and hopefully to stand down. I'm quite good at that. I've had such conversations before, and things have always been alright."

"But this time was, different, perhaps?"

Bernadette kept her tone mild, neutral. As if she was simply conducting an interview. This was important when questioning one's own witnesses. You could not be seen to be prompting the witness to answer in a certain way.

"Yes, first of all, six officers came out to meet me. Six. It seemed excessive. Then before I could make a decision about what to do, the Sergeant said that... thing. I just lost my head, as I told you."

Bernadette nodded, there was no need to repeat the words. They'd been heard several times in open court already.

"What happened after that?"

"Well, I hit out. Then I felt them restraining me. I came to my senses. They arrested me, charged me, let me go. That was it."

"So, everything after the incident was quite calm?"

"Yes."

"Nothing else was said?"

"No."

Bernadette moved on, there was no need to dwell on it. The jury had seen the video footage, there wasn't any need to go over the details.

"Do you regret what happened?"

"Of course, I do, I really do but I can't change it. I stand by my testimony. He said what he said."

"Thank you, Maneet." Bernadette turned to Justice Buckley. "No further questions, Judge."

She didn't really need too much from Maneet as it turned out. Now Priteshi could attempt to do her worst.

He smiled and nodded. "Very good, very good, Mrs Mackenna. Now, Mrs Patel, do you have some questions for the witness?"

"Oh yes," said Priteshi standing up. "Oh yes, I have."

This was perhaps meant to be intimidating, however, Maneet regarded her with some distaste.

"Ms Johal-Lynch," said Priteshi fixing her with a determined stare. "You claim Sergeant Maguire said the words you put in your statement, and yet in his testimony he denies it, supported by five other Garda officers who were also there. How is the court, or the jury expected to believe you?"

As she said this, Priteshi cast a glance to the jury with a smile which indicated how preposterous she found Maneet's assertion.

"Yes," said Maneet, "because it's the truth."

"But it isn't, is it? It's a fabrication, a lie. Isn't it?"

This was an instant attack. Bernadette mused that if she had been in the same position, she would have tried to build up to it. However, Priteshi opted to go at it right out of the starting gate. This may or may not serve her well. Bernadette watched as it played out with interest.

"No, it's not."

"I put it to you that it is, you lost your temper, and you went for the officer, and now you're trying to get out of it by making up a story. A story that you were racially abused." Priteshi raised her voice a little and became more assertive.

"Well, I was."

"Really? Because there is no evidence to back you up, is there? No footage, nothing. Just your word against six Garda officers. Who yes, yes swore an oath to the Garda and in this courtroom, to tell the truth!" Priteshi punched this home as hard as she could. However, Maneet was not fazed.

"It is the truth, nevertheless," said Maneet implacably.

"Is it? Is it indeed?" Priteshi pursed her lips in annoyance.

"Yes."

"Do you lose your temper often?" Priteshi asked in a milder manner.

"No, I don't lose my temper."

"But you did, didn't you, *that* time?" Priteshi persisted.

"As I said I don't know what came over me."

"I can hardly imagine that you have never lost your temper, and that you suddenly did so just then. That's stretching credibility rather too much, wouldn't you say?"

"I wouldn't no. If someone had called you an Indian bitch. A fucking Paki whore. A fucking little black slut, a cocksucking black piece of shit Indian dog, wouldn't you be upset?" Maneet countered.

"I'm the one asking the questions not you," said Priteshi visibly rattled.

"You asked me a question and I'm simply pointing out the circumstances were very unusual." The reply was calm, sweetly made even.

Priteshi looked at Justice Buckley but he seemed disinclined to intervene. It almost seemed as if he felt since she had got herself into the situation, she should get herself out of it.

"I ask you once again, you are asking the court to believe you've never lost your temper in your life until then, and I am putting it you that is a blatant exaggeration, if not an outright lie!" Priteshi thundered. Maneet had managed to get under her skin.

"I've been annoyed obviously but I've never lost my temper and hit out like that either. Nobody has ever called me a piece of shit cocksucking Indian dog though, not before the Sergeant did."

There was a suppressed giggle from one of the jurors, and although Justice Buckley looked over sharply, they were all impassive when he did so. Bernadette was finding the fact Priteshi was so discomposed extremely amusing too.

It seems Priteshi found herself at a stand. By opting for a direct attack, she left no space for anything else. No other manoeuvre. Had she built up to it, she might have found other lines of questioning which may have softened up Maneet.

"No further questions, Judge," said Priteshi throwing in the towel. She would most likely rely on her six witnesses to push the jury to a guilty verdict, Bernadette reflected.

"Really?" Justice Buckley looked surprised. It seemed unusual to give up so early on a key witness, particularly the defendant. "Mrs Mackenna?" Bernadette shook her head.

"Very well, Ms Johal-Lynch, you may step down, thank you."

Maneet got down from the stand and returned to the dock.

"I think we'll take our morning break," said Justice Buckley. He stood up, the Tipstaff asked the court to rise, and the judge left the room.

✻ ✻ ✻

In the meeting room, there was quite some merriment while they drank their coffee.

"You certainly had her on the ropes," Imogen said to Maneet laughing.

"It was definitely something, witness destroys counsel. Well done," said Bernadette.

"I was just being me." Maneet shrugged.

"You did it very well."

"I'm glad to see you took that bitch down a peg," said Hughes with feeling. It seemed most of them had taken Priteshi in dislike.

"I just remained calm," said Maneet. "Like Bernadette told me to do."

"It's great what you did, truly," said Bernadette. "But I'm not sure how much it's going to help us overall. It is still your word against six Garda officers."

She didn't like to rain on Maneet's parade, but the facts were still the facts. They were not really in any better position than before, in spite of Priteshi's less than impressive cross examination.

422

Maneet was about to speak when there was a knock at the door. Zhang opened it and Maneet's fiancé was standing outside it.

"Akshay?" Maneet said, surprised.

"Maneet." He looked a little sheepish.

"What are you doing here?"

"I..." He looked around. "I had something to tell you."

"Come in then, don't stand there," said Maneet although she made not move to stand up nor go to greet him.

He did so and stood looking a little lost.

"What is it?" she asked.

"Can we talk in private?"

"No," Maneet said firmly. "They already know you've been an arsehole, so whatever you've got to say you can say it here."

The others exchanged glances. Maneet's attitude seemed extremely harsh, even to them. However, Akshay took it.

"OK," said Akshay. "Well..." he hesitated. "Well..."

"Spit it out, Akshay, for fuck's sake!"

Bernadette saw Imogen's jaw almost hit the floor and suppressed a laugh. Maneet certainly had the whip hand as far as Akshay was concerned.

"OK, the thing is... the thing is, some of this could be my fault."

"Some of what?" Maneet looked puzzled.

"This court thing."

"What?"

"It was me, I tipped off the Garda. I told them about the rally. I was the one who rang them up and I said there was going to be a lot of trouble, violence. That's why they came after you."

Maneet stood up, unable to believe her ears.

"You're fucking joking, aren't you? Aren't you?"

Bernadette could hear her temper rising.

"No, I'm not. I just thought, if, well, maybe you'd give it up if..."

"If what? Akshay? If fucking what?" Maneet was advancing on him now.

"If maybe you got arrested or something. I thought maybe you'd stop and become a homebody, like I wanted you to... and... have kids and be proper wife..." he trailed off seeing her explosive demeanour.

"Fuck! You fucking shit, fuck!"

Bernadette read the signs and before Maneet could raise a hand to slap his face, she inserted herself between them.

"Enough, that's enough!" she said firmly. "Sit down, Maneet, before you make things even worse than they already are."

Maneet's eyes flashed momentarily but she subsided and returned to her seat folding her arms. She shot dagger looks at Akshay. Bernadette turned to Imogen. "Darling, can you run and try to get us another ten or twenty minutes, please?"

Imogen didn't wait to ask why but hurried from the room accompanied by Zhang to speak to the clerk of the court.

Bernadette turned to Akshay. "Can you just explain to me, exactly, and I mean exactly what you did?"

Akshay coughed politely, embarrassed, and said, "I rang the Garda station, and that Maguire person, he answered. I said look I've heard something through sources that the rally in Phoenix Park is going to turn ugly. I said that some far-left agitators were coming with weapons and stuff like that to cause trouble."

"I see." Bernadette felt disgusted but did not allow her frustration to show. "Why did he believe you?"

"I told him who I am. I said I'm her fiancé and I was worried for Maneet's safety. I told him I want to get her out of there, for her own good. He said don't worry, 'I'll take care of it.'"

An oath escaped Maneet's lips when she heard this.

"'I'll take care of it', what did he mean by that?"

"I don't know," said Akshay. "But this isn't what I expected."

"What did you expect?"

"I don't know. Maybe they would grab her, get her to safety or something." He shrugged.

"You just told Maneet that perhaps if she got arrested, she'd see the error of her ways, didn't you? So surely you thought it might be a possibility?" Bernadette wasn't happy with his answers at all.

"Yes, but I just thought she'd realise this profession wasn't for her after all, it would make her think differently, get married, settle down..."

There was a snorting noise of derision from Maneet.

"You were wrong there, weren't you?"

"I see that now," he said shamefaced.

"Why has it taken you so long to come forward?"

"I still hoped she might give up."

"You're a fucking idiot!" Maneet said angrily.

Imogen returned and nodded to Bernadette. "He has allowed us twenty more minutes."

"Great," said Bernadette, she recapped what had been discussed with Imogen who looked completely nonplussed at Akshay's behaviour. Bernadette turned back to Akshay.

"Now then, Akshay, are you prepared to say all this on the stand?"

"Sure, of course, anything." He seemed eager to try and put things right.

"Good, we're going to ask the judge if he'll accept you as a witness, and then I'm going to ask you this all over again in court, OK?"

"Yes. Yes, I will. I'll do whatever it takes."

"You can settle things with Maneet afterwards. But until this case is over, I want the two of you to stay away from each other, is that clear?"

"Well, I don't want to see him anyway," Maneet said still angry.

"But, honey bear," Akshay began.

"No contact, understood?" Bernadette interrupted.

"For sure, OK." He held up his hands in surrender. Surely by now, he must have realised how much he'd fucked up, Bernadette thought, but he might also have just gifted them some assistance with their case.

"Good, so let's..." Bernadette was about to say they should go when Olivia appeared a little breathless.

"Fuck, it's all going on today," said Hughes with amusement.

"I'm glad I've caught you," said Olivia to Bernadette.

"OK, why is that?"

"Because you need to recall those officers, well, three of them anyway."

"What?"

"They're ready to recant their statements. Brogan assures me of it."

"Really? Are you sure?" This sounded like manna from heaven, but Bernadette wanted to be certain.

"Yes, just do it, get the judge to agree. I've got them here, and they have minders in the witness waiting room, so nobody can get to them."

"OK, fine. This is going to be very interesting indeed. As long as you're sure."

"Don't take my word for it, take Brogan's," said Olivia with sincerity.

"You can believe her," said Hughes. "If Brogan said that then they'll do it for sure."

"Alright," said Bernadette standing up. "Looks like we've got something of a show to put on, let's do this!"

"Woohoo!" said Hughes standing up too.

"Now we'll see some fireworks." Imogen laughed.

"Yes, well, first I have to persuade the judge to allow it, after that we might be home and dry."

With that, she led her contingent out of the meeting room and they all headed for the court.

✳ ✳ ✳

Priteshi looked over at Bernadette suspiciously. She hadn't missed the extra people who suddenly appeared as part of Bernadette's entourage and took seats on the benches. Olivia positioned herself not far from the officer at the courtroom door after a whispered conversation with Hughes.

The Tipster entered the courtroom and was followed by the judge.

"Mrs Mackenna?" he said once he had taken a seat and checked all seemed well in the courtroom. "Are you ready for your next witness?"

"Judge, I have a somewhat unusual request," Bernadette said.

"Oh? And what might that be?" He regarded her with interest.

"A witness has just come forward with material evidence and I would like the court to admit him as a witness."

"Indeed? And who might this witness be?"

"It's Akshay Pandit, Ms Johal-Lynch's fiancé."

"Judge, I object," said Priteshi at once, jumping to her feet. "The witnesses were set before the trial and bringing extra witnesses at this stage has not given us any time to prepare."

"Mrs Mackenna has told us he's only just come forward, so she could hardly be expected to have notified the court before now, could she?" the judge said reasonably.

"Nevertheless, we've had no time to prepare!"

"I'm sure you can make notes during his testimony and then if you need some time, I'm sure we can find it for you." Justice Buckley looked at her as if daring her to object further.

"Thank you, Judge," said Priteshi having had the wind taken out of her sails. She resumed her seat.

"Judge, there is more," said Bernadette.

"More?" Justice Buckley looked surprised.

"Judge, it's come to my attention that three of the prosecution witnesses may have new testimony and I'm asking to recall them."

"Judge! I absolutely object! My witnesses have been tampered with and I can't accept this request by the defence!" Priteshi was on her feet once more and being very forceful.

"I see," said Justice Buckley mildly. "However, it's not your place to accept the request, it's mine."

"Yes, Judge." Priteshi was calming down from the initial shock of Bernadette pulling the rug from under her feet.

"Secondly, do you have evidence of witness tampering?"

"No, Judge, but..."

"In which case, should you suspect it you'll have plenty of time to question them on the subject, will you not?"

"Yes, Judge, but..."

"Will you not?" Justice Buckley fixed her with a hard stare.

"Yes, Judge," said Priteshi admitting defeat. Her expression indicated things were not going well as far as she was concerned.

"Good." The judge was all smiles once more. "I'll allow your requests, Mrs Mackenna, did you want to call the new witness now, before your second witness?"

"Yes, Judge, and then the recalled witnesses, please," said Bernadette.

"Fair enough, then that is how we will proceed." Justice Buckley sat back to wait.

"I call Akshay Pandit to the stand."

Akshay came in, took the stand, and took the oath. He stated his name and occupation for the court.

"Akshay," said Bernadette, "I would like you to tell the court, what your involvement in the incident at the rally was?"

"Yes," Akshay replied.

"Go ahead."

"I'm Maneet's fiancé, and I was concerned about her continuing to work after we were married. So, I'm ashamed to say that I came up with a plan which seems so stupid now."

Justice Buckley was listening intently as were the jury to this sudden addition to the evidence.

"What was the plan?"

Akshay paused for a moment, shot a guilty look at Maneet and then continued, "I decided to call the Garda and tell them the rally was taking place and it was likely to turn violent."

"Did you know the Garda had not been informed?"

"Maneet had mentioned it, yes. I mean, we talk about her work, a *lot* about her work. Too much in my opinion."

Maneet scowled at him on hearing this.

"So, you carried out this plan?"

"Yes, I did. I phoned up on the day of the rally and I spoke to Maguire..."

"Was that Sergeant Maguire?" Bernadette interrupted, wanting this point to be clear.

"Yes, it was him."

"And what did you say?"

"I said I had some reliable information the rally was going to turn ugly, there was going to be violence. I said left wing agitators were coming and they were going to start something."

Maneet rolled her eyes on hearing this.

"And was any of this true?"

"None of it, I made it all up," said Akshay hanging his head a little.

"What did Sergeant Maguire say?"

"He asked who I was. I told him I was Maneet's fiancé. I said I was afraid for her safety and I wanted to get her out of there. I said she would not listen to me but maybe they could assure her safety for me." He stopped again, he appeared very shamefaced now.

"What was his response?"

"He said, 'Great, I've been wanting to get those bastards for a long time, and now you've just given me a good reason. Don't worry though, I will make sure your fiancé is safe.'"

"I've been wanting to get those bastards for a long time, you are sure it's what he said?" Bernadette wanted to make sure and also emphasise this for the jury.

"Yes, he said that."

"Were you expecting him to arrest Maneet?"

"No, not really. I mean, maybe just to keep her safe, but I wasn't expecting her to be arrested for hitting him."

"Right. And why didn't you come forward before, why now?"

Akshay hesitated. "It's because I... I thought even then she might come to her senses."

"Come to her senses?"

Maneet suppressed a squeal of frustration.

"She might realise she should give up all this gallivanting around the world, settle down and be my wife. I mean, I'm more than able to take care of her. I'm well off, she doesn't need to work."

Bernadette had to keep her own face straight at this. It was totally from the chauvinist's playbook and she could hardly believe her ears. It wasn't for her to pass judgement, however.

"So, to understand you. You wanted Maneet to settle down, give up her job and be your wife. You decided that the best course of action was to have the Garda go and break up a rally she was leading and potentially risk her arrest, am I right?"

"Yes." He nodded.

"I still don't understand why you didn't allow this trial to run its course, why did you come forward? Surely if she is convicted then you would have achieved your aim, would you not?" It was a reasonable question and she needed to get to the truth.

"I know you think that, and I'm an arsehole, I know it. Sorry... Judge." Justice Buckley waved a hand dismissively. "But I'm not and the thing is that I do love Maneet, in spite of... in spite of what you or anyone might think of me. I've been stupid and I realised how wrong this was going to go for her. I couldn't let it go on without coming forward."

"Right. You had a crisis of conscience would that be fair to say?"

"Yes, yes I did, and I'm truly sorry for everything." Akshay hung his head.

Bernadette paused to think. Was this enough? It certainly cast some doubt on the case for the prosecution. She had another thought.

"You didn't by any chance record the conversation, did you?" she wondered. He worked in finance and if he had made the call from his work there might well be a recording.

"Yeah well, I thought about it. But I didn't in the end." He shook his head.

"OK." This couldn't be helped although it would certainly have strengthened their case. She decided to end things there and see what Priteshi could do. "Thank you, for your honesty. No further questions at this time."

Bernadette sat down.

"Jolly good," said Justice Buckley. "Mrs Patel?"

"Yes, Judge, I'd like to ask some questions," said Priteshi standing up.

"You don't need some time to consider?"

"No thank you, Judge, but thank you for asking."

"Very well, proceed."

"Thank you." Priteshi turned to Akshay. Bernadette had a shrewd idea of her line of attack and she wasn't disappointed. "So, Mr Pandit, that was extremely convenient how you suddenly appeared with that testimony, was it not?"

"I wouldn't say so," he replied. "I just felt things had gone far enough."

"Far enough." She echoed his words. "So, you say. Far enough. You perhaps thought things would go in her favour and when you saw they weren't you decided to come forward and I right?"

"Yes, yes that's it."

He had not picked up on her underlying intention, but he soon found out from her next question.

"You could see she was unlikely to win, so you concocted this fabricated story to inject some measure of reasonable doubt into the proceedings, am I right?"

"No, I didn't make it up, it's what happened."

"We only have your word for it, do we not? I'm sure if we get Sergeant Maguire back on the stand he's going to say otherwise."

"I don't care what he says, it's the truth."

Akshay was beginning to sound nettled.

"You said so yourself you've no proof the conversation took place at all. I mean..." She gave a light laughed. "Look how it appears to the court. You come out of nowhere and make a preposterous allegation which you can't substantiate, and then we're expected to believe you somehow incited the Garda to go to the rally. I mean, how ridiculous can you get?"

"Well," said Akshay, "I can substantiate it to a degree, because I can show you the call, I made to the Garda on that day on my call log."

Bernadette could happily have kissed him at this point. She hadn't thought of that.

"What?" said Priteshi, suddenly having the wind taken out of her sails.

"I have it on my phone," said Akshay getting out his mobile.

Justice Buckley motioned to the clerk of the court. She came forward and after a whispered conversation with Akshay, she took his phone briefly and in short order, they had a picture of the call log on the screen. One of the entries was underlined.

"Mr Pandit, just for my benefit, that is the call log from your phone?" Justice Buckley asked him.

"Yes, Judge," Akshay replied.

"And the line underlined is the call you made to the Garda station in question?"

"Yes, Judge."

The clerk of the court spoke quietly to Justice Buckley, who then said, "The clerk informs me that is the number for the Garda station where Sergeant Maguire works. So, Mrs Patel, there's your answer."

"Thank you, Judge," said Priteshi. Her entire line of questioning had just been annihilated.

"Do you wish to ask this witness anything else?"

"No, Judge." Priteshi pursed her lips and sat down.

"Mrs Mackenna?" He turned his attention to Bernadette.

"No, Judge," she replied.

"Excellent. Mr Pandit, you may stand down. Thank you for your time and your testimony." Justice smiled at Akshay and watched him leave the court. Bernadette glanced at Maneet, she did not seem to look in the least forgiving, even though Akshay may well have saved the trial, along with the witnesses she was about to bring back.

Justice Buckley looked at his watch. "I think," he said, "we'll take lunch, and then afterwards we can hear from the recalled witnesses, Mrs Mackenna."

"Thank you, Judge," said Bernadette.

The Tipstaff was in the room in short order, and Justice Buckley gave a short bow and left.

Once he had gone, Priteshi strode up to Bernadette and said angrily, "I don't know what you're trying to pull, but I'll be going to the Bar of Ireland about this."

"Be my guest, if that's what you want," Bernadette shrugged, knowing Priteshi had no case against her whatsoever.

"You've got nothing," said Imogen fiercely standing up and facing her off, "So why don't you back off and stop being

435

a sore loser. If you can't take the heat, then you shouldn't be in the courtroom."

"Well, well, whatever! It's bang out of order!" was Priteshi's parting shot before she marched angrily from the court. Carole followed behind her giving Bernadette a thumbs up which Priteshi did not see.

"What a bitch!" said Imogen.

"You told her." Zhang laughed.

"Bar of Ireland indeed, fucking cheek!"

"Let's get lunch," said Bernadette.

✳ ✳ ✳

In the meeting room, they dug into the box of filled baguettes. Bernadette was happy with the way things had gone but hopefully, testimony from the Garda officers would put some more nails in the prosecution's coffin. So far, so good but it was still some way from getting the verdict she wanted or even the case dismissed. That would be an excellent outcome if it could be achieved. However, it would really hinge on how far the officers were willing to retract their earlier testimony.

As they were eating and sipping their coffee. Akshay appeared at the door once more.

"Oh God, what the fuck do you want now?" Maneet said putting down her egg mayonnaise roll.

"Maneet, please, can I talk to you?" he pleaded.

"No!"

"But I love you, I know I fucked up, but I still love you, really, I mean..."

"Akshay, for fuck's sake!" said Maneet despairingly.

Bernadette intervened. She stood up and went up to him. "When I said no contact that is what I meant!" she said firmly.

"But…"

"No buts, you can talk to her when the court case is over and not before, so best you go."

He regarded her for a moment and then nodded.

"Right, I'm sorry."

"I appreciate what you've done but now you need to go, OK? Don't try to call her or message her either. Not until this is over, OK?"

"Yes, yes, fine, sorry… I'm going… I'm going…" He backed off and she watched him until he disappeared around the bend in the corridor.

"Thank you," said Maneet picking up her baguette and taking a bite.

"It's OK." Bernadette took a sip of her coffee, and then took hold of her own salami salad baguette.

"He seems very eager," Hughes remarked.

"Oh, he's just so frustrating!" Maneet said in exasperated tones.

"Not to mention he's not the man you want to marry anyway," said Imogen impassively.

"Oh, well…" Maneet blushed.

"She doesn't even want to marry a man," said Hughes.

"You should follow your heart! You will be unhappy forever if you do not!" said Matelda.

"OK, guys, OK! Can we stop talking about me? Please?" said Maneet holding up her hand.

The others laughed and resumed eating.

"How do you think it's going to go this afternoon?" Imogen asked Bernadette.

"I guess it depends on what they say."

"They won't let you down, I promise," said Olivia who had also joined them.

"Who will you get up first?" said Imogen.

"The one who wavered the most, the first time, he'll be the one to attack."

"Sounds like a plan."

"Let's hope, considering where we started the day, I think we're doing pretty well." Bernadette finished her baguette and sipped her coffee.

"Absolutely."

* * *

Court resumed and once Justice Buckley had returned to the room and settled, he addressed himself to Bernadette.

"Now, Mrs Mackenna, would you like to recall the first of the witnesses on your list?"

"Yes, Judge." Bernadette stood up. "I call Garda Richard Hamble."

Richard Hamble appeared, looking nervous but once more with his uniform smartly turned out. His blonde hair was very tidy, and he shot her an apprehensive glance with his blue eyes. He took the stand, and the oath before restating his name and occupation.

"Garda Hamble, you've been recalled because I understand you have something to say about your previous testimony," said Bernadette.

"Yes."

"And what was it you wanted to say?"

Hamble hesitated before speaking again. This was a big step for him.

"I wasn't quite truthful with my testimony."

"In what way?" She looked at him in a friendly manner, trying to reassure him it was all OK.

"It's not true Sergeant Maguire didn't say those words to the defendant, he did say them."

This was her cue, and she breathed a sigh of relief inwardly that he had retracted, just as Olivia said he would.

"OK, so can you turn page three six one in the evidence book, paragraph two, and just refresh your memory?"

Hamble did so and then he nodded, to indicate he'd read it.

"Those are the words he said?"

"Something like that, yes, I can't remember exactly but I heard him call her some of those things."

"Thank you." Bernadette paused, now was the time to get him to admit why he had lied to the court. "Can you explain why you didn't tell the truth before?"

"Yes, and I'm also ashamed, I just want you to know that."

"OK, I'm sure that's noted, so go on." She coaxed him gently. What he said now was crucial.

"Sergeant Maguire spoke to us all afterwards, after she was arrested and charged. He said we were all in this together. He said the Garda is like a brotherhood. Nobody ever rats on anyone else in the Garda. He said this was the greatest sin. If we backed him up on this then he'd always have our back. He'd make sure we did well, got good reports.

We'd be his boys and girls. He said he would look out for us."

"I see. Did he threaten you at all, any of you?"

"Not exactly."

Bernadette pressed him. "What does not exactly mean?"

"He hinted at the fact that people who grassed up fellow officers might find themselves outcasts. He said outcasts might find themselves on the wrong side of a baton, or bullet in an incident one day. He said nobody forgets a grass and their career would be over before it had even begun."

"So, he did, threaten you?"

"Yes, I suppose you could call it a threat."

"Does it not sound like a threat to you?"

He paused for a moment thinking about it.

"Yes, yes it does."

"And why did you come forward today to change your testimony?"

"I felt it was wrong. I didn't join the Garda for this. I joined it to uphold the law and what Sergeant Maguire did was wrong. I don't hold with racism."

"Before you went up to the defendant during the rally, did Sergeant Maguire say anything to you?" She wanted to know this because this would indicate some measure of premeditation.

"Yes, yes he did."

"And what was it he said?"

"He said, 'here comes that Indian bitch lawyer. Watch this, I'm going to wind her up, this is going to be fun. None of you is to say anything, got it?'"

This was even better than she had hoped for.

"None of you is to say anything, that's what he said?"

"Yes."

"So, you didn't say anything?"

"No."

"Until now."

"Yes."

"Has anyone coerced you to be here, made you come here today?"

"No."

"You came of your own free will?"

"Yes, I did."

"And you are aware that there are potential penalties for perjuring yourself in court?"

"Yes, I am."

"Not to mention in your own organisation?"

"Yes, I am, and I'm prepared to accept those because in the end honesty is more important."

"And do you confirm that everything you have now told the court is the truth and the whole truth?"

"Yes, I do."

This series of questions had handed her a trump card of sorts. She had two more potentially and then they would see how the dice fell with the jury after that.

"Thank you, Garda Hamble, no further questions." She sat down and waited for Priteshi who would surely come at him.

"Mrs Patel?" said Justice Buckley. "Do you have questions?"

"Yes, I do, judge, and since this was my witness, I'd like to treat them as hostile," she said quite heatedly. It was clear to Bernadette, Priteshi was discomposed by the turn of events.

"I think you can do that, yes." The judge nodded slightly.

"Thank you." She put her attention on Hamble. Given her style up to now, Bernadette expected a full-frontal attack. "Garda Hamble, I'm going to put it to you that you've been coerced into coming here and changing your statement, what do you say to that?"

Bernadette was not disappointed. Priteshi seemed to regard cross examination rather like beating someone with a blunt instrument, as opposed to a subtle but perhaps more effective build-up of a line of attack.

"I say that's not true. I'm here of my own free will, and because of my conscience."

"Your conscience, sure, of course." Priteshi's tone became acidic. "It's funny how your conscience struck you now, after you had sat there on the witness stand and sworn quite the opposite don't you think?"

"I told you, I was never comfortable with it," he replied somewhat doggedly. Now he'd got the weight of the lie from his chest, he seemed more able to hold his own.

"Well, I think you've lied to the court, for whatever reason best known to yourself. So, here's a chance to put things right. Will you now admit that you've lied here today?"

"No, I stand by what I've said." Hamble stared her out. She looked away. Her attack dog approach was not yielding results and had not done so at all during the proceedings so far.

"Who made you come here?" she continued after a moment to gather her thoughts.

"Nobody," he replied without hesitation.

"Come on, there are three of you, all decided independently to retract your statements, I don't believe that. I don't think anyone here would believe it. So, who was it, asked you all to come here?"

Hamble sighed, slightly irritated by her manner. "We got together and decided we'd had enough, the truth needed to be told."

"Oh really, and why is that?" She pressed him looking for a chink, a gap in his story.

He hesitated and looked around for a moment, then evidently decided to bring out another revelation. "I wasn't going to say a thing but it's because Sergeant Maguire asked Erin for..." He stopped and took a breath., "For sexual favours and that's not on."

"Sexual favours?" Priteshi appeared nonplussed.

"Yes, you can ask her."

This was gold to Bernadette. She wrote down some notes for Erin when she appeared on the stand.

"Like what? What did he ask her?" Priteshi rather than soften her tone became belligerent.

"He wanted her to sleep with him," Hamble said with emphasis, it was clear he was goaded by her tone.

"Oh, oh I see." Priteshi thought for a moment. "But that's hearsay though, you didn't witness it."

She said this as if she knew it for a fact. However, what Hamble said next destroyed even that thin lifeline.

"I did, actually, I was down the corridor when he cornered her and asked her. So, I heard every word."

She stopped again. It wasn't going well, and she was fighting a losing battle. Priteshi decided to quit.

"No further questions, Judge," she said rapidly taking a seat.

Justice Buckley could not resist a smile to himself, before asking Bernadette, "Mrs Mackenna, is there further for this witness?"

Bernadette stood up, "Yes, Judge."

"Continue." It seemed quite obvious he was enjoying this turn of events hugely.

"Garda Hamble, can you please tell us about the events involving Sergeant Maguire propositioning Garda Lawson?"

She flicked a glance at Imogen who was smirking quite openly.

"Sure, yes. It was yesterday after we left the court. We were all back at the station, and it was quite late, I was about to go off shift. I went down the corridor to the lockers and I heard voices."

"Whose voices were those?"

"Sergeant Maguire and Erin. Maguire was saying, 'come on, Erin, you owe me now, I own your arse, bitch, and she said, 'fuck off Maguire', he said 'no, if I want you to drop on your knees and suck my cock you will, bitch, and if I want you to bend over so I can fuck you, you will. I can ruin you, remember that.'"

There was silence in the courtroom on hearing this. It was quite shocking. Some of the jurors, particularly the females were open mouthed and looked utterly disgusted.

"What happened then?" Bernadette nudged him to continue. She remained impassive even though inside it made her skin crawl.

"Erin said 'fuck you, Maguire, you're a dickhead and you always will be.' She walked off and Maguire called after her 'I own you bitch, you're fucking well mine, do you hear me?' She gave him the finger and then I stepped out. Maguire saw me and walked away quickly. Then me, Erin, and Paddy talked. We decided it was time to put a stop to it. She's laying a formal complaint against Maguire with the Garda."

"Thank you," said Bernadette, "thank you for your honesty and for having the courage of your convictions."

"It's OK." Hamble smiled.

"No further questions, Judge."

"Very good, very good," said Justice Buckley. "Mrs Patel?"

Priteshi shook her head vigorously. Asking Hamble anything more was definitely not on her agenda. He had damaged the prosecution's case quite enough on his own.

"Thank you, Garda Hamble," said the judge, "you may stand down."

Hamble left the courtroom. As he did so, Hughes who had been watching the armed officer on the witness entrance quite intently went over to have a quiet word with Matelda and then with Olivia.

Justice Buckley glanced at his watch. It probably was around time for a coffee break but evidently, he decided to press on.

"Call your next witness please, Mrs Mackenna?"

She called Paddy Bannock. He was a bluff red-haired Scott of around thirty years old with quite a few years in the Garda. When questioned he answered quite bluntly and corroborated what Hamble had said. He was also much clearer in recalling what Maguire had said, which was almost word for word as Maneet had told it. He concurred with the reason for the change of mind and Bernadette was sympathetic to the fact he had a career which might well be ruined by him perjuring himself. Priteshi declined to question him, and the judge asked her to call the next witness, who was the third Garda officer to retract her statement.

"I call Garda Erin Lawson," said Bernadette.

Lawson had her raven black hair tied back in a bun, and she had pretty green eyes. Overall, she was classically a good-looking Irish woman, Bernadette mused. Lawson took the stand and affirmed her oath.

"Garda Lawson," said Bernadette, "two officers have retracted their previous testimony regarding the incident involving the defendant. Are you here to do the same?"

"Yes, yes I am," said Lawson.

"Please turn to page three six one in the evidence book, paragraph two."

Lawson did as she was requested, although she had obviously seen it before.

"Are those the words which Sergeant Maguire used?"

"Pretty much, yes." Lawson nodded.

"And are you prepared to stand by that now?"

"Yes, I am."

Bernadette wanted to cover the reasons for her retraction but decided first to tackle the sexual harassment.

"I also understand Sergeant Maguire attempted to coerce you into having sex with him, am I right?"

Lawson's voice was loud and clear as she answered, "Yes, yes he did."

"Was that the first time he had done so or sexually harassed you?"

"No, it wasn't."

"I see, we will come back to that. For now, can you take us through what happened last night, when you were overheard by Richard Hamble?"

Lawson took a deep breath. "Yes..." she began and then without warning things took an unexpected turn. To Bernadette, the world suddenly appeared to go into slow motion.

There was the unmistakable sound of an SMG rifle being cocked, and from the corner of her eye, she noticed the armed officer on the witness door was jumping forward and raising his weapon. However, Hughes had seen it moments earlier and at the very same time, she was vaulting up and over their bench with her Glock pistol drawn.

"It's time for you immigrant lovers to die, fuck all of you, damn you to hell!" shouted the armed officer.

Matelda had not missed Hughes' rapid movement and was also drawing her weapon.

Hughes levelled her Glock and fired in mid-flight at the officer, emptying her clip. Simultaneously Matelda opened fire. The armed officer pitched backwards hit by multiple rounds, and his SMG went off briefly and harmlessly into the ceiling before it stopped, and he lay still. The noise from the two Glocks firing was deafening, people on the public benches had screamed and were diving for cover.

Silence ensued, which was broken by Olivia shouting, "Don't even think about it or you are fucking dead!"

Glancing to the main door of the court, Bernadette could see Olivia was standing with her gun pressed against the temple of the second armed officer who had apparently raised his own weapon and was now in the act of lowering it.

Zhang moved swiftly to cover her. "Drop the weapon and get on the fucking ground now!" she shouted. The armed officer hesitated. "Drop it I said, now!"

He did so, after a moment, and having seen the fate of his colleague. May approached and picked up the SMG as he lay on his stomach. Olivia cuffed him and said, "I'm arresting you for conspiracy to commit murder, you are not obliged to say anything unless you wish to do so, but whatever you say will be taken down in writing and may be given in evidence. Do you understand?"

"Yes," came the muffled reply.

The doors burst open and several Garda officers appeared.

"It's fine, it's under control," said Hughes, who had recovered from her diving shot and rolled back onto her feet. Matelda was checking over the first armed officer who was evidently dead.

"Will someone tell me what on earth is going on?" said Justice Buckley as it became evident the dramatic events were over, and people began to sit up and look around in a bewildered fashion.

"Judge, this officer over here," said Hughes pointing to the dead armed officer, "attempted to open fire on the court. I assessed him to be a threat and acted accordingly. We are certain that the other officer over there is also involved and would have attempted the same, that's why he's been arrested."

Justice Buckley seemed somewhat appalled by these disclosures but simply said, "Ahem, oh, right. I see. Well, if someone can remove the officer who has been detained, then I think we'll clear the court of those not involved in the proceedings, and then I'll decide what to do."

"Yes, Judge," said Hughes.

Olivia and Zhang helped the cuffed officer to his feet, and then Olivia took him out accompanied by the other Garda who had just arrived. The press and spectators reluctantly left the room too. When this had been accomplished. Justice Buckley appeared to have recovered his composure. In spite of the circumstances, he nevertheless had a duty to ensure order was restored.

"Right," he said with decision. "Evidently we cannot continue with the proceedings today. However, we will continue and complete these proceedings as soon as practically possible. Such attempts at interfering with the course of justice will not be tolerated. However, in the meantime, no doubt there will need to be some sort of statements, made and an investigation. So, I suggest the jury retires to their room to await further instructions, and if I can prevail upon counsel to also remain, then we'll see what's what. Does that seem like a plan?"

"Yes, Judge," said Hughes who had somehow become the involuntary spokesperson.

"Good, good, well you seem to be the one to take charge for the moment. I shall go to my chambers and await word from you. I can obviously give a statement as needed."

"Yes, Judge," said Hughes.

Justice Buckley waved the Tipstaff away and left the courtroom abruptly.

"Are you OK?" said Imogen to Bernadette.

"Yes, yes, darling, are you?"

"Yes, I am."

"Thank God for the armed protection."

"Absolutely," Imogen agreed with feeling.

Over on the prosecution bench, Priteshi seemed to be rooted to the spot in horror. Carole was talking to her and she didn't seem to pay her any mind.

Hughes came up to Bernadette. "Sorry about all this, perhaps you can wait in a meeting room until we've sorted things out a bit."

"Sure, sure, darling," said Bernadette. "You're a hero, you saved us."

"Oh, I wouldn't say *that*." Hughes blushed.

"I fucking would, if you hadn't seen him, God knows what would have happened," said Imogen.

"If you can wait with Matelda and May, I'll get things sorted," Hughes said getting back to business.

"Sure, we will," said Bernadette.

* * *

It took some time for things to straighten out a little. Court proceedings were ended for the day, and armed Garda conducted a thorough search of the building. Seamus Gallway arrived with his number two in tow and took over from Hughes who returned to her duties as Bernadette's protection officer. A Tech Team arrived to do the forensics and an investigation team was formed up whilst arrangements were made for the body to be removed once the forensics were completed.

Bernadette, Imogen, Maneet, Hughes, Zhang and Matelda were sat in the meeting room chatting to Brogan, who had naturally arrived post haste on hearing the news.

"Fucking hell," he was saying, "whatever next? Fucking traitors and terrorists opening fire left right and fucking centre. What is the world coming to? I just don't understand it."

Seamus arrived in the meeting room just then. He was in his mid-thirties, good looking and well-muscled under his suit. He had brown eyes and a close-cut beard. Most of those who knew him held him to be extremely handsome.

"I've err... got some more information... if you'd like me to brief you, sir," said Seamus to Brogan.

"Ach, come in, come in, you can do it here, there's nothing these good ladies don't need to hear," said Brogan amiably indicating Bernadette and Imogen in particular.

Seamus nodded to them and sat down. He knew Bernadette from a murder case he had been involved in. Hughes popped her head out of the meeting room door and hailed a Garda officer who was on hand outside, to ask them to obtain some more coffee. She resumed her seat.

"Well, Kathy and her team made a breakthrough on the Dark Web," said Seamus. "Apparently in no small measure due to someone called Micky who was assisting them."

"Oh, Micky." Imogen smiled.

Seamus looked at her enquiringly.

"He's my lead investigator, I offered his help to Kathy," said Bernadette.

"It seems he's been more than helpful. They cracked an organisation called *White Ireland*, and guess who's a member?" Seamus grinned.

"Ach don't tell me, that fucking tossbag Maguire," said Brogan visibly annoyed.

"Yes, yes indeed, and we've discovered this goes into the Garda just a bit. We suspect that those two armed tactical officers were also members. There appears to have been quite a plot."

"Has there? Has there indeed?" said Brogan standing up and pacing the room. "Fucking hell! If there's one thing I cannot stand it's fucking racists. I want all of these turdballs arrested forthwith. I'll have their fucking badges I will, and their fucking guts for garters. Yes, more bad fucking apples in the bucket, fuck me, I'm over this. We're going to fucking well make sure we find every one of these fucking little tossbags and kick their arses to kingdom fucking come, or my names not Paddy O'Shanter, which of course it's not but never mind!"

Seamus smiled wryly at this rant and it appeared he was more than used to boss' ways, treating the rant with equanimity and waiting for it to finish.

Brogan seemed to calm down all of a sudden and sat back down as if nothing had happened. "So, you were saying?"

"Yes, sir. Maguire is being arrested as we speak, as are several other members we've discovered. The team taking over the investigation will be questioning them all as to their part in this and other crimes they may well be responsible for."

"Good very good, let's get these fuckers nailed and in prison where they fucking well belong, tossbags the lot of them!"

"We're doing our best, sir."

"Yes, I know, anyway once you've done your bit you can hand it over to the task force I'm forming up."

Seamus nodded. It was quite a big operation now and the Foxcatchers job was investigating church crime, not internal Garda problems or racist organisations.

"What about the armed protection?" Seamus asked him.

"Yes, I think we can keep that for a little bit longer until things have got sorted. You're not on any active cases at the moment."

"No, sir."

"Excellent. Ah coffee." Brogan smiled as the Garda officer came in with a tray of cups.

While the coffee was distributed Seamus spoke to Bernadette, "You and Imogen will need to make statements of what you saw of the incident, but you can do that at home I'm sure. Aileen and May will see to it."

"Of course," said Bernadette.

"How's the trial going anyway?" Seamus asked sipping his coffee with satisfaction. He was known to be quite particular about his coffee so the fact he liked it showed it must have passed the test.

"It had taken a turn for the better before those officers decided to try and spray the courtroom with bullets."

"Ach, those tossers recanted I hope," said Brogan interrupting.

"Yes, they did."

"Good, good. I had those five up in my office, read them the fucking riot act I can tell you. Two of the fuckers wouldn't change their story. I wasn't happy about that. We'll see how a spell on traffic duty will suit them. The other three saw the error of their ways I can tell you."

Since Bernadette could well imagine the image of Brogan giving them a dressing down, she was hardly surprised.

"You know there was also sexual harassment involved, don't you?" said Bernadette.

"What?"

"Maguire tried to get Erin Lawson to do some sexual favours for him. Hamble was a witness."

"Did he by God!" said Brogan leaping out of his chair at once. "Fucking hell, whatever next. First fucking white supremacists and now fucking sexist tossbags too? What the fuck is going on in this force. I want that fucker charged with everything that can be thrown at him, I'll make sure that dungball goes to prison and no mistake! And don't bring him anywhere near me or I won't be responsible for my actions."

He resumed his seat and picked you his coffee.

"That fucking bastard, I will rip his fucking balls out from his body!" said Matelda fiercely out.

"And don't let her anywhere near him either!" Brogan added.

The room dissolved into mirth at this. The story of Matelda's ball crushing propensities was known to all of them.

"Just five minutes with him, is all I need," Matelda persisted.

"No Matelda!" said Seamus with a smile.

"Ach, this is what he needs. You just don't understand."

There was more laughter at this and even Matelda joined in.

"OK," said Brogan once the coffee was consumed. "If there's nothing else, I'll be off, I've got to brief the AC on all of this. He's going to lose his rag I can tell you. Then we'll have to have a press conference, all that, it never stops."

He drained his cup and left in short order. Soon afterwards, Bernadette, Imogen and Maneet were allowed to go and left accompanied by their respective armed protection. Bernadette drove back to the office, while Carragh picked up Imogen and Zhang in the Merc. They had avoided speaking to the press who were hanging around trying to get a statement from anyone coming out of the building. Bernadette wisely left this to Seamus or the new task force leader.

* * *

When they got home, Eve rushed to the front door to greet Bernadette.

"Thank God, you're home, I was so worried," she said flinging her arms around Bernadette's neck.

"But I did speak to you earlier, my love, you knew I was OK." Bernadette kissed her.

"I know but even so." Eve pouted.

"I'm happy you were worried about me."

"Of course, I would be!"

In the meantime, Healy had kissed Hughes, and said, "Come on, let's have dinner, you must be hungry, and I want to hear all about it."

"Your fiancée is a proper hero," said Bernadette kicking off her shoes and hanging up her jacket.

"Oh stop!" Hughes blushed all over again.

Over dinner, Hughes and Bernadette retold the story of the eventful day in court. Healy seemed a little sad she had missed all the action, but Hughes reminded her of the role she played on the rooftop of the HQ building in Dublin with the rogue Superintendent. They talked about that and then Hughes and Healy admitted this was when they had first got together. This inevitably led to Bernadette and Eve retelling their own journey to love.

"What do you think is going to happen with the court case?" Eve asked Bernadette, returning to the subject in hand.

"I don't know. I would hope the prosecution would withdraw their suit. After all, their main witness not only perjured himself but he deliberately provoked Maneet. Then we have three others who recanted their testimony."

"Do you think, they will?"

"Your guess is as good as mine, the prosecuting counsel is a bit of a loose cannon, to be honest." Bernadette shrugged.

"A right bitch," Hughes put in. "I've heard she's not well liked by the Garda officers she has had to deal with."

"Carole said she knew her witnesses were lying."

"A nasty piece of work to be honest."

"Let's hope she doesn't last long then," said Eve.

"Going to do your witchy stuff on her?" Healy giggled.

"She's certainly done it on this beautiful meal." Bernadette laughed.

It was a Thai green chicken curry with rice and salad.

"We made it together," said Healy.

"It's delicious, darling, I hope you can make it for us when we're back at home," said Hughes.

"With pleasure." Healy put her hand in Hughes', and they smiled at each other.

"I'm glad you two aren't going yet," said Bernadette.

"We're only going once the threat is over, and we've no indication that it is," said Hughes.

"Yay!" Eve clapped her hands.

"You know they can't stay forever. They've got a home to go to," Bernadette said gently.

"I know but I've enjoyed having Iona around, I'll miss her when she's gone."

"We both will, and Aileen but they can come and visit."

"You can visit us too, in Ballysruth," said Hughes.

"We'll need a bigger house," Healy put in.

"All the more reason to find one, and to get married soon."

"That would be nice, a place of our own."

"The financial part of our divorces should be finalised soon, then we can look for somewhere."

Healy's eyes sparkled at this and she leaned across and kissed her fiancée.

"Our divorces have both gone through," said Hughes by way of explanation. "However, there were properties to be sold and so on."

Bernadette nodded, as a lawyer she knew the complications of divorce proceedings. "Were there children involved?"

"I have a son," said Hughes. "He's staying with his father. He's mad at me right now for leaving and for being a lesbian. Hopefully, he'll come around."

"I'm sure he will."

"It's hard but he won't even see me at the moment, let alone Iona."

"Give it time, it'll work out, I'm sure."

"Let's get dessert, Iona," said Eve starting to clear the plates.

"We made apple pie," said Healy.

"And custard."

"I can hardly wait!" Bernadette smiled and watched the two of them taking the plates into the kitchen.

CHAPTER ELEVEN

wo days later, they were heading back to court, having been notified by the judge that the case was to resume. In the meantime, statements were taken, endless news programs were aired filled with bulletins about the incident in the courtroom. It turned out someone had captured it, illegally, on their phone and the media had got hold of it. The video was currently going viral and the culprit who took it could not be identified. There had been talk of seeking an injunction, but it seemed almost too late for that, the video was already global. Hughes was very shy about her role in it all, although because of the video she had been hailed as a national hero. This was the second time she had been famous, the first being when she'd been videoed chasing down a suspect at the airport in her bare feet and been dubbed "The Barefoot Detective."

Arriving at the courts with Imogen, Hughes and Zhang, Bernadette noticed there was a large press contingent outside.

"Are you going to say something?" Imogen asked her.

"I may as well, I guess." Bernadette stopped at the top of the steps, turned and held up her hand. Microphones and cameras immediately swung in her direction.

"What's going to happen today?" shouted a presumptive hack.

"I don't know," she replied truthfully. "What I expect to happen is for justice to now be done. I'm sure you've all been made aware of the perjury committed by prosecution witnesses and that my client's story is one hundred percent true. The main witness for the prosecution is in custody accused of a number of crimes. Given all of these events, I cannot say what will transpire today, but I'm looking for a positive outcome."

"Were you scared, Bernadette?" A reporter who regularly fired questions at her from the Irish Sun had asked this one.

"Let's say I was surprised, it all happened so fast. I didn't have time to be scared really before it was all over. I'm very grateful to our armed protection officers and the Garda for keeping us safe."

This diverted the attention to Hughes.

"Aileen, can we have a statement?"

"Come, Aileen, let's see those famous feet!"

Bernadette judged it was time to cut things short and turned away at once. They rapidly made for the door ignoring all the questions.

"See those famous feet," Hughes snorted. "My feet are all over the internet."

"Well, you do have very pretty feet though," Bernadette smiled as they made their way to the meeting room. She had seen them often at home and admired them. Bernadette had a definite thing for women's feet and she never missed the sight of a pretty pair of toes or ankles.

"Thank you, yours aren't bad either" Hughes chuckled.

Bernadette happened to be wearing a pair of high heeled strappy sandals that day with a grey skirt suit and light blue top.

"Do you think so?"

"Very sexy, yes."

"Thank you."

They arrived at the meeting room where Maneet and Matelda were waiting. Maneet had had the foresight to order coffee so it was ready and waiting.

"Oh great, coffee," said Bernadette gratefully accepting a cup.

When they were seated, Maneet asked, "What do you think will happen today?"

"I'm not sure, to be honest," Bernadette replied. "In truth, the prosecution should withdraw, and I expect the judge to push for it. He could also elect to dismiss the case or even order a retrial, but I suspect he will want a resolution which will mean it can't return to court."

"I understand," said Maneet who had evidently hoped she would be able to see the back of the case.

"Don't worry I think one way or other things should go our way."

Maneet subsided and went back to her coffee.

"Why did the reporters want to see your feet?" Imogen asked Hughes not having been privy to the backstory and probably having missed the press on it at the time.

"Oh, that... well..." Hughes related the tale and then was prevailed upon to show her feet to the rest of them. They were pronounced very pretty, and this was followed by all of them comparing their own feet to Hughes'.

Bernadette chuckled and was glad the meeting room did not have glass walls. Anyone passing would have wondered what on earth they all were doing, twisting their bare feet this way and that.

Glancing at her watch she had to call time at last. "As fun as this is, we need to get into the courtroom."

"I bet it was fun for you," Imogen said slyly.

"I do like a well turned out foot, it's true." Bernadette shrugged without batting an eye.

"Oh? So do I, I love them," Hughes agreed.

Still discussing the merits of a good pair of feet, they made their way in a body to the court.

* * *

They resumed their positions in the courtroom, which was predictably packed. Hughes checked the armed guards very carefully this time before sitting down. Priteshi arrived and kept her gaze averted from Bernadette. It seemed perhaps the events of the previous session had hit her a little hard. Carole shot Bernadette an encouraging look behind Priteshi's back.

Very shortly after this, the Tipstaff arrived and announced the judge. Justice Buckley came in, looking as unruffled as ever and took his seat. After checking the courtroom carefully and glancing warily at the armed officers on the door, he addressed the court.

"Now, I think we are finding ourselves in a hopefully better circumstance than two days ago. Given the unusual nature of the events, I believe perhaps some consideration should be made regarding the disclosures and let's say revelations which transpired. Mrs Mackenna, since it was effectively your turn is there anything you want to say or bring to the court's attention before we move on?"

This was Bernadette's chance to add something further, and she had already discussed with Hughes that it would be in order for Hughes to say something. She stood up.

"Judge. I think it might be useful for the court to hear from DS Hughes as to the matters with respect to the incident from the last session. If it pleases the court, could I ask her to make a statement?"

"Yes, indeed, a good idea, for sure."

"Thank you, Judge," Bernadette resumed her seat and gestured to Hughes.

Hughes stood up and pulled out her notes.

"Judge," she said, "I would just like to recap on a number of points from the events and also what has proceeded from that with regard to the Garda investigations."

"Certainly, certainly, continue, I'm all ears," said Justice Buckley.

"Judge, to understand the events as they unfolded, I must inform the court I had some concern about the armed Garda on that day. The main reason is they were unknown to me. DCS Brogan who is in charge of the Special Tactical Unit had appointed that unit to supply the security for the court. I, therefore, assumed they were nevertheless OK. However, it did not prove, as you know, to be the case. Investigation has since revealed them to be members of an organisation known as *White Ireland* who had planned an atrocity in this courtroom. Their aim, I'm sorry to say, was to murder as many people as they possibly could."

She paused. The effect was dramatic. There was complete silence, even Priteshi looked incredibly shocked. The press were scribbling frantic notes.

"It's part of our training to identify threats, and I became aware the armed Garda on the witness door was cocking his SMG. There was no reason to do this, and then I saw him moving to a firing position while shouting out his intention, as you no doubt heard. This is why I took the action I did to neutralise the threat, which as you know, Judge, we were successful in doing. I'm sorry, of course, for the disruption but it was wholly necessary to open fire."

"And I'm very glad you did," said the Judge with feeling. "I am sure you saved many lives in the process."

"Thank you, Judge, I was just doing my duty as were my fellow officers here." She smiled.

"You all performed it very well." He inclined his head graciously.

"Sergeant Maguire has since been implicated in the plot and has been discovered to be a secret member of *White Ireland*. We believe it's possible he deliberately provoked the attack by Ms Johal-Lynch in order to precipitate a court case, although at this stage we have no proof. He has been arrested and is being charged with multiple offences, along with a number of other Garda officers who have also been discovered to be members of the same white supremacist group."

"I see." Justice Buckley thought for a moment. "Is there anything further you wish to tell the court?"

"Judge, that's the state of play at the moment."

"Thank you, for this enlightening summary, DS Hughes, it was very helpful. Although you were not under oath, I think I can accept this into evidence and the jury will take note of what has been said."

"Thank you, Judge," said Hughes and sat down.

Justice Buckley spoke to Bernadette, "Mrs Mackenna, is there anything else you wish to say?"

"Judge, I think as it stands, we heard sufficient testimony from the witnesses and also coupled with this statement. So, I feel we must await the court's decision on what happens next."

Bernadette sat down.

"Yes, indeed," said Justice Buckley looking pensive. "The court's decision, yes, indeed."

He sat for a moment deep in thought before electing to speak to Priteshi.

"Mrs Patel, your main witness has been arrested and certainly discredited, and by his own colleagues. Three of your witnesses admitted to perjury. Where do you feel you stand with your prosecution now?"

Priteshi stood up. "Judge, in spite of those issues, the fact remains that Ms Johal-Lynch committed an act of assault. There is nothing in the law to allow an assault to take place because of provocation so she has nevertheless committed an offence."

The judge considered what she said for a moment clearly not happy about it at all. "It is true what you say about the law, however, should we not consider perhaps some sort of process of shall we say natural justice?"

Bernadette could see he was trying hard to drop a hint to Priteshi that should drop the charges but apparently, she wasn't having any of it.

"Judge, I would counter with natural justice dictating people should not assault Garda officers, and that's what is at stake here. We cannot allow such actions to go unpunished and an example needs to be set. Therefore, the prosecution is not willing to withdraw the charges." She stuck her jaw out in defiance.

Bernadette saw Imogen's face twist into a scowl momentarily and then it was gone.

Justice Buckley stared at her very hard for a few moments, but she returned his gaze without flinching.

"I see," he said at length.

Bernadette wondered if the prosecution service had instructed Priteshi to continue or whether she was doing it off her own bat. If so then she would probably face repercussions if she did not secure a conviction, and even if she did get a guilty verdict it was likely the judge would mitigate the sentence down to nothing. He had the option of dismissing the case himself, but the danger would then be it could go to appeal on the basis that in law he had no authority to do so. Bernadette knew technically Priteshi was correct, and no defence of provocation existed in the current legislation, and in fact, it had been repealed. Her defence of duress was also tenuous. However, she was fully prepared to fight this with an impromptu speech to the jury, if necessary.

He sighed almost imperceptibly and said, "Very well, do either of you wish to call any further witnesses?"

"No, Judge," said Priteshi.

"No, Judge," said Bernadette.

"In which case, we'll proceed to final statements and the jury may decide the outcome with their verdict." His tone held a distinct note of resignation as Priteshi had effectively hamstrung him with the law.

She flushed in triumph at his speech, and it appeared to Bernadette that Priteshi felt she was guaranteed a win. This was all that mattered to her it seemed. Winning was all. The judge had also given her a hard time on occasion, and she was now exacting her revenge. Overall, Bernadette felt it was a bad strategy, but she also took note that Priteshi was vindictive, and this would be something be aware of should they clash again in the future. She also could tell Maneet was trying to mask her evident anger at the intelligence that the trial would still continue.

Justice Buckley though outmanoeuvred wasn't disposed to give Priteshi any time to prepare and said, "Mrs Patel your closing remarks if you please."

Priteshi stood up. It was obvious to Bernadette from her demeanour that Priteshi had, nevertheless, prepared. No matter, Bernadette reflected, she'd give it all she'd got when it was her turn.

"Judge," said Priteshi with a smirk, "members of the jury. While you may have witnessed some extraordinary events in this courtroom, there are some things which remain crystal clear."

She paused with a self-satisfied smile.

"It's true Sergeant Maguire did lie, and he did make provocative racist remarks to the defendant. These things the prosecution was certainly not aware of at the beginning of this trial. It's also true his fellow officers did perjure themselves and they will be severely dealt with I can assure you."

Bernadette caught a look from Carole, who rolled her eyes. It was as if to say, "but she knew and now she wants to punish them." Bernadette returned her attention to Priteshi's speech.

"Even so, there is one fact which remains constant. An assault took place. You all saw it and it cannot be denied. An assault, members of the jury which by law is illegal and punishable by a fine and also imprisonment."

She looked around again as if a Queen holding court.

"You may ask yourself why Ms Johal-Lynch should be punished. He provoked her. Surely that is sufficient cause. Well, I am here to tell you that it is not! There is no statute of provocation, an assault is an assault. Where would we be, if members of the public feel justified in attacking our hard-working law enforcement officers? I will tell you. Anarchy, members of the jury, pure anarchy and that we cannot have!"

She fixed each jury member in turn with a fierce gaze daring them to contradict her, daring them to say that she was wrong. One of two them flinched to her evident satisfaction.

"No, we cannot allow the law to be flouted, Garda officers to be assaulted and anarchy to reign on the streets of Ireland. I will not allow it!" she thundered.

Bernadette looked at Imogen, this had become a tad overdramatic. The judge seemed none too impressed either. It wasn't her place to make those kinds of statements.

"In the eyes of the law and by the evidence brought to this court, Ms Johal-Lynch is guilty." She banged her fist on the podium making several people jump.

"And guilty you are duty bound to find her, no exceptions! That is all. Do your duty in the eyes of the law, for it *is* your duty to find Ms Johal-Lynch guilty as charged. Thank you!"

She looked around reminding Bernadette of a petty dictator making a speech in front of the masses. This was once more almost more political than a legal argument, and perhaps Priteshi had her sights set higher than just the bar and was looking to end up in parliament backed by these theatrical performances.

"Right, thank you, Mrs Patel," said Justice Buckley in as neutral a tone as he could muster.

Priteshi might think she now ruled the roost in the courtroom, but the judge had a few tricks still to play. Having indicated they would get no time to prepare, he suddenly announced, "I think we'll break for tea. We'll return in half an hour."

Before Priteshi had even time to think of framing an objection, he had called in the Tipstaff and left the courtroom.

Taking advantage of this, Bernadette led out her troops to their meeting room, grateful for a few moments to pen some thoughts. Unlike Priteshi she had not really considered her closing arguments, anticipating there would probably be no need.

* * *

"What an utterly fucking vile vindictive bitch," Maneet said bitterly sipping a cup of coffee.

Bernadette was busy writing notes for her speech and didn't look up.

Imogen answered, "I agree, dreadful woman, God knows how she got to the bar."

"She probably threatened to execute them all if she didn't get appointed," Maneet said darkly.

Hughes let out a crack of laughter at this.

"What?" said Maneet. "She is perfectly vile, abhorrent."

"Oh, don't get me wrong, I agree but you've got quite a turn of phrase," Hughes replied mirthfully.

"She acted like a little dictator in there," said Imogen. "I can't stand her."

"Well then, let's hope we can have the last laugh, hey?" Bernadette finished her notes and passed the pad over to Imogen to look over. She picked up her coffee and drank it gratefully.

Imogen nodded her agreement and passed it back.

"She is a bad woman," said Matelda who decided to enter the fray.

"God don't tell me," said Hughes, "she's got no balls to squeeze though."

The others laughed.

"Ah, who needs the balls, I just squeeze, and she will cry for mercy!"

"You really do have a one-track mind," said Hughes.

"Ah, you Irish are too soft, in Italy, we just go for the bollocks no?"

"Oh, Matelda, what are you like?" said Zhang to more general laughter.

"How's your speech?" Hughes asked Bernadette.

"I think it will do."

"Do you think Priteshi can still win?"

"On technical grounds, yes, but there is more than one way to cut the cake," said Bernadette cryptically.

"I can't wait."

"You won't have to, it's time to go back in."

They finished up their coffee and headed back to the court.

Priteshi was sitting quite smugly at her station when Bernadette walked in with her team. She figured Priteshi thought it was in the bag, however, Bernadette knew it wasn't over until it was over. She arranged her notes on the podium and waited for the judge.

It wasn't long before he was announced by the Tipstaff and entered the courtroom. Justice Buckley took his seat though he had evidently hoped not to still be there. He settled himself and after a brief look around said, "Mrs Mackenna, are you all prepared for your closing remarks?"

This was a pointed question which made Priteshi scowl. Justice Buckley seemed as if he was a past master at courtroom games and Bernadette suspected nobody would get the better of him in the long run.

"Yes, Judge, all ready," she said. She considered rubbing in the fact she had had some time to prepare but recalled it wasn't wise to kick people when they were cornered.

"Excellent, then off you go." Justice Buckley sat back once more as if he was expecting something good.

Bernadette stood up. Surprisingly she did not feel as nervous as she usually did, but she religiously went through her routine. She took a breath, created her circle of excellence in her mind and then rehearsed her opening line. She closed her eyes for a moment, opened them and began.

"Judge, members of the jury. This trial has been a matter of intolerance. The deliberate intolerance of the race of the defendant. The deliberate provocation of the defendant. At the start, I quoted William Shakespeare who wrote, 'There's no trust, No faith, no honesty in men. All perjured, All forsworn, all naught, all dissemblers.' And wasn't that exactly the case? Every one of the witnesses for the prosecution lied. Three of them admitted it but the other two by default must also have lied on the stand. Perjury, members of the jury was committed in the court!"

She raised her voice a little, became strident but not too loud. Her voice cut through the silence, and she could see the jury taking it in.

"Sergeant Maguire, a member of a white supremacist group in the past, has been found to be a member again. Did I not say, in this very room, a leopard does not change its spots? And so, it has proven to be. A plot was discovered and foiled only by the swift actions of DS Hughes and her colleagues. A massacre was prevented. And was this, we could conjecture, the aim all along? Did Akshay Pandit, Maneet's fiancé play right into their hands by his misguided attempt to persuade her to give up her career aspirations and become a housewife?"

She paused for a moment to allow these thoughts to register.

"We may never know the answer to any of these questions. However, we do know this. Maneet Johal-Lynch was placed under duress targeted by extreme racial insults directed against her personally by Sergeant Maguire. Duress which caused her to lash out."

A glance at Imogen gained her a nod to indicate she was doing well.

"She did lash out. We know and that is not contested. She was provoked, and it's true to say that is no defence in the eyes of the law. However, Justice Buckley mentioned in this courtroom natural justice."

She caught the judge's eye and a fleeting smile appearing and gone in an instant.

"What is natural justice? The dictionary defines it as principles, procedures, or treatment felt instinctively to be morally right and fair. The law depends upon natural justice as its foundation. Treatment felt to be instinctively morally right and fair. Every justice system including this one recognises the principles of natural justice, and so it would be wrong not to consider them today."

The judge did not speak up to demur, and so she continued working towards her final point.

"Therefore, when you do consider your verdict, consider this. Would it be morally right and even fair to find Ms Johal-Lynch guilty considering the duress, the intent of Sergeant Maguire and the racial hate speech she was subjected to among other things? Because I put it to you, members of the jury, that the fate of justice for Maneet is actually in your hands. It is within your remit to come to your own conclusions and if, taking all the circumstances into consideration, you feel the defendant is not guilty, then so you should find her. Thank you."

She sat down and could see Priteshi was no longer smirking. Her speech might actually have a chance of hitting home. Bernadette certainly hoped so. Imogen smiled at her indicating her approval.

"Thank you, Mrs Mackenna," said the judge looking pleased. This could also be because the trial was drawing to an end, and it had undoubtedly been stressful for the judge, Bernadette mused, for all he did not show it.

"Now, then members of the jury," Justice Buckley continued, "it's not for me to direct you in this case. On the contrary, you've heard the arguments, and it's for you to decide. You may feel in the prosecution is right and Ms Johal-Lynch should be found guilty, or you may agree with the defence and that she is not guilty. I'm going to leave it entirely up to you, and at your discretion. As they say in the vernacular, it's your call. And with that, I ask you to withdraw and consider your verdict."

The jury filed out under the direction of the clerk of the court, and the Tipstaff called the court to rise, while Justice Buckley left the room.

"What now?" said Imogen when he had gone.

"Let's hang around, I've a feeling this won't take long," said Bernadette.

* * *

Back in the meeting room once more, they waited for the verdict.

"What do you think is going to happen?" Maneet asked Bernadette.

"One of two things." Bernadette smiled a little sardonically.

"No! What do you feel will *actually* happen?" Maneet made a face.

"I don't know, and that's the honest truth. We've got a chance of them finding you not guilty, but they may just as easily be swayed by the prosecution. There is no arguing you are guilty in the eyes of the law, but it would be cleaner for all of us if you were found not guilty." Bernadette smiled properly this time and tried to sound reassuring. In truth, she didn't really know which way it would go.

"Oh."

"I'm not a mind reader, darling, and I don't have witchy powers like Eve." Bernadette laughed.

"Is she really, though, a witch?" Maneet was diverted.

"Fuck yeah, that woman is spooky," Imogen said with feeling.

"She's certainly got powers over me." Bernadette chuckled.

"Your wife is a wonderful person. Iona says so. She's awfully patient, chilled," said Hughes.

"Oh God, yes, she's a hippy chick in lots of ways but without the kaftans."

"Eve is a beautiful soul, and she's most probably got magical powers," said Imogen with feeling.

"I've met her, and I agree," said Maneet.

"What about *your* partner?" said Bernadette changing the subject.

"Akshay? I'm still very angry with him!"

"No, your real partner, I meant."

Maneet's face softened suddenly. "Oh, Lunara."

"Yes, Lunara, what about *her*?"

"I don't know."

"OK." Bernadette pursed her lips. If after all this, Maneet was still on the fence, then Bernadette felt there really was nothing she could do.

"Oh God, don't look at me like *that*." Maneet's bottom lip trembled slightly.

"I'm not looking at you like anything, darling. But consider your options, maybe? Just a bit, when all's said and done?" It was a mild reproof.

Maneet dropped her eyes. Next to her, Matelda reached out her hand and stroked Maneet's back lightly, as if she was comforting her. Maneet looked at her gratefully. Bernadette imagined Maneet had probably confided in her. She let the subject go, now wasn't the time.

"Do you think it will be much longer?" Imogen asked.

"I don't know, why?" said Bernadette.

"I was just wondering about coffee... oh, hang on, no need." Imogen looked at her phone which had just buzzed. "The verdict is in!"

* * *

They made their way back to the court in a state of anxious anticipation. For Bernadette, this was always the very worst part of a trial. During the trial, one had at least a measure of control and the ability to direct things through opening and closing statements, cross examinations, and one's own witnesses. However, once that was all done then it was up to the jury or the judge. This was a point where all bets were off. The safe bets had sometimes come out against her and those she thought were lost, she had surprisingly won. So much so that Bernadette would now never take a bet on a verdict at all. It could go either way. Juries were fickle beasts and sometimes their decisions were incomprehensible. However, in the eyes of the law, once a jury had decided, that was it. The only recourse was an appeal process.

The court was unusually silent, although still completely full. Reports would have already been made and teams of media outside would be awaiting the verdict, as would the protesters who had still been very much in evidence when they arrived. Bernadette shot a sideways look at Priteshi who appeared to be more confident than Bernadette felt, however, this meant nothing in the grand scheme of things. Priteshi would have no better idea of the outcome.

The Tipstaff entered the room and announced the judge. He entered smiling and this was no doubt in anticipation of the end of the trial. Overall, Bernadette felt he probably wasn't enamoured of the proceedings, but duty dictated he presided over it, nevertheless. Sometimes cases were brought which a judge probably thought were pointless, and this was very likely one of them.

The clerk of the court supervised the jury who filed in and took their seats. Then she asked Maneet to rise. Maneet did so and gripped the edge of the dock, the strain palpable on her face. It was very possible she might be facing a conviction and the prospect very likely filled her with dread. Bernadette was convinced the judge would mitigate the sentence if it happened but Maneet would still have a criminal record. It would make life difficult for her in the future.

The clerk turned to the foreperson of the jury. She was a middle-aged woman, with greying locks and a kindly face.

"Members of the jury, have you reached a verdict?" the clerk asked her.

"We have?" said the foreperson.

"And is this a verdict upon which you are all agreed?"

"Yes, yes, it is."

Bernadette involuntarily held her breath. She felt Imogen's hand slip into hers under the table and shot her grateful look.

"Do you find the defendant, Ms Johal-Lynch guilty or not guilty of the charge of assault on Sergeant Maguire?"

There was an infinitesimal pause which seemed as if it might go on forever while everyone waited for the spokesperson to speak. Bernadette's heart started beating quite fast and she could not quite prevent the slightly nauseous feeling she got when a verdict was given.

"We find the defendant..." The spokesperson paused again just long enough to make everyone hold their breath too and then she said it. "Not guilty."

There was a sudden uproar, cheers and bursts of applause from the back where Maneet's colleagues had congregated, as well as from the press contingent. Maneet sagged slightly with relief but Matelda was there to hold her up. Bernadette could see Priteshi looked like a thundercloud.

The spokesperson sat down, and the clerk resumed her seat. Justice Buckley was smiling broadly. Bernadette was certain this was the outcome he wanted.

"Now that due process has been done, and the jury has found you not guilty," he said to Maneet, "you are acquitted by this court and you are free to go! It remains me to thank both counsels, the jury and particularly the armed guardian angels in whom I shall forever be in their debt."

He was, of course, referring to Hughes and her colleagues.

"Excellent, excellent," he continued. "I now pronounce this court adjourned and the case closed."

With great alacrity he was up from his seat, only just allowing the Tipstaff time to call the court to order before exiting as fast as he could. Bernadette chuckled at this, but her attention was soon claimed by Maneet who was hugging her tightly.

"Thank you, thank you, so much!" she said over and over.

"You're welcome, you are so welcome," said Bernadette smiling.

From the corner of her eye, she saw Priteshi stalking out of the courtroom. Normally the opposing barristers would shake hands, but no such courtesy was to be afforded. When she was gone Carole came over, and said, "Well done, that fucking bitch got what she deserved!"

"Oh really?" said Imogen.

"Oh yes, they wanted her to drop the case, but she insisted. Quint told her if she fucked up there would be hell to pay. But she wanted her pound of flesh. Well, she didn't get it!"

"No, by God, she did not!"

Carole's face wore an expression of distaste. "Anyway, I'm glad, she's a real bitch to work for, just the worst. None of the other barristers is as bad as her."

"Perhaps she won't last long," Bernadette mused, Maneet having let her go. "Listen, Carole, why don't you ring me next week, let's do lunch, have a chat."

"OK? Any reason?" Carole wondered.

"I just want to have a chat, see if there is some common ground," said Bernadette blandly, unwilling to pursue it further just then.

"Oh, OK, I will," Carole said quickly as if she caught Bernadette's drift. "Anyway, I'd better go, she'll be wondering where I am."

"Call me!" Bernadette said as they watched her hurry out.

"What are you up to?" said Imogen.

"You're the one who said we might need another junior."

"Oh! Yes, good call, can I come too?"

"Of course! I naturally included you in this."

"Of course, and well done!" Imogen gave her a hug.

"Now that's over, I think we can make a statement, don't you?" said Bernadette smiling.

"Oh yes, let's do it!"

* * *

They made their way happily and somewhat triumphantly to the courtroom steps. Although Bernadette could not really claim all the credit for the win, she had certainly turned in a good performance. She had done her best but Akshay and Brogan had tipped the balance, plus the sterling work done by Micky. She thought she ought to chat to Andrew about some kind of financial reward for Micky, perhaps a salary increase. She'd consult Imogen too, perhaps also a paid for meal for Micky and Alison at a posh restaurant might be in order.

Out on the steps, the press were waiting out in force. They were expecting Bernadette and were not going to pass up on the opportunity to get a statement. Over to one side, Bernadette noticed Maneet's colleagues, Judd, Lucy and Lunara among others. Bernadette felt sorry for Lunara, but it couldn't be helped. Maneet would have to work out her problems for herself, Bernadette had done her bit.

She stopped at the top of the steps, held up her hand and was immediately surrounded by microphones and cameras.

"Today," she said, "has been a great day for justice. Natural justice was done. A prosecution which should never have been brought was comprehensively put to bed by the jury. We've had perjury, proven racism and a main prosecution witness who was a member of a white supremacist group while also being part of the Garda. We've had attempted murder, and the murderer shot dead in court. We've had high drama for sure, but in spite of all of that, it's a testament to our justice system that my client Maneet Johal-Lynch was found not guilty. She was set up. She was provoked and, it seems, as part of a wider plot. I won't conjecture on that but I'm glad Maneet can now get on with her life. I am happy to have been instrumental in achieving this result for her. Thank you."

She smiled, batted away a few questions but the focus of the press now shifted to Maneet.

"Maneet, can you give us a statement?" they shouted.

Maneet looked at Bernadette who nodded. It was Maneet's show now. Bernadette's time was over. Maneet smiled and stepped forward. From the corner of her eye, Bernadette noticed Akshay hovering in the background. She wondered what was going to happen in his regard. However, she put this from her mind as Maneet was speaking.

"I am very pleased and grateful for this outcome," she said. "I can't thank Bernadette and her team enough for their work. I also want to thank the Foxcatchers and my bodyguard Matelda. Without their diligence and quick actions, there might have been a very different and fatal outcome. So, I am glad for all these things." She took a deep breath. "However, there is more... it's time to come clean now that this is over. I've had some time to consider a lot of things and when you don't tell the truth, eventually it comes back to bite you."

The press frantically shoved their microphones closer sensing something big was about to happen.

"It's nothing to do with this case, but in a way, it's everything to do with it because the events of this case have brought home to me matters I have not been confronting. I've spent my whole life hiding something, because of disapproval, because of my upbringing, my parents and yes, even my job." She paused once more. Bernadette regarded her with approval realising Maneet was finally going to come clean, this was a crucial moment in her life.

Maneet paused before taking the final plunge. She had started well but the emotion began to show in her face, her eyes were starting to glisten. Her voice began to crack. "I'm gay. I've been gay all of my life and I've been lying about it my whole life too. Yes, I'm gay, I like women and well, particularly one woman." She turned and called out, holding out her hand to her lover who was standing not far away. Tears were beginning to track down her cheeks.

"Lunara."

Without a moment's hesitation, Lunara came up to her. Lunara was crying too and Maneet put her arm around her possessively. She tried to compose herself a little brushing away the tears and gulping on sobs. "This is the love of my life. Meet Lunara. She's my girlfriend, partner, whatever you want to call it." After a few moments more, Maneet seemed to come back stronger. "We're together, and we have been for a long time, just not very publicly, until now. It's a huge relief to get this off my chest and finally say it to the world."

There was a stunned silence for a few moments. Nobody had been expecting this it seems. However, the media recovered quickly from their surprise and questions began to be asked.

"What about your parents?" a reporter shouted.

Maneet teared up once again and became very emotional. Lunara squeezed her hand tightly and Maneet smiled at her gratefully. In a voice once more chock full of intensity, she spoke.

"Hi, Ma, Dad, I'm sorry, so sorry..." She choked up and continued, "This will come as a shock to you but there's no other way to break it to you. I love you still, both of you." She composed herself, and finally began to sound more confident. "I'm sorry it won't be the fairy tale you wanted with the rich husband. We can still have the kids. You can still be grandparents. Love you lots!" Maneet waved almost as if she knew they were watching the screen.

She turned slightly, Akshay had moved closer and had been listening to this with an open mouth, and then he walked away.

"Akshay," shouted some of the reporters, "can we have a statement? Akshay?"

Akshay shook his head and didn't look back. He held up his hand while photographers tried to take his picture and walked away quickly down the steps.

As the questions continued, Bernadette decided to leave Maneet to it. This was her element, and she was comfortable in it. She gave Maneet a brief hug and then walked down the steps with Hughes, Imogen and Zhang. Matelda remained beside Maneet on duty.

At the bottom of the stairs, they ran into Akshay, he appeared to be waiting for her. Bernadette stopped as it seemed he wanted to say something.

"Did you know about this?" he demanded.

"I'm sorry, it's part of my job to know things. It's not part of my job to tell people my client's secrets." Bernadette shrugged.

Akshay looked very upset. "I really love her you know. I really do. But now..."

"You can be angry, and I'm sure you are upset, but you can also try to be her friend, that might be the better outcome if you are looking for one."

"She's one in a million," he said quietly.

"Yet you had secrets of your own, did you not?" Bernadette cocked an eyebrow.

He hung his head momentarily. "I know. It was stupid of me, and now this."

"Isn't it better to know now?"

"I... I just..." he stopped. "Anyway, I'll pay the legal bills don't worry."

"Sure, thanks." Bernadette smiled.

Akshay turned and started to walk away.

"You'll find someone else. You just don't know it yet," Imogen called after him.

He raised his hand in acknowledgement but didn't look back.

"I can't have too much sympathy for him considering what he did," said Hughes.

"But he did come forward, and that's part of what broke the prosecution's case," Bernadette replied.

"True, anyway I suppose all's well that ends well."

"Exactly, as the great bard said."

They all laughed and made their way to the car.

※ ※ ※

Back at the office, Imogen and Bernadette were sat once more in Bernadette's office on the sofa drinking coffee.

"Thank God that's over," said Bernadette with feeling.

"Yes, it was a pretty tough one, for a simple case of assault." Imogen sipped her coffee.

"I really thought we were going to lose."

"And I said something would come up."

"A shootout at the OK Corral wasn't what I had in mind." They both laughed.

"On another note, darling, we've set a date." Imogen smiled.

"You have?" Bernadette's eyes lit up.

"Yes, we're doing what you suggested. A small civil ceremony and then a celebration at our house."

"I'm so happy for you!" Bernadette reached across and squeezed Imogen's hand.

"I'm happy for me, and for D'Arcy."

"Your month is also pretty much up, isn't it?" There was a twinkle in Bernadette's eye.

"Yes, I know, but the paddle is staying in the drawer for now."

"Really?"

"Yes, because we've agreed it needs to be more of a game, like you and Eve. I was starting to get serious and that's wrong. I'm trying to wean myself off it a little." Imogen shrugged.

"I'm impressed." Bernadette secretly wondered how long it would last.

"I get cravings too, just like Eve."

"Does D'Arcy get cravings?"

"Yes, yes, she does, and when they get too great, we'll be getting out that paddle, believe me."

Bernadette laughed. "More power to you, darling. And now, who are you inviting to the wedding?"

"Well..."

* * *

That night Eve snuggled into Bernadette and kissed her softly.

"I'm glad it's all over," she said.

"Me too."

"I'm looking forward to being on our own again soon, even though I'll miss Iona being around."

"Oh, and why is it you are looking forward to it so much?" Bernadette teased.

"Because I'll have you all to myself. Because I can meet you at the door and let you fuck me in the hallway. Because I can be as loud as I want to... and other things."

"What other things?" Bernadette nibbled lightly at Eve's lips.

"Well, you know... I've been misbehaving myself all this time... and..."

"Shibari?"

"Yes... I want it... I'm really needing it..." Eve told her with a low moan.

"I'm sure it can be arranged."

"Yes, please." Eve started to kiss her more passionately, harder.

"I'm going to really tie you up this time, Mrs Mackenna, really tight, all over, to the wall bars." Bernadette's fingers moved downwards, going to work.

"Oh... fuck... yes... I want it... yes..."

"And then, I'm going to fuck you and you won't be able to do a thing about it."

"Oh... yes... oh... do it... faster... mmm... like that... oh God... fuck..."

"Maybe I'll have to slap your backside a little." Bernadette knew perfectly well this was a trigger and it worked.

"Oh... God... fuck... yes... yes... oh... fuck..."

"Make it nice and pink, is that what you want?"

"Yes... oh... oh... oh... fuck...ohh!" Eve tensed as she climaxed, kissing Bernadette hard, pulling her in close, squeezing her legs on Bernadette's hand.

"Oh fuck... fuck..." Eve gasped.

"What that what you wanted?"

"Mmm...hmm..." Eve nodded. "Now it's my turn..."

CHAPTER TWELVE

On a bright sunny summer's day, a month after Maneet's court case, Imogen and D'Arcy were formerly married at a registry office with Bernadette and Eve in attendance. Standing outside the registry office, the four friends embraced and then headed back to what was now to be properly known as D'Arcy and Imogen's mansion for the celebration ceremony.

In a similar fashion to Bernadette and Eve's wedding, an open sided marquee had been erected in the back garden. There were caterers in attendance, parking attendants, and also very tight security. *Hello Magazine* had been given exclusive access to take the photographs and document the wedding. D'Arcy's agent Oscar Childe had used his astute negotiating powers to negotiate a lucrative deal. The magazine was happy with a scoop which they could then syndicate for a massive price around the world, in addition to helping to sell one of their magazine issues.

Bernadette and Eve went upstairs to change into their bridesmaids' dresses and have their hair and makeup done, all courtesy of the blissful couple. With her hair styled and curled, Bernadette put on her light beige long soft fabric dress, with a front split and embellished cowl at the front. She had a pair of gold strappy sandals which she had bought for the purpose. Her nails were painted a light pink matching her lipstick.

"Wow, you're so beautiful," said Eve, kissing her very lightly so as not to disturb her lipstick.

"So are you my honey," Bernadette said returning the compliment.

Eve had a pale pink wrap lace front dress in a similar fabric, and a shoestring strap to secure it around the back of her neck. It also slit open at the front and Eve was wearing silver high heel strappy sandals. They had been out with Imogen and D'Arcy to choose the dresses which D'Arcy had insisted on paying for. Eve's hair was partly up and falling down in ringlets in a slight nod to Regency hairstyles but with a modern twist. Eve's lips and nails matched the colour of her dress.

"Shall we see if the brides are ready?" Eve smiled.

"Yes, why not."

They made their way to D'Arcy's bedroom and knocked lightly. D'Arcy and Imogen were both getting ready together defying tradition. Since they had helped each other choose the dresses there seemed little point in being apart. They had also spent the night together, along with Bernadette and Eve down the hall. The distinctive sound of the slap of a leather paddle on bare flesh accompanied by gasps from D'Arcy indicated they were perhaps celebrating their impending nuptials in their own way, much to Eve's delight who was instantly aroused by the sound.

The door was opened, Eve and Bernadette went in.

"Oh God," said Bernadette looking at Imogen and D'Arcy. "You two are utterly beautiful."

"Stunning," said Eve nodding in agreement.

"Oh, thank you, my darlings," said D'Arcy. "It's my Imogen who is the beautiful one."

"No, you are far more beautiful than I will ever be," Imogen demurred.

"Come on now, no arguments before the wedding." Bernadette laughed.

"Give us a twirl then," said Eve.

D'Arcy's dress was surprisingly plain but lovely, nevertheless. It was a pristine white ruched bust dress with a drape sleeve. The dress flared out at the back in a slight train. She was wearing high heeled silver sandals with ankle straps and a diamante butterfly toe strap. It suited D'Arcy to a tee.

"Wow, those are lovely shoes," Bernadette exclaimed.

"Oh, I knew you'd like them," D'Arcy trilled. Her hair was styled into a French plait with silver diamante threads running through it.

Imogen was wearing an ivory floral and embroidered dress with an open back. It had a high front and was sleeveless. It was otherwise plain with an underskirt. She was also wearing ivory satin mules, with diamante heels. A pair which Bernadette also fell in love with. Imogen's flaming red hair was styled beautifully in a set of curled braids with some hanging strands.

"You are so lovely, darling," said Bernadette.

"Thank you." Imogen blushed.

"You're beautiful, you make a pair of beautiful brides," said Eve.

"We are going to walk down the aisle together," said D'Arcy which was another break with tradition. "You two will walk in front."

"Are we ready to go? Is it time?" said Imogen glancing at the clock.

"Yes, when we have our bouquets."

These very soon arrived, a white floral display for D'Arcy and a red one for Imogen.

With one final check that everything was in place, the four friends left the bedroom and descended to ground level by the main stairway and out onto the back lawn.

Just as with Bernadette and Eve's wedding, the path to the Marquee was carpeted as was the aisle inside it. Plinths carried vases with flowers, red on one side and white on the other. Bernadette wondered if maybe Imogen should have had a red dress, but this would have been too much. Instead, Imogen had red lipstick and nails, whereas D'Arcy had opted for white nails, and pink lipstick.

Inside the marquee, the guests were all seated and waiting. Photographers and a videographer employed by Hello Magazine were on hand to record and photograph it all. They had taken some photographs at the formal ceremony where they had all worn smart formal clothes but not their wedding attire. Invited guests were mainly close friends or family in Imogen's case. All of the Foxcatchers had come with respective partners, as well as Brogan and his wife. D'Arcy's agent and assistant were there, as well as Carole and Olivia. All of the office staff and colleagues from Bernadette's firm had also come with their partners. Maneet and Lunara were invited as well. Imogen's family were, of course, also present too. However, Imogen had not elected to let her father give her away. She was definitely calling the shots with her family in that regard. They were slightly in awe of her marrying D'Arcy for real and not disposed to argue now their daughter had married one of the most famous and richest women in the country. A few select people who D'Arcy knew from the movie business had been asked but the guest list had been pared down to those who she and Imogen considered to be essential.

"Ready?" said Imogen to D'Arcy who seemed to be tearing up.

"Yes," D'Arcy replied in a small voice.

"You two go first then, and try not to cry, D'Arcy my love, or you will set me off too," said Imogen to Bernadette.

Bernadette and Eve stepped forward in front. As they did so what sounded like an orchestra struck up. Bernadette and Eve had had a string quartet, but D'Arcy had obtained a larger group with strings, and other instruments. A mini orchestra in fact. A larger marquee had been hired to accommodate this. They were playing something which sounded like Bach and then became a medley of other famous pieces.

After they had walked a metre or two, D'Arcy and Imogen began to walk behind them holding hands. As they approached the tent, Bernadette could see a similar raised podium at the other end with a very ornate arbour draped with ivy and other greenery. It was a nice magical effect. Although it was daylight the marquee was festooned in fairy lights which twinkled all around them and would become far more prominent that evening. Up ahead was the celebrant who in this case was female in a white suit. She was smiling as she watched their slow procession down the aisle. Eventually, as they arrived at the podium, Eve and Bernadette assisted D'Arcy and Imogen to get up the steps, and then moved away to take their seats at the front. D'Arcy and Imogen took their positions facing each other.

The orchestra stopped and after a moment, the celebrant spoke.

"Hello, all of you beautiful people. I am Celia, and I'm here to help us to celebrate the marriage of D'Arcy and Imogen who you see before you today. I can't think of when I have seen two more gorgeous brides or two people more obviously in love."

She paused while a smattering of applause broke out at this.

"Which brings me nicely to love. For this occasion, is all about love. It is a celebration of love between two people and a public declaration of their love for each other. It is a vow too, of constancy, loyalty and commitment to one another for the rest of their lives. It is not something to be undertaken lightly nor frivolously, but solemnly and with all of the serious intent it holds."

She smiled checked on both her charges and continued.

"Having said all of that, this is a joyous event and should be filled with laughter and merriment, once we have completed the exchanging of vows and rings."

Celia took one of D'Arcy's hands and placed it in Imogen's and repeated this, so they were holding both of each other's hands. Celia did not say the usual part about objections because they were both legally married, so it would have been superfluous.

"Now, D'Arcy and Imogen, are you ready to exchange your vows?"

"Yes, I am," said D'Arcy.

"Me too," said Imogen.

"Very good, Now do you, D'Arcy Brown take Imogen Stewart to be your lawful wedded wife? To have and to hold, to cherish and to love, and to keep faithfully unto her as long as you both shall live?"

"I do!" said D'Arcy with a smile.

Imogen smiled back her eyes very moist.

"And do you Imogen Stewart take D'Arcy Brown to be your lawful wedded wife? To have and to hold, to cherish and to love, and to keep faithfully unto her as long as you both shall live?"

"I do, I really do," said Imogen in a voice full of emotion.

"Oh, oh," said D'Arcy welling up at once, and beginning to cry.

Celia reached behind her and retrieved a tissue from a box which she offered to Imogen who patted D'Arcy's eyes gently dry. D'Arcy took the tissue and blew her nose to a few giggles from the audience.

"OK now?" Celia asked her.

"Yes," D'Arcy said quietly.

"Good, now you can both say your vows, perhaps, Imogen, you can start?"

Imogen looked at D'Arcy and seemed to be about to cry herself, however, she overcame it after a few moments, and began.

"D'Arcy. I don't know what I can say that I have not already said. I love you so much, from the moment I first saw you until I realised, well, that I was gay, and all the days since then I was in love with you, my darling. I just didn't know it at first, and then I didn't want to admit it, but I'm so glad I finally did. If I had lost you then, it would have cut me to pieces, my darling."

D'Arcy was visibly welling upon hearing this.

"Now, you know I'm still crazy about you in every way. I promise to be faithful to you always. I will never keep secrets from you, and we will share everything from now on. What I have is yours, what I am is yours. I give myself and my love to you unconditionally forever. I could not imagine such happiness as I've had with you and I do have with you. You're the apple to my pie, the peaches to my cream and the sugar in my coffee. I can't ever live without you, my darling, I hope you accept me as I am for always, because from now on I'm yours and yours alone. I love you. I love you and I always will."

She finished and D'Arcy let a tear pass unheeded down her cheek.

"God that was so nice, so lovely," she whispered.

"It was, wasn't it?" said Celia. "Extremely heartfelt and moving. Now, D'Arcy, do you have some vows for Imogen?"

"Yes, yes I do," said D'Arcy. She paused to gather her emotions before she was ready to speak.

"Imogen. From that day by the pool that you..." she stopped and blushed. "Where we..." A few people laughed catching her drift. "Well anyway, since then, I best not say what happened... I fell for you, hook line and sinker. I was afraid to tell you for a while but then when you finally said that you loved me, you took down all of my defences and I was yours completely. You are the person I've been searching for my whole life. All the silly stupid things I've done were leading up to the one sensible decision I ever made, and that was to be with you. The day you proposed, it was the very best... the best day of my whole life... until now, until this day... you have no idea... you have no..." D'Arcy broke down and Imogen was crying too. Overcome with emotion there were tears all around as Imogen squeezed D'Arcy's hands and waited for her to recover.

She did so, and after another few tissues were offered and taken, she was ready to resume. "My darling, you've stolen my heart and I never want it back. You can have it for always it's yours. All I have is yours and mine, we are in this together from now on, you and me. I promise you I will always be faithful, and you know I will. I promise to mind what you say, and to be your very willing... erm... wife for always... well, you know what I mean." D'Arcy giggled at this. Most people would not get the private joke, but Bernadette and Eve were fully aware of what she meant.

"I will love you. I will cherish you for always. I am yours from now on unconditionally and I will love you forever too. My darling, darling, darling, Imogen."

Imogen was smiling and her eyes were shining with love. Bernadette held Eve's hand and both of them had cried as they listened to both their friend's beautiful words. There were not many dry eyes in the marquee, and Imogen's mother was sobbing her heart out.

"That's lovely, what a lovely couple you are," said Celia. "Now we shall exchange the rings."

D'Arcy and Imogen had left the ring ceremony for this occasion rather than the registry office because they both felt it meant more in front of their friends.

Carragh who had been assigned to mind the rings stepped forward and passed a small velvet bag to Celia. She removed the rings and held them both up for everyone to see.

The rings were matching in platinum, and had inset diamonds, which they had chosen together. There was an inscription inside them which said, "Imogen and D'Arcy forever along with the date of their wedding day."

"Hmm," said Celia, "I see the date in here, that's one way of not forgetting your wedding anniversary."

This gave rise to some polite laughter before Celia moved on.

"Now these rings, are a symbol of ending and infinite love."

"Imogen, take D'Arcy's left hand and place the ring on her fourth finger."

Imogen did so.

"Now repeat after me. With this ring."

"With this ring," Imogen said.

"I thee wed."

"I thee wed."

"I will love and cherish you."

"I will love and cherish you."

"Until the end of our days."

"Until the end of our days."

"And let this ring be a symbol of my vows to you and my everlasting love for you."

"And let this ring be a symbol of my vows to you and my everlasting love for you."

"Excellent," said Celia, "Now D'Arcy you will take Imogen's left hand..."

The ceremony was repeated with D'Arcy saying the lines.

When this was done, Celia said, "And so by the exchange of vows, and rings, before all these lovely people present, the ceremony is complete, and it gives me great pleasure to pronounce you both married. You may now kiss the bride!"

D'Arcy took Imogen into an embrace immediately and their lips met for a passionate and very long steamy kiss.

The marquee erupted into spontaneous applause with clapping and whistling until it the kiss was over. D'Arcy and Imogen stood holding hands for a moment and then the mini orchestra struck up Handel's Wedding March as they walked out down the aisle and back into the house.

Bernadette and Eve followed to give them their first congratulations. There would shortly be the meeting of all of the guests and then photographs and the wedding feast. The magazine had already taken lots of photos of D'Arcy and Imogen around the mansion, which included them in their dresses. There were, of course, group photos to be done and the final couple photos too.

After the meet and greet, and everyone had circulated a little and stretched their legs, the wedding feast was announced, D'Arcy and Imogen came into the tent when everyone was seated. They sat at the podium table with Bernadotte and Eve on either side to enjoy a selection of sushi for starters which had fish, vegetarian and meat selections. This was followed by a Thai Green Curry and Malaysian Laksa, with rice and naans, with selections also for vegetarians. Finally, a tray of small desserts such as mini apple pies and other delicacies topped it off. Bernadette noticed Imogen stayed quite sober to avoid a repeat performance of her drunken bad behaviour at Bernadette's wedding. D'Arcy looked on with approval. The petit fours arrived with coffee and Bernadette who was the 'best woman' for both brides stood up to make a speech.

"Hello, hello," she said when they had everyone's attention. "It's fallen to me to make a speech but never fear there's no Shakespeare in it today although a sonnet would not have gone amiss."

There was a ripple of laughter from those familiar with her courtroom speeches.

"Anyway. I just want to say how wonderful it is to be here for Imogen and D'Arcy's long overdue wedding."

D'Arcy made a mock pout at this and Imogen giggled.

"I'm sure you'll agree it's been a beautiful loving occasion. All of us have cried I'm sure, I know I have. I'm personally so very, very happy to see them married, and I know Eve, my wife, is too, as I'm sure you all are."

Cries of "hear, hear" sounded around the marquee.

"However, it behoves me to say something about Imogen and D'Arcy. I could say a lot, in fact, but much of it would not be for public consumption."

Everyone laughed out loud at this including the two newlywed brides.

"So, we'll stick to subjects which as they say are safe for work."

"Thank God for *that*," said Imogen to more laughter.

"So, I've known Imogen a long time now, because of course we are colleagues and she's a junior partner in my firm. And a very good one she is too, and one day she'll be a fabulous senior barrister I'm sure, but we're not here either to talk about work."

"Hear, hear!" shouted Andrew to a few guffaws from his colleague.

"Thank you, Andrew, but moving on. What I wanted to say, what I wanted to say... is that Imogen, is so much more than that. So very much more." Her voice suddenly filled with emotion and her eyes welled up. Imogen looked up at her at once brim-full of tears.

"No, Imogen is the sister... I never had... and the sister Eve deserved to have." Bernadette choked a little on a sob and tears were running down Imogen's cheeks. "We love her with as much passion as anyone can love a sister. Imogen... is like family to me, to us both. We love her so very, very much. And now, we have not one but two sisters, because we also have D'Arcy. Our darling beautiful D'Arcy."

"Oh..." said D'Arcy dissolving at once into tears and having to be consoled by Eve who was sitting beside her. "And what can one say about D'Arcy? A beautiful soul, generous to a fault, perhaps too generous sometimes for her own good, but that's OK. She's loving, caring, she's been nothing but kind to us both. We can't thank her enough for all of the things she has done. And on top of this, she's married our very best friend, our adopted sister, my darling Imogen."

Bernadette had barely managed to get through this without bawling herself. She stopped to compose her emotions a little before continuing.

"So now here we are, like a little family, sisters under the skin. Two of the loveliest people who deserve all of the happiness they can get and more. Now, having said all that and without more ado, I'd like you to raise your glasses in a toast to Imogen and D'Arcy!"

"Imogen and D'Arcy," the toast rang out through the tent.

D'Arcy got up and hugged Bernadette tightly thanking her over and over and giving her a big kiss. This was followed by Imogen who sobbed in Bernadette's arms and said that her words had been profoundly moving, and her own best woman speech had been shit by comparison. Bernadette assured her this wasn't the case. Then D'Arcy and Imogen had to also hug Eve, and once this was all done. They made two very moving speeches of their own.

After the meal, they circulated around the tables chatting to their friends, and then the party broke up for a couple of hours while the marquee was prepared for the evening. In the meantime, people were free to use the pool and relax. The brides and the bridesmaids went upstairs to change.

In the evening there was an Irish band who could play all sorts of music. Maneet taught everyone Bangri and Bollywood dancing, there was folk dancing, followed by rock and roll. The guests all enjoyed themselves hugely.

Finally, much later that evening, Eve and Bernadette, a little breathless from dancing, walked together barefoot and hand in hand to a secluded part of the garden. In the background, they could hear the merriment continuing, and the moon shone brightly above. They sat together in a rose arbour near a small pond where tiny frogs quietly croaked their love songs.

"What a beautiful day," said Eve leaning her head on Bernadette's shoulder.

"Wasn't it?" Bernadette put her arm around her wife and pulled her in close.

"You made a lovely speech."

"Thank you, I was almost in floods."

"Well D'Arcy and Imogen were, and quite a few others."
Eve chuckled.

"Yes."

"Do you think they'll like the present?"

"Which one? The secret one or the proper one?"
Bernadette giggled.

"Oh well, the secret one, of course. They will *love* the
proper one."

Eve and Bernadotte couldn't afford something like a
holiday to Thailand which was D'Arcy and Imogen's present
to them. However, they had paid for a week in a very
expensive exclusive hotel in the south of Ireland, and
Bernadette was sure they would like it just as much.

"Will they like the white leather flogger with a diamante
handle? Hmm, let me think, knowing those two like we do,
I reckon so."

Eve sniggered.

"Where do you find these things?" Bernadette
continued. "What sites have you been browsing, wait no,
don't answer that."

"Oh, you know..."

"I don't know, Mrs Mackenna, but no doubt you'll tell me
anyway at some point." Bernadette kissed her softly.

"Oh, but I will, and it's possible I might have bought
some things, you know as props for my drawings." Eve
nuzzled her back.

"Is that a fact?"

"Yes." In the half light, Eve's eyes were twinkling.

"You are such a little witch."

"I know."

"And I love you so much."

"I know that too."

Nothing more was said for quite a while, as they kissed softly under the light of the moon.

ACKNOWLEGEMENTS

I would like to mention and acknowledge my wife Trish, who has loved me unconditionally and supported me throughout our journey together. She has breast cancer which is currently in remission and I can't get over the stoic nature of all she has had to bear. Many operations, and procedures but she keeps going, a testament to courage. Throughout this, she worked until she could work no longer and wouldn't hear of me giving up my Doctorate until I finished it, which I did in 2020. I have looked after her, tried to cherish and love her through all of her trials and tribulations. It's brought heartache and pain, anxiety and many other things. However, Covid brought us closer than ever, and for the most part, we live in harmony. She continues to be my greatest advocate and supporter as a writer, and I'm constantly grateful for that. I would not have done many of the good things I've done without her support, drive and encouragement. I can truly say she completes me and cannot thank her enough for all the years she has given me. I hope for many more, God and the universe willing.

In many countries of the world today, people can still not publicly reveal their sexuality, their differences from what others may consider the norm. Thankfully, after many long and hard-fought years, LGBTQ is recognised in so many nations, with more to follow. For what is love but simply an expression of human emotion, regardless of sexual identity, race, creed, colour among other things. Discrimination is unacceptable, in any form and should be fought hard whenever and wherever it occurs. We are all human and we have inalienable rights. These apply to all of us without exception.

With this, the fifth book in the Mackenna series, Bernadette endures as one of my most favourite characters, along with her partner Eve, her friend Imogen and D'Arcy. This book also deals with racism which is another intolerance we have to combat in this world. I make no pardon for the steamy nature of the prose or perhaps their kinks which is all part of the modern idiom in which we now live. I like contrasts and that's perhaps why I contrast their private and public life in this way. Who doesn't want to know what goes on behind closed doors? Witness the plethora of reality shows. I think they are larger than life but also, I feel they could be real. That's how I like to portray them. I can imagine them having the conversations they have and doing the things they do.

The series is dedicated to love and courtroom drama. It's not trying to change the world. It's just written out of love. Love is love, and that's all that matters. It comes in all forms, and I've simply tried to portray some of these. Bernadette Mackenna being gay is simply part of her story, it's part of who she is. I hope you enjoy the romance, and the spice, and everything else, and the other characters. I hope you can love Bernadette too, and the other characters with it.

If you would like to keep up to date with all the Bernadette Mackenna news, then please subscribe to my newsletter here. There will be news, insider knowledge, be the first to know about upcoming releases, special offers and much more. Join up as a subscriber and you can always write to me too if you like.

https://www.subscribepage.com/DIGallwaySubscriber

ABOUT THE AUTHOR

D.R. Bailey was raised in a family of bibliophiles. From an early age he developed eclectic tastes in fiction including; SciFi, Romance, Crime, and the Classics. Some of his favourite authors remain Gerald Durrell, Jane Austen, Peter James, Ellis Peters, and Isaac Asimov.

At the age of eleven he wrote his first fictional story about his toy teddy bear clan. Since then he has gone on to have some of his non-fiction article published in magazines and also a fictional crime series.

He has engaged in several different careers and says that these life experiences have all contributed greatly to his penchant for storytelling. Bailey has now penned his debut full length crime novel, which is a genre he is particularly fond of.

Printed in Great Britain
by Amazon

70203232R10305